A CONTEMPORARY ROMANCE

UNDER the BLEACHERS

AUTHOR OF UP IN THE TREEHOUSE

K.K. Allen

Books
by K.K. Allen

Copyright

This book is a work of fiction. Names, characters, places, and incidents either are products of the author's imagination or are used fictitiously. Any resemblance to actual events or locales or persons, living or dead, is coincidental.

For more information, please contact K.K. Allen at SayHello@KK-Allen.com

ISBN: 154313503X
ISBN-13: 978-1543135039

To my father. I love you and miss you. It's never too late. <3

UNDER the BLEACHERS

Prologue

My lungs put up a fight as the burn intensifies with each sip of air. Adrenaline overrides every ache, pumping through me as my feet pound unforgivingly against the pavement.

Just another hundred yards.

I'm not sure why I decided to come. It was a last-minute decision, one I had talked myself out of before. To love someone despite their inability to love us back may be selfless, but it also leaves us vulnerable. Defenseless.

For two years I thought cutting ties would eventually numb the pain, but I'm starting to forget him … and that just might be worse.

Rounding the corner, I see the bright lights of the high school stadium. They shine down like heaven to reveal one hundred twenty yards of lush greenery glistening from the dewy grass. Even from this distance, everything is in focus.

Players huddle near the sidelines as their quarterback's booming voice leads a chant that is echoed by his team. With a synchronized clap of their hands, it's like a bomb has just dropped at their feet. They fly apart like shrapnel, heading to their respective positions on the field. Their coach, average height with dark and thick stubble barely disguising the nervous tick of his jaw, hangs back, pacing and rubbing his palms against his outer thighs in anticipation.

And then comes the snap.

A boy wearing red and black grips the pigskin as his feet dance inside the pocket. They call him the Rocket because when he lets go of the ball, you can practically see the smoke trailing behind its spiral. But his arm isn't what makes him a star. It's when he moves outside of the pocket that the real show begins.

Speed carries him like he's the chariot of the sky, an unstoppable force. No one knows what he'll do next, but it doesn't matter. The field is his. His movements are so quick that he barely touches the ground, dodging one sack after another until he's lunging downfield in search of his next target.

I'm not nearly as fast, but a burst of energy tears through me as I skip the main entrance of the stadium and circle the perimeter. The disguised opening in the fence was created six years ago. I know, because it was my father's shears that cut into the steel.

When I press into the barrier it lifts easily from its pole, and I slip through.

Trespassing. Totally worth it to avoid a possible confrontation.

Before the loose fence slaps back against the post with a thwack, I take off again, my body cloaked in the shadows of the stands. For tonight, I'll let the bleachers be my mask.

I weave around the support beams, slinging myself forward like they're vertical monkey bars and this is my personal playground. Using the last beam to steady myself, I scan the slits between the stairs to find the best view of the game.

I can see at once that the boy has found his target. He rears back, preparing for launch while offense works like a well-oiled machine around him. His grace, unbridled. His timing, flawless.

And then, in the most perfect arc I've ever seen, the ball sails through the air and straight to the end zone, dropping easily into the arms of the receiver. Impeccable execution.

The crowd's roar is deafening as six points light up the jumbotron. A glorious rush surges through me as the spectators in the stands erupt into cheers and a thunderous beating of feet to wood surrounds me, making my nerves jump like Pop Rocks in my chest.

I adjust my blue and gray cap to ensure protection from the random articles that inevitably fall during every game as dirt and mold swirl through the air. All around me, food droppings, loose change, and God knows what else hit the gravel.

As much as I'd rather be in the stands with everyone else, stomping my feet and screaming until I'm hoarse, being part of the crowd is too risky.

Curiosity won. I'm here to see him … but I'm not ready for him to see me.

The wounds are fresh. We're all still bleeding. But I'm not the victim in this story … and I sure as hell am not the enemy.

STEP ONE

Dessert

"THE FIRST 90 MINUTES OF THE MATCH
ARE THE MOST IMPORTANT."
— SIR BOBBY ROBSON

Chocolate Covered Everything

Monica

Where's a buttery nipple shot when a girl needs one? *This* girl needs one. All this effort put into my Superwoman outfit, but not one hero or villain has asked me to dance tonight. Am I losing my touch?

It's not like my options are plentiful, anyway. The limited number of hot guys at this event are either off-limits or paid to be here and otherwise occupied with photo ops for the majority of the night.

BelleCurve, the creative agency I work for in Bellevue, Washington, has long been known for their work with nonprofits, but this event is far more impressive than any campaign I've seen. Heroes and Legends, the theme of the evening, is an awareness event that recognizes kids who have lived through bullying. The room we've secured at Melrose Market in Seattle is alive with laughter and chatter, and comic sketches decorate pop art backdrops on every wall to match the theme.

But as great as tonight has been, with just an hour left of the event, I'm ready to hang my heels.

Like the resourceful chick I am, I've managed to make do riding the buzz of flirtation to get me through this night. And

I've done so void of the same fairytale expectations most girls have. My heart isn't set on finding Prince Charming among these superheroes in tights. Tights are hot and all, but let's face it: Prince Charming is as real as those pretty packages nestled snug between those muscular legs. Every time I see a costumed man with that ridiculous bulge I want to grab hold of the decorative swell, give my potential prince a seductive smile, and whisper—*we all know it's a sock.*

I laugh, shifting my focus to a plate of goodies being carried by a passing Wonder Woman. Taking in the sweet scent as it floats by, my mouth immediately waters. Now *there's* a pick-me-up. There's no better distraction than this beautiful arrangement of white and dark chocolate, melted and hardened upon the most perfect set of strawberries.

I think I'm in love.

I track Wonder Woman to the dessert table on the other side of the room where a chocolate fountain draws a small crowd. Why didn't I see this earlier? Because there it is: the only thing sure to turn this night around for me. I snake my way through the crowd and toward my own personal heaven.

Chocolate. The food of the gods, as my grandma used to call it. And I totally agree. It's the answer to prayers. Emotional relief. A form of currency. An aphrodisiac. Raw and dark. White and saccharine. Milky sweet. Mouthwatering. It's all good; I don't discriminate.

My mom, my sister, and I moved in with my grandmother a year after my parents' divorce. I was thirteen and having the most awkward year of my life. Newly separated parents, new school, new home—and a sister who was in every way, shape, and form perfection. My grandmother, who had taken a turn for the worse after a broken hip, spent most of her days reading the newspaper, watching CNN, and mumbling to herself or to anyone who would listen. Usually, that anyone was me.

She had spent most of her adult life working as a tour guide at the chocolate museum in Cologne, Germany. She reveled in the history of the Mayas and the Spaniards and the cacao trees that produce fruits the size and shape of a football. Every now and then she'd get extra sentimental, and we would watch *Willy Wonka* with a box of assorted chocolate she'd sneak into the house. My mom would have murdered us if she had known. It would have been worth it. I'll never forget the sound of Grandma giggling when Augustus Gloop fell into the chocolate river.

Sorting through the memories of that time in my life is never fun, as it's mostly filled with confusion and false hope. But I can always rely on the moments of comfort with my grandmother and chocolate to bring a smile to my face. Like now, as I'm weaving through a thinning crowd to get to the dessert table.

When the waitress I've been stalking steps away, I swoop in, snatching a strawberry from the collection and planting it between my lips. Closing my eyes, I sink my teeth into the sweet fruit and rich chocolate, swallowing with a deep moan.

Holy mother of flying bananas, that's good. I go for another bite, this time closer to the stem, the berry filling more of my mouth as I bite down.

Someone clears their throat behind me in an obvious attempt to get my attention. I ignore it.

Seriously? Worst timing ever. I'm a little busy here.

"Glad I stuck around for this."

Panic shoots through me the instant I hear his voice. That subtle Texas drawl that takes me back to my life before moving to Washington. A drawl that he probably doesn't even realize he still has after living in Seattle for three years. Over the two years I've known him, it's certainly faded.

Swiveling around, I lock eyes with the host of tonight's event.

Zachary Ryan.

Otherwise known as the sexiest man to walk planet Earth. That's my definition of him, anyway. He's more commonly known as Zachary Ryan: NFL quarterback, Super Bowl champion, and Washington's most eligible bachelor (according to Seattle Magazine). And now he's watching me go to town on a chocolate covered strawberry like I'm in bed with it.

Zach suppresses a smile beneath his unshaven stubble as I nearly gag on my dessert. Please tell me this is not happening right now.

He's a mesmerizing sight with ocean-filled eyes that stare back at me from under the curve of his brow. And his light brown hair, closely shaven at the sides, is long enough on top to style with his signature lift.

Giving him an awkward, crinkly-eyed smile, I hold up my hand in a gesture for him to wait. I grab a Batman cup from the table, spit into it, and toss it into the nearest trashcan.

What a waste of a perfectly good strawberry. Then again, if Zach is my consolation prize, I'll take it.

After using my tongue to swipe my teeth clean, I look up to find Zachary, who's given up the fight to hold back his amusement. His laugh is deep and rumbly and all sexy man.

It's a sound I've quickly become familiar with since he seems to always be laughing at me.

Who does he think he is?

I tilt my head and glare at him. "Can't a girl eat some dessert without getting interrupted? I could have choked to death."

His laugh settles into a teasing smile. "Good thing for you I know CPR."

Now that wouldn't have been so bad.

Zachary's lips curl and he nods to the plate of desserts. "*That*, Monica Stevens, was the best entertainment I've had all night."

Now it's me trying to hold back a grin. First, why does he feel the need to always address me so formally? *Ugh.* Politeness is a weakness of mine; I'll admit it. And Zachary Ryan is the epitome of polite. And charming. And handsome. Unfortunately, the list of positives is far too long to go over in this moment. The man can't be perfect, but I've yet to find a single flaw.

Second, the fact that he even knows my full name … six points to him. But I won't let him have the extra point.

"Not saying much about yourself, since you're the entertainment and all."

His eyes narrow, but he never loses his smug expression. "I'm just the host. I wasn't entertaining anyone tonight."

"I think if you're hosting an event, you're considered part of the entertainment. Besides, your profession *is* broadcast to millions, which means you *are* an entertainer. No getting out of this one, Zachary Ryan." I throw his full name at him like he did mine, but it doesn't have the same effect. I don't know why, but I feel like this puts me at a disadvantage. I don't like that. In fact, I don't like that Zachary might always have the advantage over me. His charm is like a stun gun to my wit.

He chuckles, low and husky. My eyes track him as he steps forward, closing in until we're almost touching. In a momentary state of paralysis, I just stand there, leaving little room for him to reach around my body to the dessert table. I might even breathe him in as he passes. But to my defense, who wouldn't want to sniff the NFL's hottest new quarterback if given the opportunity? It would be silly not to.

My lungs expand, pulling in the crisp, woodsy scent that wafts off his body. If heaven had a scent, this would be it. Whatever it is contrasts with the strong citrus blend coming from his carefully styled hair, bleeding seduction. Heaven and seduction. A potent combination. A dangerous elixir to my already raging hormones.

He rights himself to standing, still in front of me, this time grinning with a chocolate covered strawberry teasing his lips. I swallow and he winks, acknowledging my reaction.

When he bites into the chocolate, I have to steady myself on the table at the sight of his strong jaw and beautiful lips in action. Zachary closes his eyes as he chews, a smile lifting his cheeks once again.

By the time he tosses the stem into the trash, I'm hot everywhere and glaring at him. He's an evil man. And now he's doing that thing where he smiles playfully and rests his teeth on his tongue.

"Was that as good for you as it was for me?"

I really do try to hold back the laughter climbing up my throat, but the way he's waiting for my reaction—he's too good.

"I think you should stick to football."

With a wink, I start to move past him. His hand, calloused and strong, catches mine, halting my steps. Everything seems to fall still except the beating of my heart, which is now thundering in my chest.

"Where do you think you're going? You owe me a dance."

Letting out a breath of air, I scold my heart for quickening its rhythm without the support of the rest of the band. It just takes off at its own pace like it thinks it's earned a solo.

"I don't recall owing you anything. In fact, I think you're the one who owes me for interrupting my meal."

"Your meal?"

"Dessert," I deadpan.

"I hate to break it to you, but dessert isn't a meal. It's a snack that comes after dinner."

My mouth hangs open. Did he just call dessert a *snack*? My grandma's probably rolling over in her grave right now. If she were here, she would set him straight.

"Okay," I say with a forced smile. "It's obvious we're not going to agree on this one, so I'm going to be the bigger person and let you change the subject."

Zachary's eyes twinkle as he tugs on the hand he's already holding. I should probably take that away from him...

"Deal," he says. "Since I owe *you*, I'll do you the honor of dancing with you." This time a full smile lights up his face, and his white, straight teeth practically blind me. "Don't break my heart. Dance with me, Monica Stevens."

"Tell you what." I start with a challenge, as if I really have to bargain with the man to give him what he wants. *What I want.* "You can stop addressing me by my full name. Then

I'll dance with you." He starts to agree; I see his head lift in a half-nod when I realize I'm making this too easy on him. "Just one dance."

With a pinch of his lips, he tells me he wants to argue, but he won't. Still, satisfaction relaxes the lines on his forehead once we fall into step on our way to the dance floor. He's respectfully silent as he guides me, as if worried a single word could blow his entire game plan.

His grip on my hand is impressive. Engulfing even—and I like it. For a fleeting moment, I imagine this is what Belle must feel like when she dances with the Beast. Small, yet important. Strong, yet vulnerable. Afraid, yet too proud to show it. And protected—not that I need protection. Though it should be noted that Zachary Ryan is a far cry from anything beastly, unless you're referring to his physique.

I glance down at the fingers threaded through mine, considering their magnitude. My friend Chloe has a theory about hands, one that I can't seem to stop thinking about now…

"What are you gawking at?"

I look up and shake my head, feigning complete innocence. "Nothing."

When we reach an empty space on the dance floor, he turns and pulls me close to his body. If I weren't so distracted by everything Zachary Ryan, I would attempt to resist him— or at least cross my arms across my chest and make him apologize for laughing at me earlier.

But who am I kidding? I'm partially to blame for this. For the past month, we flirt, we laugh, we poke fun at each other, and then when he has me all flustered, we part ways. So far it's been frustrating, but safe.

I'm not sure what's changed.

One Month Earlier

"Well, look who's making a statement. Fashionably early suits you, Zachary Ryan. But I'm afraid your fanfare hasn't arrived yet." I give him a dramatic bat of my lashes. "Your appointment with Chloe isn't until eleven."

Forming an overly exaggerated pout, I attempt to distract him from my efforts of blindly clicking the mouse, fumbling to minimize the open window of my computer screen.

He isn't fooled. I swear he hasn't taken his eyes off me since he walked through BelleCurve's main doors, but his expression wears all the conviction he needs to torment me. He already saw.

"Plants vs. Zombies, huh?" He struts closer, straightens his arms, and wraps his thick fingers over the edge of the counter. "The water levels are the hardest."

I clear my throat, fighting a blush while darting a look at my screen where my favorite game is prominently displayed. There's no point in hiding it now. The executives are at a conference in New York and everyone else who matters is already in meetings. Zach wasn't supposed to arrive for another thirty minutes.

I quickly tap on the computer's sleep icon anyway, fighting the heat that rushed through my body the moment his tall and wide frame pushed through the glass doors. Am I embarrassed to be caught messing around on the job? Sure. But more than anything, I'm thinking Zachary Ryan should come with an alert signal so everyone can prepare for his arrival. Or maybe he should carry a fire extinguisher to blast away the heat he leaves behind his every move.

Yeah. That.

His looks are off the Richter scale, but it's those big, blue eyes that speak directly to my ovaries and capture my attention whenever he's near.

Folding my arms on the desk, I try to pretend I'm not affected by the hard lines of his jaw shielded by a layer of closely shaven stubble or the light brown of his hair that's begging for a rough comb-through of my fingers.

"I'm on a cigarette break."

His face twists with disappointment. "Monica Stevens smokes?"

"Of course not, but good to know that would have been a problem for you." The corners of my mouth turn up into a full-blown smile.

Ignoring my insinuation, he leans into the reception counter. "Funny girl. Humor me. Why do you need a smoke break if you don't smoke?"

I shrug as if the answer is obvious. "Smokers are rewarded with breaks throughout the day. That's discrimination to nonsmokers. Nonsmokers must demand equal rights."

A throaty chuckle passes his lips, making it hard to not stare directly at them and imagine how well they'd fit with mine. "I'm sure your fellow nonsmokers would be proud of your advocacy."

"Oh, they would be. Aren't you?" My cheeks lift before I can stop them.

"Am I proud of you?" There's a twitch of his lips before he speaks again. "That depends."

Tilting my head, I have to bite my bottom lip to keep the ridiculous smile on my face from gaining wattage. "Depends on what?"

He nods to my computer screen. "Show me your strategy."

My jaw drops in mock horror. "You can't have my secrets. We barely know each other."

With eyes locked on me, he stares a little too long. "If you won't give me your secrets, I'll find them out, Monica Stevens. Trust me." And then he stealthily moves around the counter.

Something stirs in my belly, but I push the feeling aside. He's on my side of the desk before I can come up with a retort, but he doesn't attack me for my computer like I expect. Instead, he pulls up the stool in the corner of my workstation and sits beside me.

"C'mon, let's see this. I've got"—he glances at his watch—"twenty-five minutes to kill before my meeting. If you can't impress me with your zombie killing skills, I might have to file a formal complaint with your manager."

"My manager?" I level him with my eyes. "I work for the CEO, and she loves me."

"She loves me more."

Caught in the undertow of his crystal blue eyes, I don't doubt it. Tearing my gaze away, I swallow and wake up the monitor. "Sandra isn't here this week, so that will be a challenge for another day."

The corner of his mouth tips up. "Looking forward to it."

Present Day

I lose my train of thought when Zach's free palm grips my waist and gently guides me toward him until I'm mere inches from his body. He's watching me intently, like I'm the football he's in possession of tonight. Never taking his eyes off the ball. I guess I don't mind. Zachary is passionate in every sense of the word. He's someone who means every gesture, every look, every syllable—and right now, he's studying me as if he's mapping out his next play.

As he moves us around the floor with progressively advanced steps, I'm both impressed and amused. He's observing me, waiting for me to break, for me to miss a step. But I don't. I won't.

Zachary Ryan doesn't know it yet, but he's just met his match on the dance floor. Just because I don't carry a deep southern drawl doesn't mean I didn't put in my time. I know every line dance, I can manage a horse with ease, and I sure as hell know my way around a shooting range. Looking at and listening to me, you wouldn't guess I'm a country girl at heart. I've learned to hide it well since leaving Rockwall, Texas, and my love for stilettos trumps my love for my embroidered leather cowboy boots. Most days.

I'm thoroughly disappointed when the song transitions to a slow one, and it's not because of the tempo change. I was just starting to enjoy this.

One dance. My words. Is it too late to take them back?

He must be thinking the same thing because both of his hands are on my hips now, and his grip only tightens, but not in a way that hurts. It feels … *good* to be possessed like this.

"That wasn't a full song. I get another one." His voice is low but commanding, forcing me to pretend that his grin doesn't ignite the wick below my waist.

I should say no.

"That's only fair."

My arms slide up his navy blue suit jacket and over his shoulders until I'm clasping my fingers behind his neck, my eyes never leaving his. Zachary is nearly a foot taller than me, and I like that I feel small in his massive arms.

Who would want to let this man out of their sight? A true southern boy living in the Emerald City is a rare find. You don't find charm like this everywhere you go. But he fits in well here, better than most, blending in easily with the city slickers in their flashy suits and designer denim.

Hell, I fit in well too, but every now and then I'll hear something in Zach's tone that brings me back to my life growing up in Texas, and I'm not sure how I feel about it. There's a reason I moved away from the small-town life and found my home in the city of Bellevue, just across the lake from Seattle. And it's not something I like to think about.

"You can dance." Surprise is evident in his voice, and the crinkle between his brow tells me he just might be impressed too.

"You're an excellent lead." It's the truth, and it earns me a smile as his hands move from my waist to the small of my back. After many months of greeting Zach when he'd arrive at BelleCurve, showing him from one room to the other, serving him cold waters, buying his catering, and booking his appointments with our staff, it's a little hard to believe that I'm in his arms now. "You're not the only one with some country in this joint, you know?"

His eyes widen at my confession. I hadn't planned on telling him about my roots. It's not something I talk about, so people just assume I'm from around here. "Rockwall, Texas," I answer before he can even ask.

"No way. Did you drop your twang on your way to the city?"

I laugh. "You're one to talk."

His smile grows bright. "My momma told me I'd lose it the moment I stepped foot over here. It didn't happen that quickly, but being surrounded by a bunch of Neanderthals did the trick eventually." He winks.

"Mine wasn't hard to drop once I moved here." Especially since I *tried* to drop it, leaving everything I possibly could behind me.

"Well, look at that. I feel right at home now. I guess I saved the best for last." He presses his lips together as his eyes lock on mine. It takes me a minute to realize he's referring to me being his dance partner.

"Not how I look at it," I say, shaking my head. "It doesn't feel so good to always be the last one picked for a team. Not that you would know the feeling."

"Oh, I know the feeling. Did you miss my speech?"

I shiver in response, because his speech tonight brought everyone to tears. I don't think I'll ever forget his experiences with bullying.

"All right, then." I shake off the distraction, putting my challenge face back on. Because this is what we do well. We spar. We flirt. We laugh. "Don't think I haven't seen you dance with every other girl in here tonight."

His chest expands, and he seems to grow taller. "So, you've been watching me."

I shake my head. "It's kind of hard to miss a two-hundred-thirty pound, six-foot-three NFL player and a giggling, doe-eyed girl twirling across the dance floor."

"Tell me, why aren't *you* all giggly and doe-eyed? You've obviously got my trading card memorized." He suctions me in, the small gap between us vanishing as I'm now pressed flush against his chest.

It takes a second to adapt to the hard body melded with my soft one.

Deep breaths, Monica. Hold it together.

"I suppose those girls felt special that you asked them to dance."

His lip curls. "And you?"

"Don't."

His smirk grows into a full-blown smile. "Hmm. Well, you should. Just to set the record straight, the music only started thirty minutes ago, and you're the only one I've asked to dance. Those other girls asked me. It would have been rude for me to say no."

Oh. "Is that right?"

"It is. I've had my eye on you."

Unease creeps through my veins. This was supposed to be a fun exchange of innocent flirtation. Why does it feel like something else?

"I'm calling your bluff," I try again. "We both know your eyes have been elsewhere."

This time I'm serious and referencing my friend and coworker, Chloe Rivers, who Zach was crushing on when they first started working together. Nothing ever happened between her and Zach, but that doesn't change the fact that he asked her out—twice. Talk about a blow to my ego.

"Ouch." He frowns. "I'll give you that one, but that's not really fair. I thought you were dating that comic artist guy, Gavin. But I figured it out about a month ago. He's really turned out to be a problem for me, and I don't even know him beyond the conference room."

I laugh, knowing how right he is. Gavin and I started working for BelleCurve around the same time two years ago, and there was an immediate attraction between us. I'd only met Zach twice the entire first year of working there. He didn't start frequenting the office until one year ago, and that's when Gavin and I … well. We were something, but we were never official. Deep down I always knew his heart belonged to someone else, and since I wasn't looking for anything serious, it worked for us both.

"So then you finally saw the shining light that had been standing in front of you for two whole years." I sigh, removing a hand from his to fan myself dramatically.

He grabs my hand back as his lips curl up slowly. "As a matter of fact, it was just like that. You were sneaking a piece of cake from the catering station outside the conference room when someone flicked on the entry light. Prettiest damn deer I ever saw. Wide-eyed and so guilty."

His laughter is infectious, but I roll my eyes, hoping to hide the fact that his honesty throws me off balance. He's playing my game, and he might be doing it better than me. There's a reason Zachary Ryan needs to be kept at a distance. I just need to remember what that reason is.

"You going to come out to any of our games this season?"

There it is. That's the reason right there: football. Not my thing.

At any other sporting event, consuming copious amounts of booze, squeezing into a youth-sized jersey, and losing my voice in the crowd would be an exceptional time for me. But not football.

"Chloe mentioned getting tickets to a game. You never know." I bat my eyes up at him. He'll get no promises from me.

There's a lift of the side of his mouth. "Ah, I can't take the anticipation. How about I leave you tickets for our first home game?"

"Really?"

He eyes me suspiciously. "I guess it depends on who you bring. Chloe, sure. A guy, no."

His directness is so surprising, I laugh. "Why not? Guys are into football, aren't they?"

Narrowed eyes glare back at me in a challenge. "Well, that's kind of the problem. We have a female fan presence quota we need to meet. If I give you these tickets, it's a girls-only deal." He shrugs in mock helplessness.

"No promises, Zach."

"Have you been to a Seattle game before?"

I wrinkle my nose. "No."

"Then you need to come. You won't regret it. The energy in that stadium is insane."

The hope in his expression lights me up just enough to ignore the warning signs, and I give him an overly dramatic eye flutter. "You mean I have a choice?"

I should remember, Zachary is competitive. If I'm going to throw sarcasm and wit his way, I should expect he'll be ready with a response. What I'm not expecting is for him to lean down and press his full lips to my ear. A breath escapes before he speaks, and it dances across my skin, raising the hairs on my arms and neck. *Ah.*

"You always have a choice with me, Monica." He doesn't pull away, and I feel my body tense in his arms, waiting for what comes next. "But just so you know, I can be very convincing when I want something."

It definitely doesn't sound like we're talking about football anymore. He leans back to study me as I swallow the ball of nerves in my throat.

"No response?" he challenges. "That might be a first."

Heat creeps up my neck as I struggle to find words. Any words will do. "I wouldn't want to distract you from the game."

He winks. "Not a chance, Cakes. And I promise not to blame you if we lose."

Cakes?

An eyebrow raise is enough of a question to get him laughing again before answering. "What? You have a problem with that name too? You're the one who made me promise not to call you by your full name." He shakes his head. "No take-backs. This one's sticking. Cakes it is, for more reasons than one."

I'm not even going to ask. There's silence between us, just as my eyes catch sight of two familiar faces heading eagerly for the door. I sneak a look at the retreating figures of Chloe and my ex-fling buddy, Gavin.

It's not weird, really, and I would never call him my *ex-fling buddy* out loud. I've been rooting for them to hook up since Gavin confessed their history to me over lunch one day. Chloe had just started working as creative writer at BelleCurve, and he was not handling it well. Turns out there was a treehouse full of issues they had to overcome. Their history is deep and complex, but it's beautiful. I'm just hopeful them leaving together now means they've finally learned how to communicate.

I'm so lost in thought that I don't notice the hand lift from my waist and turn my chin, commanding my attention. When I stare back into Zachary's eyes, my heart does a chaotic dance of its own. He's a beautiful man, with kind, blue eyes that transport me to the Caribbean. His brows, slightly downturned toward his nose, give away his permanently curious nature. But my favorite feature is his aquiline nose that speaks to his strength and dominance. It sits perfectly above those full lips—lips that turn up into perfect curves and widen into the most teasing and beautiful smile—a smile that makes it impossible not to grow taller in his arms, as if he's the sun and I'm powerless without his light.

It's at this moment that I need to remind myself that no man is perfect. Not even Zachary Ryan. I admire him for what he stands for, for his charm and playfulness. I like him, even. But I know guys like him too well, and while I'm more than happy to partake in some mutual flirtation, he isn't fooling me.

For the past month, the back-and-forth banter has been steady but fleeting. Every time he comes to BelleCurve, he stops by my desk without fail. We banter and flirt until it's time for him to run off to practice, or to a press conference, or wherever the heck it is he goes. It's never been a big deal. Besides, flirting comes as second nature to me. It's how I communicate with guys, ensuring I always maintain the upper hand.

It's good to feel wanted, but it bothers me that there's more effort involved than usual in maintaining the upper hand with Zach. It makes me uneasy. Something tells me this man could crush me if given the chance.

In arms that feel far too good—too addictive—I recognize this for what it is, what it should be … and what it cannot be.

Zachary Ryan is a fairytale. And I don't believe in those.

Having Dessert Either Way

Zachary

When it comes to beauty, Monica Stevens takes the cake. Pun intended. The girl does love her desserts. In fact, it might be her one and only weakness, if you can even call it that. Otherwise, she's the most strong-willed, confident, gorgeous, stubborn, and feisty woman I have ever met.

Somehow, I've managed to convince her that dancing with me for the rest of the night is her best option. Three songs after the song and a half she agreed to, and she's still in my arms. Stepping perfectly to every beat, giggling and batting those sexy lashes at me like she owns this interaction. As if she has control enough to walk away whenever she wants.

I love it.

I love that she's acting as if she has the upper hand when she's already given in. I love the way she reacts when I hint at who really has control—as evidenced by the tiny bumps that rise on her skin every single time I speak into her ear.

"Tonight has been a magical night," booms a female's voice through the speakers.

The song that's been playing fades into the background. Monica and I stop dancing and turn our attention to Sandra Spencer, the CEO of BelleCurve Creative, who's just taken the stage.

Monica makes a move to dash away, but I take advantage of the hand that still embraces her tiny waist, instinctively pulling her closer and tightening my grip. I'm not ready for her to escape just yet.

She freezes, and I can feel her tense beneath my hold before relaxing back into her stance.

"To everyone who made tonight possible, you should feel incredibly proud of what you've been a part of. I know I am." Her eyes wander around the room, softening when they land on me. I give her a nod in return.

Sandra, or Sandy, as I call her, is a longtime friend of my coach's wife. When she found out I'd been drafted to Seattle, she contacted me immediately to congratulate me. And then with a simple phone call to a leading travel company, she helped me land my first endorsement deal. Before I knew it, BelleCurve assigned me a publicist, and they've been helping me ever since.

It was a wild ride, that first year, being a rookie on a fierce but struggling NFL team. The worst part? Being doubted by so many. During my third year of an accelerated college program, I was on track to graduate early and decided to enter the draft. The naysayers didn't stop me. Not even close. I managed to learn the ropes and set multiple rookie records.

My second year only got better. I was technically considered a veteran at that point, but most of the team was new to the league—all hungry and very much naïve to the system. We pissed off a lot of people with our undefeated home wins and unprecedented crowd. It was a Division win that season, and a Conference Championship the next—but once we got a taste for winning, once we figured out a formula that worked for us, once we learned to trust in one another, we went on to win our first Super Bowl. We hope to do it again this year.

Sandra leaves the stage after announcing they'll play one more song before ending the night. When I turn to Monica, I can already see the rejection forming on her lips. With the amount of flirting we've done over the past month, I would have never thought I'd have to work so hard to keep her attention.

But the truth is, I've never *wanted* to work so hard to keep a girl's attention. It usually comes so easy. A simple look, a mutual smile—that's all the confidence I need to ask someone out. But for some reason, Monica's resistance only adds to the list of what intrigues me about her.

"What time do you have to run off and save the world?"

She looks confused for a second and then surprises me by laughing. She knows I'm referring to her Superwoman getup, complete with suspenders, a tight blue shirt with an S proudly displayed in the center, and a skirt that shows off the natural curves of her hips. "I should be heading home."

One look in her caramel eyes, and I know she's bluffing. I see the war between her desires and her conscience. I'm trained to read my opponents, and right now I have no qualms about using that skill to my advantage.

"Did you bring your car?"

She nods, her eyes exploring mine as if she's considering something. I don't give her any more time to find an excuse to leave.

"I'm hungry. And you never did get a chance to eat your dessert. If the way you were taking down that strawberry is any indication of your appetite, I think you should come with me. I know a place."

The way her cheeks darken a shade as I hold her eyes with mine fills me with need.

"Is this your clever way of asking me out?"

I cock my head, studying her. *Does she want me to ask her out?* Taking a gamble, I shake my head with mock arrogance. "Definitely not."

Her slowly spreading smile is all I need to know I've won this battle. "Okay, then," she concedes. "Dessert first. And then dinner."

"No way!" I argue. "That's breaking the rules, and my momma taught me better than that." I deepen my drawl on purpose, knowing what it does to most women.

She giggles, and I think I might want to bury my face in her throat just so I can hear that sound again. Then maybe I can get a whiff of that wild strawberry and mint body spray I saw on her desk at work.

"What's the difference?" she asks. "I'm having dessert either way."

"Is that a promise?"

"I don't lie about food."

"In that case, dinner is definitely first. I'll need the sustenance to handle watching you and your foodgasms."

Without a beat lost between us, I gesture for her to walk in front of me, guiding her toward the valet with my palm on her back. My black Jeep sits at the curb. When the teen at the valet booth sees me, he scrambles into the driver seat, starts it with the push of a button, and then hands me the key remote.

I give him a tip, thank him, and help Monica into the passenger seat. "I'll drive you to your car later."

"Are you sure?" she frowns. "I could meet you wherever we're going." Pretty silly of her to say this now that she's already strapped into the passenger seat.

I lean forward, my hands clutching the frame of my Jeep with my fingertips. I don't miss the subtle way her eyes drift over my body. "Your car is safe here. But if you'd rather drive, you can follow me." I make no move to let her leave, hoping she'll take the hint. The last thing I want is to give Monica an easy escape. I'm going to need all the time I can get with this one.

She hesitates for a few seconds and then leans back in her seat. "Parking around here is insane. One car is fine."

With a pleased smile, I pull back and shut the passenger door. Tonight, I finally make my move. Certainly the saying is wrong, because I fully intend on having my cake and eating it too.

Edible Desire

Monica

When Zach drives down Pine Street and parks just a block from Pike Place Market, my heart is racing. *Where is he taking me?* Pike Place is closed, and the only businesses open this late are nightclubs.

"Is this where you take me into some dark alley and murder me?" I don't really believe Zachary is capable of murder, but if I didn't know him, I'd be clutching my heels between my fingertips by now. Fashion can be deadly if needed.

Zachary chuckles and switches off the engine. He turns his body to face me. Even now, awash in a red glow from the neon Pike Place sign, he's drop dead gorgeous. I hate him.

Ugh. Not really. Not at all, actually.

He's looking back at me curiously. "I told you I knew a place. Do you trust me?"

Yes. "Should I?"

The corner of his mouth curls. "You should. I think you'll appreciate where I'm taking you."

"Where *are* you taking me?"

Zachary steps out of the car, walks around to my side of the Jeep, and helps me out. I move back toward the door so my body is flush against it and take in the two-story building in front of us.

"You seriously think I'm going to walk down a dark alley with you and into one of these buildings?" I'm still teasing, but the fear in my voice is playing off something else … another emotion that I consider just as dangerous: I like him. We're alone. And I'm kind of nervous, which is strange because until Zachary Ryan came along, I was the one making guys nervous.

He steps forward and reaches for my hand. "You'll find out as soon as we walk up those stairs."

My eyes grow wide as I look around again, and then I dig my heels into the concrete. "Is this your apartment?"

I never would have guessed Zachary lived here. Most ball players live on the outskirts of Seattle where there's more land and privacy. They don't live in popular tourist areas like this. It's not adding up. And I certainly will not be entering his lair, even if he is the hottest QB to grace this state with his presence. I might be a flirt who dabbles in casual sex, but I'm not *that* girl—the one you can expect it from without even trying.

He groans and tugs on my hand. "C'mon, already. It's not my apartment. I'm not trying to sleep with you." *You're not?* "We're hungry and I'm not in the mood to fight Alaskan Way traffic or risk being recognized right now. This"—he nods up to the top floor— "will have to do. Unless you're not hungry anymore." The way he raises a brow tells me he already knows what my response will be.

"Okay, fine." I roll my eyes and let him tug me along, down a narrow passageway and up a flight of stairs. We come to a stop in front of a door with a logo that reads:

EDIBLE DESIRE
Make it, bake it, take it.

Interesting. In smaller script below there's a message telling people to please use the front door.

Zachary disarms the security code and uses a key from his ring to unlock the back door.

"You have a code and key to this place? How?" I ask, already peering inside.

He flips on a switch and the entire room lights up. I gasp. It's one big open space, a lot like a loft, but it's definitely not an apartment.

There's a massive kitchen on the other side of the room. Beside it, mini work stations fill the floor, each complete with an oven and a stove with stainless steel cookware hanging overhead. There's a long wall of shelves housing cooking supplies and dinnerware. I've seen enough of those cooking shows to assume we're in some sort of culinary school.

To our right is an oversized living area with couches and a coffee table covered in cooking and entertainment magazines. And in the back corner is a massive dining area that could entertain thirty people, at least.

"A cooking school?"

Zachary nods. "That's part of it. I like to call it a community. The space is used for all sorts of activities; instruction is one of them. We have workshops and classes, sometimes private lessons. We cater private events. And we're in the process of creating one of those precooked meal programs—but instead of cooking the meals for our customers, they come in, cook the meals, and take them home."

"We?"

He stares at me for a second. "I own it."

My jaw goes slack. This guy cannot be serious.

He chuckles at my expression. "Well, I'm more like a silent partner for now, so don't tell anyone. I own the space and materials and take care of the finances. My buddy, who's also the chef, manages everything. I went to school with the guy. He just needed to catch a break, you know? It worked out, and he's done a helluva job with the place."

Zachary walks to the kitchen as I take my time looking around. It seems like it would be a lively place during the day. I can imagine it housing an elegant party one night and a casual one the next.

Vibrant lifestyle photos of prepared meals and fresh ingredients decorate the white walls. But one photo in particular catches my attention. It's a close-up shot of a bundle of grapes beside a pair of hands that are wrapped around the stem of a wine glass. There aren't many clues about who the hands belong to, but I recognize them right away as the same hands that engulfed mine earlier tonight.

My cheeks heat when I hear Zach approach from behind. Thank God he can't hear what I'm thinking.

"White or red?"

I flip around to find him holding two bottles of wine. Red always seems to take effect quicker than white. Red would be dangerous tonight.

Meeting his eyes, I point to the red.

"What made you want to open this place?" I ask, following him into the main kitchen.

"I guess I have a thing for food too." He winks.

That's all he gives me and I don't push him, although I'm certain there's more to the story than that.

I watch him work with the corkscrew as he speaks. His sleeves are rolled up past his thick forearms now, and suddenly I'm picturing him in his element, muscles reacting as he sends the football down the field. The way this man goes to work on the field, dominating every play with precision and speed ... *sigh*. I may not be a crazed sports fanatic, but I would have been blind to not catch Zach's skills in a post-game highlight reel blasted all over social media.

That pass in game six of the regular season when Seattle was down six points with three seconds left on the clock solidified it for me. He's the best of the best. He knew just what to do, and when the ball flew from his hands, it was hands-down the most beautiful pass I've ever seen—a record-breaking Hail Mary that won the game. The man is magic on the field. Apparently, he radiates the same intoxicating energy in the kitchen too.

"It just seems a bit odd," I say. "Why would you want to start a business at the beginning of your football career?"

"Honestly, Cakes, people don't get it, so it's not something I usually tell." His words are strange, but his tone is genuine.

"Maybe you should hand me that wine and then start talking. You dragged me here, so fess up." I smile.

He pours the wine and slides a glass across the table. I take a seat at the island and watch him reach into the refrigerator to grab one of the premade dishes. He moves to the oven and preheats it before taking a sip of his wine and leaning into the island opposite me.

"Back home, my parents owned a restaurant. A small, fine dining, family establishment where we served American cuisine. My mom cooked, my dad tended bar, and we had a few staff members that did pretty much everything else. The locals loved us at first…"

Something about his tone that changes for a second, but he quickly gets back on track. He smiles. "My brother and I would rush to the restaurant after school every day. Sometimes we sat in the corner and did homework. Other days we'd help bus tables or wash dishes. We'd even help my mom in the kitchen.

"We were her taste testers. I think it was her clever way of getting us involved in the kitchen so we'd eat everything on our plates. It worked a little too well. My palette was so sophisticated by the time I was twelve, I couldn't stand eating school lunches."

I laugh with him, ignoring the unexplainable discomfort in my stomach and picturing little Zachary snubbing the lunch lady's cardboard pizza.

His face loses its smile, and he clears his throat before looking at me. As his eyes search mine, I know there's a bad end to this story, and I'm not so sure I want to hear it now.

"The restaurant business wasn't the most profitable for us, and it took up all my parent's time. My mom loved it, but after a while I think my dad started to get tired of barely making ends meet. He started drinking more booze than he was serving, if you know what I mean."

I nod, understanding all too well how failed careers can change a person.

"I was fourteen, a month shy of high school football tryouts, focused on my training to earn my spot on that team, when everything changed. One night after closing, my dad stayed late. Drinking, of course. We were all home asleep when we got the call. He crashed his car into a telephone pole." Zach clears his throat again. "He died on impact."

My hand flies to my mouth to smother my gasp, but the ache that pricks my eyes can't be hidden. "I'm so sorry," I manage to choke out. After all the Zachary Ryan Googling I've done since meeting him, this story never came up. I knew his dad had passed, but not like that.

"It was a long time ago," he says with a shake of his head. "I didn't want to upset you, but it's all kind of part of the story." He frowns for my benefit, and that only makes me feel worse. I place a hand over his and squeeze.

He glances at me before moving his hand so that it's covering mine on the island. I don't know why this feels like the most natural thing in the world, us holding hands, but it does.

"Fast forward to three years ago," he continues. "When I was first drafted into the NFL, I wasn't paid well in comparison to other quarterbacks, but it was still more than I ever anticipated making in my lifetime. It was always about playing football. The money was never the motivation, so when I got paid, I figured I could do something meaningful with it.

"My mom was torn between moving to Seattle to be close to me or staying in Texas until my brother finished college. It seemed like the perfect opportunity to give back to my mom for everything she'd done for us, and selfishly, I wanted her here." Zach laughs. "It was impulsive, but I went for it."

"You created all this for her?"

Zachary nods, but his eyes are crinkled at the corners as he laughs. "She chose my brother. Can you believe it? The people she sold our restaurant to needed a cook, so they hired her on." He shrugs. "She's happy."

The thought of Zach doing all of this for his mother is so sweet, but I can't help the laughter that rolls past my throat. "And you didn't ask her first?"

He wrinkles his nose. "It's awful, I know. The most impulsive decision I've ever made. I could have sold it. Tons of offers came through once word got out that I was considering putting it back up for sale. But the location is prime real estate and I got a great deal. I couldn't give it up.

"Anyway, the buddy of mine I knew from school … he didn't have much of a family. Got into some trouble in high school but decided to put himself through culinary school, even if it meant student loans up to his eyeballs. Said he just wanted to make something of himself. When my mom turned down the place, I called him up and asked him what he thought of partnering with me."

I tilt my head, my chest warm with compassion for this man who obviously does so much for others.

Silence passes between us and I feel compelled to ask. "What's his name?"

"Desmond." Zachary tilts his head at me and quirks a lip. "Why? You interested?"

I grin. "You said he can cook, didn't you?" I nod to the frozen dish sitting next to him. "I'll bet he prepared that too. I love a man that can cook." Wiggling my eyebrows has the desired effect.

Zach's eyes narrow and he tugs at my hand from across the island. "C'mere."

Without letting on how fast my heart has started beating in my chest, I step around the slab of granite just as he's pulling what looks like a menu from a drawer. An assortment of exotic desserts decorates the page. "Which one do you want to make?"

"Me?"

"No, the other hot superhero in suspenders."

I smirk and scan the menu. It doesn't take me long to start salivating over the triple chocolate cake. There's a strawberry garnish on the plate in the photo, so I figure it's more than appropriate for this evening.

I point to it and Zach's deep rumble shakes his chest. "I'm not sure why I even asked." He works his way around the oversized stainless steel kitchen, grabbing ingredients I could never name. The low lights hum around us as he works. I watch him, turned on by his passion for something other than football. Intrigued by the history that has clearly influenced him. And amazed that such a big guy can move around all domestic-like and make it look effortless.

He wouldn't be impressed with my cake baking skills, but I'm not about to announce my flaws in the kitchen while he's so darn confident.

We don't talk much while he's gathering ingredients, but when he's standing over a bowl of sugar he asks for me to join him. He positions me so I'm centered in front of him. He goes first, adding the butter and vanilla into the bowl, and then he places an egg in my hand before starting the electric mixer.

The cold, hard object feels odd in my hands. I know what he wants me to do with it. I've seen people do this. Unfortunately, every time I've tried to crack an egg I've ended up with shell in my teeth.

With heat in my cheeks, I turn my head to meet Zach's amused eyes. The buzz of the electric mixer stops. "Do you have something to hold your hair back?"

I remove the elastic from my wrist and grin. "Yup."

In a swift move, he takes it from me and turns my head back to the food. *This is new.* Before I can stop him or offer to do it myself, he's moving his fingers through my hair, working it into a ponytail. Chills break out over my skin when he leans down again. This time he reaches over me and grabs an egg, cracking it perfectly in one palm. I watch as he carefully releases only the clear bits before tossing the yolk in the sink beside us. No shell in the bowl.

How did he do that?

I watch him do it again with the second egg and confirm that his hands are, in fact, made of magic. As he starts up the mixer again, I make a move to step aside—I'm obviously in the way—but Zach uses his arm to keep me in place. He's done that a lot tonight. I like that he doesn't let me walk away so easily.

"We're doing this together, Cakes. Half cup of sour cream up next. Can you do the honors?"

We mix the cake batter and set it aside, its rich sweetness scenting the air. Moving to the boiling pot on the stove, we add in cocoa and chocolate chips, melting it down as his hand rests on mine. We stir the thick, velvety mixture until it softens and cascades off the spoon in a slow stream.

There's a thrill racing through me as I watch everything come together. No one has ever taught me to bake. My grandma was too forgetful to use the oven, and mom stayed away from the kitchen like it was the devil's lair.

Zachary hands me a wooden spoon and places his hand over mine. This—watching him cook, feeling his hand on mine as he moves me around his kitchen … it's sexy. But not any kind of sexy I've experienced before. I'm starting to think I wouldn't mind the night ending in a heady make out session. After the last month of build-up, we kind of deserve it.

"Rockwall, huh?"

"That's right."

"How'd you wind up here?"

I find myself rushing my words, trying to avoid answering a slew of questions about my background. Other guys have tried to get to know me before, but it's always been so easy to distract them with an extra bat of the eye or a touch of the arm. I have a feeling Zach won't let up until he knows every detail. And that can't happen.

I swallow, wondering how well my vocal chords will work against my nerves. "Unfinished business."

I feel him lean down. Hot breath escapes from between his lips and hits my neck. That's the moment I realize how close he is to me. He's right there, master conductor to my every nerve ending. Then he intertwines his fingers with mine and gently touches his nose to my neck. "I won't let you get away with that answer for long, Cakes."

A chill causes my entire body to tremble beneath him. He doesn't miss a beat. I hear his light chuckle as he picks the wooden spoon up from the chocolate mixture and blows on it until it's safe to taste. He nips at it and licks his lips, then holds the spoon close to my mouth. I open up to take a taste, never breaking eye contact.

"So good." I'm not trying to be seductive. It's truly mouthwatering.

His lids lower at the sound of my voice, and then he moves to turn the knobs on the stove to their off position and sets the heated pot to the side. There's a hitch in my breath when he leans into me, planting a sweet kiss in the crook of my neck. "Is this okay?" he questions, mouth hovering over my skin.

My senses grow hazy as I nod.

He kisses me again, this time beneath my ear. A groan rumbles low in his throat. "You smell amazing, Cakes. Like chocolate, strawberries, and just a hint of mint. My new favorite scent." His nose grazes my neck again. "I need to bottle you up so I can steal a taste whenever I have a craving." He presses his lips to the tip of my shoulder.

There's no hiding my reaction to his raspy words and his mouth on my skin. My breath stutters and my body shudders. Each kiss to my neck is like a zap of electricity lighting up my insides.

Seduction swirls through the air, tangling with the richness of heating food and dessert. After a moment, Zach steps away to check on dinner. It's a good thing, giving me the time I need to clear my head and get my shit together.

I shiver, because it's impossible to clear my head when all I can think of is the way he pressed his body into mine just now, and how I could most definitely feel every single inch of Zachary Ryan.

This is bad. Very, very bad.

Doggy Bag

Zachary

She devours dinner almost as ravenously as when she went after that strawberry earlier. I'll never get over that sight. Plump lips suckling the juicy fruit. Eyes closed, long lashes fluttering against the top of her cheeks. The moan that called to me like a bottle rocket in the night.

Monica is a unique beauty. Creamy skin and light, golden brown eyes, but otherwise dark, exotic features. It's intriguing. She's intriguing, and not just because of her physical beauty and obsession with food.

How could I have walked into BelleCurve the past two years without seeing how completely radiant she was? It's no wonder why I haven't had a serious relationship in years. Not that I haven't noticed her. I have. But with so much focus on my football career and the kitchen, my perspective of everything else was off.

Monica has it all. She's funny without even trying, which makes her personality addicting—maybe even more addicting than the taste of her skin. I wasn't planning for that to happen—the tasting her skin portion of the night, that is. While Monica might have thought I was trying to lure her into my bed, I meant exactly what I told her.

It's getting harder every day for me to walk around this vibrant city without getting noticed. I love the fans; the adrenaline they give me is stuff addicts would trade worse habits for. But that doesn't mean I need everyone in my business always. Like tonight, when I finally have an opportunity to talk to a girl I've been crushing intensely on for some time now, are not ideal to be stopped in public to take a selfie. Time is precious, and I don't want to waste a second of it. Especially not tonight.

Conversation and wine flow effortlessly. I give her a glimpse of what my next week looks like with preseason starting: the travel, intense workouts, comradery, tape reviews, press conferences, coach lectures—the works. It's nonstop, and in a way, I want to warn her. I like her, but let's be honest; the girls I've dated in the past don't deal with the distance well—not to mention taking second place to my career.

"I may not be a traveling pro athlete," she smiles into her wine, "but working full-time at BelleCurve keeps me pretty busy too."

God, I love watching that mouth. "What about school? Have you graduated already?"

She adjusts herself, looking uneasy. "Got my associate, and then I started working at BelleCurve. I took some time off from school to figure out what I wanted to do next." When she peers up to meet my eyes, something catches in my chest.

"Isn't there anything you enjoy that you've considered making a career? What about when you were young?"

"I wanted to be a model." Pink fills her cheeks, like the words flew out of her mouth before she could stop them. Is she embarrassed by her own dreams? "I'm sorry. It's been a long time since I admitted that, but it's all I wanted to do growing up. It was practically forced on me, though. My mom was a model. My sister, Maggie, has been modeling for as long as I can remember. I traveled with them to every gig, played dress up in the green rooms, had my own portfolio created—"

"I could see you as a model." The lines of her face and her high cheek bones. The softness of her curves. Her light eyes. Full lips. The way she carries herself. She's definitely got the confidence. "What happened? You said *wanted.*"

Her head turns down, which is by far the most un-Monica-like thing she's done all night. Where's my little firecracker now? As if she hears my question, she looks up again and blushes.

"I wasn't tall enough. I don't know how it happened, but I'm the shortest one in my family. Not even these things help me fake it." She kicks up her leg good-naturedly to show off her heel, but all I see is her skirt rise, exposing her glossy thigh. I have to swallow my lustful thoughts to hear the rest of her words.

"They also said I was too curvy." She peers down at her body and shrugs. "That isn't going to change anytime soon." She laughs again. This time it's nerves I detect, and anger heats my chest.

"How old were you?"

"Fourteen. Worst year of my life," she says, scrunching her nose.

"Who told you that shit?" What kind of asshole would put Monica down? At fourteen, no less. She's undeniably gorgeous. And I'm not just talking about her face and curves. You don't mess with a smile that genuine, a heart that kind. She's real. Inside and out. It's why I haven't been able to take my eyes off her.

With a wave of her hand, she tells me it doesn't matter. "It's fine. I wasn't meant to model. It was just a little girl's silly dream because it was the world that surrounded me. And I'm not just saying that because someone denied me. It was the best thing to get that out of my head at an early age. I started focusing more on school and getting the hell out of Texas."

I chuckle. "Amen to that. Seattle is more my style too. Does your family still live there?"

"No. When I moved here my mom and sister moved to LA. My mom thought it was the best place for my sister to get more exposure."

"Has it been?"

She shrugs. I grab another bottle of wine while she speaks. "Maggie doesn't want to model anymore, so it's kind of a hostile situation between them. Acting is where she belongs. At least being in LA gives her more opportunities, but I don't know. The competition is ugly. She's been turned down for more acting roles than I can keep track of, but she's still booking nice-sized modeling events. She's doing a lot of promotional gigs too. But I'm afraid if she doesn't nail an acting job soon she's going to lose it."

"That's a tough business, but I agree; Cali is the right place to be." I still can't shake this shit about Monica not being good enough to model. I straddle the bench beside her, placing the bottle of wine down and reaching up to cup her chin lightly in my hands. "You realize you're perfect, right? No asshole who tells you anything else is worth listening to. I'd have pinned you on my wall." She laughs and tries to avert her gaze, but I gently turn her back to me. "I still might."

There's a hitch in her breath and her laughter fades. My gaze drifts from her eyes to her lips, and then to her neck. I've never wanted to kiss a neck so badly. After the first taste, it's safe to say I'm hooked.

She averts her gaze and shakes her head. "Zach, thank you, but it's okay. Really." I can tell she means it. "Losing that opportunity didn't change what I thought about myself. I'm happy with my body, always have been. It was just a reality check. It made me question a lot of things. Most importantly, it made me question if I ever really wanted to model, or if it was something I thought I was supposed to want. And there's no way I'm ever sacrificing a meal to appease a few dickhole gatekeepers. I'd rather run a few miles a day than starve."

Thank God for that.

"You have curves that men love and most girls would kill for. And your height"—my lips turn up slightly at the thought of how beneficial her height really is for ... spooning and less innocent activities— "is preferable." I don't care if I'm laying all my cards out here. There's something about this girl that's worth any gamble.

There's that blush again. I love when I can see her react to my words. Before tonight, Monica has only ever exuded maximum control over her responses. Taking her away from the crowd was the right thing to do. Inhibitions down. Just us.

"And your curves." I lean in to brush my lips across her cheek. "You have the *sexiest* curves. You're perfect, Cakes."

She shakes in my hold, so I make my move. Gliding past her cheek to her ear, I smile against her skin, catching a whiff of her luscious scent and groaning. I imagine we're in a field with wild strawberries and mint leaves, a hint of chocolate still lingering in the air. "I'm trying to be a gentleman here, but I'd like to kiss you."

When she releases a smile, that's all I need to let my lips travel, placing kisses from her ear to her jaw, and then along her collarbone, until her lips are parting for me. "You're going to kill me with that mouth, Cakes." I breathe her in, then take her bottom lip with my teeth and tug gently.

A high-pitched moan enters my mouth. I swallow it and continue to press my lips to hers, gripping her waist with one hand while the other moves from her chin to the back of her head so I can deepen the kiss.

Sweet Jesus, this woman will end me.

Her lips are just as I imagined and ten times better. Soft but firm, experienced but moving as if made just for me. She's perfect. And the taste of her—mouthwatering.

Sensing my body and mind are reacting too fast, too soon, I pull away, leaving her with a soft kiss on the nose. Pretending I don't notice her heavy breaths and dazed expression, I pour us both another glass of wine, launching directly back into conversation without pause.

"Have you ever considered a profession suited for BelleCurve? You love it there, it makes sense to explore the creative side a bit more, don't you think?" She seems to still be recovering, so I continue. "Entertainment business, graphic design, video production…"

"Styling and retail merchandising," she offers. "I love to shop." She smiles and takes another chug of wine. "And I always loved the backstage hustle and bustle during the shows my sister booked during New York Fashion Week… I don't know," she says with a shrug. "Maybe you're onto something."

"I know nothing about fashion."

She eyes me up and down. "Sure, and that Gucci suit you're wearing tonight magically appeared on your doorstep."

I'm mid-gulp when her eyes roll, causing me to choke on my wine. "Wow," I say through my cough. "Calling me out. Okay. So, I buy expensive suits. Only because my publicist would shoot me if I showed up to an event wearing the same thing as every other guy."

Her laugh is loud, probably from the buzz, but she's laughing at me. "I hate to break it to you, Zach, but I doubt the guests of honor at tonight's event could tell the difference between your Gucci suit and what *every other guy* was wearing. It may be classy and expensive, but to them—it's all the same."

I bite back a smile. "Told you. Not into fashion."

She nods, agreeing my point is made. "You want to be original? Hire your own stylist so they can give you your own look, not the other way around."

Now I'm the one that laughs. "Sorry, Cakes. There's no way I'm going to let someone follow me around telling me what to wear when I can walk straight into Target just like everyone else and buy a white button-down shirt for a nice dinner." I consider my answer for a second and then grin. "Unless it's you."

There's that eye roll again. I'm starting to get used to it. "This, coming from the man wearing Gucci."

"For your information," I say, "I happen to love Gucci. And it *is* original. Besides that, I look hot. I feel crisp. Isn't fashion about the way you feel?"

She relaxes back into her seat, a smile settling on her face. "Yes it is, Gucci."

I chuckle before running a hand through my hair and locking eyes with her again. "Really? Is that *my* nickname now?"

She shrugs, eyeing me in a way that makes me want to pull her to me again. "You wear it well."

Ah, there's my girl. "Thanks, Cakes. You wear Superwoman well." I wink. "Ready for dessert?"

She narrows her eyes and then quirks her lip. "I can't believe you had to ask me that. Clearly you haven't been paying attention."

"Ah, but I have. I was just being courteous." I stand and move to the kitchen to dish out one large slice of triple chocolate cake.

"Where's yours?" she asks when I set the cake down in front of her.

I sit down and stab into the chocolate. Only inches from her, I hold the bite-size piece to her mouth. "What's yours is mine."

"I think you mean what's mine is yours." She eyes the forkful.

"Exactly." I bite my lip, just as she opens her mouth to taste the first bite.

I wish I could have videotaped this. Her eyes droop closed as her entire body relaxes around the forkful of dessert. I can hear the tiniest moan from where I sit, which isn't nearly close enough. And after she swallows, she sighs like she's in some kind of euphoric spell.

It would be the smart thing to hand her the fork and walk away. To let her eat the damn dessert and call it a night. To pour out the rest of the wine and grab the bottled waters from the fridge. Take her home, then drive to my condo and take an ice-cold shower.

I don't do any of those smart things.

My finger dips into the chocolate, pulling out a dollop of frosting. I taste it with a flick of my tongue before offering the rest to Monica. She leans in and covers the tip of my finger with her mouth—not one single ounce of hesitation. I'm a little surprised she doesn't fight me on this one. I'm even more surprised when she gently bites into my skin before dragging her mouth away, skimming my finger with her teeth.

Yup. Bad move on my part, but now she's guilty too.

Game over.

I slide one hand up her cheek and into her hair. The other moves up the fabric of her skirt until it's resting at her waist, gripping it firmly. My mouth is on hers. Tasting every last bit of chocolate; groaning when I crave more. She's a drug. And in no time at all she's become my addiction. I feed off the first taste and tell myself I just need a little bit more. *One more taste and then I'll let her go.* The thought is on repeat, battling my senses until my senses take over completely.

She reads me well. Her lips part, allowing my tongue to dive deep. Her touch mirrors my every move. Her appetite is just as greedy, proof that our connection is mutual and very real.

Monica grips my shirt, pulling it from my pants and slipping a hand up my back. It's all her fault now. If she hadn't done that, I probably wouldn't be pulling her onto the table so that her legs can easily wrap around my waist.

But just as I'm pressing her back against the handcrafted wood table, she pushes against me so she's sitting and I'm standing between her legs. My heart might fall out of my chest if this ends right now.

A panicked look takes over her face. "The cake!" Her concern is sincere and ridiculously endearing. I was careful enough to move her away from the cake before she sat on it. When she sees this, pink colors her skin.

I turn her face back to mine with just the tips of my fingers, running my eyes greedily down her body. "Leave it, Cakes. We have doggy bags."

It takes a second before her expression relaxes. "Good. I'm not leaving here without my cake."

"Neither am I," I growl, burying my face in her neck and breathing her in.

One Kiss

Monica

One kiss can change everything. It can grip you, weaken you, resolve you, strengthen you. It's beginning; it's end.

His kiss saved me.

And then it destroyed me.

He thinks this is our beginning...

I know better

STEP TWO

BelleCurve Creative

"THE ONLY CONTRIBUTION THAT WE WILL EVER MAKE IN THIS WORLD WILL BE BORN OF OUR CREATIVITY."
— BRENE BROWN

Private Affairs

Monica

Annoyed, unfamiliar faces glare back at me as I burst into the main lobby of BelleCurve Creative. The guests' visible disappointment grates on the surface of my recently exfoliated skin. I've kept them waiting too long—five minutes too long to be exact. Their meeting was supposed to start promptly at one o'clock, but since most of my lunch hours are spent volunteering with photo and video shoots for the production department, I lost track of time.

"Lotter & Jones," I say, putting on my brightest smile. "I'm so sorry if I've kept you waiting." The group of attorneys eyes me, stony faces unchanging. "I'll show you the way to your conference room."

They follow me down the hallway to the all-glass main conference room toward BelleCurve's top three executives, Sandra, Charles, and Barker, who are patiently waiting for their guests to arrive.

Letting the group walk in first, I peer around the room. "Can I get anyone anything to drink?"

Sandra beams at me as she always does. She is the kindest of the three, with Barker at a close second. Charles is all business, no small talk; always seeming to have a stick up his—

"Thank you, Monica. I'm okay. Anyone else?"

The attorneys mumble their orders without meeting my eyes, and then Sandra's eyes dart to the clock in the corner of the room. She turns on her business face and clears her throat. "We're a little behind schedule, so let's get started, shall we?"

Guilt seeps into my system as I bow out of the room. It's not like me to be late or get so flustered, but ever since the Heroes and Legends event, things have felt different. Not just at work, but at home too. I've been stir-crazy, wanting to do something more. Something valuable.

One could argue that my position as office manager *is* valuable, and it is, but it's not for me—not anymore. I love this company. I love the people. But something is just— wrong.

When I drop off the drinks in the conference room and Sandra catches my eye, my heart sinks. I know that look, but it's never been directed at me before. She's disappointed, upset, and maybe a little angry, and I don't question the reason why. *Those little snitches.*

No doubt we'll be having a conversation about this, and I'm already cringing. What am I going to say? If I tell her the truth—that I'm having more fun running errands for Richland, BelleCurve's Creative Director, than doing my own job— she'll fire me. *Instantly.* Sandra's nice, but she's a businesswoman first and foremost, and this company is her baby.

Distracted, I walk toward Chloe's cubicle right outside the conference room. It's my happy place. Usually when I need a break from the monotony, I infiltrate her space, plant myself on her desk, and talk her ear off. She always listens. Then she feeds me chocolate. Unfortunately, I remember too late, she's with Gavin in California.

Because of his work at Heroes and Legends, Gavin's been contracted to work for the main sponsor, Mastermind Comics, to enhance their bullying prevention program. It's not his first trip to the Golden State, but this time Chloe took off work to accompany him, which means this is definitely going to be a pouty kind of day.

Only one thing can fix me: chocolate.

I reach into Chloe's bottom drawer and dig through her bag of Halloween candy from last October. I know she doesn't eat the stuff; she keeps it here for me. Because she's an amazing friend, and she knows it's the only way to calm me down. And shut me up.

The moment the chocolate touches my lips, I feel my entire body relax. Magic.

Just as I'm sinking into the comfort of my weakness, a fit of giggles on the other side of the cubicle interrupts my moment of relaxation. I recognize the voices as belonging to the gossip queens—an unofficial title, but an accurate one—Gracie and Trinity from public relations.

They're nice enough, but because they share a cubicle and see a good amount of scandal daily, they can often be found whispering about some new development in the sports entertainment world. You'd think their boss and the top publicist at BelleCurve, Meredith Greene, would rein them in a bit, but with the gossip queens distracting the office from her own evil schemes, she won't.

The queens jump when they see my head pop around the corner. "Hey, hotties," I say, feigning nonchalance.

"Geez, Monica. You scared us."

"Sorry. Just walking by," I lie. My eyes dart to the screen.

Trinity rushes to hide the social media window. But it's too late. It's impossible to unsee what just vanished from her screen. I've already gotten a glimpse of the most beautiful set of Caribbean blue eyes on that face I find myself frequently wishing out of my mind.

The time I spent dancing with Zach at Heroes and Legends didn't go unnoticed. There were stories for weeks about my desperation for the unattainable QB. It was embarrassing, but I did my best to let it roll off my back. There are worse things they could have said about me, and the stories did die down … eventually.

"Was that a picture of Zach?" I smile, hoping they feel at ease enough to let me in on their private joke.

The girls exchange a look and then shrug. "Yeah."

"Was he with someone?" A twinge of jealousy hammers on my nerves. As much as I don't want to care that I saw a beautiful blonde on his arm in that photo, I can't help it. Whoever it was looked awfully comfortable with him. I just hope it wasn't—

Gracie smirks and brings up the photo again. She can't keep a secret to save her life. Neither of them can. It's a mystery how they ended up working in public relations.

When I see the blonde in a black cocktail dress who's hooked nice and snug under Zach's arm, my heart sinks to my stomach.

Trinity bites her lip. "Meredith took some photos of Zach a couple weeks ago when they went to a charity dinner. We're supposed to grab a couple shots for his website, and we came across these."

This day just went from shitty to extra shitty in less than ten minutes. Why does my heart hurt over this? It's not like there was a future for us to begin with. It's not like I agreed to a real date when he asked. The only person I can blame for letting Zachary Ryan slip through my chocolate-covered fingers is me. And now I'm just torturing myself.

"They look good together." The words hurt, but these girls are used to my rock hard exterior and bubbly nature. If I let my guard down now, I'll be opening myself up to an inquisition.

And they do look good together. Meredith is the type that looks expensive. Everything about her screams *Real Housewives of Beverly Hills*. She's been grooming herself for someone like Zach her entire life. Short angled blonde bob, perfectly straightened. Always a fresh manicure on her massive claws. Her body, tall and slender, always walking high and slow with determination.

"Do you think they're—?" I can't even bring myself to ask the question.

Trinity and Gracie both nod emphatically.

"Oh, yeah," Gracie says, in full gossip mode, voice hushed and talking fast. "Meredith tries to play it cool, but they're always going to events together, and they do look extra cozy in these pictures. She's been after him for a while now. It wouldn't surprise me if they finally hooked up."

"Meredith's kind of a celebrity whore," Trinity adds, scrunching her face.

"Can she do that? Zachary pays her to manage his publicity, for heaven's sake. If that got out it wouldn't look too good for BelleCurve."

Gracie snorts. "It's not like she'd need a job if she landed Zach." She sighs and stares at the photo again. I want to unplug her computer and chuck it over the cubicle to make the image go away.

Geez, Monica. Aggressive much?

"Did you catch that last game?" Trinity's eyes light up. "That boy is a miracle worker on the field."

A miracle worker on the field and other places. "No, I worked a shoot with Richland, so I missed it." I don't mention that Richland had the television on, volume off, and I couldn't help but stare at the QB god every chance I got. The last game was the playoff match that got the boys into the Super Bowl, so it would have been impossible to miss.

"What?" they both shriek.

"How could you have missed it?" Gracie demands. "We were down at halftime and Zach threw, like, four touchdowns straight into the end zone. It was crazy."

I force a smile. "Wow. Sounds like an awesome game."

Actually, Zach threw two passes into the end zone. One failed and resulted in a field goal instead, and the other touchdown he ran in himself. But I won't clarify for their benefit.

Gracie laughs and turns back to her computer, unable to comprehend my lack of enthusiasm, I'm sure. "I have to get these photos edited and uploaded like, now, or Meredith will have our heads." She looks at Trinity, suddenly in panic mode. "Did you write the copy?"

Trinity poises her pen over her notepad and grins. "No, but I'll have it in a jiffy."

I force a big smile and wave as I slip from their cubicle and head down the hall toward my desk, which sits just inside of the main entrance. I spend the next two hours responding to emails, importing business cards into the electronic directory, and setting up appointments. I'm bored out of my mind.

When a tall woman with dirty blonde hair walks through the main doors, I perk up. "You must be the firefighter."

The girl nods and shoves her hands in her front jean pockets. She's beautiful, and even with her long-sleeved shirt on, I can see how ripped she is. *Damn.* Girl must work out constantly.

"Nancy," she introduces herself. "I think my shoot is with Richland?"

I smile, then hop out of my chair and circle the desk.

"Wow," she says, looking me up and down. "I love your outfit."

Beaming, I pause to run my hands down the front of my DIY romper. The black, silk short-shorts would totally be inappropriate for office wear if it weren't for the floral printed tights underneath them. My top, black and bearing the words "Avec Toi Je Suis Moir"—*with you, I am me*—is slightly on the baggier side and sewn into the shorts. To top it off, I added a long zipper in the back to get the dang thing on and off. Not that you can see it beneath my long, beige trench coat—my favorite thrift store purchase to date.

"You like it? Really? I've been playing around with some old clothes at home. It's been ages since I've sewn anything."

Her mouth drops open. "You made that?" Her eyes move to my desk and then back to me.

I shrug. "Yeah. It's nothing, really. Trust me. I grew up in the fashion industry and have seen the best of the best. I was just messing around."

Nancy lets out a laugh. "Well, you should do it more often."

A buzz of adrenaline washes over me and I hook my arm in Nancy's. I'm grinning like an idiot, but I don't care. "Right this way. Richland's all set up for you. I'm Monica, by the way."

She gives me a thankful smile.

"I've never met a female firefighter before. It must be a dream getting to work with all those hot guys." I wink. "And distracting too, I guess."

"Most of the guys in my department are much older than me. Sorry to break it to you." She's smiling when we make eye contact again. "But they're great guys. Let me know if you're into the silver fox type and I can probably hook you up."

I shrug. "Why not? Silver fox. Balding. Ski cap for hair. As long as he can keep up with me, I'm game."

Nancy is laughing when we walk through the doors to the studio, and I grin at Richland, who's already standing there fiddling with his camera. "I've got your model." My singsong voice gets his attention. "I was just telling Nancy here she should hook me up with one of her silver fox firefighter friends. What do you think?"

He doesn't miss a beat. "I think you should stick to your own kind, Monica. Those boys couldn't handle you."

"See," I tell Nancy.

"Monica here needs loads of attention. Having her man gone for days at a time wouldn't sit well with her."

My mouth snaps shut and I bunch my brows in shock. Wait a second. I had no clue Richland was going to make this personal. He's smiling, so maybe he's kidding. But what is it they say about jokes? There's always partial truth to it?

"You serious, Rich? I can handle a few days of separation. Please." I roll my eyes and reach for Nancy's arm. "Come with me, doll. I'll show you to your clothes and get you into hair and makeup while Richland over here works on his apology."

Technically, I'm supposed to say goodbye here and go back to work. But Richland needs me, and this is the only part of the day I actually enjoy. The dressing room is already set up for Nancy, thanks to me, and I know right where to go for her clothes. Handing her the hanger, I look her over once more. Fair complexion. Flawless skin, but a little on the dry side. Beautiful brown eyes. That's as much information as I need to prepare her makeup while she changes.

"Monica." Richland's surprised voice carries relief too as he sees me setting up the makeup station. "You are the best."

Giving him a wink, I concentrate on testing lipstick colors on my skin. "I'm not that busy today and the execs are in a meeting, so this should be fine."

He looks as if he wants to argue with me but turns away instead, probably realizing he can't afford to lose me right now. Why BelleCurve doesn't give Richland a better production budget is beyond me. His business has quadrupled since I started with this company.

Richland is in his late twenties, on the stocky side with hard, square jaw, lightened somewhat by his full beard. His seafoam green eyes, small in proportion to his size, can shine with laughter and then zoom into focus at the snap of a finger.

Unfortunately, he works too hard to settle down. His girlfriend of seven years recently gave up on him. As focused as he is, even a stranger would have thought he didn't care about her—but I knew different.

After she left him, he started working even longer hours and smiled a little less. I think it all came down to a choice, and he chose the job. He's married to the damn place.

Maybe he's right; I could never be with someone like that. Passion is great, but not when it's entirely focused in one direction. A woman should always come before a man's career. Sure, you should love your job, but one day that career is going to end and all you'll have left are washed up memories.

Obsession with his career aside, no one will argue with the fact that Richland is a brilliant visionary—especially me. He's my rock in this place, and he was the first one to pick up on the fact that I needed this department as much as it needed me.

Over the past two and a half years, the production suite has become my secret getaway, but not just because it's somewhere to decompress. Richland has a hard time admitting that he needs the help. He's too proud, and if he had to do it all on his own to save the company a few dollars, he totally would.

I've been around long enough to see the proposals go from his desk to Sandra's, requesting additional help. He's yet to gain a production assistant, always forced to negotiate with outside resources to get the work done.

Whether it's hair, makeup, fittings, gofer duties, stand-ins, or inventory of some kind, I always find a way to show up when Richland needs me in the studio. If it weren't for this, I'd be completely lost.

Career Adjustment

Monica

I've just reapplied Nancy's lip sauce—my term of endearment for lip gloss—and am returning to my station when the door to the studio bursts open, revealing a heated Sandra.

Everything is silent and still except for Sandra and the pending explosion on her face.

Shit.

"Richland, do you mind if I borrow your *assistant*?"

Richland nods his head. "Of course. We're almost done here anyway."

Traitor.

I shiver with fear as I follow Sandra out the door.

"Thanks, Monica," Nancy calls as I'm slipping out the door behind Sandra.

I give Nancy a wave that I hope comes off as casual—even though I'm feeling anything but. In all my time at BelleCurve, I have never experienced the wrath of Sandra Spencer. I know she can be a lioness when she wants to be, but never did I expect that I would find myself the victim of her ire. Well, I guess I suspected it after she gave me that look earlier. But then I got distracted with Richland and completely forgot … *which is precisely the problem.*

Inside the executive suite, Sandra leads me to her corner office. With large windows, Tiffany blue walls, and simple but elegant décor, I'm struck by how true to Sandra this office is. Classy but kind. Rich but modest. Feminine but neutral. Smart but daring. She's an impressive woman with a lot to show for it. The opposite of what I've become over the last few months.

I've only been in here a handful of times, mostly to drop off flowers from her husband because he still treats her like they just got married—eight years later. It's sweet, and I'd love to be the kind of girl who snaps a photo and hashtags it #RelationshipGoals, but that's not where my mind goes.

I'm not suspicious of all men, just the ones that try to get close to me. So, when I think of a man sending me flowers, I see red flags. I see exit signs and getaway cars. I don't see grand gestures and proclamations of love that will last an eternity because our souls are entwined.

Sandra takes a seat behind her desk and gestures to the chair across from her.

Sitting slowly, I sink into the plush fabric, careful not to get too comfortable. I watch Sandra expectantly, wondering if now is a good time to start praying again. I wasn't born into a religious family, but we attended a non-denominational church on occasion. At first, my parents wanted to instill values in Maggie and me. We were a perfect family, dressed in our Sunday best for years.

Until life got too busy and church became an inconvenience. A conversation piece at nice dinners. A way to keep up appearances. Because that's what our family started to become near the end of my parent's marriage. Not so much for my sister and me. We believed in the lie. It was my parents who could have won Oscars for their realistic displays of love and affection.

When my dad started going on week-long job hunts, I prayed for his safety. When week-long job hunts extended for a month at a time, I prayed that the next time he came home, he would stay. Two years later, when the last extended job hunt became permanent, I stopped praying. I stopped believing.

If prayer did anything for me then, it gave me peace in the moment. Filled me with hope and allowed me to take it one day at a time. Today, staring back at my stern boss, I might need a little bit of that hope.

Sandra leans back in her chair, hands interlocked in front of her as she taps her thumbs together. "Care to explain why my guests had to wait to be greeted this afternoon?"

Man, not even an icebreaker. Okay. There's no way out of this. "I'm sorry, I was running errands during lunch and lost track of time—"

"Personal errands?"

"For production. Richland had a busy day…" She shakes her head from side to side without a word, and I swallow hard. "I don't think they waited long."

"*They* were ten minutes early. *You* were five minutes late. Try again."

I bow my head. "I'm sorry."

Sandra sighs. "Monica," she says sternly, "nothing has changed here. When a client walks through that door, they should be greeted. It's why you were hired. This has been happening a lot lately, and I've let it slide because everyone here loves you. But something needs to change."

I widen my eyes, feeling a squeeze in my chest. Total panic sets in. Oh my God; she's going to fire me. Time to start begging. "I promise, I won't let it happen again."

She tilts her head, eyes softening. "I wasn't surprised to find you with Richland just now. And I know he's grateful for your help, but that doesn't mean you can abandon your post whenever you want. This isn't the first time. You've become disengaged, and I've tried making sense of it. I've even tried waiting it out. Nothing seems to be working. There's only one solution."

Her eyes harden as she stares back at me, confirming my worst fears. "You have a responsibility here, and you failed. I'm afraid I need to let you go."

Dread weighs me down like an anchor in a bottomless sea of my own making. I've never seen her be so fierce and cutthroat. After two and a half years. I'm out—and now what? That means no more Chloe, no Richland, no catering leftovers, no promo events. Suddenly, my stomach feels like a heavy bucket of slosh.

"No, Sandra," I choke. "Please don't let me go. I'm so sorry. You have no idea how sorry. It gets lonely when no one comes to the front, so I help Rich out. He's so grateful for it. The amount of money I've saved this company on wardrobe, hair, and makeup should mean *something*."

"It does." She nods in agreement. "So you admit it; you don't love your job anymore."

I can't argue with her, even if it is to save my job. "I've just been confused lately about what I want to do with the rest of my life. I love BelleCurve and everyone here, but I know I can be of value doing other things. But I'll stop. Message received loud and clear. I can't lose this job."

"Well, that brings us to the next part of this meeting."

There's more? I gasp for air. For hope.

"Remind me: you're how close to getting your degree?"

"I have my associate, but I took a break to decide what I want to focus on." Why is she asking me this, and how does this have any relevance to my job? Or ex-job? Shit.

"And have you decided if you want to go back to school?"

I nod. "I want to. I just haven't picked an area of concentration." I sigh. "I thought working here would guide me a lot quicker than it has."

Sandra tilts her head to study me. "Really, Monica? You have no clue what it is you want to pursue?"

I shrug. "Something creative, obviously. Video production, maybe, but I don't necessarily want to do what Richland does. I've thought about going to beauty school, but I think what I love about BelleCurve is having the versatility to do it all."

"Sounds like you have some big decisions to make."

This ball in my throat intensifies. I can't believe I've just been fired. "I-I guess." Not that I can afford school if I lose my job without picking up a student loan I'll be married to for the rest of my life. Ugh. It's times like these I wish I could cry. I've only ever cried over one person—one heartbreak. It shattered me, and nothing else has felt significant enough to shed tears over since.

"What if I told you I'm willing to make you a deal?"

My entire mood shifts. "Really? I can keep my job?"

She shakes her head. "No, we've already been working on your replacement. She starts at the end of the month."

My heart sinks in my chest. "Oh." I blink as I process her words. "You've already been working on my replacement?"

Her face is so stony that I'm having trouble recognizing the woman who hired me on a whim. If I'm being honest, I got the job out of sheer luck. I walked in at the same moment the previous office manager told Sandra she was pregnant and quit on the spot, leaving her in an awful predicament during her busiest season. When I handed her my resume with only an associate degree and some volunteer hours at fashion events, she looked beyond it all and threw her arms around me, and that was the start of something special.

"Yes. But Monica, I'm willing to create a new position for you."

I freeze.

"I hear Richland is looking for a full-time PA," she continues." Someone to assist him with shoots, create production schedules, and maybe do some budget forecasting and vendor negotiations." She winks at me.

"Wh-what?"

"Sweetie, look. I don't want to lose you. You've been here for almost three years, and until recently you've been an all-star employee. You're extremely hardworking when you're motivated. Everyone here loves you. I just think you're ready for a change—and maybe a little nudge in the right direction."

She eyes me closely. "We have a close relationship with the Art Institute of Seattle. There are tons of options for someone like you. I'd like to put you on a scholarship program. We'll pay for fifty percent of your schooling if you can manage to put in thirty hours a week and keep your grades above a three point five GPA. We won't be able to boost your salary, but I think the offer is more than fair. What do you say?"

I'm stunned. Not sure what to say, except— "Why would you do this for me?"

"I'm calling it an investment. I like you, Monica. So does Richland." She reaches into her desk and pulls out a colorful pamphlet with the Art Institute logo printed on it. "Here," she says as she hands it to me. Take some time to look this over. Visit the school. Think hard about your future. You'll have to register by the end of March to get in for summer quarter. Do we have a deal?"

"Thank you. Yes! Oh my God, yes!" I want to get up and skip to the door, but I need to clarify something first. "So I didn't get fired?" I wring my hands up in front of me, bracing myself. "I just want to be clear."

She laughs. "You did. I fired you, and then I rehired you. Congratulations. We'll just tell HR you were promoted. They wouldn't appreciate the extra paperwork."

A freaking promotion?

I beam back at her. "Thank you, Sandra."

"You're welcome. I'll need you to train the new hire. Her name is Jessa Young. She's a freshman. Single mom. Attending school online. She's hungry for work and her passion is client services and organization, so at least I know she won't abandon her job post anytime soon."

I ignore her subtle insults. "I'll be happy to train her."

And it's a done deal. We hug, because we're both huggers, and then I head to my desk to start gathering my things. I'm more than ready for this transition. I'll deal with the other massive task of choosing a degree program later. One step at a time.

Tickets
Monica

"You got fired and hired on the same day? By Sandra?" Gavin's entire body shakes with laughter. "That is classic."

I give him a friendly shove, but he's still too caught up in the humor of it all to notice.

It's thirty minutes before game time, and the room is already buzzing with a fierce energy I can only attribute to football. It's Super Bowl Sunday, and I'm afraid of what will happen if Seattle loses.

I probably shouldn't say that out loud, considering I was almost kicked out when I showed up at Gavin's Bonney Lake home wearing my pink sweats and not a single article of Seattle gear. I know there are some hardcore fans here, but damn. I'm not used to being booed by a houseful of drunk men.

Chloe, being the awesome friend that she is, rushed me away to change into one of the many jerseys Gavin bought her. I don't even know why he bothers. Chloe has never been the biggest sports fan. She's a good girlfriend, though, and she looks hot in a jersey. Apparently, I'm jumping on the bandwagon now too.

So yeah, I'm wearing a Zachary Ryan number four jersey. I'm cool with it. At least the guys won't give me shit, and Chloe and I are twinsies for the day. Can't complain about that. We're both on the shorter side, curvy, and fit. Our physical differences mainly lie in our faces. I like to call Chloe a timeless beauty. With big, light blue eyes and the soft curves of her cheekbones, Chloe arrests you at first glance. And Gavin completely surrendered.

"It's actually a promotion," I shoot back at Gavin, hoping to finally shut him up.

"She even got an office," Chloe brags. "And a scholarship to the Art Institute."

Gavin jaw falls open. "You got a free ride?"

"Fifty percent," I correct him.

"Damn, Monica. You know, that's actually a smart move on Sandra's part. She owns your ass now."

I shrug. "Fine with me. And Richland's thrilled. He's been trying to get a PA for years."

"Well, congrats." Gavin grabs his sandwich from the coffee table and grins down at us, already over the conversation. "Game time!" he announces." You two need drinks."

Chloe tucks her feet under her butt and curls into me. "We'll grab something in a bit."

He leans down and kisses her. She pulls him in for more and I roll my eyes, lifting myself from the couch. That's way too close for comfort, even for me. "That's my cue. Time to break out the tequila."

"Ooh! I'm coming!" Jazz calls from the other side of the room.

Jazz is Chloe's best friend from junior high. She's a brash one, but funny. We've bonded over our love for Chloe and our passion for snack foods. While she's more of a chip lover, my cravings gravitate toward sweeter items. But food sisters all the same.

"Why can't Gavin have any hot friends?" I pout as I reach for the knife and cutting board.

"Uh, Gavin has plenty of hot friends," Jazz corrects me, and I know she's talking about her new husband, Marco.

"I mean single ones, obviously."

"What about Blaine?" Jazz perks up.

Chloe chooses that moment to walk in and gasps. "Oh my God. Blaine! Do you like him?"

"Wouldn't they be cute together?"

I shake my head, but it's too late. They're yammering on, already planning the wedding.

"Hey!" I raise my voice to silence them. "Blaine's not my type, okay?"

"Hot and single isn't your type?" Jazz challenges.

Chloe wraps an arm around my shoulder and grins. "More like, relationship material isn't her type."

I booty-bump Chloe away and return to the cutting of the limes, something much more interesting than this conversation. "Shut it and grab the tequila."

Jazz does the pouring and Chloe grabs the salt. "Now that we're talking about it," Jazz starts, "I've never seen you with a guy."

"I haven't dated anyone in a while." I shrug, darting a sly look at Chloe, who blushes. Chloe's fully aware of the casual fling I had with Gavin, and she's cool with it—as far as I know. We don't discuss it, ever … because then it would be weird.

"You went out with someone recently," Chloe, eyebrows raised. I know she's trying to pivot the conversation away from Gavin. But just the thought of Zach brings a pout to my lips.

"Six months ago," I remind her. "Anyway, it's not a big deal. We don't need to talk about my relationship status, thank you very much. I'm perfectly happy with tequila and cheese dip over here. They happen to make me very happy." I bite into a chip and roll my eyes in mock ecstasy, making the girls laugh.

Chloe's laughter is quickly replaced by a sympathetic look. She's the only one who knows the details of my night with Zach, and she's smart enough to put the topic to rest. All is much safer when we start talking about her California trip.

We toss back our shots, grab a bag of chips, and head to the living room. Everyone's in animated discussion as they stand around the giant television. The game is about to start. Jazz jumps excitedly and joins Marco, who stands beside Justin and Phoebe, another couple Chloe and Gavin know from school.

I might be the only outsider here, but I don't feel like one. Everyone treats me as if I graduated right along with them.

Chloe sticks next to me during the game. No matter how much she loves Gavin, she can't seem to force herself to learn football enough to get excited about it. One would think since my dad played pro football, I should automatically be obsessed with the game too, but that couldn't be further from the truth.

My eyes flicker to the screen just as Zach's face appears. The announcers go over his record-breaking season stats, but my senses only focus on the things I remember: his touch, his kiss, the electricity coursing through my body as he whispered in my ear. And now all I see is that damn ocean staring back at me, so deep and wide I could drown happily, never needing an ounce of air again.

My entire body becomes a current of energy as I remember that smile that felt as if it was reserved just for me. That unshaven jaw my fingers couldn't stop touching as he kissed every inch of my neck. And those hands as they held me, strong enough to crush an opponent but gentle as they caressed my sensitive skin.

A shiver breaks out over all the places he once touched … until I remember the photo of Meredith cozied up to Zach and bury my face in my hands.

As I try to banish the image from my mind, I feel Chloe press her arm into mine. "You okay there, Mon?"

I give her the best smile I can muster. Every bit of my expression is filled with regret. "Yeah. Go Seattle!" I cheer with a sarcastic pump of my fist.

"Why aren't you girls watching this game?" Blaine yells at us from the other side of the room. "It's freaking fourth quarter and tied!"

I flip him off and turn back to Phoebe to finish my story about the chocolate covered strawberry disaster at the Heroes and Legends event. We've all had way too much to drink at this point, so I don't care how many times Zach's name comes out of my mouth.

"Wait a second … so you seduced Zachary Ryan and he asked you to dinner?" Phoebe is way too loud, sobering me some.

I glance around and notice some eyes on us. Shit. Looking back at Phoebe, I shake my head. "We were kind of friends already. It wasn't a big deal."

Chloe detaches herself from Gavin's arms and stumbles over to us. "You're so cute when you talk about Zach. You get all pink and agitated."

"Nothing happened!" I insist. "We just ate dessert and stuff."

"Stuff!" Phoebe shrieks at points an accusing finger at me. "Oh my God, you had sex with him."

I'm pretty sure everyone is staring at us now, but I don't look around the room to confirm. "No! We just made dessert, and then ate it." I'm not drunk enough to mention the hot make out session involving cake and taste tests of … me.

"Maybe you should call him," Chloe says.

"Why?"

"Why not?" she challenges.

This isn't the first time we've had this conversation. I told Chloe the entire story at work the Monday after Heroes and Legends. Of course, the moment she heard everything, she told me to call him. But why should I? It was an innocent make out session. Nothing more.

At least that's what it was supposed to be.

He wasn't supposed to send me flowers and season tickets a week later. He wasn't supposed to text and call until I finally blocked his number from my phone. But that was six months ago.

"He's seeing someone."

"Who?" she challenges.

"It doesn't matter," I shoot back. "Zach plays football. I know far too much about what it's like to jump into a relationship with one of those guys. They're rarely home. Girls are easily accessible at every turn. Their lives are free for public criticism. It's just not a fun situation to be in."

"Geez," Phoebe says with wide eyes. "How many football players have you made dessert with?"

I laugh and throw a couch pillow at her curly blonde head. "Enough!" I say, attempting to end the conversation.

"You could have at least taken the damn tickets."

I gasp. Chloe claims she rarely drinks. I call bullshit, but she gets mighty brave with some alcohol in her.

"What?" she asks, clueless to the problem with announcing my season tickets to the entire group of ravenous football fans. "You make out with the guy, he sends you season tickets to his games, and you cut off all lines of communication."

I bury my head in my hands, feeling like she's just cut me open in a sea full of sharks.

"Season tickets for what?" Marco's head swivels away from the television to ask. Sure enough, all the guys' eyes are on me. I groan.

"Seattle!" Jazz tells him, pointing to the television. "Zachary Ryan gave Monica season tickets." She flips her head to me, which I spy through the cracks between my fingers. "What did you do with them?"

Once again, my face heats with embarrassment. This time, Chloe looks ashamed for outing me. I go to cover my face again, but Phoebe holds my hands to my sides. "Sorry, babe. You're going to have to explain this one."

"Please tell me they haven't been sitting in your Zachary Ryan box of love this entire season. So help me, Monica."

Blaine's now in on the conversation, shaking his head. They're all staring at me like I'm crazy.

"No! Geez, he should have never given them to me."

Jazz's hands move to her hips. "And you couldn't go? Or didn't want to go?"

I glare at her. It's no one's business what I did with those tickets. I could kill Chloe for mentioning it. "I've been busy! I gave the tickets to Children's Hospital with the promise that they would go to a different family each game and that they would know they were from Zachary, not me."

"Ahh!" the girls gush.

"That's sweet, Mon." Chloe smiles.

"Why would Zachary Ryan give you tickets in the first place?" Gavin's edges his way closer to us and Chloe wraps her arms around him, holding him back.

"You don't have to answer that!"

"Yeah, way to step up, friend." I roll my eyes at her and hold up my empty beer. "Getting a refill. You all can keep talking about this if you want, but you won't get any answers from me." I point to the television. "Oh, and your favorite QB just threw an interception with two minutes on the clock."

In unison, heads snap back toward the game. I use the opportunity to sneak into the kitchen for another shot. Chloe walks in behind me, an apologetic look on her face. "If it makes you feel better, no one doubts that you and Zach could be a thing. That's saying something."

I smile, because for some reason that does make me feel a little better. I'm extra grateful when she hides the bottle of tequila in the crook of her arm and pulls me upstairs into the guest bedroom. We call this my room since I claim it every time I'm too drunk to drive home, which is most times we all hang out.

"Have you ever talked to Trinity and Gracie?" I blurt out, suddenly racked with jealousy over Meredith and that stupid photo.

Chloe scrunches her nose. "Not really. They kind of make me uneasy. Always whispering and giggling in their cube. I try to ignore them."

"They were looking at pictures of Zach and Meredith last week. She went to some charity dinner with him. The girls think they're together and hiding it. What if they're dating, Chlo?"

"Ignore the gossip queens. You can't believe a word that comes out of their mouths. You know how jealous they were of you at Heroes and Legends. I wasn't even there to witness all of it, but from what I've heard, they were mean mugging you the entire time you were with him. Meredith too. They're just trying to hurt you."

"They showed me a photo," I try. "They looked ... cozy."

Chloe sighs. "I mean, they do attend events together. It's her job. But tell me something: why do you care so much?"

Biting the inside of my lip, I nod. "You're right. I'm being stupid. Maybe I have some regrets." *But I can't act on them.* Reaching out to Zach will only shine light in a cave I've been hiding in for good reason. For reasons that I might have a hard time remembering if I let him get close to me again.

Chloe squeals. "Monica, call him! Even if he blows you off, just get it over with so you stop feeling bad about whatever happened. Maybe you two can start over. He's such a nice guy, I'm sure he'd understand."

I shake my head, but not because I don't think Zach's nice. He *is* nice … and sexy … and smart … and hot. Nice guys aren't usually all those things.

He was never supposed to get so close. He was supposed to be the popular football player who I flirted with on occasion. And then he was supposed to disappear.

Why won't he just disappear?

Distractions

Zachary
Six Months Earlier

Teeth dig into my skin as a light sigh escapes her lips. A breath tickles my shoulder. I'm pulling her close. I've managed to remove the suspenders, but kissing her feels too damn good to press for more. I want to savor this. Devour her slowly. Never mind that tight Superman tee that I'm gripping in my fist. It's begging to disappear.

A moan enters my mouth as Monica runs her fingers up my back. She's a biter from what I gather—or maybe she's still hungry. I'm not quite sure. All I know is that if she removes that top, there's no chance in hell we'll be smart enough to stop what we've started.

It's like a competition. She grinds into me, and I remove or adjust a piece of her clothing. Then she removes something of mine and we start all over again.

I pull away from her to give us a moment to think about what we're doing, and as I do, I gently tug on her bottom lip. I'm not sure that helps our situation. I wrap my hands around her wrists and lift them from my chest. "Cakes, you're too addicting."

She grins. "I think you're tasting your triple chocolate cake."

My nose touches the spot between her neck and shoulder. "No, it's definitely you." I nip at her skin and follow it up with a kiss. "Maybe a little of both." My groan falls into her mouth before I pull away again. "Damn it. Chocolate has never had this effect on me before."

"You aren't so bad yourself." She moves in to kiss my neck, and I'm overcome with an urge to make a belt of her skirt so that she's exposed to me. I want to bury myself in her however she'll let me.

You'd think I was prying a pebble out of a cement block instead of putting a measly inch of distance between us so I can speak. "Ah, you have no idea how much I want to see Superman fly right now," I say tugging her shirt and then finding her eyes. "I like you, Cakes. You should know that before we take this any further."

Her pout is almost as sexy as the way she's rubbing her thighs together to quell the ache I know she's feeling. "Don't worry, Zach. I'm not one of those girls you need to make promises to."

I chuckle and pull her into my arms again, taking her mouth in mine. "I have an early flight that I haven't even packed for. Maybe we should wait until I'm back in town. I'll take you out, do this right."

"Like a date?"

Why does she sound appalled at the idea?

I brush a loose strand of hair behind her ear and fall into her caramel eyes. "Yes. A date. That thing that usually comes before I tear your clothes off."

She shivers in my arms. "I wasn't complaining."

Laughing again, I press my forehead to hers. "If I'm being completely honest, I want to take my time with you."

Something in her expression changes. My eager, flirty girl's eyes lose their tenacity, like her thoughts have launched her into another place and time. "Cakes," I whisper against her mouth. "Where'd you go?"

Her eyes snap up. She's back, and pushing me away. "I should get going," she says. "You promised me a doggy bag."

And just like that, she's hopping off the table.

No, no, *no*. What did I say?

Her suspenders are back on, her skirt flattened into position before I can even get up from the table. She's searching for something now. Her shoes or purse, maybe. I'm too busy watching the way she moves in that tight little skirt, mentally berating myself for interrupting what could have been. An uncomfortable feeling twists in my gut—a feeling that tells me I've lost Monica for good.

Instinct nudges me in her direction. I wrap my arms around her from behind and kiss the side of her head, giving her reassurance if that's what she needs. "I get back into town next Monday. I'll call you."

She flips her body around, rejection evident on her face. "Zach—"

"Cakes," I cut in before she can say anything. "Did you have fun tonight?"

She nods.

"Do you want to see me again?"

She bites her bottom lip, then nods, but I don't miss the hesitation. "Yes, but I can't—"

Does she think I'm trying to bail on her? "I really do have an early flight."

Her expression softens. "I know. I believe you."

"Good," I assert. "Then I'll call you next week. We'll make plans."

Monica reaches for my chest and slides a hand up my dress shirt. I already miss the feel of her hands on my bare skin.

But then she says the unthinkable: "I think it's best if we end this tonight."

What the hell? Her words are a vacuum sucking the air right out of the room.

I take a step back. I knew Monica would be someone I'd need to prove myself to. That's why up until tonight all I've ever done is smile, compliment her, and ask her about her day. I could see from a mile away that she wasn't going to fall victim to my charms. Not the way I need her to. But after what just happened … I was certain we'd be seeing each other again.

"You're serious?" I ask, unwilling to accept her words. Did I completely misread everything about our flirtation? Our banter? This entire night? I'm missing something.

Confusion and hurt are the two emotions I've always had trouble controlling. Sometimes they collide, forming a knot of anger ready to unravel at any moment. I can feel it now, the battle that radiates from my chest outward, blistering my senses as I try to sort through my thoughts.

"I'm willing to put more time into this, but I won't chase someone who doesn't want to be chased."

She swallows against the bite of my words, and I imagine it's regret she's pushing down with it. "I don't want to be chased, Zach."

There it is. She couldn't have put it clearer than that. I mean, geez. It's not like I haven't been the one to pull a

Monica. Make out with someone and push them away when I'm not feeling it. But she *was* feeling it. There's no way that what just happened was one-sided.

So then what is going on?

"All right, then." I stuff my dress shirt into my pants and walk into the kitchen, trying my best to snuff the fire in my chest and give her what she wants. I snatch a large plastic container to scoop the cake into and place it in a paper bag. She wants cake.

Without a glance in her direction, I walk to the back door. "Ready?" I ask roughly over my shoulder.

I still can't look at her, my emotions clearly brewing something ugly. Something dark that, mixed with the sexual chemistry between us, brings my need for her to a boil. Every inch of her exposed flesh—and then some—has been marked with my touch. It feels wrong to end things this way.

There's an awkward silence before she starts shuffling to the door behind me. This time, she doesn't try to stroke my ego with an apology. "Yeah," she sighs. "I'm ready."

Game Over

Zachary

Our season may not have ended the way we would have hoped, but it was a personal best for me. Most passing yards in a single season. Highest passing rating. Four touchdown passes and zero interceptions in six consecutive games. And now it's over after a tough Super Bowl loss that could have easily gone the other way.

Not going to lie, though; two weeks later, the loss still stings.

Hopping on a private jet along with my business partner and best friend, Desmond Blake, seemed to be the best idea ever. So here we are vacationing in Maui, lounging on the deck at our rented villa on a private beach and sipping ice cold beers. And it's heaven, a little piece of paradise on earth. A gentle breeze coming in with the high surf, crystal blue skies painted across a gradient of blues and greens, and a fragrance so intoxicating it's impossible to ignore each intake of air.

My phone rings for what seems like the hundredth time today, cutting into my tranquility like a sharp blade.

"Damn, you need to mute that shit. Or shut it off. I'm over here dreaming of that hula girl from last night." Desmond's eyes are closed, but his brows furrow as he adjusts his body in the lounge chair next to me.

"Sorry, dude." I don't need to glance at my phone to know who's blowing me up. I can't ignore it again. With a groan, I pull myself from my lounge chair and press the answer button while walking back to the condo.

"Hey, Trevor."

"Jesus Christ, Ryan. Who do I need to screw to get you on the phone?" My agent's typical Jersey volume blasts my eardrum.

"I don't care who you screw. Just stop messing with my vacation."

Trevor chuckles. "Oh, trust me, I—"

I don't want to know how many chicks he's screwed since the Super Bowl all because he's "Zachary Ryan's agent." Desmond pulls that shit too, and I try to ignore it the best I can, but it bothers me that they use my name to get laid.

"I told you, Trevor. I'm taking these two weeks off. I'm doing nothing but baking in the sun, watching crappy television, and sipping girly cocktails. You don't get to boss me around for two whole damn weeks." I pause, and then add, "And don't call me Ryan."

Trevor knows I hate it when he calls me by my last name, but he obviously did it to rile me up because I hear laughter on the other end of the line.

"I'm hanging up," I threaten.

"No, wait! Just give me five minutes."

"Fine. One sec."

Stepping through the sliding glass doors, I force myself into work mode. Passing the palm tree-inspired sitting area and stark white kitchen with a blue tiled backsplash to match the home's exterior, I push open the French doors to my makeshift office where tropical light pours in from the large windows.

Even though the work is inescapable, the sand and the sky and the faint sounds of waves crashing onto the shore bring me peace. Just because I've told everyone I'm out of pocket for two weeks doesn't mean I've stopped checking emails, unfortunately. I might as well have a nice view while I get shit done.

"All right, Trev. You've got your five minutes, starting now."

"Well, thank you so much for giving me a few precious minutes of your time." His voice drips with sarcasm. "Look, you've already got a contract renewal to sign. We need to respond as soon as possible. It's a big money deal. Four more years, my man. Everything we've negotiated and more. No surprises. Let's put these fuckers out of their misery. Seattle's shaking a little at the fact that you haven't signed, so if you need me to go back to sweeten the—"

"Send it over. I'll sign it today." I've already looked at the terms, and I'm confident with the deal. No need to squeeze the lemon any harder. Not when Coach and I already negotiated at length and came to an unofficial agreement. That's a type of trust I would never break.

Coach Reynolds and I have a special bond. One that dates back to high school when he gave me an ultimatum between joining the football team he coached or continuing down the reckless path I found myself on after my dad died. It was an easy decision, but not one I would have made on my own. That ultimatum got me here.

There's silence while Trevor switches gears. I can almost hear them churning. "Okay, then. Good. Next order of business—"

"You've got four minutes."

"The camp." He jumps in without missing a beat. "We've locked down a location. Bigger than the last, as discussed, but we need branding and a theme. And I don't think you're going to get by this year without getting some big sponsors involved—not with the number of sign-ups we've gotten already. We're looking at hundreds, dude. We'll need the help. Marketing, sponsors, creative. The works."

I perk up a little. Now this is a subject I don't mind talking about. "Good thinking. Let's get that ball rolling. Have you talked to Sandy?"

"The broad from BelleCurve? I have not."

I roll my eyes. Trevor is such a schmuck sometimes. "Yes, but don't call her a broad, please. You know she's like family to me. Set up a meeting with her two weeks from now. Her team can help with sponsorships and marketing. I have a few other ideas too. Just keep on the venue and get notifications out to the schools. We don't necessarily need anything branded until closer to the event."

"Shouldn't Meredith be doing that?"

I pause at the obvious annoyance in Trevor's tone. He's referring to Meredith Greene, my publicist. He's slowly coming to the end of his rope with her, and I don't blame him. "I trust you two to work out those details."

There's a brief pause. I know Meredith is a handful. And maybe she gets sidetracked by personal agendas more than I'd like, but she's been my publicist for three seasons. That type of knowledge and trust is hard to replace.

"You got it. Glad to get some of that off my plate. Your endorsement offers are looking great too, kid. You're going to have one hell of a year. Just sign the deal for Coach and enjoy your vacation. But Zach, answer your phone next time I call."

I roll my eyes. "You're a good man, Trevor. Thanks, bud."

By the time I send back the signed contract and step outside, the sun is sinking through hues of oranges and purples that paint the sky.

Desmond's finishing a call of his own, so I sit back in my lounge chair and memorize this moment as my senses hum with all things tropical. A fresh, salty breeze washes over my skin as scents of plumeria and pikake flowers infiltrate my nose. I need more of this. So does Desmond. I turn to my friend.

"Calling your lady friend from last night?" I tease Desmond as soon as he gets off the phone.

"Screw you," he quips. Then he smiles that goofy, dimply smile of his that seems to work well for the ladies. "As a matter of fact, I was. That one was hot as hell. I might have to bring her back tonight, if you don't mind."

I make a face. "Did you just ask for my permission to screw a local? This is our vacation. Do what you want. Just bag it. The world isn't ready for mini Desmonds to run rampant. It's already crazy out there."

"Har har. What about you? I haven't seen you on the prowl for a while now."

I move my hands through my hair that's been salted by sand and surf and let out a laugh. "I got rejected at the beginning of the season, man. Still licking my wounds from that one."

Desmond makes a face like he's truly in pain. "That bad, huh? Sorry, dude."

I shrug. "I could have pressed her a bit more. There was something there, but with the season starting and the pressure from the league, I wasn't in the right headspace."

"Wait. Is this the girl you brought to the kitchen?"

Nodding, I try to remember when I told him about Monica. It was during preseason. There was one night Desmond and I hung out, celebrating a successful month of business. That night was the last time I drank more than a single beer in one sitting until this vacation, and that was all it took for me to tell my best friend everything.

"You're still thinking about her, huh?"

Shrugging seems like the safest response. "It's not like I've had anyone else to distract me."

"Well, let's fix that!" he enthuses. "We're in Maui, for fuck's sake. Let's go out! Find you a distraction."

When Desmond winks at me, I'm blasted with unease. We're two different types of men when it comes to dating. He's looking for the one for right now, and I'm … not. At least not anymore.

"Count me out tonight. I'm here to relax, not party. But you should go. Bring the girl back if she's willing."

"Oh, she'll be willing," Desmond jokes. "So what were all those calls about? Trevor hounding you again?"

I throw him a knowing look. Desmond's all too familiar with Trevor's constant need for urgency. "It was all good stuff. I signed the four-year extension, and he's setting up a meeting with the agency to discuss the football camp over spring break. You should get involved this year, man. Maybe cater it or something."

"Can't. I'll be in Texas for a couple weeks visiting my old man." He sits up, his dark blonde hair falling into his eyes. He pushes it back before slapping his hands to his knees. "I forgot to tell you. Mrs. Peterson invited me to speak to her Food and Nutrition class while I'm in town."

I laugh. "Let me guess. You still have the hots for her." Desmond's fascination for older women was sort of a problem when we were younger. He's like a permanent toddler who will break the rules just to spite them.

The dimple that sinks into his cheek tells me all I need to know. "You know what?" I hold up a hand like a shield. "Don't answer that."

If you had told me four years ago that I would have gone into business with the dude who made my life a living hell throughout my early teens, I would have never believed it. Then again, if it weren't for Desmond, who knows if I would have had the drive to beast it up in the gym to show him I wasn't someone he wanted to mess with. Without that push, I may have never found the bleachers. Or played ball. Never would have gone on to play in college, never would have entered the NFL draft, and never would have scored a phenomenal deal with Seattle.

Desmond put me in the position to use my good fortune to help him. Not that he needs my help anymore. He's turned his life around and has paid it forward in other ways—most notably through the charities we jointly support. Sometimes all a person needs is an opportunity to break the negative cycle. Desmond is living proof of that.

"You gonna come around the kitchen this off season?" he asks. "The regulars keep asking about you."

"I'll stop by some time, man. Just don't go announcing when I'm coming. We don't need any distractions."

I don't need to elaborate on my reasons for staying away during business hours, although Desmond disagrees with them. Some of the regulars know about my position with the company, but they also know to keep it to themselves. I want the business to succeed for the right reasons. No need to turn the place into a hotspot for paparazzi and hopeful fans. Desmond, on the other hand, wants exactly the opposite.

He barks with laughter. "You mean your Wifey Club? Let 'em come. You know I'll entertain them just fine."

Annoyance gets the better of me. "Why do you always bring them up? They're just fans." I sigh. "Excited fans."

Over the past few years, Desmond has seen my fan base grow—and he's been more than happy to reap the rewards. When my publicist, Meredith, suggested starting a social media group to give my female fans a place to congregate, I had no clue it would blow up the way it has. And it's only been live for three months. I almost had the entire thing taken down when I found out what they called it: *The Wifey Club.*

Desmond flashes his pearly whites at me, and a boulder sets down in my stomach.

He's practically cackling now. "I created a fake profile. It's hilarious, dude! These women go nuts for you. You should read some of the stories—"

"I don't want to see any of it." I could kill him for even joking about that club. In my opinion, it's been the worst move made by my PR team, but they disagree. Supposedly the goal is to boost my popularity in a safe place where they can monitor traffic and conversations. So far, it's just been a trainwreck of a group that needs to be policed constantly.

He shrugs. "Oh, calm down. It's entertaining, that's all."

"You know what? If you're going to be on there, I don't want to hear about it. I'm tempted to demand Meredith take it down."

"I'm honestly surprised you haven't. You seem all bent out of shape about it."

"I wish I could, but Meredith had a good point. What if another one gets created in its place? Then we can't delete posts or monitor the information being passed around. At least this way we can stir up positive gossip. Talk about the organizations and not my dating life."

He clears his throat. "Lack of dating life."

"Seriously, dude?" I warn.

"What? It's like you have your own personal dating site! Just pick one." He smirks. "Or two."

I slam my arm into Desmond's chest. "You're making me wanna drink. More."

"Good. Drink. And then let's go find you a distraction." He winks, and I shake my head. Desmond will get it one day when he meets the right one. The kind of distraction he's talking about, passing the time, isn't something I'm interested in.

But maybe that's my problem. A distraction from Monica is probably the perfect cure for this slump I'm in. Then again, how much of a distraction would it actually be if I'm going to see her again in two weeks when she's forced to greet me as I walk through the agency doors?

Truth be told, I don't think anything will distract me from Monica—the girl who rejected me. Who didn't return a single one of my messages or acknowledge the tickets I sent her. The one who didn't just *get* away. She ran.

STEP THREE
First Assignment

"THE FUTURE BELONGS TO THOSE WHO BELIEVE
IN THE BEAUTY OF THEIR DREAMS."
— ELEANOR ROOSEVELT

Beginnings and Endings
Monica

When I arrive at BelleCurve, Richland is waiting in my office with a fresh bouquet of flowers. *In my office.* I feel like a freaking queen. He congratulates me on the promotion with a hug and a doorstop disguised as a fuchsia patent leather pump. We share a laugh, because this is Richland. Serious about work, but there's a goofy side to him too that not many people get to see. I'll have to work on bringing that out of him more.

He rushes off back to work, leaving me with some standard orientation packets to read that take up the rest of the morning. I glance around at my little box of an office, big enough for a large wooden desk, two cushioned chairs, and a bookshelf. My inner interior designer is already at work planning the décor.

It's quiet in the suite today. No clients, no shoots. Richland tells me these are the days he treasures the most. He gets to spend time reviewing potential work to bid on, working in the editing bays, or storyboarding with the production crew. He's with a group of illustrators right now, reviewing final sketches for a government PSA project.

Since I've basically been Richland's only assistant for nearly three years, I don't need to ask how to keep busy. I tidy up the main room, restock the break room, take inventory of supplies, and start prepping for tomorrow's shoot.

The morning flies by, and when lunch rolls around my stomach is growling like a starved lion. I pull up my chat window and type a quick message to Chloe.

Monica: My first day is officially half over! You are now the friend of a production assistant. You're welcome. Now take me to lunch to thank me.

Chloe: Nice try. I took you to lunch last week.

Monica: Gasp! That was BEFORE I started. This is huge, Chlo Chlo.

Chloe: Fine. Give me 15 minutes to wrap up and I'll take you to the corner store for yesterday's hot dogs.

Monica: Yummmm.

I smile. Richland might be my favorite person to work with at BelleCurve, but Chloe's quickly turned into my favorite friend. From the moment I met her, I could tell she was genuine. She's the type of person that bleeds raw emotion. Truth be told, she looked like she could use a friend like me. Someone who wouldn't let her hide in the corner. Turns out, I needed a friend like her too.

I don't have to worry about Chloe lying or gossiping behind my back like I would with Trinity and Gracie. Chloe works hard, like me. She loves hard, like me. And she's real, like me. Basically, I'm friends with myself.

I try to tell her we're sisters, but she won't take the bait. Says we're too different to be sisters, and I guess that's true too. While she's on the quieter side, I'm unafraid to be the life of the party. Maybe that's why we gel so well together. I'm her entertainment, and she's my chill pill.

While I wait for Chloe in the front lobby, I smile at Jessa, the new office manager, who has the phone glued to her ear. She doesn't notice me, so I use the opportunity to scroll through my social media accounts on my phone. Lots of loves and likes and a few comments to my latest selfies, but I don't stop to check them.

Chloe's flying down the hall to greet me. She looks extra done up today, rockin' a chic black pant suit that reminds me of the genius Yves Saint Laurent's "Le Smoking Suit" campaign, with a fitted, white button-up blouse and matching patent leather heels.

"Dang, girl," I call, giving her my approval rating with two hands up in the air. "You're a total ten. But it's just lunch. You didn't need to dress up for me."

Chloe huffs and clomps past me to open the door. "Client meetings all morning," she says briskly. "Let's go get you fed, woman."

"Good. I'm hungry."

"What's new?"

We fall into step once we reach the busy downtown sidewalk lined with corporate high rises and high-end retail shops. I give her the side eye. The one I give her when I'm afraid to turn to face her completely. Serious Chloe can be scary. "Man, what crawled up your butt?" I ask.

She groans. "Nothing, sorry. I was up late with Gavin. He left for Cali this morning."

"Again? Weren't you two just there?"

"Yup." She doesn't appear to be too happy about the fact that Gavin is traveling again. "Mastermind asked him to move there. They want him in the studio."

My jaw drops. "No! Worst news ever. Take it back."

She shakes her head, waving off my shock. "He told them no. He would never leave Washington, not even for an awesome job. But he does love working for them. He's worried he's going to lose everything now that he turned them down. So he decided last night that he would fly there and try to work something out."

"There's no way they'll let him go, Chlo. He's too important to the campaign."

She sighs. "That's what I believe too, but he's stressed over it."

"Then do your job. Be his stress reliever."

She laughs. "Why do you think I'm tired this morning?"

I gasp. Chloe did *not* just toss me a sex joke. "Wow. I'm impressed."

"Shut it!" She pushes open the door to our favorite French café, Belle de Jour, and holds it so I can walk in behind her. *So chivalrous.*

The restaurant is casual and quaint, packed with the usual crowd of business professionals. Each wall is warm with beige tones, contrasted by the blueberry-splashed, wide arched windows that face the sprawling courtyard fountains.

"Hey, you should come over tonight," Chloe offers as we stand in line to order. "Girly movies, wine, and popcorn?"

"Can't." I make a face. "We have an early shoot tomorrow. You should come to my place instead, that way I can kick you out at bedtime or you can crash there. But you'll have to take the couch. I'm not in the mood for a late-night cuddle session when you start dreaming of Gavin again." I shudder at the memory.

She laughs. "You're no better. Last time I slept on your couch you moaned out Zach's name a few times."

"Liar!" Even as I say this, my heart does a little flip at the sound of his name. It's hard to think about Zach and not recall our night together—not to mention the disappointing way it all ended.

Monica
Six Months Earlier

The air is thick with tension. Rain spits against the passenger window, and I know its aggression is aimed at me. Yes, I think the rain hates me. I think I hate me. Even this barely eaten triple chocolate cake that sits between me and Zachary hates me.

Zachary parks his Jeep in the Melrose Market lot beside my car. I don't get out yet, biding my time and caressing the red, leather-trimmed seats. There are many words that remain unspoken, and I'm not sure if any are meant to be shared.

His jaw is set, expression pointed forward. I think he's contemplating something, but I'm afraid to look at him for too long for fear that my willpower will completely dissolve under his spell.

This has been the best night of my life. Why am I sabotaging it?

That's the million-dollar question.

There's a rustle of fabric and then a thump on the headrest as Zachary leans back. The thick cloud of intensity permeating the air has dissolved some, thank God.

"Did you have a good time tonight?" he asks.

"The best."

A hand crosses the space between us and takes mine. "Then I'm not going to pretend I'm okay with ending things like this. I like you, Cakes."

I turn my body to answer him, but his eyes trap me, catching me off guard. They're filled with hope. Hope I have no right to give him.

"Zach." My head falls forward, and I remove my hand from his. I have to tell him something, even if it's not the whole truth. This isn't fair to him. "You're leaving tomorrow and you'll be gone for a week. You'll come back busier than ever with practice and games. Then you'll go out of town again. I know how this works. Realistically, how can we get to know each other when you're traveling and consumed with football?"

"Easy." He answers without thinking, so I give him a second to consider his own words.

It's not easy. Easy would entail him not playing in the NFL.

"Football players date. They get married, have babies, take care of families even. It doesn't matter what time of year it is. Football is demanding during the season, sure, but we have lives outside of the game." He tilts his head as if it finally clicks. "Is it that? Is me playing football a problem for you?"

I shrug, not meeting his eyes. We're getting far too close to broaching topics I can't talk about with him. "It's not the kind of relationship I want."

"This"—he points between us— "is just two people getting to know each other. How can you possibly know this won't work for you?"

"I just know!"

He flinches as if I'd slapped him, and I instantly regret my reaction. But Zach makes me feel ... unbalanced. Like he knows me better than I know myself, which is impossible. He doesn't know half of it. If he did, we wouldn't be having this conversation. Taking a breath, I continue weakly. "And it sucks."

With that, a piece of my mask falls. I may look put-together and confident to everyone else, but I'm just a girl with a confused heart who hides behind bold outfits and perfect makeup. This guise, I learned from my mother. Maybe we're more alike than I've ever wanted to admit.

"Thank you for dinner tonight, Zach. I'll never forget it."

I shuffle out of the Jeep and approach my car, key shaking in my hand. I'm stepping into my car when I hear Zach's door open.

Turning, I almost expect him to demand more from me— or maybe I *want* him to demand more. But it doesn't matter what I want. What he wants. I've seen firsthand where this kind of attraction could lead. It's like fate has already decided for us. And a bomb waits, ready to explode with one step in the wrong direction.

No. Our paths are laid out for us, brick roads made of different colors, leading in different directions. He'll go his way. I'll go mine.

My heart spasms in my chest as he steps forward, but when he hands me the box of leftover cake, it seizes with disappointment. "Don't forget this."

He's not even looking into my eyes anymore. Zach will forget all about me in a few days. He'll be busy with football and distracted by the beautiful women who would never turn away at a moment like this. Tonight was memorable, but fleeting. And I have no choice but to be okay with that.

I take the cake and slip it into the passenger seat before standing to say goodbye. "Good luck this season."

He lifts his tight jaw in acknowledgement, but his stare drifts off into the distance. We stay like this, quiet, for several seconds. Every single one brings a pang to my chest.

Our eyes finally lock, and instinct tells me to step forward, to bridge the small gap between us. But I hesitate, because it doesn't feel small. It feels deep and gaping. I could fall and there's no telling what waits on the other side.

Fuck it. I take the step and let my arms circle his waist, drawing his eyes to mine. His expression softens, telling me so much about him, more than I've already learned tonight. Zach's emotions run soul-deep, and he's not afraid to express them.

I bite back a smile before I speak. "Pain heals. Chicks dig scars. Glory … lasts forever."

An infectious smile blooms on his face before he can stop it, and I find myself smiling too. "Impressive and appropriate. *The Replacements*, huh?"

I shrug. "It's one of my favorite movies."

Just when I think the tension has been defused, he places his thumb on my bottom lip and draws a line across the sensitive skin as if memorizing the texture, wanting to burn it into his memory. "Thanks, Cakes."

There it is. The nickname that awakens every nerve ending in my body. I'm going to miss it.

When his forehead lands on mine, my eyes fall shut. I never want to let him go. But I have to. This man might have already ruined me, but I won't ruin him.

His lips brush mine, and instead of pulling away like I should, I cave.

It's just one kiss.

One.

Last.

Kiss.

Our lips only caress for a moment before he slides his mouth to my ear and releases a breath that has me clinging to him. "It goes against everything I believe in to let you drive away." I shiver in his hold. "So don't you dare for a second think that I want to."

I smile into his chest and then climb into my car with a heavy heart. I want to look back. I almost do. But this is for the best ... I hope.

The Anti-Chef
Monica

Chloe and I walk out the BelleCurve doors at five o'clock on the dot, which is a rare occurrence for us both, and stroll arm-in-arm to my apartment. I live just two blocks from the office in an insanely nice building on First Street, but looks can be deceiving.

With seven hundred and ten square feet, I have what I need. Because I live so close to work, I rarely need to use my old clunker of a car. The place is safe and convenient, and although the price is steep for the square footage, I'm saving money in other ways.

When I first moved to Washington I'd chosen a cheaper place south of Seattle and regretted it for an entire year. Not only was traffic ridiculous, but the money I was spending on gas was insane, and the apartment wasn't even worth it.

As I change into my comfy clothes, Chloe gets a call from Gavin, so I tidy up. I start with my sewing crap in the living room, which I toss on my bed, and then I step into the kitchen to find us something to snack on while I wait. We might get takeout later, but I grab two cans of tuna and a box of crackers to tide us over.

I plop down on the couch and turn on the TV, flipping channels until I've found an entertainment news station. Chloe walks in and joins me just as I'm digging into the tuna.

"Yum," she moans sarcastically.

"What?" I say, clutching the can in defense.

"Is this all you have at your house? When are you going to learn how to cook?"

I roll my eyes. "Never. Who needs to cook when there are perfectly nice establishments within walking distance from my home? There are professionals who get paid to cook. I am not one of them."

Cooking was always a sore subject in my childhood home. There was a time our housekeeper made all our meals. Before the threat of losing financial freedom ended causing a million and one problems between my parents. Sophie was let go, and my mom was expected to do more around the house. Only that never happened, which ended up causing a bigger divide between my parents.

Unfortunately for me, Chloe won't let the subject go.

"You've heard that the way to a man's heart is through his stomach, right? There is truth to that. You should learn how to cook. At least to make basic stuff. Like popcorn. Or sandwiches." She snorts at her own joke.

I toss two pillows at her head in quick succession. "I can heat popcorn, and I know how to put a sandwich together."

"What about baking chicken or throwing food into a crockpot? It's so easy and takes no time at all." She gasps, and her eyes light up. "You should go to Zach's cooking school! Maybe he'll be there." Then she sighs deeply. "And it will be like a second chance at love."

I really wish I hadn't run out of pillows so quickly. "Not interested."

"You are the flirtiest person I know. Honestly, Mon, your hang-up with Zach is confusing. Do you want to just be a tease for the rest of your life?"

Wait, what? How did we go from my lack of cooking skills to my issues with Zach and relationships?

Holding up a finger, I shake my head. "A tease doesn't put out. I, on the other hand, do." I pause, realizing how slutty I must sound. Luckily, Chloe knows better. "You know, if I like the guy enough."

"You're a relationship tease. You hook up with a guy, and then once you've punctured his little fishy mouth, instead of reeling him in, you rip the hook out."

"Oh my God! Worst analogy ever. Who the hell pays you to write?"

Chloe grabs one of the pillows and smacks me with it. "It was awesome, actually. Think about it. You toss them back in, and then they bleed out."

"Right, because if I reel them in, what would happen then? You'd prefer me to gut and eat them? Stuff them and mount 'em on my wall?"

Chloe makes a face. "Okay, yeah, *bad* analogy—especially for a foodie."

"So bad."

She laughs. "Then what? What would make you give in?"

I have a feeling it wouldn't be as hard as she thinks to give in to Zach. Physical separation from him helps, but it's not enough to get him off my mind. My pull to a man has never been so strong, and it's all for nothing.

What can I tell Chloe? She's become my best friend in Washington, and I know she would accept every single flaw that comes with me, including my daddy issues. But this is different … and with Zach, with his career, it's beyond complicated.

"I'm not sure," I finally say. "I freak out about relationships in general. It's just scary to think about settling down with someone for the long haul."

Her eyes relax into sympathy. "You just need to find a guy that completes you."

I bat my eyelashes at her and smile. "But you complete me, Chlo Chlo."

Making her best attempt to adopt a serious look, she tilts her head, suppressing laughter. "Then you need to find a dude version of me."

Not a bad idea.

"Zach is a dude version of me," she says, perking up.

I narrow my eyes. Chloe hates my death stare. *Seriously, what is her obsession with Zach?* "How so?"

The way her face transforms to confusion tells me she has absolutely no clue why she just said that, but I'm amused and patient as I wait for her response. Her eyes widen and she straightens her back.

"We both used to sit alone at the lunch table. We've both got the silent but strong thing working for us. Oh! We both like to journal—"

"Zach likes to journal?"

Her eyes go wide. "Every night."

Why does it bother me that Chloe might know more about Zach than I do? She has to interview the guy for events, so it shouldn't get to me, but it does. Clearly. Our night was fleeting, but something about it was special. Even I'll admit that much.

"Told you, Monica. You need to get to know the guy."

"It's too late already, okay? Even if I wanted to pursue something with him, which I don't, he's probably forgotten I even exist by now. He could have anyone. Like Meredith." I shrug. "I had my chance, but even if I had another one, nothing would change. It would never work out."

"Why? I feel like you're not telling me something."

The sound of the doorbell saves me from coming clean. I'm surprised to see Chloe jump to her feet to open it.

"I invited a special guest to make this party complete!" she says as she throws the door open.

When Jazz enters carrying a large pizza like she's Vanna White strutting past a tile of glowing letters, I laugh. "Yes! She's hot *and* she fills bellies."

Jazz winks. "That's right. When the boys are away, the girls will play. And by play, I mean stuff our faces with calories because our men will love us anyway."

A pang hits my chest when the girls talk about their "men," because maybe I feel just a little bit left out. Deep down I think it would be nice to have a constant. A best friend who's a little more than that. But every time my thoughts head down that road, I think of Zach, and I'm pulled back by the certainty that I don't want all the bad that would come with that relationship. I've been through it once—and once is more than enough.

The Setup

Zachary

It's only been six months since I last visited BelleCurve, but everything feels different the moment I walk through the wide double doors. The music coming through the speakers has changed from pop country to soft rock. The colorful décor that used to scatter the front desk has gone neutral. Even the scent of wild strawberry and mint is gone, replaced with vanilla. It's all changed.

My eyes are quickly drawn to the figure behind the reception desk, expecting to see *her*—but that is another thing that's changed.

The blonde receptionist's blue eyes widen and pink stains her cheeks, but she pulls it together quickly. She swallows, then blinks nervously. Everything about this girl is the complete opposite of Monica.

The stranger staring back at me straightens a stack of papers and adopts a far too serious look for the occasion. Monica never pretended to act professional. She was the most charming combination of cordial, professional, and snarky.

Where the hell is she?

"Mr. Ryan," the woman greets in an overly formal tone "Mrs. Spencer will meet you in the private conference room today. I'll take you back there now."

I should give the girl a chance. She's obviously new—by no more than six months, anyway. And she's nervous. That'll go away after she gets to know me. "You can call me Zach. Everyone here does. I haven't seen you here before. Are you new?"

Something sparks in her eyes, and she looks pleased to be asked. "I am. I'm Jessa—Jess. Everyone calls me Jess." The pink in her cheeks deepens.

My laugh is subtle, but it can't be helped. I'm used to girls acting nervous around me, but it's usually followed up by a request for an autograph or photo. Jess will do none of those things, because she's a professional. At least she's trying to be.

"When did you start? I haven't been here in a while." I lean in, letting my elbows land on the counter. This is my way of getting her to talk about who she replaced and to hopefully ease her nerves, but we're interrupted when Sandra comes strolling in from the hallway.

"Zachary Ryan, are you chatting up my office manager? Be nice; she's new."

I wink at Jess and give Sandra a look of complete innocence. "It's not my fault you hire all the pretty ones. She was keeping me occupied since you're always late for our meetings."

Sandra's jaw drops in mock astonishment before she laughs and pulls me in for a hug. Backing away, she puts a finger near my face. "I am never late for our meetings, young man. I resent that." She nods at Jessa. "Thanks, Jess. I'll show Zachary back." Turning to me, her eyes narrow into a glare, and then she gestures with her head for me to follow her. "Let's go, showboat."

"Nice to see you too," I tease. "I see you've scared another office manager away."

"You mean Monica? Let's just say she moved on to bigger and better things. I caught her playing around in the production suite instead of doing her job, clearly bored. Had to do something about it."

"Seriously?" She's got to be kidding. The Monica I remember was the best at her job. A little loud at times and a klepto when it came to food, but nothing irredeemable. But fired? Geez.

She turns and cracks a smile at me. "Don't worry, Zach. She's in a better place now."

"I hope you weren't the one to give the eulogy."

"Oh, but I was." She wiggles her eyebrows.

Once we're in the private conference room, Sandra closes the door behind me. She prefers not to use the see-through room when we're discussing potential projects. It causes too much gossip and speculation in the workplace before a deal is even signed. Honestly, I'm surprised she doesn't sneak me in the back entrance when I visit too.

"Congrats on a fantastic season, by the way. I haven't had the opportunity to talk to you. John and I were biting our nails until the very end of that last game. It was nothing short of exhilarating. Gave the fans what they wanted—well, except for a win."

I clutch my chest and fall back into my chair. "Ouch. That was painful coming from you."

"Hey! I said it was a good game."

I wave a hand in the air jokingly. "Thanks. It was a great season. Looking forward to the draft. Fresh meat on the team always inspires us to get creative on the field."

"Speaking of creative."

"Ah, check out that segue."

She beams. "So, another project, huh? Let's hear it. You know I'm a huge fan of your community outreach initiatives."

BelleCurve is known for turning simple stories into inspirational messages that resonate. Not to mention, their network of potential sponsors is invaluable.

"For the last two years I've held youth football camps in the spring. I rally a few of the guys together, we meet with the kids a few days somewhere in Seattle and then wish them luck with their future. Heroes and Legends inspired me to go bigger and give the camp more meaning. So..." I clap my hands together excitedly. "We're making it bigger, better, and badder than ever. One camp. Twelve coaches. Speakers. Activities that promote leadership. A scrimmage, and an awards ceremony."

I see her face lighting up already, but I hold my hand up to tell her I'm not done. "Best part of this? We'll be with the kids for a full week at a real camp somewhere. We're still working on that. And the response we've already gotten is incredible.

"I love it. Where does BelleCurve come into the picture? We don't own the anti-bullying campaign anymore. Heroes and Legends was sold to Mastermind Comics in August, so I'm not sure repurposing any of that content would be possible."

I can already see her wheels turning. Holding up a hand, I wiggle my fingers a little to get her attention. Her head snaps up to find my amused face peering back at her. "I don't want to repurpose Heroes and Legends. I want to speak directly to young athletes about community and leadership and empower them to set positive examples. It's not just about how to throw a spiral or pummel their opponent. Sure, we'll do some of that too, but there should be a theme, and we'll need some help getting sponsors."

"That's great, Zach. You know I'm happy to help you however I can." She taps her chin thoughtfully. "Let's talk about funding. If we want big sponsors like we had at Heroes and Legends, we'll need big incentives." She leans back in her chair as she tosses some ideas at me. "What's the charity?"

"My charity," I say. "Together in Sports. The proceeds go into a fund for each school that joins the program and is used to pay for things like uniforms and travel for those who may not be able to afford it otherwise. Give everyone an opportunity to play."

Sandra smiles warmly. "It's wonderful. BelleCurve will stand behind you one hundred percent. Marketing will help us get the ball rolling on branding." She pauses for a moment. "You said you needed a theme, so we'll work on that too. If we need to get Chloe on board to help with the speeches, just let me know. You two worked well together before." Her eyes light up. "What about production? Maybe that's how we get the sponsors to really pay attention."

This reminds me of a thought that came to me in Hawaii. "Could we document the entire event? I'd love to create PSAs for the local schools. We interview the kids, talk to them about their own experiences, their struggles, and how they're going to work to overcome them. We can incorporate the sponsors throughout the messages somehow."

Having heard enough, Sandra stands. "I'd say it's time to go round you up a team."

Several meetings later, we've effectively planted the bug. The marketing team has already started brainstorming ideas for the theme, and the director of corporate partnerships is ready to reach out to sponsors. Sandra wants to talk to the production crew next, but since they've been in a shoot all morning, she hasn't been able to get ahold of Richland.

Sandra leads me to a familiar cubicle. "Look who came to visit."

Chloe swivels her chair, and a huge smile quickly illuminates her face. "Hey!" She stands and throws her arms around me.

Returning her enthusiasm, I lean away from her and smile. "Nice to see you too, Chloe."

She looks between Sandy and me curiously. "What are you doing here? Do we get to work together again?"

"Possibly," Sandy cuts in. "You two can talk about it over lunch if you're free." She makes a cringe face. "I talked poor Zach into staying the rest of today, but I have a noon appointment I'm already late for."

Chloe nods. "Of course, yes. Let me just shut down."

As Chloe finishes up an email, Sandra does some tapping on her cell phone. "Great!" she announces. "Two o'clock is confirmed with Richland. Have fun at lunch."

Sandra waves and rushes off for her next meeting while I hang back with Chloe. I fully intend on asking her about Monica at lunch.

Until— "Shit."

"Whoa. Did you just cuss?" I've never heard so much as a *damn* from Chloe's mouth.

She flips her hair to look at me. "I cuss sometimes when I royally screw up. Like now. I have a one o'clock appointment I need to prepare for." She grabs her things and pulls on my elbow. "Come with me. I have an idea."

Chloe drags me down the hall and through the corridor that leads to the production suite. "Where are we going?"

"Richland's PA is free for lunch. You'll eat with her."

"The PA?" I stop in my tracks. "Chloe, this is weird. I'll just go grab lunch and come back."

Something about the smile that's about to crack on her face makes me take a step back. "Wait. Richland doesn't have a PA."

Chloe is a horrible liar, so the moment the comment is out of my mouth, she blushes profusely. "Okay, confession: it's Monica. I really do have a meeting to prepare for, but I figured you two could talk about … stuff."

At the sound of Monica's name, my heart does some palpitation nonsense, and I'm having trouble stringing a complete thought together. My mouth is safer shut.

"I'm sorry for trying to be sneaky, but it sounds like you two will be working together, so you might as well get the awkward part out of the way."

I just stare at her for a second. *How much does she know?*

As if she read my mind, she says, "I know about the night of the event, and I'm a horrible friend for even saying that much." She cringes mid-thought. "I just—well, she's the new PA." Chloe throws her arms up in embarrassment. "I suck at this."

"Are you trying to tell me that she wants to see me?"

She sees my smirk and raises me a glare. Walking back in the direction we came, she points behind her without making eye contact. "You can find her right through those doors."

"Chloe," I call after her, making her stop and look at me. "If you know about that night, then what makes you think I want to see her again?"

I almost feel bad when her face crumbles into shards of shame. "I just figured…"

I back up to the door that separates me from *the one who ran away* and finally release a grin. "Thanks for the setup. I'll take it from here."

Lunch Guest

Monica

Just before noon, Richland and I wrap the first video shoot we've had since I've officially been on his team. It was fun—a short interview with a homeless man dressed up as a clown. Literally, he dresses as a clown daily. And his reason is actually a good one: people stare at him anyway, so at least now they aren't staring at *him*, but a disguise. My heart ached for the man, but his smile was brighter than any I've seen in a long time.

Just in case he didn't come with his costume on, we were prepared. But the red curly wig was left untouched, so I place it on my head along with the spongy nose, and I snap a selfie. Richland left for lunch a few minutes ago and I'm waiting for Chloe to get here so I can show her my new look. I can't wait to scare the shit out of her.

When the door finally opens, I grin maniacally and wait for a reaction I'll never get—because the figure that crosses the threshold is not Chloe. It's not even Richland. It's not anyone I'm expecting to see. *What the—?*

Zach's face is filled with surprise at first, and then amusement as he realizes who's behind the disguise. A full-on belly laugh erupts from him, complete with a stomach grab as he keels over.

I slowly pull off the nose, then the wig, and stare back and the guy that's owned my thoughts and dreams for the last six months.

Damn. He looks better than I remember. Dressed in fitted jeans and a blue button-down, average attire for an above average man, he numbs all coherent thoughts.

What is he doing here? And where has he been?

His naturally creamy skin is a golden bronze. His hair, freshly trimmed. A careful shave in just the right places give him that rugged charm look that always drove me crazy.

Who am I kidding? It still does.

I can smell him from here—that crisp, woodsy scent mixed with his citrus shampoo—and I'm flooded with memories of that night. Now here he is, in the flesh, doing unfair things to my heart.

"Hi, Cakes."

Cakes. I wish I could say it's been months since I've thought of that nickname, but I would be lying. I've spent too much time imagining that deep, raspy voice seducing me with his words.

And now I'm thinking of his lips on mine, dragging across my sensitive skin. His hands roaming…

Shit. "Hi, Zach."

The production room always feels sweltering after a shoot, and I'm still feeling the effects from the blistering lights. And being in the same room with Zach again certainly doesn't help. Setting the clown attire on the chair beside me, I reach for my water and guzzle it down. The distraction is useless, especially when I dribble some down my chin. *Smooth, Monica.*

His smile dims as if he's disappointed in my reaction. Not that I'm giving him much of a reaction at all. My tone was even when I spoke his name. My expression, blank. Which is funny, because I feel anything but blank. A freaking parade is stomping through my chest, a celebration at the mere sight of him.

That confirms it. Six months is far too long to go without a Zachary Ryan sighting.

"It seems we have a predicament," he says, shoving his hands in his front pockets. "Sandy pawned me off on Chloe, and Chloe mysteriously had something better to do than entertain this guy right here." Zach points to himself. "So I've been sent to you. The new PA. You get to take me to lunch."

Did he just…

"I *get* to take you to lunch? Because no one else wants to go with you?"

I probably should think through my responses before speaking. I don't want to be rude. He's done nothing to deserve my cold shoulder, but seeing him again does crazy things to me.

"I guess that's what happened." Even Zach's nervous laughter is charming. So annoying.

I look around, quickly coming up with a list of chores that will keep me busy throughout lunch and up until the end of today and beyond if needed.

"I've actually got work to do." I swallow the lie. It tastes disgusting in my mouth, which is why I try to avoid lying always. But this is a special circumstance.

His expression dims, and I'm reminded of the way I left him in that parking lot. Same expression, once again twisting my insides in knots.

He backs away. "Cool. I'll just run out and grab something. Or maybe I can track down Meredith." He turns away.

That stings a little—not that he means for it to. He has no idea I'm aware of his rumored fling with his publicist.

Why am I acting like such a bitch? He's not asking me out; it's just a lunch thing. A *work* lunch thing. Nothing like the last meal we shared together.

Unfortunately.

"Wait," I call out.

He turns and raises an eyebrow. When I don't say a word, he sighs. "Monica?"

There's a tightening of my heart when I hear him speak my name instead of his nickname for me. It sounds all wrong. He gives up again and turns toward the door. That's when I finally move. Rushing forward, I meet him at the door. We're so close now, I could reach out and touch him, but I don't. "I can take a short break."

"Great," he says evenly. "I'll drive."

"We can walk." Getting in his Jeep again is a bad idea. The sexual tension between us the last time we rode in that vehicle was almost too much to resist.

Three blocks later I push through the door to Belle de Jour before he can open it for me. "We'll just grab something from here and take it back to the office." He follows me past the main restaurant entrance and to the back of the takeout line.

The place is classy enough that even if someone recognized him, they won't make a scene.

"Sandy said somewhere nice."

"Oh, this place is nice. We just aren't eating here." I grin at him, feeling giddy from the familiarity of our sparring.

He puffs out his chest. "It's not my fault everyone had other plans today."

"We've established that I'm the fallback."

"You had your chance to be first pick."

I swivel my head to shoot him a glare. "Seriously? It's been six months."

His face twists as if I have no right to be upset at him for bringing that up. "Yeah. Six months ago you rejected me, and now you're treating me like shit. How does that work?"

It's like his words just body slammed me an inch from the end zone. A reminder that whatever issues I have with my past are hurting someone else, and he's not letting me off the hook. But hurting him was never my intention.

"I'm not treating you like shit, I'm just…"

He nods. "Treating me like shit."

Facing forward, I feel my cheeks heat.

"You should really warn people before you show up at their place of work. I wasn't expecting to see you today."

"Says Fuzzy the Clown." Zachary chuckles at his own joke.

I'm simultaneously amused and annoyed that he's not taking me seriously. I elbow him in the chest.

"Ow!" he exclaims. "You realize my entire body is insured, right? I could sue you just for touching me unkindly."

I shift my pressed lips to one side. "So now touching is an issue for you?"

His expression matches mine while he leans in closer. "No, Cakes. Touching is perfectly fine." His eyes move to my lips and I suck in a sharp breath. "Light strokes, scratching, a nibble here and there. Just no bruising or drawing blood, 'kay?" He winks before pulling back. "Besides, I was at BelleCurve to see Sandy today."

"What for?"

"A project." His eyes narrow. "You're the new PA, huh? What happened to going back to school?"

"I'm still undecided, but I've been looking at my options. I'm starting at the Art Institute this summer. And my old job was no longer meeting my expectations, so Sandra promoted me."

He laughs throatily. "You got canned. She already told me."

My head jerks to face him. Are Sandra and Zach really that close? That piece of information should have been none of his business.

"She was pissed, so she was teaching me a lesson. For about fifteen seconds I honestly thought I was out of a job. She noticed how much time I was spending with Richland in the production suite and knew he needed the help. It worked out for everyone."

"I guess so. Looks like we'll be working together," he says.

"What are you talking about?"

He raises his chin, motioning for me to move forward in line. We order, and when he tries to pay I move his hand aside, the simple touch searing my skin with his heat. I yank my hand away and reach for my company credit card.

"This is on BelleCurve."

He doesn't argue.

We get our food and start walking toward the office. I glance at Zachary, still waiting for an answer to my question.

"What do you mean we'll be working together?" I ask again.

His eyes examine mine for a second. "I'm hosting an event. A football camp with a leadership theme." He shrugs, and I get the impression he's afraid I won't like his idea. "I want to repurpose my speech from Heroes and Legends. Create something meaningful for the kids that I can identify with and raise money for kids who can't afford to play sports."

"How does the production team fit into this?"

"I didn't know you were with the production team when Sandy and I started talking," he says with all seriousness. "I want to document the event and see how we can spin PSAs out of it. We have a meeting with Richland today to see what his thoughts are."

The excitement in Zach's tone hits my heart with a pang. It's so easy to be crazy about this guy. He's always passionate. Always thoughtful. Always looking for ways to help others. Why does he have to be so damn perfect?

"That's a great idea," I offer.

"You think so?"

I nudge him. "Yes! Those kids are lucky to have someone like you as a role model. You have a touching story. One that's relatable. The feedback we got after Heroes and Legends was phenomenal, partially thanks to you."

He smiles, pleased, and nudges me back. "So you'll be okay working with me? I know you have a crush on me and all. It could get awkward."

"Sounds like I'll have to find a way to manage my attraction for you, bleeding heart and all."

His cringe smothers his smile. "So graphic."

When we arrive back at BelleCurve, I lead Zach through the private hallway that empties into the production suite and head to my office.

"This okay?" I ask him, taking a seat behind my desk.

He smiles. "Fine with me." My eyes focus on the door he's closing behind him. I open my mouth to tell him to leave it open, but he shakes his head, reading my mind. "I like to eat in private."

He's full of it.

My mouth remains shut. We tear into the bags, unwrap our sandwiches, and eat silently for the next few minutes until I realize he's watching me. My mouth specifically. I swipe at it with the back of my hand, suddenly self-conscious that I'm getting food everywhere. Missing breakfast is not good, but it's been happening more and more lately with this new flex schedule Richland is allowing me as I scope out the Art Institute and attend meetings with their academic advisors.

I reach for a napkin to wipe my hand and then my mouth again while I swallow my next bite.

"What's this?" he asks, reaching for one of the frames facing away from him on my desk.

I go to grab it, but he's faster. His eyes move from my face to the picture, and then back to me again.

When I got my own office, I searched unpacked boxes in my closet for photos and décor to decorate my new space. The photos I chose are a lie. Forced smiles. Broken dreams. That's all they represent. But they're also sentimental, a reminder of the life and people I left behind.

He's holding a picture of me when I was fourteen, standing proudly beside Maggie after her first bigtime runway event. My mother is perched behind us, beaming brightly at the camera.

Everyone thought we were the most adorable family, both before and after my father left. My mother, sister, and I stuck together, though my mother was more into attention and fame than anything else. Modeling came before everything, which was something I admired as a child but eventually grew to resent. There was simply no other option.

She managed my sister, who was a hot commodity in Texas by age sixteen. It helped that my mom's former model days gave her an in with the right talent scouts, but even so, my sister was born to be on a stage. Acting is her life's passion, but modeling is what got her foot in the door.

"Wow, you girls look a lot alike."

"My sister and mom." I slip the frame from his hands, but he just grabs the other one, which was taken four years later. My mom had some photos taken of me for a graduation memento, and as weird as it is that I have a picture of myself on my desk, I like it. I can't remember ever feeling so beautiful.

"Holy smokes, Cakes. Even as a teen you're hot." His eyes dash up to mine. "Wait. No. That sounded pervy. You're much better looking today."

Laughing, I try to grab the frame from him, but he pulls it back. "You could have totally modeled."

My body heats under his stare. How does he still have this effect on me? It's been months since we've seen each other, but I feel like it was just yesterday. "I have nothing against modeling, and it was great for my sister. But moving here on my own was the first step in figuring out my own path instead of living life the way I've been told to live it."

His expression softens. "I think that's a beautiful way to look at the crossroads in life. It must be cleansing to give yourself a chance to assess the value of your decisions. We're too close to our own demons sometimes, aren't we?"

His words lift my cheeks. Of course he understands. Looking down at the picture, it's hard not to remember the hustle and bustle of backstage life as everyone flocked around in utter chaos right before a runway event. That's where I had the most fun before my sister's shows. I never strutted at a runway event. My gigs were mostly for stock photos and local advertisements. Nothing big. Nothing that reached outside Rockwall.

After two years of suffocating in my dying dream of modeling, I chose to replace the negative thoughts with bigger smiles, louder laughs, and a resilient attitude. By the time I moved to Washington, the exuberance that was once an act had become part of me. And I was free to do with it whatever I wished.

It's been a trial-and-error process, for sure. I'm making mistakes all the time, but I'm also righting wrongs, turning burdens into blessings. I'm figuring it out. For the first time, I feel like wherever I end up will be where I belong. Even better, I'll have no regrets.

When I set the picture back on my desk and look up, Zach's staring at me with a question in his eyes. "You're gonna let me in at some point, Cakes."

I shrug and take a gulp of my water, hoping he can't tell he just tripled the cadence of my heart. I don't fault him for being curious. The pictures invite unwanted questions, but I can't remove them. They remind me how far I've come. How much stronger and independent I am without the silent disapproval of my mother weighing on me.

"Are you three close?"

He couldn't have just dropped it.

"We used to be. Not so much anymore."

"I'm sorry."

Something about Zach makes me want to pour my heart out to him, tell him stories I've never shared with another soul.

"It's okay. We just drifted apart," I tell him. I want him to understand me, I really do. It's just, sometimes I have a hard enough time understanding myself. "My sister and I text on occasion, usually when she's got some big news or when she's annoyed at Mom for being Mom." I laugh, realizing how much I miss our shared eye rolls over the ludicrous things Mom would say and do. "Neither of them agrees with why I'm here."

"Why are you here? Bellevue is a long way from your family."

"I told you," I say, retreating into my shell. "Unfinished business."

He doesn't look convinced, but he seems to get the hint. He searches my desk further, probably for more conversation points. I've got nothing else. He looks to the bare walls.

"I just moved in here."

"Ah." He nods. "That explains it." Then his eyes set on mine. "Are you seeing anyone?"

Looking back at him, I can feel everything about my demeanor soften. "Nothing's changed, Zach."

"And you're happy?"

"Yes, I'm happy." There's no need to think about this one. I'm a happy person in general. Sure, I have some issues when it comes to men, but that doesn't mean my life is ruined over it. I've learned how to cope with my feelings, with my insecurities, and my needs are fulfilled. Well … if we're talking about *needs*, it's been quite some time since they've been fulfilled, but that's beside the point.

For a few seconds he just watches me, studying me as if my silence might help him understand me. "You didn't come."

"Huh?"

"The games. The tickets I sent you. I didn't see you once."

Oh. I swallow. "You looked for me?"

"Every game."

"That was a sweet gesture. I should have thanked you, but—"

"You could have said *something*. Or shown up. That would have been thanks enough."

I want to sigh or roll my eyes and tell him he's ridiculous for expecting me to actually use those tickets after we'd already said our goodbyes, but I can't. The gesture was a thoughtful one, and at the time, it made my heart beat a little faster. But taking them would have given him false hope, and that would have been a problem for both of us.

"I had too many conflicts. I gave them to Children's Hospital and told them they were a gift from you. They were distributed to patients and their families."

His eyes crinkle in the corners. "That's not fair. I can't really be mad about that."

Our conversation has grown uncomfortable, and our surroundings are far too quiet. The silence between us makes it worse. I take a step to leave the room and can hear him following me. I'm not sure what to do now that lunch is over. No one gave me instructions. So I wing it.

I give Zach a tour of the full production suite, not worrying if he's already seen it all. When we're done, we land in the small production meeting room. I grab a notebook from the cabinet before probing Zach with questions about his event. At least this way I can update Richland when he's back in the office.

It sounds like whatever we end up doing for Zach will last until the end of April, maybe later depending on how long the PSAs take to edit. That's two months of working closely with the man. I can do this. It wouldn't be the first time I've worked with someone I had the hots for.

Lucky for me, I'm resilient when it comes to relationships. I don't suffer from fear or rejection. My heart was broken once a long time ago, and that was enough for me. Besides, I've already warned Zach that our attraction will lead us nowhere. Nothing has changed. That's why it's a good thing we'll be too busy working on this campaign in the safe space of the agency to be tempted into anything more.

At least I'll keep telling myself that.

Location Scout

Monica

I've somehow become the designated note-taker at this planning meeting. Richland and Meredith are tossing ideas back and forth for Zach's event like it's a competition, and none of them have anything to do with the project as Zach explained it to me.

Sandra, Chloe, and Sharlene, one of BelleCurve's project managers, are all here too, but none of us can get a word in edgewise. To be fair, Meredith and Richland have massively different agendas to fulfill. While Richland wants rich and classy, Meredith wants hot and sweaty. Her goal is to sex everything up. I'm sure there's a reason Zach hires her as his publicist, but I hope this isn't it. She's completely off the mark.

Everyone in the room is familiar with Zach's bullying story. Chloe is closest to it, since she helped Zach organize his message last summer. I can see her gritting her teeth, dying to jump in and break up the bickering so that Meredith and Richland don't continue going down the wrong path, but I know she won't.

There's a second of silence while the two take their first real breaths. Words roll off my tongue before I can stop them. "Zach is looking for engagement opportunities with the kids. The calendar shoot idea for sponsor incentives and raising money for the campaign are great, but the focus should be on the camp and what they're doing to enrich these kids' lives."

All eyes are on me now, and I'm shocked I haven't been interrupted yet. "The message is about leadership, teamwork, and community. We should encourage kids to talk openly about the real issues they face at school. And of course, we should be documenting the kids' practices and activities. We get the media talking about what Zach's doing. We post about it all over social media.

"We create a sports calendar, sure, sell it to help raise money for Zach's organization, but that's not the message we need to be concentrating on right now. How do we get the message out there? The camp will be the hub of all the excitement, and *that's* what we need to capture."

I'm full of energy, looking around the room and waiting for someone to jump in and play off my ideas. Meredith's mouth hangs open, and I'll admit, that pleases me quite a bit. Chloe's smiling but not speaking, and her eyes are focused on something behind me.

"Everything she just said." The voice in the back of the room startles me. We all look at Zach, who's gliding from the closing door to the seat beside me, a charming smile plastered perfectly on his face. He swivels a chair around and sits in it backwards while looking around the room. "Hey guys. Hope you don't mind. I'm a little early, and my ears were burning."

Sandra chuckles. "Not at all. It's better to do this with you here. Anyway, it sounds like Monica's on a roll. Which is a good thing, because Richland and I discussed it, and with Sharlene deeply involved in several other campaigns right now, we were thinking Monica could take on a lot of the coordination." Sandra looks at Sharlene and then me. "What do you ladies think?"

Sharlene nods without hesitation. I know she's slammed. But me? I've been roped into coordinating various tasks within events, but never an entire event.

I nod, because I'm not about to tell Sandra no in front of all these people, especially Zach. Not after the opportunities she's placed in my lap. I'll deal with whatever reservations I have later.

"Are you sure, Sandra?" Meredith jumps in, looking more uncomfortable than I've ever seen her. "She's new to the production department, and she's only a PA."

Only a PA, Chloe mouths to me, and we both silently laugh.

"Zach needs someone more experienced on this campaign. Let's be smart here."

Meredith doesn't get to me the way she would most girls. Sure, the photo I saw of her and Zach makes me uneasy, and she obviously has something against me, but the fact that she's trying so hard to push me out is telling.

She's right; I'm no project manager. I'm a former office manager-turned PA with a love for all things creative. That hardly makes me one to lead such an important project. But the fact that she just said that out loud...

"Considering the fact that Monica's the only one who truly gets it at this point, I think it's *best* that she takes the lead," Zach declares, turning to me.

After the shock in the room subsides, I sit taller and face Sandra. "I agree. And I can't wait to get started."

I purposely don't meet Meredith's eyes, but I lick up her wounds with salt on my tongue and a smile on my face as I watch her in my periphery.

"All right, sounds like we've got that figured out." Richland claps his hands and stands. "Monica, set up some meetings for us this week, and make sure to invite Zach whenever he's free. I trust you to work with his team on the scheduling." I jot down some notes on my laptop while he turns to my left. "Zach, do we have a name for the campaign or location for the camp?"

"Marketing was supposed to be working on the camp branding, and my agent is locking down a camp on Orcas Island as we speak. I can send the information your way if you'd like."

Richland nods to me. "Give it to Monica. She'll do some research on the location. I don't think we'll need to scout this one, but if you have any field plans, Zach, that would be helpful. If not, Monica can work with graphics to mock something up. Then we can all discuss."

"Definitely," Zach agrees.

The team walks out the door, but surprise, Meredith hangs back. "Mind if I have a word, Zach?"

He seems distracted by his phone before pulling his eyes up to meet hers. "Not now, Mer. I'll have Trevor set up a meeting with you this week."

After another lingering look at Zach and a death glare at me, she walks out, letting the door close behind her.

If I had any questions about a potential relationship brewing between Zach and Meredith, this interaction answered them with a firm no. Their selfie on the gossip queens' monitor has hovered over my mind like a looming cloud, raining doubt upon me every time I thought of it. It's possible they had a thing once and it ended. But I think it's time to let my jealousy go.

I'm able to exhale once Zach and I are alone, but he's not going to let me off that easy. "What's wrong?" He nudges my side.

Does he have to call me out on everything? Normally I'd play this off like I'm the best decision anyone could make. Why *wouldn't* they choose me? I could play that card now. Ease whatever tension there is and deal with my doubts on my own time. But Zach... He hands me the key to let down my guard with a subtle nudge, allowing my strength to surface over fear. And I trust he'll allow me to stumble along the way.

"Nothing," I finally answer. "It just hit me. The responsibility is not something I'm used to. I'm not a project manager. I'm barely a production assistant. Maybe Meredith was right."

He makes a disgusted face. "Don't listen to her. She's just jealous of you."

"Me?"

Zach's eyes drift from my eyes to my lips. My stomach clenches, and I realize how much I've longed for him to look at me like that again. His lip curls up and he lifts his chin as if my thoughts are obvious. "Yeah, you."

He doesn't elaborate, and I'm not going to ask him to. Instead, I raise an eyebrow. "Well, I've never, not once, led a project. I think you're letting your lust for me seep into your common sense."

He throws his head back and laughs. "My lust for you? Arrogant much?"

I don't back down. Our faces are inches from each other, but I don't care. I'm angry. I also like being close to him. Such a bad combination.

"You don't need to do much," he says, his husky timbre softening. "Marketing is slacking on coming up with the theme. We need one, like, yesterday. Maybe since you seem to have a good grip on what this is all about, you can help me come up with something. As soon as we have it locked down we can start branding and planning production. We can go to Orcas Island if that will help."

Orcas Island, as in, the campgrounds where the event will be? Orcas Island, as in, the destination that happens to be three hours and one ferry ride away? He's not fooling me.

"We?"

"Yes. Let's go this weekend."

"Absolutely not." Folding my arms across my chest, I lean back in my chair.

He mimics my movements, challenge written in his expression. "I bet it would impress Richland if you made the trip. Aren't you all about going above and beyond?"

"Yes, but not with you!"

Why won't he just drop it? I'm agreeing to work closely with him on this project. I was even honest about my comfort level in taking something like this on. The last thing I need is for the two of us to be alone and trapped in his Jeep for an extended period.

A chuckle rises from somewhere deep in his throat. "I'm sorry to break this to you, but this is my project. I want to check it out and do the research."

"Then go. But I can't come with you. It's not … professional. Not after what happened between us." I stand up and close my notebook, hoping the conversation is over. That's as straightforward as I can get without divulging the root of the problem.

Zachary stands too and leans down so his face is near mine. "I get it, *Monica*."

I suck in a breath, feeling the wave of heat that rolls from his body to mine. God, he's intoxicating just to stand near, but I'm not too gone to realize he's using my name as a weapon now. *Cakes* when he's seducing me. *Monica* when he's mad at me.

"You don't want me to be into you. Guess what?" He narrows his eyes, and I swallow against his intensity. "I'm not. What happened, or didn't happen, between us was six months ago. But you're as excited about this campaign as I am. I heard it in your voice earlier. I need someone like that on my team. So just cut the bullshit already. I'm not going to make a pass at you. I won't even try to be your friend if that freaks you out. We'll work together. That's all."

I don't get a chance to even breathe before he turns away from me and walks back out the door.

Crap.

Catch 'n' Throw
Zachary

My morning workout is a complete waste. My trainer gave up yelling at me and left over an hour ago, but I'm still here, determined a good run on the treadmill will cleanse my thoughts of the one person I'm not supposed to think about. Unfortunately, Monica's resistance toward me is only making me more curious about her, and that won't do.

When Monica and I met last summer, she was fearlessly flirty. Unapologetic about her boldness. Sassy to a fault. And funny without even trying. When our eyes locked through the conference room glass while she was sneaking off with a piece of leftover chocolate cake from our meeting, I was intrigued. Monica struck me as daring and beautiful with impenetrable confidence—a combination that jumpstarted something inside of me.

That wasn't the first time I'd seen her, but it was the first time I saw beyond the flawless exterior and wanted to know more. My next trip to BelleCurve was a few days later. I purposely showed up early so I'd have a chance to talk to her.

She didn't disappoint.

Monica kept me company, talking a mile a minute about nothing in particular and keeping me engaged with every syllable. She was irresistibly bold and passionate about life.

I liked her. She didn't expect me to entertain her with stories about my success. She didn't clam up around me or treat me differently from any other guy. She didn't try to play a game of disinterest, hoping to garner my attention. She was just—Monica.

When I saw her at Heroes and Legends, I knew I had to ask this girl out. I didn't expect her to shut me down or to stop being the Monica I'd come to adore. I don't know why, but kissing her changed everything.

After letting her drive away, I wasn't planning to think about her again. I wasn't expecting thoughts of her to linger like we had unfinished business. There was clear closure in our last conversation. But a week later, it was a struggle not to call her and pretend like it was just a friendly check-in. Instead, I took the chickenshit approach and sent her the tickets, hoping she'd have a change of heart. Desperate, I know. And when she didn't show up to that first home game, I finally called her.

Now here I am six months later, an hour into my cardio, burning way more calories than my system can afford, while once again thinking about Monica Stevens. I'm not even sure I like her anymore after the way she's been acting.

No. That's a lie.

I might want her more than ever now that she's added weight to her defense. But even if I do, it doesn't matter. She's made herself clear, and I made a promise. From here on out, it's all business between Monica and me.

My phone rings, forcing me to end my workout. I use the back of my shirt to wipe my face before answering.

"Coach." I use the pause to catch my breath.

A chuckle answers on the other side. "You all right there, Zach? Don't tell me you've already lost your endurance. You've only been out of practice for a month."

"I'm at the gym." I smile into the phone.

Coach Reynolds was one of the reasons I was excited to join the team in Seattle. He's a family man, an introvert by nature, and very well-respected. Not just within the league, but within the college and high school sports communities too. The man is someone to be admired, and I've looked up to him since he took me under his wing my sophomore year of high school.

"Good. I won't keep you," he says. "Trevor called. Wanted my permission to involve some of the boys in your little fundraiser."

"It's a charity event, Coach. Like previous years. Nothing little about it." I laugh at his attempt to rile me. "Did he give you the details? You should come out, at least catch the scrimmage at the end of the week."

"He filled me in. And I approve." The line grows silent for a second, and I wonder if Coach has more to say. It seems like he does. Finally, he lets out a breath on the other end of the line. "Zach, you can come to me with these things. Don't keep making your agent call me."

"Sorry, Coach," I say sheepishly. I know he hates when I send Trevor in my place, but time has been tight lately. Delegating and letting Trevor and Meredith schedule me has given me time back to do other things. But he's right. He's family. Not by blood, but in all the ways that matter.

"Trevor's been working all the logistics while I work with the creative team at BelleCurve to nail down the theme and production."

"All right. I just wanted to tell you that I gave him my approval and offered up my time if I can be of any help. Coaching, janitorial work. Whatever you'd like."

I let out a laugh. "Coach, you're tempting me here. I might have to get you to show these boys how to run some two-point stance sprints."

"Ha. Better not scare these boys away so young." I hear a smile in his voice. "Look, the wife and kids have been asking about you. They haven't had a chance to congratulate you on last season. Plan on coming to dinner one of these nights, okay? Actually, how about tonight?"

My thoughts turn to Monica. "Can I let you know a little later?"

"Sure thing. Just come over if you've got the time. You know we'll have enough to feed you."

I chuckle. Mrs. Reynolds does always overcook. "Yes, sir."

I'm pulling up in front of Monica's apartment, which is only a block from BelleCurve. We made a mutual decision to forego the trip to Orcas Island, at least for now, and instead spend some hours over the weekend brainstorming theme ideas.

When the door to her apartment building swings open and Monica pops out, I get a good look at her petite body in leggings, black leather boots, and a long-sleeved red and black checkered button up. It's going to be hard to not stare at that all day, but the plan is to avoid eye contact and play it cool. I'm a man of my word.

I start to open my door and then shut it. It goes against everything I believe in to not open the door for her, but if I'm going to prove to myself and to her that I can be around her without a hidden agenda, then I'm winning. In other words, I'm teaching myself how to be a dick for this girl. Awesome.

"Hey," she says breathlessly, slipping into the passenger seat.

I want to look. To see if her face is as flush as her tone hints. Did she run downstairs? Is she nervous? I bite my curiosity off at the head, refusing to give in. A true disciplined professional; that's what I am.

"Hey," I answer casually as I pull away from the curb. "Where to?"

"There's a community field a few blocks away. Figured we'd start there. Could've walked, but street parking is lame around here."

"No problem." I take the next right before adjusting the volume knob to the radio. It's presently set to my favorite country station, so I leave it and focus on the drive. Silence slices through the music as I drive, so much that I want to laugh. Two people purposely forcing themselves to act like the opposites of themselves, all to deter an inevitable attraction. Pure comedy.

"We were expecting you at BelleCurve yesterday," she finally says.

I pop a mint in my mouth and offer one to her, keeping my eyes on the road. She shakes her head.

"I couldn't. Had a prior engagement with Meredith set up."

It's the truth, although the plan was to hang with some members of the Wifey Club for a few hours and then spend the afternoon at BelleCurve. Plans changed when Meredith convinced me to join her at an early happy hour to discuss my latest endorsement deal.

She's been extra needy lately, and I hate when she gets like that. It just means she'll come up with another outlandish idea to reap more attention to my brand, and I'm not that excited about what she's done for me lately. I understand that being a sex symbol of sorts comes with the territory when you play for a championship-winning team, but she's taking it too far.

"No problem. It's just, I've got a schedule to put together and I kind of need you for that. There are a lot of unknowns at this point, so I was hoping you could help me fill in some of the blanks."

I glance at her and a pang of guilt hits my gut. "I'm sorry. I thought it was just another planning meeting, and Meredith thinks she owns me." I laugh at my own joke, but I see the perturbed expression Monica tries to hide.

What's that about?

I turn back to the road.

She sighs. "Planning involves scheduling. Without you I can't prepare the schedule. It's fine. Just call and let me know next time."

I bite the inside of my cheek to stop my smile. She's cute when she's upset. Maybe she's even jealous, but I won't get my hopes up. "Will do, Coach."

"Don't call me that."

"Then what do I call you now that Cakes is out of the question?"

There's another awkward silence before she responds. "I didn't know that was out of the question, but I suppose you could call me Monica? It's kind of my name."

Her tone carries zero flirtation, but at least the Monica I know is still there somewhere.

Instead of explaining to her why Cakes is no longer allowed in my vocabulary, I just nod in agreement. "Monica it is."

Maybe today was a bad idea. I want us to work well together, but if it's going to be this much of a challenge, maybe I should have her speak directly to Trevor.

"Zach," she starts.

See, I already know her so well. I know she's about to question why I'm not undressing her with my eyes per usual.

"Yes, Monica?" I turn and give her the most dazzling smile I can manage.

She folds her arms across her chest. "Okay, smartass. I know what you're doing. Can't we just go back to being ourselves? You're acting so … weird."

I shake my head. "No. If we both act like ourselves, we'll like each other, and that's not allowed, remember?" Parking the car, I glance at her again. "Your rules, not mine."

Without missing a beat, I reach into the backseat, feeling Monica's eyes bore into me. And then it's like a magnetic reaction. I have to look at her again.

Her eyes are lighter in hue now with the sun casting light on her face. A translucent honey instead of rich caramel. Fucking beautiful. Peach skin that pinks easily. And her hair, long waves that brush against the top of her breasts. Yeah, I definitely shouldn't look at her. Ever.

"What are you doing?" She's peering into the backseat now, trying to get a glimpse of what I'm grabbing.

With a curl of the side of my mouth, I bring up the football and wave it in the air. "We're going to a field. Might as well bring this."

"Are we playing tackle or did you bring flags too?"

The question is unexpected, and it makes me laugh. "Neither, *smartass*." I wink, then reach for my door handle so I can't look back at her again. Every time she speaks I want to plant my lips on hers and swallow her words, stroking each syllable with my tongue. That's the effect she has on me when she makes me laugh. She doesn't even have to try.

"Just catch and throw, Ca—Monica." Shaking my head, I hop out of the Jeep and shut the door before I can say anything else.

Avoiding her door, I walk straight toward the field, using long strides to get me there as fast as possible. She's practically running to catch up. I can hear her coming, but I don't expect her to punch the ball from my grip as she passes. My mind is on other things, like the fact that I hate the way I'm forcing myself to act. I didn't think I needed to guard a football in Monica's presence, but once again, she surprises me.

The pigskin flies into the air and we both reach for it at the same time, but she's already ahead of me, grabbing it and tucking it under her arm.

"What the…?"

She takes off running and laughing. I give her a few seconds before going after her, mostly because I need to calm my instant arousal. After that, it's game on.

It only takes me four quick strides to wrap my arms around her waist. She shrieks when I reach over her and steal the ball back. Holding it over my head, I turn and walk backwards to the field. She stalks me with a smile, and just like that, our axis has stabilized. This is where we need to be.

"Can you throw a football? Or do I need to show you how this works?"

Her eyes narrow a little at my challenge, and then she smiles. "I guess you'll find out."

Surprising me once more, my eyes widen a little before my walk turns into a jog to gain some distance. "All right, then. I need to see this."

We're only twenty yards apart when I throw the ball right to her. I know my strength, and I give her none of it. She's able to catch it easily, but before I can appreciate the technique of the catch like I want to, she's throwing it back to me.

It lands against my chest with a powerful thud. "Geez, Monica. That's an incredible arm."

She smiles and waves for me to move further back. So I do, and then I throw it again. She catches it and immediately rears back to throw a bullet my way. *What in the world?* "Where'd you learn to throw?"

"My dad," she says easily. We continue to move away from each other with each pass. Now I'm just curious how far away she can target with that arm. I've never seen anything like it. powderpuff leagues would kill to have her on a team. She gets to about forty yards when I notice her start to lose aim slightly. Still, that's damn good.

"Throw it for real," she says. Even from forty yards away I can see that her skin is glowing with exhilaration. She looks radiant standing there, ready to take another ball to the chest, with wisps of hair coming loose from her ponytail and cheeks now blooming pink from adrenaline.

I don't dare deny her, but I have to laugh because she obviously doesn't know what she's asking. "I don't think you want me to break your ribs, doll face."

Hands move to her hips and she cocks it out a little. "I can handle it. Just do it."

My hand moves to my temple to rub the tender spot while I think about what to do. If I were to throw it as hard as I could, it would knock her over—or worse, knock her out completely. Without pads on, that little body of hers would snap in half. But I could still give her some heat.

Winding back slightly, I wing it to her, cringing when I realize how fast it leaves my hands. Faster than anticipated. She squares herself up, jumps slightly, and it plows into her, throwing her back and onto the grass. The ball jolts from her hands the moment she lands, so she reaches up and snatches it, holding it tightly to her chest.

"Shit!" I run the forty yards and drop to my knees to find her laughing hysterically.

"Ow," she says through her laughter. The ball is still tightly in her hands. "First down," she jokes.

"Sorry to tell you, but you fell before you had possession."

"No!" She makes a face and turns to the side, letting the ball fall from her hands. "It was mine."

Now I'm laughing. "You took that one well. I'm sorry, Monica, I didn't mean to throw it that hard."

She rolls onto her back again and locks eyes with mine. "I'll forgive you under one condition."

I'll do whatever you say. "What's that?"

"Don't call me Monica ever again."

A wide grin slowly spreads across my face.

"You got it, Cakes."

Under the Bleachers

Monica

Zach's tossing the ball up in the air and catching it while I snap a few pictures of the field. He's been silent for a while now, seemingly deep in thought. We're supposed to be brainstorming the camp's theme, and I'm feeling pressure from every angle. Marketing couldn't get the job done to Zach's satisfaction, so now the task belongs to us. I'm clueless as to what he's looking for, but surely I've captured enough of the field.

Slipping my phone in my shirt pocket, I peer at Zach out of the corner of my eye. We're walking the track now with no intended purpose, but I'm reminded of walks I would take with my elementary school crushes. When a boy I liked would hold my hand or subtly brush into my shoulder. The innocence of those moments was simple, yet magnified. But that was back when fairytales felt real.

My life changed drastically between then and high school. It didn't take much to lose my innocence after I learned that fairytales were nothing but false hope based on lies. I guess you could say I was lost and looking for any means of affection. I gave it up to a guy I thought could never hurt me—the anti-football player. Math clubbing, chess playing, jazz loving, zit popping, high-water wearing, Victor Rubio.

He was supposed to be safe. The way he looked at me with those puppy dog eyes and followed me around school like I was God's greatest gift, I genuinely had hope. The jocks were the ones rumored to be creeps with a rising tally on conquests, but when the "safe" boy I lost my virginity to blabbed the news all over school, he became the hottest thing on campus—a legend to the males, a god to the females. Because Victor Rubio got with the daughter of an NFL superstar. Talk about regrets. The worst of it? Turns out I wasn't even his first.

"Don't you have something better to do than walk around an old high school field on a Saturday? I thought you famous types are always busy with some media engagement or cocktail party," I tease.

Zach presses his lips together and shrugs. "Not me. I like to lay low in the off season. You know, Netflix and chill, workout, and do the occasional charity event. Besides, I couldn't think of anything better than hanging out with you."

He holds up his hands in defense, gripping the ball in one hand while realizing he just slipped. "*Not* hitting on you," he reassures me. "You're just fun to hang out with, that's all."

The moment I opened the Jeep door this morning, I knew what I was walking into. Zach made himself clear the other day that he would maintain complete professionalism, and then he just walked out the door leaving me reeling with confusion. He claims he's not into me anymore, yet when I'm with him, I feel like he's fighting this pull between us just as much as I am. And his words earlier ... he's right. If we act like ourselves, we would wind up where we were six months ago, tangled in each other's arms and losing ourselves to the chemistry that binds us.

So here he is, doing exactly as I asked, and I hate it. As much as I want to push him away, I want to cling to him at the same time.

With a flick of his wrist, he tosses me the football. "Time to fess up, Cakes. For someone who doesn't think too highly of football, you sure know a lot about it. What else did your dad teach you?"

"Everything." I force a smile in Zach's direction, desperately wanting to explain to him why I resist his charms—or at least why I'm attempting to resist them. I'm failing miserably.

We stop walking and he brushes a strand of loose hair from my cheek. "You've got a story to tell." *He thinks he's so smart.* "People say I'm a good listener, and I'm great at keeping secrets. I also give really good advice, but only when it's requested."

The stupid grin that lights up his face next carries too much sincerity it makes me fold like well-kneaded dough. How does he do that? My secrets are mine, and I've carried them alone for so long. No one has ever pried into my background. Not even Chloe.

I'm the master of distractions, but Zach throws me off at every pivot. He plays life like it's a football game. Every time he's denied a first down, he's back at it fighting his way toward his goal.

A deep breath and slight laugh does little to soothe my nerves, but being here like this with Zach, walking beside him, his sweet words ringing in my head—maybe I'll let him gain a few more yards.

He follows me to the bleachers and sits beside me while I slide my finger around the threads of the ball, slowly, just like

I would do when I was little. My palms were so small it was a miracle I could get a good grip on the thing, but I got used to the way the leather felt beneath my fingertips. Smooth and rough in a single stroke. Solid and airy in one toss. "Don't hold it so tight," my dad would say. "There you go. See that gap between your hand and the ball?" He moved my arms, so the ball tipped up, my arm above my head. "Look up, M. See the sky?"

When I got older, I became as resentful of the pigskin as I was fascinated by it. I no longer cared about the intricate stitching and inflation measurements. I cared about chucking the ball downfield as far as possible, wishing it would take my pain with it so I could finally forget. Because forgetting would be preferable to what I've put myself through all these years.

"My dad played ball professionally," I confess. "Played until I was ten. He was in the prime of his NFL career when he suffered a season-ending ACL tear."

I look up, gauging Zach's reaction. No football player enjoys listening to stories of injuries on the field. Especially injuries that end careers. But Zach gives nothing away except patience.

"His contract was up by the time he recovered. Rumors spread that he would never play the same, and no one would give him a chance. That was it for him. A horrible end in the prime of his career.

"He got depressed. Fought with my mom constantly. Everything fell apart. They separated." I shrug. "One day he was my world, and the next, he was gone."

Taking a breath, I concentrate on my heart's pacing. For so many years, it was just my mom, my sister, and me who knew about our father's betrayal. No good would ever come from telling anyone about our heartbreak. *So why am I letting Zach in, of all people?*

A hand lands on my back. "That's shitty. I'm sorry, Cakes. Where is he now?"

My nervous laughter doesn't fool him. His hand drifts up my back to my neck, which he gives a quick squeeze, sending a buzz of comfort through me.

"It doesn't matter. I haven't spoken to him since I was fourteen. That was a long time ago." Kicking at the rocks of the track, I shrug. "Sometimes I come out here to think—about my dad, my future ... everything, really. It might sound stupid, but he was my hero. When it all went wrong, I was in major denial. How could the perfect family just ... collapse—like it was built with rubber cement instead of the good stuff?" I smile, because as sad as it is, it's honest, and I'd like to lighten the mood a bit. "I'm still mad at him, but that's why this place is great. I feel connected to the good memories when I'm out here."

"Have you tried talking to him since then?"

Shaking my head, I swallow the need to spew more hurt words.

"I don't think you're in denial at all. If you can't understand his reasons for leaving, then how could you move on from it? Sounds like you need closure."

I shudder. It's not cold, but that word makes my stomach roll with discomfort. "What if I don't want *closure*?"

My throat constricts. When I realize I'm leaning on Zach, I pull myself upright. The only support I've relied on for years is my own. Independence and self-reliance are my strong suits. That isn't about to change today.

"I don't know if this is inappropriate to ask, but I'm curious," Zach starts. "Would I know of him? I'm assuming he played for Dallas." He eyes me warily. "Maybe I don't want to know."

Dread swarms my stomach. Zach grew up in Dallas. He probably slipped out of the womb wearing a Cowboys jersey and had the active roster memorized before he could speak.

I must hesitate too long. Zach shakes his head. "I'm sorry, Cakes. It doesn't matter. I shouldn't have asked."

A hall pass I very much appreciate. I've already told him too much.

It's silent for a few moments as he runs a gentle hand up and down my back. A comforting touch; no more, no less. I don't expect him to say anything now. No words could ever remedy the years of damage caused by the man I loved most in the world. A man I still love but may never understand.

"Injuries like your dad's can shred lives. I get it. I've seen it. I'm sorry you had to go through that." Zach's voice carries pure sincerity, making my chest swell with emotion.

There it is. The reason I feel like I can tell Zach almost anything. He gets it. He doesn't judge. He understands enough now to let the rest of what I'm not telling him go.

I sigh. "When I look back on it all, I think about my mom and how awful she was to him when he was recovering. Every argument was about money. She just couldn't stand the thought of not having it. I know it stressed him out. But at the same time, he knew what he was marrying into." Amusement lifts my cheeks. "She happily retired from modeling after I was born. Marrying into the NFL, she didn't have to worry about money, but of course that changes with an injury like my dad's. Football salaries are meant to last a lifetime, and she felt short-changed. Suddenly there was all this resentment over her career ending, as if it was my dad's fault. All she talked about was the supermodel she would have been if she hadn't given up her dream because she relied on his to survive.

"I guess in a way it's true, but to blame someone you love for a decision you both made?" I shiver. "I was twelve and knew she was wrong. I love her more than anything, but it doesn't mean I have to agree with her decisions."

"That's a grown-up way to look at things at twelve years old."

"What can I say? I have an old soul." I laugh. "As much as I didn't agree with the way my mom reacted to the accident, I do feel like it's unfair to be angry at her when my dad's the one who left us."

"You beat yourself up a lot for how you feel," Zach says, his voice coating me like a soft blanket. "Don't do that. You're allowed to be angry, sad, whatever it is. Even years later. It's unfair to set rules on your feelings."

"Yeah, over ten years later and I'm holding onto something I'll never get back." I hand him the football which he palms with one hand. "I used to love football, but it's hard to watch now.

"That's why you couldn't go to my games?"

I nod. "It's been a long time since I've watched a game from the bleachers." Patting the bleacher step, I feel some weight lift from my chest. I didn't realize how good it would feel to talk about all that. Maybe now he can respect the boundaries I've created—even though I kind of don't want him to. It's a painful conflict between attraction and fear.

Suddenly something changes in Zach's expression. "I'd like to think something like that would never happen to me. Not just the injury, but the aftermath." He shrugs. "I've had good mentors who taught me that football won't last forever. I've always looked at the kitchen as not only my side gig, but my plan B too. Funny—I created it thinking that it was my mom's dream, but … maybe it's mine."

By the time he's done talking, he's woven our fingers together. I don't make a move to shake him off. Instead, I find myself relying on his comfort and strength. It feels good to let someone else carry the weight for once.

I want to believe Zachary is a better man than someone like my father. There's no doubt in my mind that he is *now*. But things change. Life changes people, and once a person stops dreaming, they become unpredictable. It's good that Zach has a plan B, but he hasn't been put in that position, so how could he possibly know the outcome?

There's something about him that draws me in, more than his good looks and charm. When we're together I can almost forget that he's the most eligible bachelor in Seattle who just signed a four-year extension that will make him far more money than anyone could ever need. It's not about any of that for him. He makes his moments, and then he lives in them purposefully. It's a beautiful thing.

Zach's eyes lock on mine, and the corners of his lips turn up. He shifts and snakes his body through the crack in the bleachers, guiding his feet to the dirt below, then looks up at me with a full-on grin. "You comin'?"

This is … different.

I slide my hand across the worn wood and blue chipped paint of the bleacher steps. The last time I had a view like this, I was ten years old. I'll never forget it...

My dad was running the track, and I was bored waiting for him and for the rain to let up. The bleacher steps were much like these, the old wooden style before safety inspections forced the stadium owners to retrofit them. The stairs were slick from the rain and made for an awesome surfing platform. I skidded from one side to the other, ignoring my dad's yells from the other side of the field. Out of the corner of my eye I saw him running for me. He must have had that parent intuition thing, because it was in that moment I slipped, whacked my head, and fell between the steps, down twelve feet or so. I remember the impact, the immediate shock of pain—and then nothing.

I woke up in a hospital bed with a concussion and two broken limbs, but the pain wasn't the first thing I recognized. A nurse with raven black hair and pink bunny scrubs stood at the end of the bed talking to my father. Even groggy, I could see that she was comforting him. *Why?* My heart flew into panic mode. Something was wrong, but I didn't feel it until I tried to scoot up in the bed. Everything in my body screamed, including me.

A shudder runs through me. There's a reason I don't relive that day. It's too painful for so many reasons.

I inhale deeply and slip through the steps of the aging wooden structure—this time on purpose—and welcome Zach's hold as he guides me down safely.

I can practically feel my heart pumping out my ears, but for the first time, it's not because of his touch. The memory of me falling is more vivid than it's ever been, but I don't understand. Why now? I come to this field often. It's become a safe place where I'm free to dwell on the past while still keeping my distance from it.

But now … Zach challenges my demons without even meaning to. And while he's someone I know I could follow anywhere if circumstances were different, I'm painfully aware that circumstances are *not* different.

Straightening myself, I watch him peer through the slit in the steps and stare out at the field. It's clear he's about to tell me a secret of his own. I want to protest, leave this space that's too close to a man I can't have. But he listened to me. I owe him the same respect.

"Dreams are a funny thing," he begins. "When I was young, dreaming felt safer than living. Fear ruled my world in more ways than one. Let's just say … I ran a lot," he chuckles. "Mostly from the punk that wanted to torture me, but not always. Sometimes I was my own worst enemy."

He faces me and lifts his arms above his head, using his fingers to grip the underside of the bleacher step. With a crooked smile, he has my complete attention. Even in moments like this, when my wall is taller than me, he disarms me.

"You've heard my speech. The story of the relentless bully who tormented me beyond measure. I've talked openly about the garbage cans and rocks, and how I overcame it all once I made up my mind to put a stop to it, but that's only part of it."

I nod. Of course I remember the story. It had some of the guests in tears by the time Zach finished his speech at Heroes and Legends. There's more to it?

He sighs. "Behind every bully there's a story that never gets told. We're so quick to judge their actions, and we in turn condemn and classify. And then we punish instead of guiding the abusers in the right direction. Don't get me wrong; there should always be consequences for bad behavior, but putting a lid on a boiling pot will only guarantee an eventual eruption.

"The moment you take the time to pull back the curtain and evaluate the issues, you'll find that there's a root to the pain. A reason. And the younger you address it, the better chance the bully has to live a better life."

The fact that he's been bullied himself and has taken his time to think about the other side is oddly endearing.

Gripping the edge of the bleacher step tighter, the taut muscles in his arms react. "Football was what I dreamed of to escape it all. That dream gave me a purpose, a drive to go after the things I deserved in life. It gave me a reason to stop hiding. Eventually. But this…" He drops his arms and looks at me. "Under the bleachers of my old high school, before I even played football, I was finally able to feel safe, if only for moments at a time."

I shiver. "From your bully?"

"Yes, but not just my bully."

Everything is so quiet. I can hear his deep inhale and exhale. "The restaurant took a toll on my family. Like I told you, it was my mother's passion, but for my father it was a burden. He was a businessman, so he thought he'd enjoy the marketing and finances, but our restaurant was small. We could have a packed house every night—which we pretty much did—but we'd only ever just make ends meet. My mother wanted to expand, but it would have taken another investment to do it. The disagreements were endless. My dad's drinking never helped.

"He became the joke of the town. The drunk that would serve his patrons and then stumble down the street at midnight instead of making sure his family got home safe after closing. My friends' parents didn't want their kids near my family. The restaurant business started dying, and suddenly I was exiled from my peers without a lifeline. My parents were too consumed with their own issues to see how they were affecting my brother and me."

My heart constricts. It doesn't take much to see that Zach and I have led completely different lives. Still do. But there's so much in his story I can relate to.

"This one boy started in on me when I was twelve. His dad had been let go from the restaurant because my parents couldn't afford to pay him after a slow month. You know, his taunting was manageable. I did my best to ignore it. But when the physical violence came, that's when the fear set in. Physically, I stood no chance back then."

"And then you bulked up," I tease, remembering the glitter of laughter that spread over the audience at Heroes and Legends when the tone of the speech turned from drama to comedy.

Zach smiles. "Something like that." He looks around us at the structure we're standing under. "One night, I decided to walk the twelve blocks from the restaurant to the high school stadium to watch the football game. I realized someone was following me and started running. I was like that Gump kid without the knee braces. Surprisingly faster than my enemy.

"There was no way into the stadium without stopping, and I knew he'd catch me by then, so I ran to the back where the fence came up against the woods and bleachers just like this one." His eyes widen as my heart pounds in my chest. "And I shit you not, I heard him calling my name. Taunting me."

With a shake of his head, Zach tears his eyes from mine. "I stumbled, only to fall right into a section of the fence that had been pried open by someone else."

"How do you know?" My voice sounds strangled when I speak. There's no way I'm hearing him right.

He shrugs. "The opening was perfectly disguised. No one would know it was there except for the person who made it. And me. It turned out to be the perfect place to watch the games. And man, did I dream of being out there on that field. A small-town hero, a boy who needed an escape from his life." His smile dims.

He has to be talking about the same fence my dad cut open to get to me after I'd fallen.

"One night while hiding under the bleachers, I resolved that I didn't want to hide anymore. My little brother looked up to me, and I couldn't sit around and let a bully rule my life. I started spending my time at the gym instead, determined to bulk up and earn a spot on that field.

"Meanwhile, things at the restaurant got worse. My dad was overspending, there was a lawsuit over a bogus food poisoning claim … and then there was the accident." His voice cracks and he clears his throat. It's the first time he's taken a pause since starting this story, and my chest tightens.

His dad's accident is something that lingered with me after Zach and I parted ways last summer. The fact that he had to deal with the loss of a parent that young shreds my insides. I'm almost ashamed for having my own hang-ups with my father. My dad and I may not speak to each other, but at least he's still alive.

My words dissolve at the tip of my tongue. *I'm so sorry for your loss. What a horrible way to lose your father. At least he didn't leave you by choice.* None of those things feel right to say.

I step forward and place a hand on his chest and tip my head down, offering silent condolences instead. Heat seeps from his body. Muscles ripple beneath my fingertips, causing me to step back as if I've been burned.

"After the accident, my anger just kept growing. I became irritable, unforgiving, reactive. I was already an emotional kid, and my father's death turned that into something dark and ugly. Thank God I didn't follow in his footsteps and start drinking." He shudders. "I didn't know what to do with myself. I just focused on my workouts and getting through one day one at a time.

"One night, I was running drills by myself on the field, angry that because of my father's death I had missed tryouts. Pissed off that it was dark and soon I would have to drive downtown to pick my little brother up from his friend's house. Pissed off at the world for anything and everything. That's when my bully showed up again and had the audacity to offer his condolences."

Zach's laugh bleeds sarcasm. "The thing is, I knew he was being genuine. He hadn't touched me in over one year, yet I was still resentful." I watch Zach's fists clench, although he's still got a sideways smile on his face. "I hit him. Hard. And then I hit him again, as if he were just some punching bag that showed up in the middle of the field.

"He tried to fight back. Got a few swings in, but my rage was uncontrollable. The high school football coach broke us up. The next thing I knew, I was getting suspended from school and then handed a spot on the football team."

A smile spreads on my face as I remember how I felt in a similar situation when I thought I was getting fired from BelleCurve.

"Didn't quite make sense at the time, but Coach said he'd been watching me before that night. He saw the work I was putting in on the field. He also knew about my dad, so he had some sympathy. He knew my anger would be put to better use on the field. I owe that man my life."

The wistful look on Zach's face reveals the guilt he still carries from that night. "What happened to your bully? Did he get in trouble for the years of abuse he caused you?" I feel defensive for Zach. He shouldn't feel remorseful for finally sticking up for himself.

He laughs. "I think I'll spend the rest of my days being sorry for hitting Desmond that night. And he'll never let me forget it."

"Desmond?" That name sounds all too familiar. "Wait … your business partner?"

"The one and only. Funny turn of events, huh? He's a good guy. Like I said, he'd had some rough times. I'd trust the guy with my life now."

Wow. It's all coming together. Zach had mentioned that the guy had been dealt a shitty hand and just needed a break. And after everything the kid did to him, Zach was the one to help him turn his life around.

I look around us and envision little Zach running for safety, breathless and scared. It's no wonder he can lead a team with such humility and grace. He's lived both sides of the coin, as aggressor and victim. *Behind every bully there's a reason.* Maybe the same is true with my father. Maybe behind every father who's abandoned his child, there's a reason too.

Probably. But is there redemption?

No. I won't pour false hope into my already salted wounds. There is no excuse for what my father did. Zach's story is about second chances. It's about opening yourself up to the opportunities that come your way. Something I'm still learning to do.

"Under the Bleachers."

Zachary cocks his head to the side and catches my eye. "What?"

I smile. "That should be the theme of your camp. Under the Bleachers. The place you hid out until you realized that you could alter your path."

He twists his lips up into a mile. "Under the Bleachers. Now that, Cakes, is why I want you on my team."

"You like it?" I'm trying to hide my schoolgirl giddiness, but it's impossible. I feel like the high school quarterback just asked me to prom.

"I love it."

Jumping up, I clap my hands, excitedly. "Good. Then that's settled. I'll talk to marketing on Monday and we'll get started with the logo."

I try to ignore the way he's watching my excitement with a grin on his face. Forcing my eyes from his, I check the time on my cell phone and gasp. It's almost four o'clock. "I guess we got what we needed out of today. Should we call it a night?"

"Sounds good. I need to get to a dinner thing." He pauses. "What are you doing tomorrow?"

"On Sundays I usually lounge around, watch *The Walking Dead* reruns, and eat all the snacks around my house so that I can go to the store and buy new ones. I'm not that exciting." I grin.

"Did you say you needed help with the schedule?"

"That would be nice. The sooner the better."

My insides melt when I see a hint of a smile light up his face. "How about I stop by your place tomorrow at noon? Or we can meet somewhere."

I swallow. He's kind for not being presumptuous, although I wouldn't mind a little Zach persuasion right now. "We can work at my place. Might be easier."

What are you doing? Do not invite him into your apartment.

"All right, cool." He steps away from the overhang of the bleachers and I pause to watch him for a second.

There are flutters in my chest at the thought of spending more time alone with him. And then heat rises in my neck as I admire how well his body moves in those jeans. Who am I kidding? This is all one big catastrophe ready to blow up in my face. And I'm not prepared to stop it.

STEP FOUR

Don't Kiss the Boy

"ATTRACTION IS ONLY INTENSE WHEN MYSTERY IS INVOLVED."
— ANDRE COSTA

Takeout

Monica

Why did I invite him here? Not only is my apartment a complete disaster, but it's small. Cozy, smells good, and the décor is true to me ... but it's so, so small. He only gives me thirty minutes to prepare for his arrival. I thought he was coming at noon. He *said* he was coming at noon. But it's eleven thirty and I'm frantically hiding magazines, plucking loose jewelry and thread from around the room, and organizing fabrics from a late-night design fest. Because when inspiration strikes like it did last night, it's like a tornado's blowing through, and I can't stop the madness.

My shower is five minutes max. I spray myself with wild strawberry and mint, circle my eyes with my favorite charcoal liner, and throw on leggings, a sports bra, and a loose tank top. If we're going to be working all day, then I should be comfortable.

When the doorbell rings, I do a frantic last minute scan of my living space. Not hideous. Quickly shutting the door to my room—because that *is* hideous—I work on calming my quickened heart rate before opening the door.

Zachary Ryan stands there looking fresh as ever with his sexy stubble and low-hanging denim. I really shouldn't be surveying him like this, but the sexiest thing about him isn't even how well his clothes fit over his athletic build. It's what he's holding that has my heart galloping like a wild horse.

A grocery bag.

He brought me food.

I think I'm in love.

Not really. But damn.

Grinning, he lifts the bag to draw my attention to what he's holding as if my jaw hasn't already gone slack. "Hi, Cakes. Figured I'd bring lunch."

I give him room to enter before shutting the door, but I don't miss the way his eyes skim my body. He thinks he's sly.

"I'm impressed," I admit, sliding onto a stool. "What did you bring me?" He's effortless moving through my too-tiny kitchen. Even with his enormous build and heavy steps, his presence in my space seems natural.

With a wink, he pulls out a container of fresh chicken breast. "Do you like lemon chicken? Figured we could just make something here."

Shit.

I freeze—on the outside. Inside, I'm a flurry of panic. I've never been embarrassed about my lack of cooking skills until this moment. Here he is, the god of all gods, standing in my kitchen wanting to cook for me, and he's about to find out I've never cooked a day in my life.

He's already rustling around, looking for cookware and whatever else is needed to prepare lunch. I'm one hundred percent certain I don't have anything he's looking for.

"Cakes," he calls after closing a third drawer.

Pressing my eyes together and cringing, I sink onto the stool. "Yes."

I open one eye to test the waters and see him staring back at me, dumbfounded. "Tell me you have pots and pans somewhere around here."

Opening my eyes and mouth wide, I pause for a second before responding, my words carefully measured. "I don't have pots and pans. Or silverware. Or salt and pepper. Or ... anything really."

He's scratching his head now. I think he's considering my words. And then he lets out a laugh. "You're the biggest foodie I know. You don't cook?"

"I live on takeout." I shrug and then perk up immediately. "Oh! There's some food left over from my dinner last night. It's teriyaki."

My excitement vanishes when I see his astonished face. "Just kidding."

I wasn't kidding.

Zach puts the groceries away and pulls out a container of cocktail shrimp. "You okay with this for now?"

"Yup." I pop my lips, hoping to distract from my blush. I've never been so mortified. Even Chloe's constant teasing about my domestic downfalls roll off me like it's nothing. It's never been a big deal. When someone comes over they either bring something, or we order in, or we go out. There are so many options. But Zach is different. He slices me open and exposes my weaknesses in a way that makes me wish I *did* know how to cook. And that's the only time I've ever had such an absurd thought.

I'm sure that's the kind of girl he's used to: someone who can take care of him, have dinner ready when he gets home from a hard day on the field. My mom never did any of those things, and my dad hated it. He never understood why she couldn't at least try.

We plop down in the living room and open the shrimp cocktail. Zach's back rests against the couch while I sit on the carpet opposite him, the coffee table between us. Studying him, I'm aware of how casually he sits in my tiny apartment. He could probably pace the entire room in three steps or less.

I stifle a laugh when he pushes the coffee table out to make more room for every inch of muscle.

With a mouthful of shrimp, he catches me staring. "You okay there, Cakes?"

I smile. "Yeah. It's just—I live alone and I don't have much, so—" I look around my apartment laughing at the handmade posters with quotes from fashion icons hanging on my walls. "It's a little smaller than you're probably used to."

"You think I'm judging your space?" He shakes his head. "No way. I think what you have here is perfect. It's safe, close to work, and the perfect size for one person."

"Right. And with your massive male form taking up space, that's two people, and I'm starting to think it's too small."

There's a twinkle in his eyes when he speaks. "I don't mind, Cakes." His head tilts. "Haven't you had guests before?"

I know what he's asking. He wants to know if there have been any guys in here with me. He waits for an answer while staring at me with a look that sears my insides. "A few friends, never someone of your … caliber." I grin, hoping to keep this conversation safe. A small smile teases his lips.

The silence that follows grows too heavy. I flip the switch on the television, leaving the volume on low. With my laptop open, I pull up my email and calendar so we can go over his schedule.

According to his agent, Trevor, Zach isn't fully aware of his own day-to-day activities. Trevor and Meredith work as a team when it comes to controlling his publicity, which means they control his calendar and send him reminders constantly. Zach recently requested they give me access so that I can see what's going on in his world.

Apparently, he doesn't feel the need to keep much private. I can see every single meeting, business and personal. I know when he works out, when he meets with his team. When he has doctor appointments, press meetings, interviews, appearances. It's overwhelming, but it's helpful for what we're trying to accomplish in such a short window of time.

"Looks like you've got some travel coming up," I finally say.

His eyes are on the handful of shrimp tails he's peeling with care. "I do?"

Amused, I peer up at him. He truly has no clue what his team is booking for him, does he? "You sure do. And it looks like you'll be crazy busy. That could suck for me considering you'll be gone for five days right before camp starts."

He chuckles and gives an upward tick of his head. "And because you'll miss me?"

I narrow my eyes. Zach's managed to fit a troupe of shrimp in his mouth, and the sight is obnoxiously cute. But the smell of salty seafood makes me wrinkle my nose. "Not if I capture this image of you right now." I pull up my phone and take a photo.

He glares back at me, swallowing the last bite of shrimp and tossing the shells in the overturned plastic lid. "At least you'll be thinking about me, Cakes. That's all I really care about."

With a lift of my brows, I attempt to respond evenly to remind him that he's not to flirt with me. Flirting is bad. But he speaks before I have a chance, effectively silencing my rebuttal. "Bring the computer around here. Let me see."

I stare at the hand patting the seat next to him on the couch and raise my eyebrows in defiance. He should know better than to call me over like I'm his pet. My posture lifts instinctively to show him his demands won't work with me. "Try that again."

He curls his lip, and if it wasn't so damn sexy I would tell him to wipe that cocky grin from his face. "Please," he says, lifting his brows and adopting a look that makes me want to go out and buy him some squeaky toys and marrow. "Is that the word you were waiting for?"

Oh geez, I can't even with this guy.

"Yup," I concede.

Bringing my computer around, I take the seat he just patted. Immediately, his woodsy scent overpowers me, but not because it's strong. No. It's a reminder of our make out session in his kitchen and the frenzy that overcame us. Every time I get this close to him, I have little flashbacks that threaten my defenses.

To make things worse, he scoots closer so our legs are touching and then leans in to my screen. One hand moves to the lid of the computer, while the other presses into the couch directly behind me. I can feel the dip in the cushion. One tiny move and he'll be touching my ass. Stiffening is my only chance to get through this one.

Meanwhile, there's a raging storm in my damn chest. I swear he's going to hear it.

After a second of staring at the screen, he huffs out a breath and slides back against the couch. His arm brushes mine, triggering goosebumps to spread across my skin. "She's got me in three different states in one week."

"Right. Which is the week we need to have everything approved for print."

Damn, it's hot in here. I pluck at the collar of my already-loose tank top and use it as a fan against my flushed skin.

I can feel his eyes on me now, but I don't dare face him. We're too close for me to trust myself when looking into those ocean blues.

"Is Monica Stevens, PA extraordinaire, stressing out?"

I wish I were stressing out. It would be a much better excuse for what I'm feeling. Letting out a deep breath, I nod. "I just didn't realize how tight our schedule was, that's all."

We only have four weeks before the event, and with Zach gone for one of those weeks, there's a lot to accomplish.

My mind is moving a mile a minute, going over the mental list of things we'll need to tackle in the coming weeks, when I feel fingers slide through my hair until they reach the base of my neck. I gasp, staying very still.

"Relax, Cakes." The silk in his voice would normally do the trick and calm me down, except he's still touching me. Gentle at first, then transferring to a slow, reassuring squeeze.

A groan passes my lips, flaming my cheeks and causing him to chuckle—and then it's over as quickly as it began. Moving his hand away to hover over the keyboard's mouse pad, Zach clicks into each appointment. The damage is done. My senses are heightened. I'm aware of every subtle brush against my arm, and I swear he's doing it on purpose now, as if his nearness isn't torture enough.

"What's a Ravaged shoot?" I ask, looking at one of the appointments he has in Chicago. "Sounds scary."

"It's my new body care line."

"You're kidding. You have a body care line? Lotions, soaps, face creams? And you named it Ravaged?"

"You'd like it, Cakes. After all, you were my inspiration for the scent."

I snap my head around to face him with laser beams in my eyes. "Please tell me that's a lie."

My expression has the opposite effect than what I'd intended. He *laughs*. "Nope. Not a lie. I told you I wanted to bottle you up, didn't I?"

Oh my God.

"And what about my scent reminded you of destruction?"

Our faces are only inches apart, so I don't miss the glance that moves between my lips and my eyes, only adding gas to the fire that lights up my insides. My breathing is heavy but slow as I try to assess his seriousness.

"You sure you want to know?"

I nod, hoping he doesn't notice my nervous swallow.

"For one: it's sweet, like you."

"Okay, stop." I roll my eyes.

He laughs. "And it's got a thick richness to it, like kissing you after you devour triple chocolate cake, because all I could think about for weeks after that night was the taste of your kiss."

Damn him.

"Zach," I warn. My voice has gone soft. I don't want him to think I'm welcoming this exchange, but it's not like I'm putting up much of a fight. One wrong move and our lips will connect, effectively obliterating any chance of surviving this—whatever it is we're doing.

It's all too evident our exchange has taken a turn from light to serious quickly. His smile is fading by the second, and then he does the sexiest thing I think any man has ever done in my presence.

His eyes are clearly on my lips now, just as his tongue darts out to moisten his bottom lip. Then he bites down, trapping the plump skin and letting it drag backwards until his lip is released.

Holy shit.

His eyes are darkening and my senses have officially been transported back to six months ago, when his touch made me dizzy and his kiss lifted me to the clouds.

Is it awful that I want those teeth to bite into me again and tease my bottom lip while Zachary runs a hand gently up my thigh?

No. No. NO.

"But there's an edge to Ravaged," he continues, his voice raspy. "One that can only be explained as a little … mysterious." He leans in slowly, and I'm extra careful to stay still.

Please kiss me.

"And seductive."

My eyes flutter closed as I feel his nose drag the length of my cheekbone.

"And devastating."

Warm air skips across my lips for the briefest second. Then it's gone.

When I open my eyes, Zach's leaning against the back of the couch, watching me. Waiting for something, I think. I'm still catching my breath, disoriented from lack of oxygen and disappointed because he tricked me.

What the hell just happened?

His eyes narrow. "For someone so adamant about staying away from me, you sure looked like you wanted me to kiss you."

Asshole.

In an attempt to hide my embarrassment, I turn back to the laptop and let my hair fall like a curtain between us. Maybe it's a good thing he's going to be gone in a couple weeks. Distance is exactly what Zach and I need. Hell, maybe I'll tell him not to come back into the office for our meetings. We can pass ideas back and forth over video chat.

No. No video chat. Just the phone. And if his voice is too much to handle, there's always instant message and email.

I try to focus on what we're here to do and get started drafting the pre-production schedule. There's a reason he came here today, and it wasn't to sample the inspiration for his new scent. Although honestly, that idea does sound more appealing right now.

"How was dinner last night?" I ask, thinking a change in subject is in order.

"It was fine. My coach's wife loves to cook and always makes way too much food." He chuckles. "He tells me he had no choice but to marry her after he packed on all the weight from her cookin'."

I swallow my shame and a little bit of anger. Geez. Back to cooking again. It was a bad idea to invite Zach here.

He excuses himself to use the restroom, and when he returns he must take it as some sort of cue when I keep my attention focused on my laptop, my fingers annihilating the keyboard.

"Do you need me for this part?" he asks.

"No," I don't look up. "Just let me get the dates into my production planner and then we can talk details." Zach slaps his knees and stands. When I hear keys jingling and scraping denim, I look up. "You don't have to leave. I'll only be fifteen minutes or so." Hopefully he doesn't think I'm being rude. I just have nothing to add when it comes to conversations about cooking, and I really do need to get started on this schedule.

"Take your time. I'm going to run to the store quickly so that we can have a decent meal."

Embarrassment claims me once again. "I'm sorry, Zach. I can order us something. Every place around here delivers."

"Nah, I'll be quick. Keep working." With a wink, he walks to the door and lets himself out.

My breath releases in a gush. What is going on with me? I'm normally so composed. Men don't fluster me. Ever. It's me who ties men up in knots—sometimes literally—but I can't do that with Zach. I can't flirt. I can't even sit near him without having the intense urge to straddle him.

Ugh. I need to focus on this schedule. Putting my grinding fantasy to rest, I turn back to my computer and aim to finish what I need to before Zach gets back.

When Zach walks through the door thirty minutes later, I'm finally saving the document.

"You should lock that when you're alone, Cakes," he says as he brings his purchases to the kitchen. "Your neighbors are way too friendly. Some chick just let me walk right in behind her. Didn't even need to buzz you." It's sweet how he doesn't try to mask his concern.

"You're right. I just got caught up in work." My mouth falls open when I enter the room and see what he's brought back from the store. "Cookware? Seriously? You have to return those!" By the looks of it, he didn't get a cheap brand either. What is he doing?

"No way. Consider it a thank-you for helping me."

"I'm getting *paid* to help you. I can buy my own pots and pans, thank you very much."

"How long have you lived here?"

"Ten months. What does that have to do with anything?"

He sets the box down on the counter and runs a hand through his hair. "Consider it a housewarming gift then." His smile almost puts an end to the argument, but this isn't right. What does a gesture like this even mean? Because it feels like it means a whole lot more than *thanks for helping me with my football camp.*

"Zach," I say louder this time, frustration intensifying.

He tilts his head and takes a step toward me, causing me to step back against the counter. "Are you about to scold me? Careful, Cakes. I might like it a little too much."

Heat floods my veins, and I have to clench my thighs together. I shake my head and try to sound calmer when I speak again, but it's almost impossible with him so close. "You know I'll never use this stuff. I can't accept it."

"Why not?" His eyes search mine.

"You know why not."

"It's a nice gesture. I think you should say thank you and stop being rude."

I move to place my hands on his chest to push him away, but I instantly know that will have the opposite effect. I set them against the counter behind me instead. "I'm not trying to be rude. We don't buy each other things. We're not even friends. You're stuck working with me for a few weeks and then we both go back to whatever it was we were doing before."

It's silent for too long because I'm a cold, heartless bitch. Daring a look in his direction, I'm met with the last expression I ever wanted to see on his face: hurt, plain and simple. It's there and it's quickly unraveling the skein of resistance I've been carefully winding.

"Zach," I try again in a much softer tone, but I can see the damage is already done.

He takes a step back and looks at the gift for a second before shaking his head and walking out of the kitchen.

"Zach, stop. I'm sorry."

He doesn't stop.

Fuck. Why didn't I just say thank you?

I follow him to the door. "What about the schedule?"

"I'll be in the office tomorrow after my workout, but you know that since you have my calendar." His chilling tone rakes my spine. "I have a meeting with Sandy at eleven. She's taking me to lunch, and then I'm free if you need me to answer any questions."

My heart is racing in a desperate sort of panic at him leaving upset. Slipping between the door and Zach, I give him a pleading look, hoping to catch his eyes.

"Can you look at me for a second?"

He does. "Do what you want with the gift, Monica. I'm not taking it back. I'm sure you'll find a nice charity that will accept it just fine." Reaching around me, he grabs the door handle.

"You can't leave like this. I'm sorry for reacting like that. It was a sweet gesture, and I should have just thanked you." I grip the bottom of his shirt, careful not to touch anything else. "So, thank you."

His eyes soften. "You're welcome." He places his hands on mine and plucks them from his shirt. "But I'm still gonna leave. I'll see you tomorrow."

With one more pleading look, I realize there's no winning Zach over. Not tonight. I step aside and let him open the door.

With guilt climbing the walls of my chest I want more than anything to rewind the last five minutes. If Zachary Ryan wanted me before, he sure as hell doesn't want me now. How do I fix this? Because I want to, even though I shouldn't.

Apologies

Zachary

It wasn't until my senior year of high school that I earned my nickname, the Rocket. It hardly made any sense being that I was more launcher than rocket, but I didn't think to point that out at the time. It wasn't the nickname itself that mattered, but who gifted it to me.

Practices were most intense over the summer—not just because of the scorching Texas heat or the grueling training exercises, but because the competition was fierce. Out of fifty guys, twelve were in the running for first string quarterback. We were all hungry, but only one would stand out. And that one would be me.

Coach kept me in check the two years prior, denying me a starter position until I put in my time as third, then second string, and filling the receiving and tight end spots as needed. I never questioned him. He was the type of man that sniffed out success and challenged it until it rained excellence.

So when he lined us up and announced me as starting quarterback, I knew I'd earned it, and so did everyone else.

"What do you say, son? You ready for this?"

With a smile so wide it could split me open, I shook Coach's hand and let him tug me in for a hard pat on the back. "Proud of you, Rocket."

My throat thickened with emotion making it almost impossible to speak. "Rocket, sir?"

He smiled. "You've learned a hell of a lot over the past two years. You're born for this, but not just because of that rocket arm of yours." *I thought that was exactly why I was chosen.* "You embody everything a great player should: leadership, maturity, intelligence... And the exhaust you manage to create with each throw sure as hell helps." Winking, he wraps a hand around my neck and squeezes. "I can't wait to see where you'll take this team."

That conversation is one that carried me through my years of college ball, and into the NFL draft. His words somehow helped to balance the pressure of it all. It helped validate that there was more to me than ranks and records. Rocket may have been my nickname in high school, but leadership has always been my secret weapon. And that's the exact message I want to bring to light at camp.

Under the Bleachers is the hot topic during my meeting with Sandy on Monday morning. She loves the theme, but I'm glad she doesn't press me for more information. Monica and I didn't get to talk about much else yesterday because of the pots and pans disaster. Not too sure what that was about, but I was one hundred percent certain it was time to leave.

I don't need to dwell on the fact that Monica is resistant to our connection. She was hurt by her father. I understand her hesitation when it comes to men, but it still pisses me the fuck off that I can't break through those walls, which she seemed to build only after we kissed last summer. As much as I wanted to do it again yesterday—and I'm certain she would have let me—there was no way that was happening. I made her a promise, and I stand by my promises.

Before Heroes and Legends, Monica was more than happy to flutter those pretty eyelashes and spar flirtatiously with me until we'd both grown dizzy from laughter. Our moments were addicting, and I always went back for more. Despite our history, I thought working one-on-one with her would be fun—in the sexually frustrated kind of way that might eventually lead to more. Her reaction yesterday was the reality check I needed to know this girl means business. There's no fighting the word no, even if it's served with a pair of Bambi eyes, stuttered breathing, and flushed cheeks.

From now on, I'll give Monica what she says she wants, even though I know she sure as hell doesn't mean it. She'll get my courtesy and professionalism during official meeting hours. We'll only discuss the event when we're together, and there will be no more off-site meetings.

Monica will stay on her side of the field, and I'll stay on mine. That is a rule I can follow.

"We'll need to get to the venue a little early."

We've been in Monica's office for only ten minutes and it's already too much. My restraint should earn me a straight pass to heaven.

"It'll give us a couple days to set up, gather B-roll, and get a bunch of interviews out of the way. We'll be too busy the rest of the week to cram it all in. I also looked at your schedule, and you're free that entire weekend. I thought we could leave early Saturday morning and have a full day and a half of pre-production time. You're still bringing Seattle players to coach, right? You could use that time to review the schedule, you know, if you need to. If you're cool with all that, I'll run it by Richland."

I shrug, aware of how fast her speech comes when her confidence starts to dwindle. "Sounds good to me. I'll have Trevor coordinate with the guys."

She eyes me a little longer than she should, likely assessing my attitude since I walked into her office and made sure to keep the door wide open. I even propped it open with a doorstopper disguised as a single pink heel.

"Maps of the camp and field mockups would be helpful," she adds. "I did some research on this place and they don't have a football setup. Are you planning on marking the field and installing bleachers?"

"Yup."

There's another awkward pause as her fingers freeze at the keyboard. Her eyes dart to mine, then away again. From the moment I sat down, she's been a true professional. She even dressed the part in a gray pencil skirt cinched at her waist, a black blouse that stretches a little too tightly across her chest, black rimmed glasses that I'm pretty sure she doesn't need, and a fucking diamond necklace disguised as a tie. It falls perfectly between her cleavage just begging for me to look.

"Okay." She quickly finishes whatever she's typing, clears her voice, and adjusts her glasses. "Now we just need a logo design and some starter copy so marketing can get to work on the fun stuff."

She clicks her mouse a few times. As she does, I take note of the m&m charm bracelet around her wrist and the sparkly ring on her pointer finger with the letter M at the center. Only Monica could make candy-inspired jewelry look classy.

"I created some mocks last night just to get the ball rolling. I figure we can give some ideas to marketing to play with. There's a dozen or so, but don't worry if you hate these. I got inspired after our talk on Saturday and wanted to try something. I meant to talk through my ideas with you yesterday, but—"

The laughter that follows is filled with nerves and insecurity. For a second, I want to reach across the desk, yank on that silver tie, and bury my mouth in her luscious neck. Instead, I scoot my chair closer to the desk and swivel the laptop to face me. I start to click through each design.

"Honestly," she cuts into my thoughts, "don't tell me you like them just to be nice."

I ignore her and continue clicking from mock to mock. "You did this?" I ask just to make sure.

"Yeah," she responds tentatively. It shouldn't bring me satisfaction making her sweat this one out a bit, but it does.

I swipe through each graphic again, stopping at my favorite one to examine it closer. At least I think it's my favorite one. They're all incredible.

Monica can't stand the anticipation anymore. My face deliberately reveals nothing. She comes around, places a hand on the back of my chair, and leans in. The scent of wild strawberry and mint is so close my muscles immediately lock up.

That's too close, Cakes. Too damn close if you want to keep me from feeling like the world will explode without you.

"What do you think?" she prods. "You won't hurt my feelings, I promise."

That voice. She's normally full of certainty, but she's clearly off her game. It's obvious she wants to please me, and I secretly love it.

I look up at her sweet caramel eyes, and my heart tells me to give up the resistance. To fight a little bit harder for this one, because damn it, she's worth it. But then I remember it's not me in possession in the ball.

Pushing these pointless thoughts away, I look back at my favorite design: the simplest one of the bunch. The words UNDER THE BLEACHERS, stylized with aging wood and chipped blue paint, rest above a simple script reading FOOTBALL CAMP.

"I love them. They're all good. Really good. But I think this is the one. It conveys the message perfectly. Interesting texture choice."

She sighs with relief and plops into the chair beside me, not flinching when her knee rubs against mine. "I used the photos I took at the field for the texture. It's hard to tell a story in a graphic, but with the wood, I can show that it's damaged but still sturdy. Still safe. Worn, but standing."

Her eyes brighten. "It doesn't matter how many times you fell down, you know? You always got back up and kept moving. It's your history, and when you look at history from the right angle, no matter how worn the film is, you can see the beauty in it. At least, that's what I see."

My eyes dart up to catch the blush that forms on her cheeks.

And there it is.

The very reason why it's hard for me to let Monica continue to fight our connection. She's incredible. Smart. Funny. Beautiful. Creative. The cons list I created last night when I was trying to flush Monica's sexy eyes from my system has self-destructed. No number of cons that can outweigh her pros, and I'll do anything to make her see that. Even if it means keeping up this act of nonchalance for a little bit longer.

Engaged to Heartbreak

Monica

The dynamic has clearly changed between Zach and me. It's stiff. Formal to the point of discomfort. Every nicety seems forced, which is the exact opposite of who we both are. I've apologized for the way I acted last Sunday and he says it's fine, but I don't believe him. How can I when everything has changed?

He only came by the office twice this week, and each visit lasted only as long as the meeting was set for. No extended banter, no stolen glances. Not even a fist bump when he approved an idea. The cut and dry version of Zach sucks donkey. And apparently I'm a pouter now. Chloe pointed that one out because she's way too damn perceptive.

The thing is, I've been beyond nice in every exchange with him. I've gone out of my way to recognize everything he does for me. Thanking him for the things I don't even think he realizes he's doing. Zach was raised to open doors for women and to take heavy items from their hands. He's always on time, always polite, and always a gentleman. So, yeah, I thank him. A lot.

I've dropped my defenses too. Not completely, but enough to allow myself some happiness. Resisting Zach wasn't making me any happier. He was tired of being rejected. Hurt by my coldness. And strong enough to know he didn't have to put up with any of it. You push someone long enough, and they might just leave.

So I'm trying to put myself out there. To make things go back to the way they were before I rejected his so-called housewarming gift. Spending my entire Sunday working on that logo was my lame attempt to get back in his good graces. Not even *The Walking Dead* reruns could pull me from my funk, but my creativity came in handy in a way I didn't expect.

It feels good to do something for Zach, even if that something is camouflaged as doing my job. I know he knows the truth, because he's always looking for a deeper meaning. That makes him intense, sure, but I don't want him to stop looking at me with that intensity.

For the first time in my adult life, I want to let this unfold—whatever *this* is—because every moment with Zach feels too good not to see it to the end. Is that selfish? To prolong the inevitable a little bit longer? To give myself a glimpse of what this could be before I lose it all?

Rushing out of the building after work on Friday, I have no plan. Zach just left, so I'm hoping to catch up with him. I don't have to look far. He's walking toward his Jeep parked just outside the main doors.

My anxious feet dance in place as I wait for a crowd of pedestrians to pass before practically jogging toward him. He must hear me even over the blaring horns and the engines idling in downtown Bellevue traffic because he stops at the curb and turns around, his eyes full of questions.

What the hell am I going to say?

"Hey, Monica. Did I forget something?"

Ugh. There's that damn formality again. I love my name, but it sounds foreign coming from Zach. I don't have time for these thoughts. Not only do I need to come up with something quick, but I also need to turn my sour mood into something more attractive.

"No. I just wanted to say goodbye. You left in a hurry, and things have been so hectic this week." I don't even notice that my eyes have fallen to the concrete sidewalk until I kick a pebble and it skips off the curb. Embarrassed by my unease, I look up and let out an airy laugh. "Anyway, happy St. Paddy's Day." I smile despite my awkwardness.

The corner of his mouth ticks up, but the move is so quick I almost miss it. "Happy St. Paddy's Day. Green was a good choice today. Wouldn't want any grabby hands pinching you."

He's giving me shit, thank God. I've missed his smart mouth. From my shamrock leggings to my oversized sweater vest, I'm definitely decked out for the occasion. The only non-green item of clothing on me is the white tank top beneath my sweater.

I shrug. "I'm a quarter Irish. What do you expect?"

"I guess that explains the light eyes and tolerance for alcohol. What else are you?"

Well, this conversation has taken a turn down Weird Road. But I guess I'll bite. "Brazilian and German from my mom's side; Swedish and Irish from my dad's." I need to swerve the conversation back in the intended direction. "Are you doing anything fun tonight?" The chickenshit in me hopes Zach takes the hint and asks me to hang out. Whether it's today or tomorrow, I need to see him outside of work. To feel what I felt last weekend. I need to know that it's still there.

To my disappointment, he shakes his head. "Didn't plan on it. Crowds aren't really my thing. Are you going out?" He eyes me up and down and laughs. "Of course you are."

Heat rises from my neck to my cheeks. Even so, I've missed his teasing.

"I'll be at a party in Bonney Lake." I open my mouth to invite him. I don't think the crowds will be too bad. Or maybe we can blow everything off and hang out at my apartment—

"Hey, Zach!" Meredith calls out as she approaches. "Thanks for waiting, doll." She reaches up on her tiptoes and kisses his cheek.

My heart freefalls to ground, landing in a pitiful splat at my feet.

"Ready?" Meredith's eyes twinkle as she looks up at Zach. When he doesn't respond right away, she turns, her face transforming like she just noticed me standing there. "Oh, hey Monica."

"Hey, Meredith." I return her extra sugary tone and step away before this gets even more uncomfortable.

Looking for any distraction, I shove my hand into my purse and pull out my phone. Without looking up, I offer a casual wave and tap the screen until I get to my recent call log. "I better get going," I say as I turn in the direction of my apartment. "Catch you two later." And I'm off down the street, suffocating the rising embarrassment in my chest.

Damn, my willpower is impressive.

I take a deep breath, press the phone to my ear, and wait for Chloe to answer. When she does, I take a deep breath and plaster a smile on my face. "Hey, birthday girl!" I say to Chloe for the second time today. Gavin had asked her to take the day off today, so I didn't get to see her at work, but I called her sleeping ass first thing this morning. She wasn't too happy about that.

She laughs, sounding much more awake now. "Hey. You're never going to believe what Gav got me for my birthday."

I grin, despite my own unhappiness. "Ooh, I know! Your first orgasm?"

"Shut up. He proposed!"

It takes me a second to sink in, and then I gasp. "No. Way."

What the hell, Gavin? Way to let her friends in on the secret.

"What did you say?" I tease. "I hope you made it extra angsty and told him you had to think about it."

She giggle-squeals. "I said yes!"

"I'm so happy for you guys, Chlo." My chest swells with happiness for my friends, sufficiently brightening my mood.

"Come to Gavin's now and we can get ready together. I got us a little party starter."

There's a second of hesitation on my end because part of me wants to run home to sink into a bath and guzzle a bottle of wine in an effort to numb my mind.

Life was so much easier when I didn't give a shit about having a man in my life. But I refuse to be that girl who chooses misery over pain.

"Monica?"

"Sorry. Bad connection. I'll see you soon."

We hang up. Once I'm in my apartment I'm like a woman on a mission, tearing apart my closet for something to wear to Babalouie's. Something that will guarantee mucho flirting—that's a must—which means zero green. Every pinch I receive tonight will be the equivalent of flipping off any thoughts of Zach and Meredith together at dinner. Sharing laughs, flirty eyes, and possibly a kiss at the end of the night.

Ugh. My best friend just got engaged, and I'm so happy for her. I really am. But it's ironic, because the only thing I'll ever be engaged to is heartbreak.

Compromising Positions

Zachary

Three beers at dinner fail to ease the discomfort in my chest. After Monica walked away, I wished I had run after her. She played it off decently enough with that fake-ass wave and high-pitched departure, but she can't hide from me.

I know when she's jealous. I know when she's disappointed.

As much as I've wanted to give Monica space after the blowup last weekend, I don't want her to get the wrong impression. I want her to feel comfortable approaching me for any reason, even if it has nothing to do with work. In fact, I'd prefer if her reasons were non-work related.

When she approached me on the sidewalk, I thought we were getting somewhere. And then Meredith happened.

It's not abnormal for Meredith and I to share a meal to handle business. We do it all the time. But even I have to admit there's something odd about tonight. And not just because she thought it would be a cute idea to kiss me on the cheek in front of Monica. Something she has never done before today. What the hell was that, anyway?

Between Monica and Meredith, my jaw hurts from grinding my teeth together, my knuckles ache from the clench of my fist, and I can't stop shifting in my seat. I'm on edge.

"Mer, why did you seat us right in front of a damn window? I can't take a bite without a camera light flashing in my face."

Her eyes grow wide and she raises a hand to call over a waiter, then turns back to me. "What's up with you tonight?" she hisses.

The waiter appears right away, and Meredith's expression transforms into a bright smile. Either I've been blissfully ignorant or she knew how to hide her true colors well, but I'm starting to see that hissing Meredith is the real her. "We'll need you to close the curtains so we can have some privacy," she requests sweetly, as if she thinks her tone will negate her patronizing words.

"Of course, Ma'am." The waiter unclips the curtains and pulls them together. "Is there anything else I can do for you?"

"That'll be all," she says, oozing with softness. Then she turns to me, narrowing her eyes. "You're like a snapping turtle starved for a meal."

I laugh, only amused because that was the point of dinner. I'm starved from running around all day with an agenda she created—without leaving me time for lunch, I might add. So I'm tired and pissed and ready to sign the damn contract she brought so I can get home and call Monica. Maybe figure out where she is.

"You know I like my privacy when I eat. How did they know I was here?"

Meredith can't be trusted, and I'm getting tired of making excuses for her. She's clearly up to something now. I'm not the type of celebrity that people care to follow with cameras unless something big has gone down. And it's not like I'm involved in any scandals or dating an A-list celebrity. It's the

Seattle fans, not entertainment media, that approach me on the street, and the encounters are mostly pleasant.

"Zach," Meredith says with a frustrated breath, "when are you going to trust me to handle your affairs as they should be handled? You try to control too much."

Dear Lord, help me. "I'm trying to have a say in what becomes public knowledge. Having cameras show up at our last-minute dinner hardly seems newsworthy." *Unless you've got something up your sleeve.*

She lets out a patronizing laugh. "Zachary Ryan, when are you going to learn? The press always knows where you are. They're like police dogs, trained to sniff you out whenever they want. Did it cross your mind that they may have gotten wind of the mysterious contract you're about to sign and followed us here?"

I narrow my eyes. Today is the deadline to sign off on a new endorsement deal—my biggest one yet for a national sporting goods company. I meet with the client in another week, but no one knows about it. This is something Trevor would normally manage, but Meredith insisted on handling it. I'll need to have a talk with Trevor about that.

"Nope." I point in the direction of the window. "They were here before we arrived."

Meredith is silent as she sips her wine and stares back at me, her expression transforming into something unreadable. I'm thankful when our dinner comes and I can distract myself by filling my stomach with food.

Eventually we settle into a conversation about the next month of activities. It's really the last free month I'll have before I'm swamped with football again, but Meredith has managed to keep me busy in the meantime. With a week of travel coming up and the work that still needs to be done for camp, I'm exhausted just thinking about it.

By the end of dinner, I'm on my feet the second she's paid the bill. Another meal paid for by BelleCurve. I almost feel guilty about it. Sandy has done so much for me over the years. I don't need them to schmooze me.

My Jeep sits on idle for us at the curb. Unfortunately, in order to get there, we need to pass an absurd number of waiting cameras. I mutter a string of curse words under my breath, knowing there's no way out of this, and take long strides to the Jeep. Meredith is practically running to keep up.

She's all grins and laughter when I open her door. She turns, placing her hands on my chest, her rich flowery French import of a perfume burning my nostrils like poison.

I have no doubts. I've been set up.

"Thank you for dinner, Zachary," she purrs, hands sliding purposefully down my chest. Dread spreads through me as she slips into the passenger seat like a snake slithering away from a meal, confirming what tonight was all about … because she clearly is not trying to hide it anymore.

How could I let this happen? Why the fuck would Meredith set me up? She spent the car ride swearing she didn't. But I saw the satisfied look on her face when she touched me last night. And as the cameras clicked furiously, each one flashing like lightning in my gut, I knew the truth.

After several failed attempts to call Monica and warn her about the photos that I know are coming, I force myself out of bed and into the shower. After my workout I drive straight to Monica's apartment and knock on the door.

Silence.

I walk to the field, hoping to find her on her morning run. Nothing.

I even call Chloe, but her phone goes straight to voicemail.

That's when I check my social media pages. Just as I suspected, they're plastered with images of Meredith and me. And the photos look ... convincing.

To the world, it will seem like Meredith and I were on a date. But I don't care about the world. Whatever I have with Monica, as awkward as it is right now, is the most genuinely pure relationship I've ever had—and I've destroyed it.

Saturday rolls into Sunday, and Sunday rolls into Monday. Not one response from Monica to my texts or voice messages. Not a single damn one. So I cancel everything I have on Monday morning, including a meet and greet with the Wifey Club—Meredith can come after me with a pitchfork if she wants—and drive to BelleCurve. I walk straight into Monica's office and slam the door behind me.

Monica jumps and immediately starts clicking something on her computer before I can look at it, though I have a pretty good guess about what she's been looking at.

When her screen goes black, she glares up at me, her nostrils flaring. "Wow. Way to make an entrance, Zach."

"Wow. Way to avoid my phone calls, *Monica*."

There's a flicker of pain that crosses her expression, but it fades quickly, and then she's turning back toward her computer. "I have a meeting in five minutes. You need to leave. I'll send you a calendar appointment for my next availability. If it's urgent you can shoot me an email and I'll get back to you as soon as possible."

The sickeningly sweet tone of her voice is too much to bear. "Then I want five minutes of your time before you kick me out of here."

She's expressionless as she gestures for me to take a seat. "Fine. What is it, Zach?"

God damn it, this woman is infuriating. "Cut it out. You're pissed at me. I figured it out when you walked away on Friday. What I can't figure out is why. Because I was with Meredith? Because she gave me a stupid kiss on the cheek? She's my publicist, Cakes. That was weird, but it was nothing."

There's a flash of something in her eyes, but it's the strange smile that creeps onto her face that rattles my nerves. Then she flips her screen around and taps on a few buttons. The photo staring at me brings back all the dread I felt in the moment it was captured. Meredith's got her perfectly manicured hands on my chest, and she's looking deeply into my eyes with a smile that would disarm most. But not me.

"It looks bad."

She nods without saying a word. She doesn't have to. After spending weeks trying to get Monica to open up and trust me, has Meredith truly sabotaged any chance of that happening?

Her expression is too firm. Too foreign to belong on Monica's face. Maybe that's why my gaze slips to her white tank top, just thin enough that I can see the cleavage spilling from her red bra. She's wearing the same suspenders from that night at Heroes and Legends, too—the ones that fell away the moment I touched them with my eager fingers.

"I think she set me up," I finally admit.

She nods again, as if she's already arrived at this conclusion.

"Nothing happened."

Another nod. "I know."

There's no way the shock is hidden from my expression. "You do?"

Monica sighs. "Look, Zach. Meredith's agenda is clear to me, and I think maybe to you too, but that's not why I disappeared this weekend. Your lifestyle—"

There's a lurch of pain in my chest. "Don't." I pace the length of her office, trying to wrangle my frustration before I officially blow up. "This isn't about Meredith or stupid pictures that landed on the internet. This is about you and me." I stop, looking at her with a hopeful expression. "What were you going to ask me on Friday before Meredith showed up?"

She's a fawn darting through the woods again, looking for safety, but the moment my flashlight reaches her eyes, everything stops. Caught, her eyes widen. *I knew it.*

"I was going to invite you to Bonney Lake for St. Paddy's. But you already had plans." She shrugs. "It was at a dive bar anyway. You wouldn't have liked it."

She's like a Girl Scout trying to earn her badge. Except the fire she's trying to build is in my chest, and she's not rubbing the sticks together fast enough. I fight through the smoke. "You can't possibly know that if you didn't ask."

Her eyes narrow. "You already had plans."

"I would have hung out with you after."

Her already darkened eyes flash with anger as she touches something on her computer screen, illuminating the photo of Meredith looking up into my eyes. "After this?"

"You said you didn't believe that crap." I'm physically shaking now. "You are the most confusing woman I have ever known."

Something changes in her expression, and she gets up from her desk, walking to me and placing her hands on my chest. When our eyes lock, the fire and smoke dissolve, but the heat remains. My hands instinctively move to her waist to pull her closer.

To my surprise, she smiles. "That right there," she says softly. "That's why I don't believe what the media wanted those photos to portray. You didn't respond to her like this."

Fuck. My heart beats in its cage. "I don't respond to anyone like this. Only you," I say, tightening my grip. I don't care if this isn't what Monica wants to hear, or if she still wants to play games with me. I'm tired of holding back when everything in me is screaming that it's right.

"Zach, it's fine. Don't beat yourself up. My issues with Friday are more mine than yours. Let's just move on, okay?"

Everything about her right now makes me want to throw her on the desk and dive into her mouth. I need to taste those lips again.

Her voice breaks through again, interrupting the hope that's replaced the fire in my chest. "I do have a meeting that I need to get to."

We can't end things like this. "Let me take you to dinner tonight. Call it a work dinner if you want."

Monica's jaw hardens and she shakes her head. "I can't. I think we need to keep our meetings in the office from now on.

With the doors open." She nods at the closed door, but I don't take the bait.

"Seriously? C'mon, Cakes. You're killin' me. You're jealous of Meredith one minute, wanting me to kiss you another minute, and now you're telling me you don't want to see where this could go? How long you going to play this game?"

"I'm not playing any games."

"But you are."

"I'm not." She pushes off my chest, but before she can get away I pull her in so that she lands flush against my body. She can't even look at me, but she doesn't try to pull away again.

"I see you, Cakes. This isn't a one-sided thing. You like me, and I like you. There's no clearer way to put it. But if you need to keep denying us a chance to figure this out, then I'll let you have that for a little bit longer. Doesn't mean I'll let you forget what you're missing." I push her back one step until her back greets the wall. Her breath quickens.

"It's never going to work," she whispers.

I use my hands to cup her cheeks, then guide her chin so she's forced to look into my eyes. When she does, I give her the most desperately pleading look I can conjure. "It will."

Her eyes glisten with unshed tears, and I'm going crazy making sense of this woman's fears. What is she keeping from me? She's fighting so hard to keep me away from her heart, but she knows she'll lose.

"I care about you and about this project," she says with imploring eyes. "I want all of that to work out. Let's get through this project first, and then we can talk about us if that's still what you want."

"So you're saying there's a chance?" I tease.

Her narrow eyes twinkle as she smiles. "Smartass."

Groaning, I bury my nose in her hair and continue to hold her tight. "I'm not giving up on you, Cakes. Not now, not ever. And to be clear." I slide my hand between our bodies until my palm rests over her heart. "It's this I want."

A few silent moments pass between us before I pull away from her completely, leaving her with a promise.

I'm not giving up.

Craving Him

Monica

Well, he wasn't lying when he said he wasn't going to give up. I've never met such a stubborn man in my life. He's armored with some type of rejection seal. Nothing will shoot him down. In fact, I think he gets stronger with each blow. Not that I'm carrying arrows anymore. What's the point? By the end of the week, I'm officially tired of fighting my attraction.

I feel the intensity between us stronger than ever. We're back to being ourselves, which is great, but it's running havoc on my emotions. We flirt because we can't help ourselves, but every time I feel flush in the cheeks or like my heart is jumping around in my chest, I remind myself why *more* is a bad idea.

It doesn't mean this week hasn't been exhausting, battling these crazy feelings for him. He's come into the office way more than usual, giving me zero time to objectively evaluate how I'm feeling because he's constantly around—eyeing me from across the room, brushing past me, subtly touching my arm or back, leaning in real close when I'm showing him something on my computer, giving me that sexy *reserved for Cakes only* smile—but he hasn't made a move on me yet.

What is he waiting for?

One thing I can't ignore: I crave his presence all the time now. I appreciate his persistence because, let's face it, Zach could have anyone. Why me? Especially when I'm so hard to crack with my tower-high brick walls.

My feelings for him haven't disappeared. I might even like him more after watching his godly restraint. It's not something I comment on, though, for fear we'll find ourselves having a conversation that will only disappoint us both. We keep it light and simple.

We haven't talked about Meredith since our last confrontation. I'm glad he's onto her scheming, but why hasn't he fired her yet? She's still running around, owning his time off like she knows what's best for him. She's a tyrant with an agenda, and I'm afraid her agenda is exactly what Gracie and Trinity said it was from the very beginning.

She wants Zach, and she's pulling out all the stops to get him to want her.

It's Friday night. We've accomplished a lot over the past five days: reviewed and provided final feedback for the apparel designs and logos, outlined one of the sponsor videos, and received the first draft of venue mockups from the design team—but I'm getting antsy at the thought of Zach being out of town next week. When he left the office earlier, he thanked me, told me he'd be back soon, and kissed my cheek. The kiss was … disappointing. There was no passion, no sexual undertone, no lingering sparks caused by his hot breath on my cheek … no promise for more. It was just a peck of thanks. For doing my job.

Why does that leave me feeling empty?

I spend Friday night trying to answer this question over a bowl of ice cream. It seems Zachary Ryan has changed me.

I'm now one of those women who sits at home on the weekend with a pint of chocolate ice cream in their lap, stewing over a boy. Ice cream has never been my go-to for self-soothing. It only makes me feel bloated and tired when I wake up the next morning—way worse than a hangover. Maybe that's why I'm punishing myself with it.

When my phone buzzes in my pocket Saturday evening, my heart immediately jumps in my chest. I hope it's Zach telling me his plans for tonight fell through. I still have regrets over the pots and pans disaster. Maybe we can cook. Scratch that. Maybe *he* can cook.

I sigh when I see Chloe's name light up the screen.

"Hey, Chlo Chlo."

"Hey, Mon Mon."

"It sounds better when I say it."

Chloe snorts. "You're snippy. Zach still playing hard to get?"

"You can say that. I've had a rough couple of days."

"That's why I'm calling. Maybe I can make it better."

I perk up. Leave it to Chloe to save the day. "I'm listening."

"Gavin got an invite to the Mastermind movie premiere in Seattle tonight. Guess who's going to be there?"

I think about the appointment marked private on Zach's calendar and my shoulders fall in defeat. "He's going to a movie premiere tonight?"

Chloe laughs. "He's giving the movie intro and sponsoring the after party. Gav got four tickets. Please tell me you don't have plans. I want you to be my date."

"Isn't Gavin going?"

"Yeah, of course."

I smirk. "Does he know you like me better yet?"

She shushes me. "Don't tell him, or he won't let us hang out anymore. Come be my date."

Sighing, I feel the pressure and want so badly to cave. "I don't have plans, but there's no way I'm going. Things are still kinda weird between us. I'm not going to crash his event. He'll think I'm a creeper. You should invite Jazz and Marco."

"Stop!" she insists. "You're coming if I have to make Gavin toss you in the car. BelleCurve set up the event, so it won't be weird that you're there. Besides, Jazz and Marco are at her parent's house. It's their anniversary. Thirty years, can you believe it? That's an insane amount of time to be with someone."

I laugh. "You and Gav have a decade already, so don't be so surprised."

"We're not married yet," she corrects me firmly. "Look, Gavin invited Justin. He and Phoebe are on the outs again. Just don't tell Phoebe if you happen to talk to her. I feel bad we're taking Justin, but they are Gav's tickets, so…"

I toss myself back on the couch and laugh again.

"Please come, Monica. It's one of those action films, so you know I'm gonna fall asleep if you're not there fighting me for popcorn."

"True," I agree in all seriousness. This is what we do for each other, always taking one for the team. Letting out a half-sigh, half-groan, I relent. "Fine, Chloe. You've got a date. When are you picking me up?"

"Yay! We'll grab you in an hour. Dress up for the after party."

"Will do. Love you, Chlo Chlo."

"I love you too, Mon Mon."

Premiere Showdown

Monica

Gavin's truck is parked at the curb of my apartment building when I push through the main doors. Chloe steps out of the front seat, revealing her curvy frame and tone body in a leggy gray dress she bought the last time we went shopping. She sees me and smiles before her eyes travel the length of my body.

"Monica! Your outfit is adorable!"

I beam, feeling pride rise in my chest. It's a white, satin slip dress, with white chiffon layering. It ends right above my knees, which in combination with the spaghetti straps makes it classy and flirty. But it's the caplet now draped over my shoulders that is my favorite part of the outfit. I found the fabric online and got inspired; the most perfect nude material with a hint of gold to match my favorite clutch purse and strappy stilettos.

"Thanks!" I gush. "I was just playing around with materials and threw it together."

Chloe is still swooning when Justin replaces her in the front passenger seat and we slip into the back.

"You made that?" Her jaw drops as she fingers the soft material. "*This* is what you should be going to school for."

"I'll make you one," I beam, ignoring her comment about school. I still haven't decided what I'll be studying during summer quarter, and I don't want to talk about it now. "I bought the same material in black. It would look cute on you too."

I turn to the guys in the front seat and change the topic. "Thanks for inviting me."

Gavin gives me a wink. "No problem. I'm all for playing matchmaker when Chloe agrees to see a Mastermind film."

We all laugh at that, but everything shifts the moment I'm reminded of Zach. I've been trying to force him out of my mind to shake the nerves. The excitement I felt seconds earlier is gone.

When I turn to look at Chloe, her face softens and she leans closer so she can talk quietly. "Maybe you two just need time away from the office together. You're always working, and you're setting all these rules about everything."

"Chlo, this is the exact situation I'm trying to stay away from. Zach will be busy tonight with his fan club. I'll be the last person he'll want to talk to."

"Not in that dress." She wiggles her eyebrows, making me laugh. "You want the truth?" she questions in warning. "I think your subtle hints are too subtle! You just need to do what you do best and be straight with him—but don't scare him."

Chloe's voice is louder now, and Gavin chuckles softly from the front seat. I wish he could see me glaring.

"What did you tell me once?" Chloe continues. "Put him out of his misery already?" Her eyes twinkle at the reference to me urging her to sleep with Gavin. "Why don't you start listening to your own advice? You're not going to like yourself very much if you let this one get away."

Chloe's right.

"I hate when you make sense, which is like, all the time. Maybe I just hate you all the time."

She snickers. "Nice try. You could never hate me because I've already won your heart with my baking skills. You're my number one batch, remember?"

I roll my eyes at her horrible play on the word bitch and tickle her side until she's breathless with laughter. "Who's the batch now?"

"Okay, okay, stop!" she squeals. I relieve her of my fingers and she places a hand over mine and smiles. "Whatever happens, you still look hot in that dress."

Nothing can stop my smile after that comment, because as usual, she's right.

It's clear we've walked into an exclusive party. The entire theater has been reserved for the premiere, and the long bar on the other side of the room is packed. Since we're a few minutes early, Gavin and Justin head to the wall-to-wall bar to order our first round while Chloe and I hang back to people-watch.

"Wow," Chloe says as her eyes catch on a woman in costume. "Were we supposed to dress up?"

The woman, who's donning full body paint, a tiny black leather skirt, and pasties covering her nipples, poses for a photo. I totally could have rocked that.

"I've been to some film premieres in LA and they can get pretty rowdy, especially since celebrities are walking the red carpet. This is tame in comparison." I hope it doesn't sound like I'm bragging.

"Speaking of celebrities..." Chloe's eyes are pointed at the other side of the room. "Actually, maybe you shouldn't look."

I see what she sees. It's Zach, smiling and laughing with a group of people focused solely on him. He looks amazing in a black button-down shirt and silver tie—oddly like the tie necklace I was wearing on Monday. Even from here, I can see the sparkle in his eyes as he works the crowd.

But that's not what she's referring to. My heart drops down the bottomless pit in my stomach when I notice who's beside him—or rather who's clutching his arm and hanging on his every word.

They're on a date. Again? I'm going to be sick. After everything he said to me on Monday, this feels like a kick in the stomach.

Chloe tries to distract me with chatter, but I can't take my eyes off him. The way he pauses to listen intently to what the others in the group are saying. The way he takes short sips of the amber liquid in his hands. The way he politely makes himself available to the next person requesting his attention. His laugh. He's a natural charmer in the most genuine way.

He's too good. Too … smooth.

At some point, his eyes shift from whoever he's talking to and drift around the room. When they fall on mine, they lift in surprise.

Great. It's not bad enough that I showed up at his event like a Zachary Ryan stalker. Now he knows I've been watching him.

I take in a helping of air and clutch Chloe's arm as Zach excuses himself from the group, leaving Meredith behind to walk toward us.

Shit. What do I say? Am I supposed to admit that I knew he would be here? Maybe I should play it off like I'm surprised to see him too.

As I'm screaming at my body to appear as nonchalant as possible, Zach runs into Gavin and Justin, who are on their way toward us with drinks in their hands. They greet each other animatedly, and then Zach asks Gavin a question. Gavin responds by handing him one of the drinks before they close the gap between us.

Zach gives Chloe a hug first and then his focus turns to me. No hug, but he extends the drink in his hand, ice clinking against the glass, and a smile rests on his perfect lips. "Hey, Cakes."

The anxiety I've been feeling about Meredith falls away, and the group I'm with suddenly becomes engaged in animated conversation. Zach and I are in our own bubble. I smile with ease.

"You look nice," I say.

That's an understatement. Up close I can see that his crisp slacks match his skinny silver tie and freshly trimmed hair— closely shaven on the sides and styled with a slight lift at the top. He's freaking gorgeous.

I glance over his shoulder, my excitement vanishing when I see Meredith stalking toward us, eyes zeroed in on Zach. A woman on a mission to claim her man. I hold back an eye roll.

Turning back to Zach, I notice his eyes drop to my dress as he inhales in the tiniest of breaths. "So do you, Cakes. I'm glad you came."

I feel my body warming from the inside out. "It would have been nicer to get the invite from you, but"—I wink, fighting to regain control of my body—"I'll let it go this one time."

His lips press together tightly. "I didn't know if it was your thing."

Anything with you is my thing.

There's a flurry of motion around us, and I realize that everyone is heading into the theater. And that's when Meredith approaches, effectively popping our bubble. She hooks her arm around Zach's, looking far too comfortable.

I've never wanted to claim a man as mine so badly. Frustration claws through me, vigorously digging in at the sight of her. She's off the charts beautiful with her short blonde bob and sharp blue eyes. It's not the first time I've noticed the way her height perfectly complements Zach's, and just how natural they look together. Perhaps that's why I'm racked with jealousy every time I picture them together. Lucky me, now I get to see it up close.

"Great to see you guys," she tells us, eyes sweeping our group and then landing on me with an unmistakable glint of challenge. I hate her.

I look at Zach, full of questions that I know are visible through my eyes. He's staring back as if he wants to answer, but Justin comes to my rescue. Placing an arm over my shoulder, he leans in to avoid screaming over the crowd. "Ready to find our seats?"

Nodding, I strip my eyes from Zach and let Justin guide me behind Gavin and Chloe. There's a hole in my chest that I know is for me alone to own. After all, it's me who's given all the resistance. It's me who's incapable of expressing my true feelings. I'm to blame, and I'll be the one to suffer.

I should have left the moment I saw Meredith on his arm. Instead, I'm sandwiched in between Chloe and Justin with Zach a few seats to the right and one row in front of me. I get to watch every single laugh between him and Meredith, every single touch. This is not my idea of a good time.

Every so often he'll turn his head to glance at me. I pretend to not see it. I pretend I'm watching the most exciting movie ever made, laughing and gasping at all the right parts. That's the fun part of being surrounded by a premiere crowd: everyone gets into the action.

By the time the movie's over, I've had enough. Meredith has made her point, and Zach clearly isn't fighting it. I'm not going to stay to watch anymore of this shitshow. I pull Chloe away from the crowd to let her know.

"Not to be a Debbie Downer, but I think I should go."

"No, stay! I've never seen you act so unsure over a guy before. Just go walk up to him and tell him you want to suck his face."

I roll my eyes. She sounds like me. "He's with Meredith."

Chloe makes a disgusted noise in the back of her throat. "Do not let that woman play you. She's obviously into Zach, but he doesn't like her like that. I can tell."

I shake my head emphatically. I've convinced myself of the same thing once before, and look where it got me.

Chloe sighs, and we take a break from our conversation to look around the room. I spot Zach immediately. He's making his rounds, taking pictures with fans, engaging in conversation, and charming the pants off anyone who looks at him.

I start saying my goodbyes. I've just finished hugging Justin when Zach appears out of nowhere. "I need to borrow you," he says gruffly. And before I know what's happening, he slips his hand into mine and pulls me around the corner into the empty theater hallway.

My heart is all over the place when I meet his glowing eyes. He's pissed.

He's pissed?

"What are you doing?" I demand.

"So you won't date me—you won't even acknowledge we're friends—but you'll bring a date to my event?" There's fire in his tone, but it's the catch in his throat that burns me. "For a second I thought maybe you were here to see me."

What the—?

"Justin isn't my date, but I can see why it may look like that." His eyes soften. "The truth is, *you* didn't invite me here tonight, but I *did* come here to see you. And *you're* the one with the date on your arm!"

"She's not my date."

"That's not what it feels like when I watch you with her."
My voice cracks, but it might as well be my mask finally
bleeding the truth.

The tension falls away at my confession, and it's replaced
with something else. Understanding, regret, determination.
Zachary's face hardens, his eyes narrow, and then he grabs
my hand again, tugging me into the nearest theater. He sits on
the back of a seat and in a swift move pulls me between his
legs.

His clean citrus scent hits me like a splash of ice water.
It's a shock to my system, and it makes everything come
alive. I'm trying to find my breath when his hand reaches my
face.

"You are making me crazy, Cakes." His knuckles brush
my cheek as his grip tightens around my waist. I want him to
pull me closer so that I can feel him. I need to know he still
wants me—the way I want him. "I meant what I said earlier.
You always look beautiful, but tonight especially."

I blink while registering his words. Because I'm sick of
telling myself I can't be with this man who I so clearly want
to be with—and because he's the first man I've ever spent an
entire week with and missed at the same time—I close the gap
and take hold of his tie, playing with it so I have something to
focus on while his face is only an inch from mine.

"Do you like her? Meredith?" I look up, my face tilted,
begging for honesty.

"No, Cakes," he whispers. "I like *you*." The rush of
breath leaves his mouth and enters mine. My eyes flutter shut
for half a second, but when I breathe in, my strength fills me
again.

I smile against the unleashed butterflies that come alive in my chest. His eyes blaze with intensity, telling me I've asked the right questions to justify his next move.

A hand runs gentle circles in the arch of my back, while his other hand cups the back of my neck, a finger lightly running across my cheek.

We're like this for a while, staring into each other's eyes, silently challenging the other to back down. Neither of us do, and I get a desperate feeling in my chest. One that tells me to kiss him without permission. To dip my tongue into his mouth and feel everything I haven't felt in over six months. I've never wanted anyone to kiss me so badly.

"When do you leave tomorrow?" I realize my voice is husky. So embarrassing—I hate when I sound like a phone sex operator.

Zachary, on the other hand, seems to love it. His nose skims the slit between my lips and then moves to my ear, releasing air into the canal before biting down on my lobe. My body goes tense with pleasure and a moan climbs up and out my throat.

"Six in the morning." He moves to the other ear and does the same thing, causing my body to shake. "Sorry to leave you stranded, Cakes. It's horrible timing, I know." The hand that was circling my back slides down to cup my ass. I gasp.

Swallowing back my fear, I plead with his eyes first. "Drive me home."

He takes a ragged breath and watches me for a second before leaning in to brush his lips across my cheek before softly kissing it. This time, I feel everything. The sparks. The passion. It all pours over me like molten lava cake. I want more.

"I want to," he admits. His lips move to my neck, and I can feel the effects cascade over my body. He groans as my lips part for him, panting with need. His hand lifts the bottom of my dress as fingertips feather over the rise of bare skin. His mouth presses harder into my neck, sucking and nipping, adding to the rising heat of my body.

He moves so his forehead is on mine and he's looking me square in the eyes. "If I were to come over tonight, I wouldn't leave. Ever."

Leaning against his forehead, I smile. "Then you should definitely come over." My finger hooks into the top of his jeans, slides around to his front, and tugs, making myself completely clear.

He groans before stopping my hands with his. "Wait, Cakes." He leans back slightly to meet my eyes. I can almost see the cloud we've just been riding on begin to lose opacity. "I know you too well already. I'll wake up tomorrow, leave for a week, and that will give you far too much time to regret whatever were to happen if I took you home tonight."

Damn him.

"But I missed you this week."

He smiles the most adorable smile and kisses my nose. "Good. Note to self: playing hard to get works."

I chuckle. "I don't want to play games."

Shaking his head, he breathes in deeply, and lets it out as if he's relieved. "No games. Not anymore. But we're not doing this tonight. A few hours won't be enough for what I have planned."

Oh.

STEP FIVE

When There's Chemistry, There's a Way

"CHEMISTRY IS A LOT LIKE COOKING;
IT IS THE COMBINING OF INGREDIENTS."
— STEVE BROWN

Long Distance

Monica

I'm on my third selfie of the day. It's only Monday, and Zach keeps asking for things. A photo of me holding one of the flyers. A photo of me holding one of the shirts. A photo of me wearing the shirt. This boy cannot let go.

Monica: Don't you trust me? I've got this!

Zach: I just want pictures of you.

I laugh and toss my phone on my desk so I can run to marketing and check on the rest of the new proofs. The deadline for all revisions is five o'clock today, and I'd hate to miss it and add dollars to the budget. We've been doing a great job so far keeping costs down while sponsorship money is rising.

Taking my time, I move through each piece and mark up anything that needs to be changed. Deb, the creative director, is waiting for my stack of pages with a hopeful expression. "They look awesome," I say with a smile for encouragement. "Just a few tweaks. Can you give it to Bethany to review before I send everything to Zach? I don't trust my eyes at this point."

"You got it."

My phone buzzes just as I'm walking back into my office. When I click into my messages, Zach's pouty face appears. I scroll above to see that he's at it again.

Zach: I need another pic.

Zach: Cakes?

Zach: [Pouty Zach Selfie]

Monica: Of what?

Zach: Your lips.

A fierce blush lights up my cheeks.

Monica: I'm working!

Zach: And your boss just asked for a Cakes original. I need a close-up of those lips.

Monica: I'm suing for sexual harassment, boss.

Zach: Fine. You're fired. Now send me a selfie and we can settle this outside of the courtroom. I'll make it worth your while.

I bite back a grin.

Monica: You should let me get back to work before I slip up and send these shipments to China.

Zach: You play dirty. Fine.

It's silent for the rest of the workday, even as I stay late to proof everything before emailing Zach and Trevor for final approval.

I'm finally home and still no word from the selfie king, so I shower and then slip under the covers, moaning at the warmth. As I lie in bed, I find myself scrolling through our text exchange from the day, laughing at his reactions to some of the photos I sent over.

A yawn captures me, and I frown realizing it's way past my bedtime. But I can't go to sleep without hearing his voice—and making sure the project is still on track. I find his number and hit the call button.

"Perfect timing," Zach answers. "I just got back to the hotel."

"I wanted you to know that I sent about thirty pieces of artwork that need your approval. The clothing and brochures need to be ordered as soon as possible, and we'll be spending the rest of the week finalizing the production schedule."

"Looks like you didn't need me around after all."

I can almost hear him pouting. I grin.

"Cakes, if you're smiling I can't see you."

I laugh. "Yes, I'm smiling. Because you're right! Turns out I'm quite capable without you around."

He huffs. "As true as that may be, I think you realized how much you like it when I *am* around."

"True. Then you wouldn't be blowing up my phone all damn day."

"You loved every second of it."

I smirk. "So confident."

There's silence on the line, and then I hear another ring. Looking down at my phone, I see that he's transferring the call to video chat. Pulling the blanket across my bare chest, I answer it and face the phone toward the ceiling.

"Cakes, I need to see you," he demands.

"Nope," I say plainly. "I'm not camera ready."

He growls. "I don't give a fuck." Whoa. That's language I don't hear from Zach that often. He must mean business. "I miss your face, Cakes. Let me see you." And just like that, his tone is smooth, melting whatever resistance I had.

I turn the phone so he can see one of my eyes, and I can see him. Holy hotness. Zach's unshaven face is so close. I want to lick him. And it doesn't look like he's wearing a shirt. Sigh. "Cakes," he warns with a growl, this time making me laugh.

I give up the battle and turn the camera fully on to me. "Fine. You win. Happy?"

An arm moves to rest on the back of his head as he leans against a pillow. Yup, he's not wearing a shirt. "Very happy," he answers with a smile. "Beautiful." His eyes scroll the frame and I notice when his eyes catch what I'm hiding. His head falls against the bed with a thud before he groans. "Not fair, Cakes."

I laugh. "Next time warn me and I'll put some clothes on."

He shifts around his bed and pulls his phone in closer. "Yeah, that's not going to happen. Is that what you wear to bed?"

I roll my eyes, ignoring his question, and pull the phone in so he can only see my face. "How was your day?"

"Would have been better if I was with you."

I grin. "So corny."

His eyes narrow. "Careful. I'm coming straight for you the moment I land. All that sassiness will come back to haunt you."

"Looking forward to it."

"Another busy day tomorrow?" His eyes twinkle, and I know he's coming up with a list of potential selfies to request.

I grin. "No, actually. I'm taking the day off to visit the Art Institute. I've been slacking. I need to pick a program and enroll this week. There won't be much time after camp, and I hate procrastinating."

He sits up in bed, and I can see in full detail how his skin rolls over the rungs of his muscles. Damn. "I was going to ask you if you've made any progress with that. I guess you've been distracted by work." I swear I hear some guilt in his tone.

"No way. You don't get to take credit for my lack of direction when it comes to school. It's just a tough decision, you know? It's a big commitment. I feel like I'm in a cage full of butterflies and I'm being forced to choose one. They're all so pretty."

"Which one will you have the most fun studying? There has to be something you wanted to be when you grew up, before modeling came into the picture."

"That's the thing," I admit. "The modeling stuff kind of threw me off track. I never had a chance to explore much else."

He doesn't look convinced. "Keep searching, Cakes. You'll figure it out. I think it's great that Sandy's being flexible with work and school. It takes some pressure off so you can focus on both. She's smart."

I can't argue with that. Sandra's taking a chance on me, and because of that, I feel a bit more pressure. But maybe pressure is exactly what I need at this point. Without it, I wouldn't be planning on starting school this summer at all.

"I'll let you know how it goes. But I want to hear how the other side lives. Other than drooling over my selfies, did you do anything else today?"

The side of his mouth curls, and I know he's drawing up a mental image of my photos. "Yeah." He shrugs. "Solidified an endorsement deal and flew to New York. I'll be here for a couple days at a press event with Meredith."

A lurch of anxiety ricochets across my chest. My face must show my obvious discomfort because he leans into the phone and sighs. "Cakes, I didn't tell you that so you'd be jealous. I just wanted you to know."

I shake my head, swallowing back my embarrassment. "God, no, it's fine. Sorry." My cheeks are so hot I could melt a block of ice in seconds. Giving him a wink, I turn to my side and stifle a yawn. "I'll make sure to bother you tomorrow with endless selfies and status updates. But I better get to sleep."

He pouts. "Okay, Cakes. I'll talk to you tomorrow."

"Night, Zach."

Decisions

Monica

It's done. I'm enrolled at the Art Institute.

Holy shit, I'm back in college. After spending countless hours over the past week buried in brochures and touring the school's many offerings, I picked my program. It came to me in an aha moment while preparing wardrobe for one of our shoots. Richland was working on a low budget project—again—and needed lingerie for an upcoming Mardi Gras-themed shoot. It was pure instinct to drag my sewing kit to work and stitch something together myself using recycled décor from old shoots. That's when the lightbulb went off.

This isn't the first time I've considered it, but this time it hit me like news of a BOGO sale at Nordstrom.

Fashion design.

I've been designing and altering everything I wear lately anyway. I've been sewing ever since I could hold a needle, and with the amount of experience I have from being on runways and production sets with my sister and mom, the entrance essays were a breeze to write.

On my trek home from work on Friday, I'm taken back to my childhood. To a time when I had the brightest stars in my eyes, the biggest dreams. Since the moment I was born, fashion was my first language. Of course, that was thanks to my mom constantly reminding us of her successful modeling days and how she gave it all up for her family after marrying her high school sweetheart—who'd just happened to become an NFL superstar.

Maggie was four when Mom enrolled her in her first beauty pageant, and the competition was fierce. She was dragged from one personal coach to another, each one with specialties ranging from stage presence to wardrobe to facial beauty. Yup. At four years old, my sister could apply her own false eyelashes. At least that's what my mom claims.

My first vivid memory was when Maggie was eight and I was six. She'd landed her first runway gig. It was for a local designer in Texas coming out with a new children's line. Not a big deal, but at the time, it felt like the biggest deal. It was the first time I'd ever been backstage among a chaotic medley of laughter, demands, zipper pulls, and the clattering of little girls' heels.

I watched that show with the highest of admiration for my beautiful sister, so confident and perfect at everything my mom made her do, like a precious little doll. I thought I wanted all that too. Why wouldn't I? It wasn't enough at the time to watch the madness unfold before my very eyes backstage. I wanted to be the one everyone was fussing over.

My mom figured it would all work the same for me, and for a while, it did. Pageants did wonders for my confidence at that age. The oohs and ahs from the crowd of strangers validated my beauty. I loved the attention. In fact, I'd be lying to myself if I said I didn't crave it. And even to this day, I kind of miss it.

When I got a little older and my sister got busier, booking modeling gigs left and right, my mom pulled me from the pageants, assuming the next logical step would be to have me model too. For years, the agency strung me along with broken promise after broken promise. Impatient, my mom asked them why I wasn't booking any jobs like my sister.

Their answer?

I was too short for the runway, and I would never fit into the clothes. They didn't have the confidence to work with me anymore.

My heart was broken. Not just by the agency, but also by mom. She lost interest in me and focused solely on my sister's career. I became the shadow. The one who would never be good enough. And even though I moved far away from my mom and sister nearly three years ago, I've continued to live in that shadow. I became the girl who *used to* have dreams because I haven't created any new ones.

Until today. The decision was easy once I walked through the fashion design department at the Art Institute and saw the exact things I fell in love with during my childhood at runway events: the high-pitched hammering of sewing machines hard at work, fast-paced seamstresses pinning fabrics for a tapered wear, and the colorful array of designs fluttering by. Never a dull moment, behind the scenes. I imagine it's a lot like how Zach's dream unfolded as he watched the games from under the bleachers.

Although I didn't realize it at the time, it wasn't the way the models looked or walked or presented themselves that captured my attention. It was about the process and the excitement—the details in the art and the reactions from the crowd. It was about *working* with the models to bring fashion to life, to develop a creative narrative using style to elicit a desired reaction from the crowd.

It's been a part of me all along. I didn't need to seek out my dream; I just needed to realize what was already in me.

When I wasn't spending my time among the fashion students in Seattle this week, I was totally slammed at work. Everybody needed me for something, and since Zach was busier than ever, Trevor called me like crazy.

Even Meredith was sending me emails—one awful idea after the next about how to sex up the campaign. She's an idiot. Sorry, but she's clueless about what we're actually supposed to be doing. Stripping Zach down to his boxer briefs and rubbing oil and water all over him won't serve a purpose other than her own selfish one. Her argument is that we need to "stimulate the parents too to get them more involved." Yes, she used the word *stimulate*, and I'm certain she wasn't referring to their minds.

Ugh. It's hard to push thoughts of Meredith and Zach together out of my mind, but he keeps me sane by sending trinkets of relief throughout the day. He never stops asking for pictures, and he calls me every night. I love the rasp in his voice when he's exhausted from one event after the other. I love every yawn he tries to muffle so I'll stay on the phone. And I love that he hides nothing about his day, even the bits about Meredith. It only makes me want him back in town that much more.

It's almost eleven at night when my phone rings, alerting me that I have a video call coming through. I smile. This is how Zach prefers to talk to me, and I'd be lying if I said I didn't like it. I do. I like that he wants to see me rather than just hear my voice. And after that first call that caught me off guard, I've been able to put together some cute outfits for bedtime.

"Hey Cakes." Zach smiles into the screen and I smile back.

"Hey back. Another stimulating day?" We both laugh. Zach thought Meredith's photoshoot idea was equally ridiculous, but he's not sure if he'll be able to shake her of it. Why he doesn't put his foot down and start calling the shots is beyond me. He puts too much trust into a woman with an agenda that doesn't seem to honor his character.

"You know it. Is that another Monica original?" Zach asks.

I hold the phone away so he can see the entire outfit, including my shiny, smooth legs. "You like?" I grin. This one is as blue as Zach's eyes. It has spaghetti straps, buttons down the front, and tiny shorts with an elastic waist.

"You know I do." I look up to watch his appreciative eyes roam the length of me. His gravelly voice is everything. "You have no idea how much I miss you, Cakes."

Warmth blooms from my inside-out, pulling my smile along with it. I fall onto my bed, bringing the phone with me and letting the down comforter conform to my body. "I might miss you too."

"Hm." He considers my response with a smile. "I'll take it." His eyes pull to the left. "What's that noise?"

I turn my head to make out what he's referencing and stifle a yawn. No wonder I'm so relaxed. Pellets of rain have begun to tap on my window. "Another rainy night. It looks like it's going to come down pretty hard. See?" I turn my phone so that he can see my window and then turn it back to face me.

We're silent for a few seconds before I speak. "My sister and I used to love curling up in blankets on the porch during

231

the thunderstorms. We'd bring our travel karaoke machine outside and follow the sounds with our voices. At some point we'd end up beatboxing and layering vocals until the storm let up." A bubble of laughter surfaces and erupts into a giggle at the memory. I miss how ridiculous we could act around each other.

Zach chuckles and brings the phone closer so I can make out the stubble on his jaw and the greenish-blue center of his eyes. "That just gave me an idea. What are you doing tomorrow night, Cakes?"

Tomorrow *night*? A lick of disappointment hits me. After a week of flirting and missing him, I can't imagine not seeing him the moment he steps off the plane in the morning. I'm being silly.

"I was thinkin' about washing my hair," I tease.

His eyes narrow. "Good. Wash your hair, and then I'll pick you up around five."

I smile. "Sounds like a plan. Are you going to tell me what we're doing, cowboy?"

He chuckles. "No, but you're on the right track with that nickname. Just make sure to wear something you can get dirty in.

Muddy Promises

Monica

Zach is right on time Saturday evening when he pulls up along the curb of my apartment. I'm glad he can't see the glow that lights me up from the inside or hear the heavy pounding of my heart.

My cheeks already hurt from smiling all day, but now that I see him leaning against his Jeep with a wide grin of his own, they just might burst.

As I close the distance between us, he offers one of those country boy nods—you know the one—but without the tip of the hat. He's a beautiful sight, standing there with his hands shoved in light gray jeans and wearing a black hoodie, unzipped to reveal a white fitted shirt.

"Hey, Cakes."

"Hey yourself."

He pulls me in for a hug and buries his face in my hair. I'm doing the same, falling into him easily while pressing my cheek to his chest.

Everything about this moment feels complete, like we could end our story right here and never look back. Unfortunately, *back* was the easy part. *Back* was safe and fun. But it can still be fun. At least that's what I'm hoping.

I'm instantly soothed by his sweet, fresh scent that has become my heaven. Paired with the strength of his arms, it's the perfect combination. At some point we moved past friendship, and my desire for more drowns out that little voice reminding me why this is a bad idea.

He groans and tightens his hold. "You feel good."

I laugh and look up, my heart lifting when our eyes connect. Can you miss something you've never had before? Because I've missed this—the way Zach makes me feel when I let him in, like he considers it a privilege. I've even missed the way his tone hums through my body when he's this close. Not to mention those ocean blue eyes, beautiful smile, and perfectly styled hair.

He lifts a hand to my cheek and swipes at it gently with his thumb. "You ready?"

His sweet smile is asking more than the obvious. Why won't my damn heart slow down? "Ready as I'll ever be."

We get on I-405 heading south when he reaches for my hand. "I'd ask you what you did this week, but I think I know every single detail. I might even have a selfie of it."

"That is probably true." I think about my time at the Art Institute this week and realize there is something I haven't told him. "Oh! I'm officially enrolled for school."

He glances at me with a surprised look. "Really? That is news. Are you going to keep me in suspense?"

I fasten a smug look on my face. "Maybe I will."

"Ah, come on, Cakes." Zach's flirtatious glance as he squeezes my hand is enough to give in.

"It's the most obvious of all the choices. It's just not something I've seriously considered before."

"Fashion design?"

My head whips toward him in shock. He says it like he already knew what I didn't.

He shrugs in response to my surprise. "I think everyone knew but you."

I steal my hand back and cross my arms across my chest. Should I be embarrassed about this? How could my friends know me better than I know myself? He laughs and steals my hand back. "You make your own clothes. You grew up in the fashion industry. You assemble all the wardrobes for production. And you designed the event logo. But nothing is more obvious than the crap thrown all over your bedroom."

I gasp, completely mortified. "When did you see my bedroom?"

His eyes crinkle with laughter. "The bathroom is attached to it. I might have snuck a peek. The question is, why didn't you realize it sooner?"

It's a good question. I'm just not sure I have an answer quite yet. "I don't know. I spent my childhood thinking I wanted something completely different. The limelight was all I dreamed of. I don't think I realized at the time what really impressed me about runway shows was the work that went into them. The set design, the choreography, and most of all, the outfits. I'd spend hours just hanging backstage watching the seamstresses and designers pick at the models until they accurately portrayed their work. It was all so fascinating.

"Maybe it's always been what I wanted, but I just didn't realize it. Sure, I practiced walking in heels and knew my signature pose by the time I was seven, but more than anything, I was critiquing designs and assembling my own outfits from carpets and drapes around the house."

"That's very *Gone with the Wind* of you," he teases.

Laughing, I get a good look at him. I need to remember this moment. "Wow. I didn't think it was possible for you to get any sexier."

He shrugs, completely unashamed. "Fashion is part of you."

"It is."

He squeezes my hand and focuses on the road ahead. We drive in silence for a few minutes while I check out his profile. It's his eyes I keep going back to. Such deep and honest eyes. But there's not an ounce of insincerity in his heart either. I love that I can feel safe with him. He's so attuned to my needs and feelings by now, I find it hard to think he could ever disappoint me.

"You never did tell me where you were taking me. I didn't know what to wear."

There's an amused gleam in his eyes, but he keeps them concentrated on the road. "It's a surprise. Hope you don't mind a bit of a drive tonight. But I'd say you're dressed just fine."

I glance down at my new outfit—I put the finishing touches on it yesterday. Heavily distressed dark denim, thanks to a pair of scissors and some sand paper, are now ripped at my upper thighs and knees. I even added some gold and silver studs to the front to dress it up a bit. Paired with an oversized, cream scoop neck sweater, it's both casual and classy. Perfect for tonight since I'm still clueless as to where Zach is taking me. And with my good luck fringed booties at my feet, I'm ready for anything. I think.

"You were joking about getting dirty, right?"

"Don't worry, Cakes. You'll stay clean." He gives me a quick wink. "Just don't get out of the Jeep."

Baffled, I just stare at him, waiting for a clue of some kind. His mouth remains zipped.

Thirty minutes later we've completely left civilization, and Zach's turning down a gravel road. A mile later, we're in a section of woods and on another path, this one fresh with mud.

"Um, Zach. If you don't want me to question whether you're a serial killer again, you're gonna want to tell me why you're driving me deep into the woods where no one can hear me scream."

He reaches over and grabs my knee this time. "Nothing to worry about, Cakes." He winks. "I'm considered a professional where I come from."

"A professional of what, exactly?"

Zach doesn't answer. Instead he removes his hand, turns up the music, and takes the wheel in both of his hands. With one final look at me, he grins. "You're gonna want to hold on there." He points to the handle above the passenger window as he revs the engine.

I latch on just as I hear the back wheels spinning, and then the Jeep takes off down the path. My stomach lurches forward. Mud flies all around us, splattering and streaking the windows. I'm screaming before I can control it. Even with the seatbelt holding me, I'm being tossed into the air like a ragdoll, my hair flying around me in vicious waves.

I hear Zach's laughter over the blaring country music and the roar of the engine. I'm laughing too as adrenaline pumps through my veins. Every bump that throws us into the air only shakes more laughter from me.

He doesn't do anything too crazy, doesn't make any wild turns or slam on the brakes. For that, I'm thankful. He just drives straight and fast until he approaches a sign that warns him to slow down.

The path opens to a large, dirt field, its center soft and muddy from recent rain. Once we've cleared the trees, he accelerates toward it until we're sinking and then spinning through the outskirts of the pit.

Each time we slow, the tires descend deep into the thick sludge. Zach knows just what to do. Revving the engine, he lightly taps and releases the gas. As he does, the Jeep climbs forward until he's found the perfect opportunity to press down on the lever and spin us out of the sinkhole.

We circle the pit a few times before heading back to the trail. He turns down the music so I can hear him. "There aren't any regulated dirt-riding paths or mudding spots around here," he explains. "Some of the players own this land just for this purpose. We've set it up so it can be as safe as possible. Mudding can be dangerous if you don't follow the rules, so we made some." He winks, and I'm instantly comforted by his consideration. He didn't have to tell me any of that, but he wants me to feel safe. And I do, because I'm with him.

"Want to do it again?"

My eyes go wide with excitement and I nod emphatically. "Yes!"

"Why haven't I ever heard of that before?"

We've made it to the end of the trail for the fifth time and decided to take a break. The music is playing from his portable speaker now while Zach moves around the Jeep, adjusting the seats and rolling out a large cushion.

"I don't know, Cakes. We used to do it all the time in Texas."

I help him open the rag top, and then I sit with my back against the front seat. He plops down near me and sets a padded cooler between us. "Hope you don't mind a simple dinner. I didn't have time to make anything fancy."

A thankful smile is all he gets from me before I'm slapping his hand away and examining the contents of the cooler. "Corn bread?" I ask curiously.

"Skillet corn bread with corn relish. A southern staple."

I set it down to pull out the next few containers. Pimento cheese and crackers, sweet tea, and ... a large jar. My face twists with amusement. "Pickles?"

"Yes." He hands me a beer and then sets the container to the side. "Think you can appreciate this?"

With a teasing glare, I grab it from his hands. "I appreciate all of it. Thank you." I look down at the can, rolling it between my hands and smile.

"Dallas Ales? "How'd you get your hands on these anyway?"

He leans back, opening his can and taking a swig. "My mom brings a case every time she visits. We used to serve it in the restaurant, and it was Dad's favorite." He shrugs. "I think it's her way of remembering him. The memories, good and bad, come alive when we open these bad boys." He winks and I know he's trying to lighten the mood, so I don't pry for more.

We eat in silence for a while, staring out at the darkness, the wind washing the trees around us. There's not much to see as the sun is setting, but the darkening purplish-blues of night hold my attention.

Synchronizing perfectly with the country tunes that play in the background, nature adds music of its own. Crickets chirp into the night, squirrels scurry up trees, owls claim their territory with each hoot, and leaves rustle in the evening breeze.

When we've finished our dinner, Zach reaches for my hand. At first I think he might be prepping to leave, but then he pulls me to the tail of the Jeep so our legs dangle over the edge. He adjusts our hands, weaving his fingers through mine. Our eyes lock and we smile, lingering there for a second before turning to face the sky.

The night is brightly speckled with stars, and they're only gaining brilliancy with each moment that passes.

"Wow," I breathe. "I haven't seen stars this bright since I lived in Texas. Living in the city, you forget to look up past the skylines. Even then, you can't see this much detail."

"Yeah. My brother and I would camp out in our backyard sometimes, but he was afraid of the dark. I'd have to take off the cover so we could look through the screen ceiling. We'd lie there and count the stars until we fell asleep."

"That's adorable." I smile. He releases my hand and snakes his arm around my shoulders, drawing me close.

A streak of light pulls our focus back to the sky. It moves so quickly I almost miss it. I gasp. "Make a wish," Zach says in a hushed voice, like the shooting star can hear us and anything louder might break the magic.

I make my wish and look up to find his eyes on mine. "What'd you wish for, Cakes?"

Shaking my head, I try to breathe against the erratic pounding of my heart. "If I tell you, it won't come true." I swallow. "I really want it to come true."

That's when he gives me a look I may never forget. Full of confidence and need. Defiance and lust. It's a lot like the look he gave me before kissing me in his kitchen, but this time there's a whole lot of build up behind it.

His finger brushes my bottom lip, and I'm certain he can hear my stuttered breaths. His touch shakes my whole body, and it only intensifies when he drops his mouth so it's only a breath away from mine.

His words tickle against my lips, and the rasp in his voice burns through me. "I'm ready to make my wish come true right now."

"Then do it," I whisper back.

He's so close. "If I start kissing you now, there's no turning back, Cakes." He says this not as a threat, but as if he's afraid. My heart dances in my throat.

He's right, but I don't want to go back … as safe as that may have been.

I close the distance, so tired of fighting my feelings. Right now, I don't want to think about anything else except Zach and how well we fit together. With one hand pressed into his thigh and the other gripping the back of his shirt, our mouths move together.

Kissing me was his wish. I bet he thinks that was my wish too. It wasn't. My wish involves rewriting history so that I never would have fallen through the steps of those bleachers.

But even now, as his tongue sweeps mine and he sucks on my bottom lip, I know my wish was made in vain. That event was just the beginning of a chain that I'm the cause of—a chain that links my past to my present. I just need to figure out how to ensure it won't continue into my future.

The Taste of You
Monica

Zach is officially courting me. He actually used those words. And while I want to rip his clothes off every time he kisses me, I let him lead. It's been all over-the-clothes hand-grabbing with a little slip of the tongue. Nothing more, and I'm starting to go crazy.

Who would have thought the freaking single hottest man to grace planet Earth would rather spend his time getting to know me when we could easily be doing other things?

It's not like me to let a man take things this far. One date is usually enough. To go on multiple dates means getting to know someone, and getting to know someone means that you develop feelings for them. I've never wanted the feelings attached to sex before, but with Zach, it's already too late.

I'm not exactly sure when he wormed his way into my heart, but he did, and now I'm suffering the consequences. Sexually frustrated Monica will get what she wants soon. Even if she—I—have to take control.

It's Tuesday and we're on our fourth date. Each night it's been something different. A shared pizza and a walk around Alkai. Takeout on the beach at Golden Gardens Park. Private nighttime access to the zoo. And tonight, we agreed to ride the Wheel, eat a light dinner, and then get dessert.

What I didn't realize was that we were going to get dessert at Zach's place. I'm totally fine with it, but he's only ever come to my apartment, so this feels different.

Part of me is curious to know how he lives, but the other part enjoys the comfort of owning the space I'm in with Zach. There's that control thing again. I'm starting to realize I might need to learn how to let go if I'm truly going to move forward with my life.

"Home sweet home." He grins as he parks and opens his door. I smile back, a swarm of flutters taking over my insides.

He's at my side of the Jeep in seconds, opening it and helping me out. This is Zach. The guy who refuses to let me open my own door or carry my own bags. I may be independent, but I certainly won't complain when a man wants to treat me right. I like that he's consistent with his actions and follows through on his words. It makes him trustworthy.

Taking the elevator to the top floor, I'm supremely aware of how different our worlds are. I've felt none of that until this moment. Nothing about Zach screams that there's a divide at all, and I don't think it has anything to do with having a former NFL player as a father. Zach is as down to earth and as real as any guy can get.

This doesn't have to be weird.

The elevator opens directly into an open view of his immaculate home. Spacious and bare, just as expected. White walls with some framed art, but nothing that tells me anything more about Zach than I already know. It's the opposite of my home, which causes me to laugh before I can stop myself.

Zach interlocks his fingers with mine and squeezes, a smile on his face. "I love your laugh."

And just that right there is the kind of thing that lassos my heart, giving me no choice but to surrender. I put up a good fight. Now it's time to see what happens.

He pours two glasses of wine. By now, he knows what I like so he doesn't need to ask. He even drops in two cubes of ice because I prefer my pinot a little watered down.

"Are you going to give me a tour?"

I love the smile he's wearing now. It carries a hint of shyness, a little pride, and a whole lot of sexy. He hands me my wine and leads me from room to room. Everything is spotless, which doesn't surprise me at all. Two bedrooms, two bathrooms, a study, a gym, and a living room later, the tour is complete. The only decoration besides some Seattle skyline paintings on the walls are the classic football photos, framed famous quotes from athletes, and a collection of family photos at the end of the hall. That's where I stop and take my time while Zach runs to the bathroom.

Now that I'm seeing Zach and his brother side-by-side, I'm amazed at the resemblance. His brother has the same strong, oval-shaped face, big blue eyes, and prominent nose. His hair is the same light brown, but it's shorter. The biggest difference is in their heights and builds. Zach's got maybe an inch more of height, while his brother's build is wider. Otherwise, they could be mistaken as twins.

"What'cha looking at, Cakes?"

I hold up the photo of his brother. "You two must have been quite the issue for your mom."

Zach's lip curls at one corner. "Oh no, not me. I was the angel. Ryan was the little ladies' man."

"Wait a second." This is the first time Zach's mentioned his name. "Ryan?"

"Yup," he says, almost sourly.

I burst into laughter, unable to help it. "Ryan Ryan?" How did I miss that?

Zach takes the picture and plops it back on the stand. "Yeah, well, he'll be the last one laughing when his fame skyrockets because of that name."

"True. He'll be hard to ignore."

I scan the rest of the photos, spending extra time on the one of his entire family. Zach must be fifteen or so, his brother around thirteen, and they're standing in front of the restaurant with giant smiles.

"That's my favorite," he says, wrapping his arms around my waist. Something tells me his hold is more to comfort him than to embrace me. "That was three months before the accident."

"I'm sorry, Zach." I'll never stop apologizing for the way his dad died. How awful it must be to live with that every day. To know that part of you is gone from this world and never coming back.

I set that photo down when another catches my eye. It's a different family, but Zach, Ryan, and their mother stand proudly with the group.

"That's Coach Reynolds," he says fondly.

"I recognize him." I smile. "You two seem close."

He laughs. "Yeah, well, he did save my life."

Zach's arms leave my waist, and I feel abandoned the moment they do. It's as if he's already become a part of me, and that's terrifying. Based on how much that simple gesture just affected me, I can't imagine what would happen if his absence is ever permanent.

"Coach Reynolds was my high school coach, too. Kind of cool if you think about it. He gave me a family then, and he's giving me one now. Same goes for Sandy. With my mom and bro still in Texas, it can get pretty lonely."

Zach has been upfront about his family and the support he's gotten from his coach, but I guess I wasn't expecting to get this close to it all. I look through the rest of the photos, trying to find something to steer the conversation to something lighter.

"Where are all your football awards? Besides this, there's zero personality here. I'm disappointed in you, Zach," I tease. "You finally let me into your world, and it's boring as hell."

He chuckles and walks me down the hall and onto the balcony. "Sorry to disappoint. I had someone come in here and decorate for me, and I haven't touched a thing. I haven't even unpacked completely. I don't see myself living here forever, and since I'm rarely here, I've left it as is. The place is a little big for me, but I bought it because of the view."

I turn to see what he's referencing, and the view smacks me in the face. Zach's condo overlooks the lush landscape of Kerry Park and a wide swath of the metropolitan area. The Space Needle sits off in the distance, prominent against the landscape. It seems relatively quiet in this part of the city as it's somewhat tucked away.

"Wow," I gush, setting my glass on the ledge and gripping the rail with both hands. "I've never seen Seattle like this."

His arms encircle my waist again and I'm grateful I decided to wear my hair in a bun tonight. My neck is like a magnet attracting his lips to my skin. He does it now, pressing down on that soft spot that's become his favorite, making me hum and tip my head to the side as an invitation for more.

"You're looking at what used to be my favorite view."

I giggle, already knowing where he's going with this.

"Oh yeah? And your new favorite is standing in front of you?"

He smiles into my neck before kissing it again. "Mhmm." Those shivers again. "I have something for you."

My body freezes and he chuckles in response. "Don't worry. It's nothing to do with cooking. Well, not really." Placing another kiss on my neck, he pulls away, no longer protecting me from the chill in the air. "Wait right there."

I turn back to the view of Seattle and wait, knowing this is my chance to redeem myself from the wretched pots and pans disaster that he'll never let die. This time, I won't screw up the thank-you.

A small black and red gift bag appears on the rail in front of me. I give Zach a smile over my shoulder before untying the string and pulling the tissue paper away. Inside, I find a small silver-framed photo. There's a picture of me on the beach at Golden Gardens. Zach and I were snacking on grapes, a heavy blanket over our legs as we looked out at the surf. The wind must have just blown when he snapped the picture. Wisps of dark brown curls wrap around my face, but you can still see my toothy smile. And there's a poem in the space to the right of me.

Sweet Tooth

Chocolate tresses cascade down your back,
Thick honey and cinnamon reside in your eyes,

Strawberry ice cream flavors your lips,
And you speak with mint bubblegum replies,
You give every piece of your apple pie heart,
And heal with your macaroon touch,
A caramel kindness fills your soul,
And you wonder why I crave you so much.
– L.H. @lhoferpoetry

The night air is cool, but heat radiates around us with intensity. Swiveling to face him, I slide my hands up his chest and hook them over his neck, still holding the frame in one hand and beaming. "I love it, Zach. I didn't know you were into poetry."

Zach's relief is so clear that my guilt simmers all over again. He tilts his head down to touch mine, looking almost embarrassed when he speaks next. "I've always loved poetry. Reading it, anyway."

"Do you write?" I'm remembering something Chloe told me during Super Bowl.

He shakes his head and laughs. "No." Then his eyes adjust with his next thought. "I copy my favorite poems into a journal and jot down stories to go with them. There's usually a reason a poem speaks to me. Each one reflects something special in my life."

I smile. "Did this one make the journal?"

He nods. "It did."

I look at the frame again. "Who's L.H.?"

"One of my favorite poets on Instagram. After he posted this, I couldn't stop thinking about what drew me to you in the first place. Sure, it was the way you ran off like a bandit with that chocolate cake, but it was also the way that you were unashamed about it. I figured if there's one way to get into that apple pie heart of yours, it's with food. If this doesn't tell you how I feel, then nothing will."

My throat tightens, and there's a swelling in my heart. "You are the sweetest man." I know I'm seconds away from letting my emotions spill down my cheeks. I don't know any way to make it stop other than to lift onto my toes and press my lips to his.

Arms encircle my waist and pull me off the ground as the kiss deepens. When he sets me down a minute later, I'm feeling light and so damn happy.

"Dessert?" I grin.

He winks and pulls me away from the rail, leading me into the kitchen where he lifts me onto the island. "Stay here," he says huskily.

He retrieves dessert from the refrigerator, a small white box, and sets it on the counter beside me. He doesn't open it right away. Instead, we sip our wine and chat about all we've accomplished in preparation for camp. We can't help it. The excitement that's been building and the aggressive planning are all coming to a head, and I'm more than ready to see how everything plays out.

"So you're going to another school this week?" I ask.

"Yup, tomorrow. They happen to be having an assembly, so the principal thought it would be the perfect time to come in and surprise the kids, hand out flyers for camp, and give out a few free tickets. Oh, and Balko will be with me."

Balko is Zach's number one tight end and possibly the cockiest player on the team, but Zach believes he has every right to be that way since he gets work done out on the field.

"Won't you be with the production crew at the assembly?"

I shake my head. "No, we're double booked and Richland wants me covering a photoshoot."

He pouts, making my heart flutter in my chest. "I can stop by your place when you're done with work," he suggests. "We can make dinner there." A smirk accompanies his last sentence. The jokes about me not cooking are endless, but I've started to like them.

"Funny. But I can't tomorrow. Gavin's out of town again, and Chloe goes a little bit crazy when he's away. We usually do girl's night and then she crashes on my couch."

"Really? Chloe doesn't seem like the clingy type to me."

I shrug. "She misses him. It's not a jealousy thing at all. Those two are rock solid. Anyway, it's just an excuse for us to watch cheesy old movies and stuff our faces."

Zach's eyes crinkle at the corners. "Sexy. Aren't girls supposed to have naked pillow fights and compare their boyfriends when they have sleepovers?"

I choke on my laughter. "Oh trust me, we do a little of that too." I wink at him, not wanting to state the obvious—that Zach isn't my boyfriend. At least, we haven't put a title on what we are yet.

Zach steps between my legs, examining my wrap dress with a wicked smile. "Have I told you how much I love that dress?"

"Only a few billion times tonight." I grin and look down at the tie holding my dress together. He eyes it like I'm his present. Holy hell. I hope he unwraps me.

There's a part of me that wants to tell him we're moving too slow. But at the same time, I'm enjoying this, whatever it is that we're building. If foreplay were a gymnastics sport, Zach would win. He's taken his time to carefully execute every move, and it's all building up to the grand finale.

Geez. The way he's eyeing me, it's like he's planning his dinner and I'm the main course. It's hot.

"Do I even want to ask what you're thinking right now?" I ask with a tilt of my head and a grin.

"Probably not."

I probably do.

He smiles before his mouth finds mine, kissing me softly while he lightly plays with the fabric of my dress. Even with the extra height of the counter, he still hovers over me in the most dominating of stances. I've never been one to let a man own me in that way. It's usually me taking the lead, but everything's different with Zach—and I love it.

When he steps back, a breeze hits my stomach and I look down to see that he's undone my dress and the material has fallen open, revealing my carefully selected black and pink lace underwear.

Zach greedily examines every inch of my body with a look so fierce I can feel it low in my belly. And when he zeros in on the lace of my bra, I watch him swallow his excitement before the quietest intake of air passes his lips. It's sexy as hell coming from the man now sandwiched between my thighs.

His eyes flicker up to meet mine, and they darken ever so slightly. I take a slow, quiet breath, trying like hell to keep my nerves at bay. But the next thing I know, I'm distracted by Zach slowly opening a box next to me. *Dessert.* "Whatcha got there, Zachary?"

"Just a little something I want to put on you tonight."

Huh?

He curls his lip at the corner and reveals an assortment of chocolate covered strawberries. They're all beautiful, but one of them is special. It's decorated with white icing like the threads of a football. And that's the one he chooses to place between my lips. I don't have time to react before he murmurs darkly, "Bite."

His authoritative tone catches me off guard, and the thrill of excitement races up my spine. There have been crumbs left along the way revealing a less than gentlemanly side to Zach when it comes to sex. Every now and then he'll unleash a hint of darkness that only makes me more curious. He's the perfect contradiction, and my body reacts to all of it.

I bite into the strawberry, eyes rolling into the back of my head, but not from the juices. Zach's mouth is on my throat, kissing me as I chew, making it almost impossible to swallow. When I do, his mouth moves to mine. This time his kiss is ravenous, yet controlled. His lips are firm and demanding as he steals my breath with every stroke of his tongue.

I'm dizzy with contentment as he bites down on my bottom lip and uses his grip on my thighs to pull me forward. I can feel him now. God, he feels good against me. Even more so when the friction of his movements sends bolts of pleasure through me.

He must have taken the strawberry from me at some point, because it's on my skin now. Coolness skates over the curve and dip of my breasts. I look down. A watery pink stream has traveled across exposed skin, leaving a sweet and sticky mess behind. The wicked gleam in Zach's eyes is enough to undo me.

Inch-by-inch, his tongue traces the strawberry's path, lapping the residue clean from my body. My thighs clench around him as his mouth wanders off path and ends up hovering over my nipple, sucking and biting through the sheer cloth of my bra. "Ah," I moan, and my hands grip the counter's edge, loving every movement that causes the bulge in his jeans to glide against my core.

When his eyes flutter up to lock eyes with mine, while never removing the suction of his mouth, I completely melt. Those dangerously beautiful blue eyes that are desperate for my pleasure are also daring. He knows what he's doing to me, and not just physically. He's after more than that. He's after my heart.

The strawberry finds my navel, or his mouth does—I don't know what happens first, because when his tongue pushes into that spot I can't hold myself up anymore. My elbows give way. I fall back flush against the island, the movement forcing his mouth lower.

"Sweet Jesus, you taste like heaven," he murmurs, his words hot against my skin. I gasp when a finger hooks into my underwear and pushes it to the side, exposing me. "And now, I'm about to go to hell."

He plays the same game with the strawberry, only this time his mouth doesn't stop once the juice is gone. He stays on me, a man on a mission with every expert stroke of his tongue. Heaven and hell is right.

It doesn't take much for me to let go, especially when he demands it from me with his gravelly voice. Especially when he pushes a finger into my core and curls it just right to finish the job.

Never has dessert tasted—or felt—so good. Zachary Ryan has officially ruined me for all desserts ... by making me his.

I've finally come down from my cloud of bliss when I feel him righting my underwear and lifting me back to a sitting position. And just when I think it's over, he places the once-bitten and thoroughly juiced strawberry between his lips and bites down, ensuring that no drop is left behind.

Oil and Water
Monica

I work like crazy the next two days, finalizing everything and checking items off our project timeline before the week-long festivities begin at Camp Dakota. It's especially helpful that Zach has been preoccupied with the school visits. After the other night, he would only be a distraction in this final week of preparation. I do miss him, though. After seeing him every night since he's been back, the last two nights have been tough. Luckily I had Chloe to console me.

It's late in the afternoon on Friday when I finally emerge from my office. Everything is ready to go for tomorrow. I'm confident about it and ready to take Richland up on his offer to let me leave early, but it looks like he's had a change of plans.

"What in flying rainbows are you two doing?" I exclaim.

I've walked in to find Zach completely bare except for a pair of black boxer briefs tight enough to reveal … everything. Richland is standing in front of him with a bottle of baby oil. I'm halfway tempted to snap a picture, stick a caption on it, and post it on Facebook. It would go viral instantly. But seriously … what the actual fuck is going on?

"Nope." I shake my head. "Never mind. Whatever sprinkles your donuts. I'm out of here."

But I'm rooted in place watching them. They're both laughing so hard that I can see Zach's abs tightening with each inhale, and Richland spins to greet me. "No! Stop, Monica. Thank God you're here. I thought you went home early."

"I was about to, but I was just wrapping a few things up." I focus on Zach for my next question. "Why are you naked?" He's finally stopped laughing, but he's still wiping tears from his eyes.

"Meredith," they say in unison.

I roll my eyes. "The oil and water photo shoot?"

Richland nods. "She wants an opening and closing video for dramatic effect, and then she wants to repurpose the raw footage for some other crazy shit she's got up her sleeve." He nods to the sheet of paper on the desk to my right and I pick it up.

Looking at the sketch, I shake my head. "I still don't get the purpose. Why does she get a say in this?"

Richland sighs. "It doesn't matter. It's happening."

I try to be a good sport like him, but I'm secretly fuming that Meredith gets away with this crap.

"Imagine a complete contrast to the bright opening number where we've got Zach frozen but on rotation in front of the camera." Richland points to a photo on the nearest wall, referencing the last shoot we did with Zach. "White shirt, happy. We'll do the opposite for this shot. Dark, covered in sweat, showing the hard work from the week. His expression determined, ready to take on anything. *That* will close this puppy out. Let's just get the shot and we'll edit it onsite."

And that's what I love about Richland. He hated the idea, but the moment he knew he was stuck with it, he committed to it and now it's his. I'm still not convinced.

Richland holds up the plastic bottle and then extends his arm to me. "You can do the honors. This is not going to happen for me. Sorry." He laughs again and walks away after setting the bottle down. "I'll be over here. Just holler when the rubdown is complete."

Richland is crazy. Out of his damn mind. There's no way I'm going to lather Zach up with a bottle of baby oil—*at work*. But then again, Richland thinks I'm a professional and that there's nothing to worry about. If he only knew.

Richland moves to the other side of the room to busy himself with the photo equipment. Zach grins. "Saving the day once again, aren't you, Cakes?"

"This is a bad idea," I say in a hushed voice.

He chuckles lightly. "C'mon, just lube me up and then you can hand me over to Richland." He winks.

I know I've got to do this—not because I think it's a good idea, but because it's my job. And I am a professional. If anyone can do this, it's me.

Except, oh my God, Zach's body. It's the first time I'm seeing it like this. Almost completely bare, rock hard abs, as if sculpted by Michelangelo himself. Strong legs with not a millimeter of fat on him. But those briefs and everything they're not hiding … whoever said black made things appear smaller never got an eyeful of this guy.

Jesus, save me. It's too hot in here. Richland should know better than to turn on the lamps too long before a shoot. I'm practically sweating, and I've just stepped under them.

"You okay, Cakes?"

I ignore him, too distracted by my thoughts to hold a conversation. I mean, geez, why didn't I get him naked the other night? *Oh yeah ... he wanted to take it slow.* I try not to laugh out loud. After giving me the best orgasm of my life, he didn't want me to reciprocate.

Way to drag this out, Zach.

And now I'm getting ready to rub down his perfect body at work.

I snatch the bottle of oil, refusing to meet his eyes. Filling my palm with liquid, I coach myself silently, repeating *I'm a professional* until it comes true.

"Cakes, eyes up here."

I'm inhaling as I look up. "Huh?"

He laughs. "It's not a big deal. Just oil me up already."

Words I never thought would be spoken to me. I might have dreamed about this once. Maybe I'm dreaming now. As I float on my imaginary dark cloud of Zachary Ryan's perfect body and all the ways I can touch him freely, I begin coating his back.

"Are you all right?" he asks again.

"I don't know," I say with mock sweetness. "How would you like it if I came to your work and took off my clothes, then asked you to rub me down so I could pose for a photo shoot?"

The moment I say the words I know how stupid they sound.

He laughs deeply, infuriating me further. "Do you really need me to answer that?"

I growl and slap a heavy dose of oil onto his back. "No," I whisper-shout. "Shut up and let me do my job."

He's still loudly amused at my unease, and I don't know why, but it sends a flare of anger through me. Here I am, trying to do my job and rub down this NFL god who not too long ago was buried between my legs, and he has the nerve to laugh at me.

Payback's a bitch.

My movements are slow. I decide I might as well appreciate this fine specimen at my fingertips. One thing that's always fascinated me is the human body. As I glide my hand along his back muscles, up his spine, and over his shoulders, I try to remember all the smart names for all the taut muscles I once learned. It's a struggle because the only way to accurately define Zach is perfection.

My fingers slide gracefully over every swelled muscle, every defined curve, digging in a little at every dip, just to get a reaction out of him. He's as still as can be. That's okay. The professional that I am is certain to cover every inch of his warming skin.

"We should take a selfie and send it to Meredith," I start. "Thank her for the idea. I'm not so sure I hate it anymore." I grin at my own joke. Well, half-joke.

Zach gives me a throaty laugh. "Such a kind gesture. Your thoughtfulness astounds me."

"Thanks, Zach." I run my hands along his back at the waist, and my eyes zero in on the black briefs wrapped around toned skin. I freeze for a second, trying desperately to pull my eyes away. Of course I'm going to check out a hot guy in boxer briefs, especially when I'm getting paid to feel him up—but damn these thoughts that come with it.

His laughter ceases, and that's when I realize my fingernails are digging into his waist, my mouth so close to his back I might graze it with my lips. The silence is what brings me to the surface of my thoughts. I gasp a shallow breath before letting him go and stepping back.

What am I doing? My nails have left a tiny imprint on his skin. I rub it gently; glad he can't see how mortified I am. "I'm sorry." I let out an embarrassed laugh, but Zach remains still, his body rigid.

I grab the spray bottle and release water onto his back, watching little beads form all over his body. As the water reacts to the oil and retracts, balling up into droplets and sliding down his slicked up back, it hits me.

Oil and water. That's us.

Zach is a sturdy creature with nothing to hide. And I'm anything but. Somehow I ended up in his world, but that doesn't mean I belong here. That's why when he comes close, I retract. Never by choice, but by necessity.

He turns to face me. I'm sure my face is flushed. Here I am, touching every inch of exposed skin on this man's body, when all I really want is to touch the unexposed ones.

"Enjoying yourself, Cakes?" His tone is low and husky.

I refuse to look up. My strength will die the moment our eyes meet, and I'm not ready to lose this kind of power. Not when he's so clearly the winner in every other interaction between us. It's finally my turn to call the shots.

Pouring more oil into my palm, I set down the bottle and eye his stomach like it's my next obstacle course. *American Ninja Warrior,* here I come. Peering around Zach's body at Richland to ensure he's preoccupied, my lips curl up slowly. I smooth the liquid over his skin, paying extra special attention to the lines that run diagonally from his shorts, up his stomach, and then back down again.

He clears his throat. "Be careful."

Batting my eyelashes up at him, I feign mock innocence. "Just doing my job. It's not a big deal, right?"

I'm fully aware of the way his eyes darken in response to my teasing. "It is now."

Shit.

Do not look down. Do not look down.

Taking a slow sip of air as slyly as possible, I continue my work, lathering the rest of his stomach and arms, paying extra attention to the valleys, ensuring every inch is tended to before setting the bottle down to complete the race.

I don't need to look up to see how unmistakably heavy his breathing has become. That's when my head tilts down and confirms what I already knew. I may have made it to the finish line, but not without awakening the beast.

My eyes fly up to meet his in a crash so fierce I nearly stumble back. He doesn't let me. Instead, he grips my arm, holding me steady and leaning in. "I told you to be careful," he growls. My heart is crashing against the walls of my chest. *Oh my God.*

We're both oblivious to anything but each other until we hear the clattering of something on the other side of the room. "Ah, shit," Richland mumbles, stooping to pick up whatever it was.

Zach releases his grip and glares at me one last time before walking off to the bathroom, and I make the trek to the makeup table, furiously trying to calm my nerves. But it's too late. What I did was beyond teasing, and the look in Zach's eye told me he won't be forgetting it anytime soon.

I need to get out of here. Now.

"Hey Richland," I call out. "He's all set so I'm taking off. Need anything else for the shoot?"

"Nope. Go on home. It's been a long day."

Relieved to get away, I pack up my things and rush out the door before a freshly oiled Zach comes out of the bathroom.

"Cakes, open up."

The knocking scared the crap out of me. I heard it from the shower and finally threw a towel around me to see what the commotion was all about.

I open the door and tighten the towel around me when I gaze back at Zach's amused expression. "Sorry," I say as I dash back to my room to change. "I didn't know you were coming over."

Hurrying, I throw on a baggy tank top and some shorts. It's not like he can stay long, anyway. Zach has an early workout and we both need to be on the bus by eight a.m.

He's standing at my bedroom door when I emerge. I jump back, my heart leaping into my throat. "You scared me."

"Sorry." He grins. "I was about to sit on your couch, and then I remembered I've got oil all over me." He cocks his head to the side. "Kind of your fault. Mind handing over a washcloth or something?"

I look over his body, still shiny and smooth, and I try to fight a blush. "You can shower." Yeah, definitely not going to be able to hide that blush. "If you want. You can't stay for long, but my couch is new…"

"Sure, Cakes. Got a towel?"

"Whatever happened to plans with Desmond tonight?" I ask, grabbing him a towel from under my sink.

Zach doesn't give me much room to leave the bathroom, forcing me to slide against him. He grins wickedly. "Something came up. So I'm here instead."

Okay, then. I exit quickly and close the door behind me to hide my blush.

Zach showers while I prepare a plate of crackers and cheese. I didn't stop for takeout since I have a pile of leftovers from the week. We'll have to make do with what I have here. After a quick clean-up, I turn on the television, which is already set on some entertainment news station, and I flop down on the couch.

A few minutes later I hear the click of the bathroom door and turn to watch it open. Holy crap. It's like the heavens part and angels start singing when Zach walks into the living room. I scramble to a sitting position. He's wearing the same outfit he had on as I oiled him up earlier. I narrow my eyes, knowing exactly what he's doing. *Not going to happen.* The grin on his face is wide as he sits beside me, making himself comfortable as if it's his own home.

"I could totally get fired, you know."

"For groping me at your office?" His head turns to me, eyes filled with challenge.

I glare at him. "I did not grope you. My boss told me to rub you down, so I did."

He laughs. "I don't think he asked for you to give me a massage while you were at it. That was all you. Trust me,

Cakes, if I did that to you it would be all over the news and I'd be under fire for sexual harassment."

I hold up my finger in warning. "Not even funny. Welcomed sexual advances are completely different."

His eyebrows lift in mock surprise. "I don't remember welcoming any of what happened back there."

I growl and bury my head in my hands. "Seriously, Zach. What if Richland had caught on to any of that?"

"He already knows about us."

I look up, shocked. It didn't even occur to me that they would have talked about us—whatever we are.

"It's obvious, Cakes. He straight up asked me tonight. Don't be mad. I've known the guy for a long time. Richland's cool with it."

"He is?" I mean, I've known Richland for a long time too, but I've never asked him for his opinion on employee-client relationships.

He nods and slides a comforting hand over my shoulders. "Said if you're fine, he's fine, and he won't say anything." Zach tucks a stray hair behind my head. "I think he has a soft spot for you."

I sigh and lean against him. "Well, that's kind of a relief."

He squeezes my thigh with one hand while pulling me tightly against his chest. "I got you, Cakes. That's why I came up here. I know we don't have plans tonight." He pauses for a moment. "You going to kick me out now?"

Smirking, I turn to catch his puppy dog face, begging me to let him stay. "There will be no kicking, but you should leave soon. I'd hate to be the reason your biceps deflate in the morning."

He lets out a deep laugh and squeezes my thigh again, this time inching it up my leg until I'm back to barely breathing. "C'mere," he says, huskily.

My focus is on his lips when he speaks, so I'm not entirely sure what he means. I'm already pressed against him. But then he cradles the bottom of my thigh and lifts, pulling my leg across his lap so that I'm straddling him.

His eyes roam from my neck to my lips and then finally to my eyes. His hand sweeps through my hair until his fingers massage my neck. "If you can't tell, I'm crazy about you. Two days away from you just about killed me."

My eyes flutter closed, relaxing against his touch, until another hand runs up my thigh and skates between my skin and my shorts, reaching the top of my thighs.

"Me too," I admit, just above a whisper.

The hand that's caressing my neck pulls me closer. Hot breath tickles my neck before he's kissing it. "Zach," I breathe out, feeling like I might explode without more.

He nips at my skin. "I was so pissed at you earlier."

"You were?"

His other hand lands on my leg, mirroring the one that's grazing the skin beneath my shorts, moving over my thigh, and then finding my ass. He grips both cheeks firmly before sliding me up his lap so that I'm acquainted with the one part of him I've been fighting to stay away from. He groans as we connect. I suck in a breath. Everything goes dark when my eyes snap shut, making his intoxicatingly fresh scent stronger.

Lips glide up to just below my ear. "Hmm," he murmurs. "You're such a tease." Chills move up my spine and across my skin until everything begins to warm under his spell.

I meet his eyes, my breath catching in my throat. He's brushing a thumb against my cheeks like they're the most beautiful pieces of me. He does the same with my chin and my lips.

I want to feel him press deeper into me, so I try to move, but he stops me with one look.

"Tell me we're not pretending anymore." His voice cracks, and suddenly I realize what this week has been about. It hasn't just been about getting to know me, or teasing me slowly until we can't take it anymore. He wants to trust this. To trust me. And he wants me to trust him.

I melt at his words and shake my head. "No, Zach. Not anymore."

"So you're mine?"

Isn't this a lot to commit to when we're both so worked up? "I'll try," I say honestly.

He shakes his head, the stubble of his chin scraping my skin. "Not good enough. I need to hear you say it," his husky voice demands.

I groan in frustration, but not because of his question. Why are we still talking? "I'm yours, Zach," I whisper. "I've always been yours."

With a curl of his lips he's guiding my head toward his again until we crash together in an explosive kiss. Because when oil and water react to heat, everything sizzles.

He finally eases his grip. My body begins to move above him, slowly, treasuring every inch of his still-clothed body. His hands find the bottom of my tank top and slip inside it, running a hand up my back before encircling my waist and pulling my body down firmly onto his lap. He groans, and then everything intensifies. Our breathing. Our rhythm. Each touch. Each sound.

He rocks up into me, pulling away from my mouth and grabbing hold of the bottom of my tank top. With one look in my eyes, he asks permission and receives it. My shirt comes off. His eyes roam over me before his hands do. And then his mouth is wrapping around the peaks of my breasts and teasing each one with a gentle suction.

He must feel me try to move. Both of his hands have moved down again so that they're on my thighs, under my shorts, rocking me into him with a firm grip as if he can't get enough. He tastes me. Licks me. Nips me. His boxer briefs and my shorts leave little to the imagination, only sending us into a deeper frenzy.

I pant into the air. My hands are equally greedy as they grip his hair and I press into him. "Zach," I say again, this time for an entirely different reason. My heart rate quickens and my muscles begin to clench. Grinding against him might just get me to where I need to be.

"You're so beautiful, Cakes," he murmurs against my skin. "Fuck. I need to be inside you." But he doesn't try to move us. Instead, he's helping me find my release as I desperately move against him, and I swear he might come too.

A sharp moan makes it past my throat as pleasure soars through me, blasting my body with shudders, and then everything goes still.

With a growl, Zach grips me by the waist and flips me onto my back. But just as he starts to tug at my shorts a phone rings—well, it sings.

What the hell? No.

Kenny Chesney's voice pours through Zach's phone speakers, and his head falls to my chest with a moan.

Running my hands through his hair, I sigh. "Ignore it."

We're still barely clothed when he starts to move above me, pressing his lips to mine. And then I hear the lyrics *"never forget you, Coach."*

I can't help it. I look over to the coffee table and see *Coach Reynolds* lit up on his phone. Yup. Moment totally ruined. I reach for his phone and hand it to him with an annoyed smile. "It's for you."

"Cakes." He wrinkles his eyes. "I don't want to talk to him right now. I don't know why he'd be calling on a Friday ni—" Zach's face changes suddenly. "Shit!"

He jumps up from the couch and dresses faster than anything I've ever seen, retrieving his clothes from the bathroom and shoving his feet into his shoes.

He presses his lips to my forehead. "I'll call you once I'm on the road. I'm so late."

I'm officially panicking now. I hope everything's okay, but there are so many questions swirling through my mind.

It takes thirty minutes for him to call me. Apologies immediately flood the phone line. I'm trying to grasp his words, and ease immediately settles in my stomach when I realize everyone is going to be okay. There's no emergency. Just a promise he made to someone other than me.

"Coach's daughter has a dance recital tonight," he explains. "I'm so sorry, Cakes. I promised her I'd be there, and I completely forgot until Coach called. It wasn't on my damn calendar." He lets out an uncomfortable laugh. "I can be back at your place around ten ... but you probably need to sleep."

His voice fades with regret. Meanwhile, I'm speechless. After giving in to what felt was so right, I never expected Zach to make everything feel so wrong. He made a choice. A choice that comes before me. A choice that brings on my darkest, deepest insecurity, making me want to wrap myself into a selfish ball.

It's a sweet thing he's doing for that little girl, but what about me? Is it so awful to want a man that will choose me first for once?

My thoughts are dark. While his reasons for leaving were innocent and honest, and his apology is genuine, that's not what my mind focuses on. All I can think about is the little girl that still breathes inside me, still heartbroken and living with wounds cast by her father.

Insecurity breeds anger. The anger intensifies, making the corners of my eyes burn as tears threaten to surface. Of course, I hold them back. I'll always hold them back. Because I'll do anything to wash away the memories of these past weeks. Weeks that slowly opened me up to the possibility of trusting someone. Maybe even loving someone.

I've seen others fall in love. I'm a sucker for a good romantic comedy. But never once did I imagine myself in the place of the girl that gets her heart won over by the leading man. Not until Zach came along and demanded I give him a chance. I should have never listened.

Zach and I don't defy the odds; we *are* the odds. We were oil and water from the beginning, and that's not about to change anytime soon.

"Don't bother." And then I hang up … because it's done.

STEP SIX

Football Camp

"THE TRUTH IS, WE ARE NOT AFRAID OF BEING IN LOVE
WE ARE ONLY AFRAID OF NOT BEING LOVED IN RETURN."
— UNKNOWN

Surprise Visit

Monica
Fourteen Years Old

"Monica! Monica, wake up. Let's go. Now! I found it."

Maggie's voice was distant, as if I had drowned and she was trying to reach me from the surface. It took me a few seconds of her rattling my body around to bring me to full consciousness. Her tone was filled with excitement, which I knew could only mean one thing. "You found Dad's address?"

"Yes," she hissed. "C'mon. We need to leave before Mom wakes up. Let's go."

I tossed the bedcover to one side and moved quickly, following my sister's pace. Ever since she got her learner's permit, finding dad has been all she talked about. Oftentimes after the lights went out and mom was snoring in the next room, Maggie would sneak into my bed and we'd talk. She would tell me how much she hated modeling and that she resented Mom for not letting her quit. And then we'd talk about how much we missed Dad. Maggie would fill me with dreams of sneaking off in the middle of the night to find him. The way she told it, our reunion would be nothing short of a fairytale.

Maggie had turned sixteen the week before, and it seemed that her dream—our dream—was finally going to come true. We hadn't seen our father in nearly two years.

I was ten when he was injured. For the following six months, he fell into some sort of depression. And then he started to travel once a month. Once a month became once a week, and by the time I was twelve, he was gone.

He stopped coming home. Stopped calling. I was twelve when I realized that I didn't have a father anymore—not in the normal sense of the word, anyway. That was also the year the divorce was finalized and we moved to Rockwall, leaving Dallas behind permanently.

"Look, it's not that far from our old house!" Maggie said, her excitement palpable. That this didn't bother her like it did me was just one of the many differences between the two of us.

"Really? So Dad was our neighbor and still never came to see us?"

Her eyes never left the road as she spoke. "We don't know that. He could have moved back after the divorce."

Maggie was as careful and logical as they come. It must have been from all that work strutting the catwalk. Patience, timing, and grace were necessities for survival in the fashion world. Perfection was the only option, and Maggie was very much perfection.

My sister was the beautiful one: tall with killer legs, a slender frame, and sharp eyes that screamed for attention. I aspired to be just like her. It felt natural to want what she wanted, and seeing Dad again was no exception.

"Where'd you find this, anyway?" I asked, staring down at the empty envelope with my dad's name and address scrawled on it in familiar writing.

"Mom keeps a safe in the back of her closet. I found it last week when I was looking for jewelry for the party."

I stared at my sister's profile. Even in the dark, I could see the shine in her eyes, and the pride in her face. "What will mom do when she wakes up?"

"Freak out, probably." Maggie laughed. "Call us a million times. Then she'll probably call Dad."

"She doesn't have his new number," I reminded her.

Maggie's face transformed into one of fury. "You don't actually believe that, do you Monica? Of course she has his number. She clearly had his address." She ripped the envelope from my hands and waved it in my face as evidence. "She's been lying to us."

"But why would she lie? Dad stopped coming around long before we moved. He's the one who left." I took the envelope from her. "Pay attention to the road."

She huffed and faced forward. "You'll see, M."

I hated that she called me M. While the two of us were Dad's m&ms—Maggie and Monica—I was his M, and she was his Mags. The nickname just another painful reminder of what he left behind.

Maggie's face narrowed into the night with infectious confidence. "When we get to Dad, I'm sure he'll explain everything."

It was two in the morning when we arrived outside a beautiful brick home guarded by a tall iron gate. I hadn't been able to sleep during the hour ride there, especially with the anticipation of seeing my father again.

Maggie was certain that Mom was the cause of his disappearance, and I was starting to believe her considering all the facts. Mom was hiding letters from him, so she obviously lied about knowing where he was. But why all the secrets? And if she was lying to us, then why hadn't he been fighting harder to see us?

Maggie parked on the curb outside the gate and looked at me, a huge grin on her face. "We should probably wait until morning. I don't want him to get mad that we woke him up." She reached into the backseat and handed me a blanket and pillow. "Get some sleep, sis. Dad will be so excited to see us in the morning."

I believed her. I slept well that night and woke up feeling just as excited as she was. At the first sign of light, we hopped the fence and ran, giggling, across the perfectly manicured lawn. We dashed up to the white doors and stood at the lavender welcome mat on the front porch.

It was in the instant that the front door opened that my world started to change. I felt the shift. The first blow to my already aching heart. A blow that winded me from the first impact. Because I knew. When I saw the familiar raven-haired beauty holding a newborn baby in her arms … I knew.

I'd never forget that tightness in my chest when I awoke to that velvety voice in the hospital after my fall from the bleachers four years earlier. Two broken limbs felt like nothing compared to the pain I felt when I saw my father with the nurse.

Maggie, of course, didn't make the same connection. She'd never seen the woman before now, but beyond that I think she was in denial.

With a tug of her hand, I silently begged for us to leave. I didn't want to see my father and confirm what I already knew, but Maggie yanked her hand away and spoke to the woman, whose panicked eyes were scanning my features as if she'd seen a ghost.

"Hi," Maggie greeted her cheerily. "We're here to see our dad, Liam. Do you know him?"

The woman's eyes darted to the baby in her arms. "I'm sorry—I—how did you—?"

"Honey?"

A familiar figure appeared behind the woman. A figure I'd always thought of as superhero strong but that I quickly realized was anything but. His eyes caught her expression, and I'm certain he knew before he saw us.

Watching my father recognize his two little girls standing on his porch—one with a hopeful expression and one with utter devastation on her face—he was no longer that superhero to me. No longer the man I remembered idolizing and thinking about with unmeasurable love.

He was a fraud.

As if my heart hadn't already been pummeled, another little girl, this one a toddler, scurried over and clung to my father's leg. She had dried snot on her nose and long, ratty but beautiful dark hair. Someone should have been there to take their picture. A family of four stared back at us now—a beautiful family who had clearly created a life together, built as if another hadn't been buried in the process.

That's when my sister finally made the connection. The light in her beautiful brown eyes dimmed, her mouth fell closed and flat, and the perfect posture she'd trained for years to achieve slouched in defeat. Whatever hope she'd held onto died that day.

There we were, standing on the porch of our father's new home with his new family. A home we didn't belong in because we'd been replaced. Our Dallas home, my mom, Maggie, me—we'd all been replaced by this perfect picture before us.

The next few moments were a blur as the woman rushed her children inside and closed the door behind them, leaving my dad alone with us. He fell to his knees. His face crumbled, and tears quickly formed in his eyes.

He wept, and he apologized, and he tried to embrace us. I know I felt stiff in his arms. It had been two years of complete silence, and I now knew his betrayal started even before that.

But why? Did he not love us anymore? Did we do something wrong? Did he like them better? So many questions, but I would never get my answers.

Maggie wouldn't embrace him and grabbed my hand instead.

"You have another family?" I could feel her shaking through our conjoined palms. "You left us!" Her scream was so loud that I swear it rang through the air for several seconds while our dad buried his head in his hands and shook.

"I love you girls so much," he cried. "You weren't supposed to find out like this."

Something about that last sentence set Maggie off and she burst into tears. "I hate you! I hate you! I hate you!" Her screams were ear-piercing and heartbreaking, and my own silent tears came in a steady stream down my face.

"Mags." Dad's voice broke, but he knew there was nothing he could say to make this better for any of us. "You have every right to be mad, but please, just come inside. I'll tell you everything. Meet your sisters—"

I felt myself being yanked from the porch and down the driveway, otherwise, I was numb. I kept my eyes on my father, not wanting to leave despite my hurt. His eyes met mine. "M," he croaked, before his expression crumbled in agony.

He pleaded with Maggie to stay. Followed us down the driveway, even. Then he reached for me and clung to my hand. For the instant our hands were connected, I wanted to cling back ... but I knew I had a decision to make.

Stay with my dad, or go home with Maggie.

I chose her.

As much as I wanted to stay, to force myself to listen to what he had to say, to make him fix the hurt with that magic glue that always solved what seemed like life's biggest problems when we were little ... it was too late. Maggie and I weren't little anymore. Two years had passed since we'd seen our father, and this was our reunion.

So I left with Maggie. She needed me. I needed her. We were two sisters, lost and broken, but at least we were lost and broken together.

The Wheels on the Bus

Zachary

Chloe is the last person I expect to show up at Monica's front door early Saturday morning. My back and neck are stiff, my throat is dry, and my stomach aches from a forgotten dinner. I've been propped against the damn wall all night, waiting. Screw my morning workout.

The moment Monica hung up on me, her final words banging through my mind like a gong in a subway station, my heart overturned in my chest: *don't bother.* Such hurtful words from the brightest light that has come into my life in a long time.

I panicked. Only a few minutes from Clara's recital, I made a U-turn and called Monica back until my calls started going straight to voicemail. *What the fuck did I do?*

Circling the conversation in my mind, I texted coach to apologize for missing the event and then sped back to Monica's. After relentlessly pounding and desperately shouting her name, a neighbor popped his head out to tell me he saw her leaving five minutes before I had arrived.

I slept as best I could sitting up, dozing off every now and then, only to be awakened by every little noise, each time expecting the sound to be Monica walking down the hall. I imagined the conversation we'd have. One where I completely misheard what she said. Or maybe she was kidding. Because for the life of me, I don't know what could have caused that reaction. It was a little … explosive. Even for her.

Okay, sure, I'm an ass because I forgot that I already had plans. I forget things. My timing sucks, too. When I think about what was about to happen on that couch I want to drill my head into the wall behind me. But what was I supposed to do?

Chloe looks exhausted and doesn't even register me sitting by Monica's door until she almost trips over a sprawled out leg. "Zach?"

I rub my eyes, my body groaning as I shift up straight. "Where's Cakes?"

Chloe purses her lips and shakes her head, then inserts a key into Monica's door and pushes it open. "Gavin's getting her drunk ass on the bus. Come in. Help me grab her stuff."

As tired as I am, I jump to my feet and hold the door open. "Why hasn't she come home?"

I'm thrown a glare over her shoulder, something I never think I've ever seen from Chloe Rivers. "You should know, superstar. Probably the same reason you slept on the floor in front of her apartment."

"Seriously? So now you hate me too? She freaked out for no reason—at least she didn't give me one. But I guess I messed up by having other plans that I couldn't get out of—"

"Couldn't, or didn't want to? There's a difference, Zach."

"Look." Why am I arguing with Chloe when I should be talking to Monica? "As soon as I realized how upset she was, I came back here. But for her to get so upset over an honest mistake like that—it kind of freaks me the fuck out."

She shakes her head at me, her face hardened with frustration. "Maybe you don't deserve her."

I lean back on my heels, my own frustration tearing through what once was worry. "What? Chloe, I've done nothing but adore that girl from the moment this all started."

"You're lucky *that girl* even agreed to spend time with you last night," she retorts. "You haven't figured it out by now?"

The dumbfounded look on my face tells her that no, I haven't.

"Monica has only ever dated *safe* guys, if you can even call it dating. I don't think she's ever had a boyfriend. She prefers guys who don't expect much from her. You're the first one, Zach. The first one she even considered letting into her life in a more significant way." Chloe sighs. "She can't handle disappointment in relationships. She plays her cards just right so that she's never let down. In her mind, whatever plans you had that made you fly out of here were more important. And she doesn't know how to deal with that."

"But why? You're telling me she would have rather me disappoint a *little girl*—my coach's daughter—to prove that she comes first? Don't you think that's a little unfair and selfish?"

Chloe's expression transforms into sadness. "I don't know why. That's something you should probably talk to Monica about. There's one thing I do know, though. Monica is the furthest thing from selfish. Sure, she might have her heart locked up tight, but who's to say you're not the one to find the key? Monica and I have never talked about why she's so resistant to relationships, but I'm sure it has something to do with the shitty way her dad abandoned her family. I don't push her on it." She shrugs. "You don't need to understand someone completely to be there for them. If you love them, you figure out how they need you most and step up."

Huh. Not even Chloe knows what stirs Monica down deep. I'm not sure whether that's comforting or frustrating. But she has a point about all that other stuff.

We grab Monica's packed suitcase and duffle bags and head out the door. If I wasn't so pissed off I would think it was cute that I'm crazy about a girl who manages to fill an entire oversized duffel bag with snacks.

"Don't fuck up anymore," Chloe says as I take the first step onto the bus. "If she even gives you a chance to."

I narrow my eyes, ready with a clever retort, but Gavin steps up behind Chloe and wraps his arms around her. Suddenly, I remember something Monica said the other day, and my expression softens. "I heard about the engagement. Congrats."

Chloe grins and holds up her left hand to give me an eyeful of the massive glowing rock on her finger. *Damn.*

"Thank you," she says with a wide smile.

Gavin presses his lips to Chloe's temple. "Thanks, man. Hey, take care of our precious cargo in there. We'll see you guys on Saturday for the scrimmage."

"You're coming? That's great."

"Mastermind is a sponsor. I'm bringing a shit ton of comics for ceremony giveaways. I'm a fan of what you're doing, dude. Anytime you need help with anything, let me know."

Gavin's a good guy. "I will. Thanks."

I climb the short staircase on the bus and walk the aisle. As I search the rows for Monica, I'm slapping hands and knocking fists with my teammates, thanking them for coming.

It's in the back of the bus I finally spot a pair of dainty, pink, sock-covered feet splayed out in the last row.

So this is why Monica needed help getting onto the bus. Her hair is strewn out in a knotted mess and covering most of her face. One of her hands has fallen limply off the seat, and her mouth hangs open.

It's obvious that last night consisted of heavy drinking and light sleep. She's passed out cold, halfway to snoring, and taking up the entire back seat. I take the row in front of her on the other side of the aisle so I can keep an eye on her.

As much as I want to wake her so we can get this all out in the air, I'm grateful for the time to think. I need to figure out how the hell to get her to talk to me. Because whatever issues I thought we were moving past seem to only be surfacing.

Monica stirs, and that's all it takes for my eyes to lift. I'm not sure if I even went to sleep when my eyes fell shut, but if I did, it wasn't enough. Today is going to be a bitch. I groan and straighten just as Balko peeks at me through the crack in the seats a row ahead of me.

"Hey, Nut-Zach." I roll my eyes at the sound of his voice. *Gotta love team nicknames.* What started out as nutsack, my team's special term of endearment for me based on my sack-free season last year, quickly turned into Nut-Zach. I don't hate it. Don't love it either.

"Hey, dude." We knock fists.

I lift myself up fully to check out the rest of the passengers. Most guys are keeping to themselves, headphones on. Others are bantering back and forth. No one likes early morning wake-up calls, but it's cool that these guys were so willing to step up and take a week out of their vacations to do this.

"Who's the girl?" Balko asks, lifting his head quickly in a gesture that points straight to Monica, who looks like she's trying to get comfortable and force herself back to sleep. I'm sure she feels like crap.

"That's Monica. She works with the production team. She's been my right hand setting all this up. Didn't you meet her when you came into the studio for photos?"

His eyes go wide. "No shit. That's the hot chick from the shoot? The guys and I were just talking about her the other day. She had some little pleated Catholic schoolgirl skirt on." He groans, and I wish I could erase that sound from my mind. Instead, I smack the side of his head and sit back.

"Don't even think about it. She's off limits."

Balko laughs. "You doing her, or planning on it? That's not right. You gotta let her choose at least. A woman has her rights."

In no mood to fight over Cakes, I force the corner of my mouth to curl up into a smile. "She already made her choice, Balko. Try anything, and you'll eat my fist for every meal this week."

He turns around, but I'm aware of the amusement on his face. He loves a good challenge. "Damn, dude, chill. I get it. You boned her. Doesn't mean she wants your meat stick again, but it's cool." He shrugs, still facing forward. "You're marking your territory. But if she crawls into my bed tonight, you keep your paws to yourself."

I know Balko's intention is to rile me up, and it's working. I need to think of anything else to calm me down. Reactions are all he wants, and when he doesn't get them, it only makes him push harder.

I've known the guy for three years, and this is him one hundred percent of the time. Always infuriating. If he so much as got an opportunity with Monica, which he won't, he wouldn't back away from it no matter whose girl she was. He's not exactly a loyal dude, per his last two wives and multiple mistresses. He's a kickass tight end, though. That's reason enough not to pound his face for joking about Monica.

Another movement from where Monica's lying drags my attention to her. She's moaning a little, still appearing uncomfortable as she shifts in her seat. After a few seconds of hesitation, I cross the aisle and help her sit up against the window.

Her eyes flicker open at my touch and then narrow into a glare. "What are you doing here?"

I probably shouldn't laugh, but I do. "Checking on you. Here." I uncap my water bottle and hand it to her.

She stares at it, scrunching her nose and twisting her lips around. "No." She shoves it away. "You need to go home."

"You're on the bus, Cakes. We're heading to camp." I shift her feet and plant myself next to her, blocking her from leaving like I'm sure she's already considering.

She turns her cute head to look out the window and groans again. "Why does my head feel like I drove it into the side of a building?"

"Maybe because you got pissed at me last night and then got wasted with Chloe and Gavin. Only, I can't figure out why you got pissed at me and why you got so drunk when you knew you had to wake up early for camp." I check my phone for the time. "Looks like we have two hours left in this trip, so you might as well start telling me why you hate me."

She shoves her entire body into me, elbows first. I don't move—much. "Get over yourself," she says.

I turn my head, utter amazement and hurt on my face. She sees it but turns away, which just pisses me off.

"Get over myself? Monica, you are so far beyond selfish at this point, I'm not even sure why I'm sitting here."

I don't care what Chloe said. Monica may be a selfless person in general, but right now, she's *acting* selfish.

"Then leave." Her voice is quiet, shaky.

Fuck.

"No." I lean in, moving a knotted strand of hair so I can see her face. "Not until you talk to me about what happened last night. I messed up, Cakes. I'm sorry. I promised Coach's daughter I would be there, but I completely forgot about it because I've been so wrapped up in *you*. When he called, I panicked. I'm sorry I left like that, but how can you possibly be this mad?"

Monica hasn't turned to face me yet, but her expression has softened. "I'm not good at this, Zach. I'm no good for you."

I swear I see a sheen of gloss coating her eyes. But Monica doesn't cry, or so she's said.

"Most girls probably wouldn't freak out over what happened last night," she continues, "but I did. I'm strong most of the time, but not when it comes to this stuff. It's embarrassing. I'm sorry."

I sigh and lean into her shoulder. "Cakes, you don't have to be strong all the time. Let me be strong for you when you need a break. You've got me, you know? Whether you want to keep me in that safe pocket of a friend zone forever or finally let me have a chance to tackle you, I'm here. I'll always choose you."

"That was so cheesy," she moans.

I laugh. "But it's true."

She bites her lip and shakes her head. "But you won't. You proved that last night. It shouldn't be a big deal; I get that. But to me, last night *was* kind of a big deal."

I grip her chin softly between two fingers and implore her to look in my eyes. "I did choose you. But you wouldn't know that because you wouldn't answer your damn phone. I turned around. I came back to you. Slept on the floor outside your apartment all night. If you had shown up with a guy, so help me—" I shudder.

Her eyes widen and then shrink just as fast. "I wouldn't have." There's a pause. "You really slept outside my apartment?"

"Yes. Check your phone." She reaches for it, and I put my hand on top of hers to stop her. "Not now. Can I ask why it upset you so much?"

She shakes her head and turns back toward the window. "I'd rather you didn't."

I place my hand on her thigh and squeeze, then lean over and press my lips to her bare shoulder. "Okay." I pause, wondering if I should ask my next question. To hell with it.

"Did you at least have fun last night? Everyone looked pretty tired."

Her face does that cute scrunching thing. "I just went there to get away, but then Chloe dragged me to the bar, and I can't remember much after a few shots. I was upset and Gavin put everything on his tab, so…" She shrugs.

I chuckle lightly. "You'll be paying for that most of today."

"You don't need to poke the bear."

I poke her thigh playfully. She flinches and lets out a laugh. "Careful. I drank enough to unleash Washington apples all over you, pretty boy."

"Pretty boy? Really?"

She shrugs. "You are kind of pretty."

With this comment, whatever tension remaining between us floats away. I lean into her again. "I'd totally kiss you right now, but I'm a little afraid of your puking status."

A grin lights up her face. "Damn. And all this time I couldn't figure out how to keep you away."

We laugh, but I just can't shake something. I kiss her shoulder, breathing her in. Even after a hard night of drinking, wild strawberry and mint still lingers on her skin. "Cakes, you know I like you. A lot. I'm just having trouble figuring out how you feel about me. I know the attraction is there and all, but I want more than that. I want all of you." I take her hand, lace our fingers together, and squeeze. "You can't expect me to be a perfect man to you if you're keeping things from me. That's hardly fair."

She toys with my fingers one by one before she speaks. "You're right, but I'm not ready to make any promises. I can't." Her eyes flutter open to meet mine. I could live in those eyes. Die in those eyes. "If you can't be with me, I understand, Zach. I never promised this would be easy. I just admitted that I wanted to try and I wouldn't pretend that my feelings for you didn't exist."

She's right. Monica hasn't made any other promises, and I need to respect that, but it still hurts. I'm falling for this girl way faster than she is for me, and that's a first. It sucks, but I'm not ready to call it quits. Not yet.

"I'm not going anywhere," I concede. "But you need to give me something."

A sigh falls from her lips. "Zach," she pleads.

"Just hear me out," I say squeezing her hand. "I need you to give me this week. No walls. No overthinking this. Just you and me, Cakes." I brush my thumb across her cheek. "If you give me this…" I swallow. "I won't pressure you anymore. Ball will be in your court if you want to take this further."

Her eyes fall closed for half a second, and then she peers back at me with defiance that I think is more aimed at herself than me.

"Okay."

Camp Dakota

Zachary

We arrive at Camp Dakota just before noon and head straight for our cabins. If I had it my way, I would have stolen one of the cabins for Monica and me. But apparently being a celebrity and the organizer of this event doesn't earn me any brownie points with the facility director, who is adamant that boys and girls sleep on completely opposite ends of the camp. Which sucks because Monica will be the only woman here until tomorrow. I don't know how I feel about letting her sleep the distance of twelve football fields away ... alone and budded up against a thick of woods.

After our group grabs food in the cafeteria, we meet on the field. All of us: coaches, coordinators, some assistants from our training facility, and the production crew. Even Trevor came out to help us get organized, but he's taking off in the morning once Meredith gets here.

Monica's been busting her ass all day setting up equipment and arranging the production crew's storage unit, which will also be sectioned off for interviews under the bleachers. The cameras will face the field. That was Monica's idea. One of her many brilliant ideas that is making this event come together better than I ever could have dreamed.

I try to make eye contact with Monica as she passes out Under the Bleachers t-shirts to the staff. She's in the zone.

After our talk on the bus and her promise to give me this week, I'm antsy for attention. She's been within eyesight all day, but I still miss my Cakes.

There's no telling how much time we'll get together this week, and that only deepens the ache. I'll just have to get creative. The excitement of a good challenge stirs within me.

Turning back to my teammates, I walk them through the agenda, starting with everyone's arrival tomorrow. Most of the event details have been kept under wraps up until now to keep the focus on what matters. It was difficult enough to convince Meredith that we weren't setting up meet and greets and cocktail functions with the parents at the end of the week. If I had it my way she wouldn't be coming at all, but we do need her social media expertise.

It's nearing dinnertime when we break to throw the ball around for fun.

"Hey, Cakes!" I've got the ball in my hand and I'm supposed to toss it to Taylor, who's playing wide receiver about twenty yards from me. Monica's standing on the opposite side of the field watching us when her head snaps to me. I grin. "You got this."

The throw sails straight to her, but it's a little short. She manages to run and catch it, and then she tosses it back effortlessly.

"Damn!"

"Holy shit. Did you see that throw?"

"PA girl's looking for a new gig, Richie. Watch out now."

I don't know when or why the guys started calling Richland *Richie*, but it's already stuck.

Monica laughs and takes a bow for her new fans.

"Throw it again, Nut-Zach. She won't get it this time," Balko calls from the end zone.

I shake my head. "No way, dude. You'll try to crush her. We're just having fun."

Monica looks between us, then to me, challenge in her eyes. "C'mon. Throw it, Nut-Zach."

I throw my head back and laugh. Hearing those words come from Monica's mouth makes the nickname a little bit funny. "Don't call me that again, and I'll throw it."

She grins. "I gotta show your friend how it feels to lose to a girl."

Hoots and hollers come from the rest of the guys. Shaking my head in amusement, I step back and toss it extra short this time, but she already figured as much, so her timing is excellent. She clutches the ball and runs toward the end zone where Balko awaits her arrival. Instead of stopping her, or letting her go—which probably would have probably been the better option—he swoops her up by the legs so she's hanging over his shoulder and carries her toward center field.

"No one gets past this tight end!"

It's all fun and games until Balko slides his hand up Monica's thigh, and I don't think he'll stop until he reaches her ass. And because it's Balko, he turns to me and winks. *Oh, hell no.* I drop the ball and stalk after them. "Hands off, Balko. You know the rules."

"What rules? There are no rules," he calls back, picking up his pace.

"Let me down, Balko," Monica says. "You're going to piss off the gorilla."

He sets her down and they laugh together as I close the distance.

"You're a real slimy bastard, aren't you Balko?" I spit.

He slaps a hand into my chest and starts jogging backward. "I think she liked my hands on her, dude. Maybe it's love." If that isn't bad enough, he looks at her and winks. "Nice ass, sweetheart."

My blood boils, and I start to go after him. I'm going to give him his damn reaction, and he's going to be sorry for it.

"You two are going the wrong way!" Monica calls as she takes off toward her cabin. She turns and jogs backwards, grinning, and then points to the other side of camp. "The cock-fighting arena is that way." She laughs at her own joke.

"Not funny, Cakes," I warn.

"Aw, c'mon, Zach. You two could dress them up and everything." There's an annoyingly huge smile on her face. "And then I can vote for who wore it better." With an overly cheerful wave, she retreats to her cabin. Behind me, Balko howls with laughter.

Sleeping Arrangements
Monica

I won't tell anyone this, especially not Zach, but I'm freaking out.

Zach drops me off at my cabin after dinner, and after a lingering kiss that's far too tentative for my liking, he's shooed from my porch by a security guard carrying a flashlight. Rules are rules.

Rules are also meant to be broken.

As Zach leaves, I slip him my key. His eyes widen and he smiles before jogging off into the dark. I immediately lock my doors, take a shower, and climb to the top bunk.

I stretch out under the small window that frames the moon, and after five minutes of rereading the same line of the climax of the latest Kristin Hannah book, I closed the case to my Kindle and sink beneath the covers.

There's an overpowering weight on my heart and mind when I think of the past twenty-four hours. The intense grind session at my apartment that was one phone call away from something more. The raging inferno in my chest when Zach ran out the door—away from me—to get to his coach's daughter's recital. Which of course led to the drunken meltdown at Gavin's house after. And then our conversation on the bus ride here … and my promise to him. One week.

What happened last night is the exact reason I avoid relationships. If my father—the man who was supposed to raise me, protect me, love me—could trade in his family for an entirely new one without a backwards glance, how am I supposed to believe that someone I choose to love won't hurt me the same way? Or worse.

Zach has the power to obliterate my heart.

My thoughts are interrupted by a light tap on my door and the sound of a key meeting the lock. I jump halfway out of my skin. I knew he was coming, of course, but this middle-of-the-woods-alone thing reminds me of the horror movies my sister and I would secretly watch late at night when we were kids.

I throw off the covers and jump from the top bunk to the floor to greet Zach just as he slips in, a mischievous smile on his face. "I haven't had to sneak around like that since I was a teenager," he says.

He leans against the door, breathing heavy. "I ran the long way around the woods so no one would see me. Wonder what they'd do if they caught me. Kick me out?" This is as cocky as I've ever seen him.

"You're not above the law, you know. What kind of example are you setting for the kids?" I raise my eyebrows, testing him.

He tilts his head. "I don't see any kids around here, Cakes." His roaming eyes move to my legs, pausing at my boy shorts, and then continue up my bare torso, coming to a stop at my half camisole top. Let's be honest; we both know he's not just here to make sure I sleep safely. I didn't wear this for myself.

My heart does crazy somersaults as he slowly approaches.

I back into the ladder, knowing I'll need the support. "I'm glad you showed up. This whole camping thing is not something I signed up to do alone." I push out a breath of air with my smile, but it catches in my throat.

He's standing in front of me now, his fingers lightly drifting up my sides. His mouth moving to his favorite place between my shoulder and my neck. "I'm with you now, Cakes." He kisses that spot that makes me shiver. It's the lightest touch, but it reverberates through my entire body.

Breathe, Monica.

He knows what he's doing to me, and I know he's smiling by the way his mouth is parted on my neck as it travels up to my ear. He nips at my lobe and breathes out, sending a rush of chills over my body. When he moves his lips over my mouth, I think I might come undone. "Do you want me to kiss you?" he teases.

God, yes. I swallow, bringing a nod with it.

He just smiles, his fingers gently brushing the tips of my breasts over the cloth of my camisole. He looks down at where he's just touched and groans, then bites his bottom lip. His eyes drag up to mine, effectively trapping me. "You like it when I touch you, Cakes?"

My head falls back to the base of the top bunk with a thud in response.

He chuckles. "I think you do."

My breathing joins the chaotic symphony in my body when his hands fall to my waist and he dips one finger under the elastic. He doesn't go far he just runs a finger along the edge between my skin and my shorts. Teasing. And then his eyes flick up to catch my half-closed eyes watching him. Waiting for the torture to end.

"Tell me what you want me to do, Cakes." His husky tone barrels over me until I'm filled with sensations too strong to ignore. The moment his lips brush the silky cloth covering my hardened nipples, I've already forgotten his request.

"Hmm?" His question rumbles low in his throat.

I inhale sharply as a finger dips lower into the waistband of my shorts, slowly gliding down until my insides are clenching with anticipation. Just as quickly, his finger moves from my shorts dragging a feather light touch up my stomach and beneath my camisole.

He reaches the curve below my breast, and that's when my lids fly open to find him studying me, amused but with a hint of vulnerability that tells me this is more than some selfish need he's trying to fulfill. He's always been patient. Gentle. And now is no exception.

"Cakes. I need you to tell me what you want."

This answer. I think he's asking for more than I can give him, but I give him the truth. "I want you." I swallow. "All of you."

Zach leans forward and kisses me lightly. I have the urge to shove my fingers in his disheveled hair and pull him to my mouth until neither of us can breathe. To make him forget whatever he needs to hear, because I know he's hesitating.

"Is that fair," he asks, "when you won't give me all of you?"

His question threatens to extinguish the fire we've started. I wasn't expecting that. I look away, but he quickly uses his fingers to turn my head back to him.

"You promised me this week. No walls, remember?" He breathes me in deeply and leans into my neck as he exhales through his mouth, blanketing me with warmth and soothing the rise of panic that started its journey through my stomach. "Help me understand why I'm not enough."

Emotion grips my throat and stings the back of my eyes. "Is this about Balko?" I grasp his waist. "Zach, you are more than enough. And I want everything you want. *Everything.*"

The way I answer—with desperation and regret—makes it clear there's more to it than I'm saying. He knows it, which is why he continues examining me, waiting for more. When I don't give it to him, he sighs and pulls away.

The hope in his eyes transforms to frustration, hurt, and anger all over again. And once again, it's my fault. He's worth more than what I'm keeping from him.

So I make a decision. I turn and take the ladder up to my bunk, stopping at the top and looking back. "There's something I want to tell you." There's another moment of hesitation before he follows.

Maybe I should have evaluated this sleeping arrangement a little better before we got on this single bed together. Zach's a monster of a guy. He's too tall to straighten out, so he pulls his knees in, unintentionally pushing me against the wall. I laugh and turn my body so my back is to him, giving us both room.

He adjusts the blankets so I'm completely covered but leaves his arms out, wrapping them around my body and pulling us closer. I'm thankful to be facing a tiny window where the moon is clearly visible above the trees. It calms me as I struggle with my thoughts, wondering what I could possibly say to help Zach understand what has me so conflicted. This isn't just about me getting hurt. It's about him … and protecting him from things he can't even imagine.

"I've seen first-hand how football rips families apart," I start. "How you can be completely in love with someone one minute, promise them the world, and then fall out of love another minute." I take in a shaky breath before continuing.

"One injury on the field changed so many lives. Not just mine, Zach. Maggie's, my mom's, my dad's... One day we were the happiest family with dreams so big, no one could touch them ... and then the next day we were broken."

I tell him everything about the night Maggie and I drove to my father's house to see him again, only to find that he'd replaced us. He's quiet the entire time, tightening his hold at the parts I struggle to say out loud.

"It still makes no sense to me, you know? How he could just walk away from a life he worked so hard to build. A life he truly loved at one point. We're always encouraged to follow our dreams. But dreams can make you selfish. He loved his dreams so much he wanted us all to be a part of it. And we were all consumed with it.

"When you fulfill your dreams, it's like a drug. It shoots you up and you're flying high, completely oblivious to the real world at your feet—until you come down off that high. My dad didn't just come down, Zach. He crashed, and he burned, and he dragged us all along for the ride until there was nothing left. That accident was the end of my father's dream, but it was the choices he made that led to the destruction." I turn to face him, hammering my point home. "What happens *after* you've lived your dream? What are you going to do then? When the high is gone and *you're* the one standing on the sidelines?"

I don't wait for him to answer.

"Dreams change," I continue. "People change. And I'll never ride on the coattails of anyone else's dreams again."

The first tear falls, but it's not mine. Somehow I'm still holding it together. Zach, on the other hand is gripping me tighter than he was before, and then he's peppering sweet kisses along my neck, my back, and my shoulder. After a few seconds, I turn to face him and wipe the lone tear from his face. That's when my throat tightens and my own tears threaten to come.

I'm colliding into another reason why it's hard not to fall for this man. He's vulnerable in the most beautiful way. I haven't even given him all the details of my story and he's already impacted by it. Which is why he can't know everything. The truth would break his heart.

He moves his forehead so it's touching mine and takes a deep breath. "What if I told you that you're my dream? More than football, more than the kitchen. I don't know how, Cakes, but in the months I've gotten to know you, you've managed to unlock something in me.

"People have always asked me to describe my perfect woman. Each time I would give them a different answer because I didn't know. I never thought I had a type. But things changed when I finally saw you. The next time someone asks me that question, I'll know exactly how to answer. Because it's you."

"I don't know what to say," I whisper.

He shakes his head. "You don't have to say anything, Cakes. Just give me this week. Give me the chance to prove that I'm someone you can trust … and maybe even love."

I stare back into his eyes under a faint blue glow cast on his handsome face.

Just one week.

He sighs when I say nothing, then leans in toward my lips. "All I want right now is to kiss you," he whispers.

"I hope you do more than kiss me."

His answer is in his smile.

Our lips dance together as we help each other out of our clothes. Zach rolls on a condom, and then tests me with his fingers. I'm ready for him. His eyes fall closed for a second as he realizes the same thing. We've had enough foreplay in the past eight months to last a lifetime. All I want to feel is our naked flesh pressed together.

Heat swirls through the room with the friction between our bodies, connecting through our hardest and softest places. But mostly, he's just kissing me, promising me this will be more than sex. More than the intense hunger we've always had for each other's bodies.

We're like this for a while, dragging out every pleasurable moment. And then he fills me, rocking into me slowly with confidence and strength that could command an army.

How can I deny this man who makes me feel so incredibly whole and wanted and loved? It's a sweet, tender, and symphonic love that I hope never leaves us. It's his heart and mine. Melding together with each thrust. I meet each one with acceptance, asking for more as my fingers press down on his skin, ensuring we're as close as physically possible.

With my legs squeezing around his waist, his strength reaches the deepest parts of me. Injecting my soul with our intense and undeniable connection.

He alternates between kissing me and watching me, his breaths growing heavier with exertion. By the erratic pounding of his chest against mine and his half-closed eyes, it's obvious that he's ready and waiting for me.

Always waiting for me.

I run my nails down his back and grip his muscular ass, pulling him deeper as I feel the first sign of my release. My mouth finds his, but our lips only brush against each other, too focused on other things.

Zach practically sighs with relief when my muscles clench around him and I let out a muffled cry. We let go together.

As much as I tried to fight it, I know I lost this battle long ago. So I concede.

At least for this week, I'm his.

Dreams Above Fear

Zachary

I love her. That's why for a full afternoon of greeting the young athletes and their chaperones as they stepped off the bus, I can't get her off my mind. The feel of her hips grinding into me. The taste of her watery lips as I pressed her into the shower wall this morning. Her gasps of warning each time she was close to letting go.

But more than anything, I remember the way her flawless skin looked in the moonlight. I've always thought of Monica's beauty as something special. The kind that doesn't need moonlight to make her glow. If anything, it's the moon that benefits from her radiance.

I was already falling before today, before yesterday. But when Monica started talking about dreams and her fear of them—it only made me confirm what I already suspected.

Screw her father for walking away from the best thing he's ever created. Who would break a little girl like that? Her father broke her heart, and she'll be incapable of giving it to anyone else until she can let him go.

"Coach Zach, you didn't call my name."

I place my hand on the little guy's shoulder and lean down, my clipboard in my other hand. "Sorry about that, buddy. What's your name?"

"Desmond White."

I grin. "Well, Desmond, I happen to have a best friend with that same name. Nice to meet you." I shake his hand, causing his face to light up.

"Let me see." I check the clipboard until I find his name and then walk him over to Sydney, Seattle's running back. "Sydney, I think you've got an all-star here. You're gonna want to keep your eye on this one."

I spend the next hour making rounds as the coaches introduce themselves to their teams and go through some basic training exercises. I can tell the kids are ready to make the most of this week. So am I.

Sometimes I forget there are cameras following us around this event. Like now, when I turn and almost run smack into one. Monica laughs from behind Buddy, and the sound lifts me above the clouds. I give her a wink, wishing I could do more than that. Every time I see her, I want to pull her into the nearest hiding spot and kiss those lips. Or better yet, kiss her smack on the lips in front of everyone.

Unfortunately, I've had to settle for less obvious displays of affection, like when I find a reason to brush by her just so that I can slide my hand along her back, or when I lean in to tell her something and graze my lips against her cheek.

Lunch comes and goes. Monica disappears under the bleachers for a few hours while she conducts an interview with some of the kids who are willing to get in front of the camera. And then after dinner, I invite the coaches onto the stage for the opening ceremony. We roll the intro video showcasing a snippet from each of the guys and their definition of leadership. It's successfully motivating and has everyone cheering by then end. Then each coach gets a chance to introduce themselves in person.

When it's my turn, I step forward to the microphone. "This week is very special to me," I begin, "so thank you all for coming. I know you're all eager to hang with the pros, get some tips, and go back home to completely dominate your competition—am I right?"

The cheer is thunderous, and it makes me laugh.

"Good!" I shout back. "Let's take a second to talk about that right there. Never lose that. That fight. That dream." My eyes dart to Monica, hoping she doesn't read too much into my words, even though they are somewhat directed at her. "Not everyone is afforded an opportunity like this one," I continue. "Not everyone is afforded the opportunity to realize their dreams the way that you have. Imagine this for one second." I look around the room at the boys' expectant faces. Waiting. "Imagine loving football so much, but you're told no. No, you can't play because you can't afford the uniforms … you live in the wrong neighborhood … you're not good enough.

"When I was your age, it was a privilege to play ball. To step into a team and prove myself every single day. But who was I proving myself to? Tell me: who are you here for? Are you here for yourselves?"

There's a hesitant cheer. I laugh. "It's okay to admit it. That's what this week is about. Are you here for your team?"

This cheer is louder, and I smile. "*That* was the correct answer." I wink at a boy who had gotten it wrong, and he chuckles. "This week isn't just about you and all the things you'll learn to improve your game—and trust me, you *will* improve. It's about improving so that we can be better for each other. For our team." I point to the guys behind me. "For our brothers." There's a deep cheer from behind me. "For our family."

I reach for Balko and pull him forward, wrapping an arm around his shoulders and pointing at him. "This guy wouldn't be half as successful on the field if it weren't for me."

Everyone laughs except Balko, who shakes his head dramatically.

"But I wouldn't be half of anything without him either." I push Balko back in line, making everyone laugh again.

"We lift each other up. We're honest with each other. And we encourage one another. That's what leaders do. And football will give you an opportunity to be a great leader if you let it."

I jump down from the stage and walk down an aisle. "Raise your hand if you know someone who can't play ball even though they want to."

Half the hands go up immediately, and then more slowly join them. I stop for a second and look around. Heat rises in my chest, and I shake my head. "That's no good. We need to change that. Will you guys help me change that?"

Everyone cheers.

I grin before locking eyes with Monica, who's clutching her clipboard to her chest. "Good," I say without releasing her from my stare. "Because everyone deserves to live out their dreams. Fear simply isn't an option."

It's movie night on the field. The kids don't mind a little drizzle as they sit on their blankets to watch *Little Giants* on the projection screen.

At some point after dinner and before the movie, when the clouds started to roll in and the sky threatened to open, Monica sprang into action, instructing the crew and coaches to cover the bleachers with a giant tarp to protect the production equipment underneath.

Once I know everyone is settled and focused on the movie, I search for Monica. She shouldn't be hard to find. As one of the only girls here, she's quite the hot topic among the boys. Well, now that Trinity, Grace, and Meredith are here, they might be topics too, but my ears only perk up when I hear Monica's name mentioned.

I spot her sitting with her crew on the sidelines, laughing at something onscreen. I move around the back of the bleachers, careful to avoid Meredith. She's been trying to get my attention all day, and I've been making it a point to ignore her. Sandy doesn't know my plan yet, but she'll be fired after this event anyway, so I'm not worried about her little tantrums anymore.

I sit beside Monica, nudge her with my shoulder, and shoot her a smile. "Hey."

"Hey," she whispers, a shy smile lighting up her face.

It's no secret at this point that I'm into this girl. My team knows, Richland knows, and I'm sure the rest of the crew does too. Based on the looks I'm getting from Meredith and the rest of the PR team, they seem to be catching on as well. I don't care, but unfortunately, Monica does.

I resist the urge to pull her away from the group to bury my face in her neck and tell her about my day. Instead, I'm a good boy. I wait until the movie is over, help the crew secure the equipment, and walk Monica back to the cabin she's now sharing with my PR team.

Once everyone has taken off in their own directions, I take her hand and hold it to my mouth, placing a soft kiss on her knuckles. We're nearing the front of the cabin when she pauses, holding me back from rounding the corner.

Monica leans against the side of the cabin just as we hear the door close, shutting out high-pitched laughter. Finally, she takes a deep breath and looks up at me.

"What are we hiding for, Cakes?"

She sighs. "I'm here for work and there are more of us now. And let's just put this out there: Meredith has the hots for you. I don't think she would appreciate that I've stolen your attention."

I make a face. "I'm pretty sure she's onto us. Everyone is. But you still want to keep this a secret?"

"I don't," she says forcefully, clutching my shirt and pulling me toward her. "Don't do that, okay? Don't start looking for reasons to pull away. Not now. I promised you this week, and I'm going to give it to you."

After last night, I'd better get more than one week. I can't even think about that right now or I'll start a conversation I know she's not ready for. She has no idea how impossible it would be to let her go, not when I feel like we're already connected in the most important ways. All I can do is nod and swallow my true feelings. She's not ready for them.

"Thanks for walking me back."

Gripping her waist, I let my head fall. "I'm going crazy knowing I can't stay with you tonight."

The twinkle in her eye tells me she already knows this. With a tug of my neck, she pulls me toward her so our lips are almost touching. "Show me what I'm missing, hot stuff."

A breathy chuckle slides past my lips as I accept the challenge. I kiss her softly at first, meaning to pull away and leave her with something, but she nibbles on my bottom lip and I forfeit. With a dip of my tongue, I slide between her lips and deepen the kiss.

My hand slips easily between the back of her jeans and her skin. I groan at the silky softness of her ass. "Damn it. Why does it feel like I'm a horny teenager with a curfew?"

"Because it's only ten o'clock," she laughs. "And you are horny." She rubs against me teasingly. "But you have an early morning tomorrow."

I shake my head. "Not me. The coaches have an early morning. I start making my rounds at nine."

She pouts. "Well then, you're spoiling yourself. I'll be out there at six. Shouldn't you be out there too if your team will be? Lead by example, right?"

She has a good point. "But it's so early!" I exaggerate my pout to make her smile, and I know it works because she reaches up on her tiptoes to kiss me.

"I'm not ready to let you go," I whisper against her lips.

Monica sighs. "Me neither."

Well, that just makes me more determined.

"Text me when the girls are asleep," I say with a wicked smile. "I have an idea." I swear her cheeks deepen in color, but it's impossible to be sure in the darkness.

"Okay."

It's almost midnight when Monica finally messages me. We meet in front of her cabin and then run through the darkness to get to the football field. The security guard is making his rounds, so we wait for him to leave the area before sprinting for the bleachers.

The truth is, I paid him off earlier to not harass me this week, but Monica doesn't have to know that. The light in her eyes at our adventure sparks something in us both I can't imagine losing.

The bleachers are still covered in the enormous tarp, protection from the rain from earlier today. It's basically one giant tent, closed on each end. I detach the Velcro so that we can slip inside, and then I seal it back up carefully so passersby won't have a reason to check things out.

Once we're inside, I use the flashlight on my phone to find the setup I prepared for us. I lined the ground with a thick packing blanket, placed the couch cushions stolen from the interview setup on top, and then covered the cushions with my sleeping bag. I found some white holiday lights thanks to my new security guard friend and strung them across the light stands to give our bleacher fort a dim glow.

Monica laughs softly when she sees what I've done. She lets me pull her down onto the makeshift bed so that we're lying together and she's cradled in my arms. When we're finally settled, I let out a heavy sigh. All this effort is totally worth it now that I have her in my arms.

"Finally."

She makes a cute little noise and snuggles into me further. "You were amazing today with the kids. Your speech … you were born to do this, Zach."

"Thanks, Cakes." I rub her back. "It feels good. It's hard to know if I'm really making a difference, but at least we can all have fun in the process."

Her fingers run over my unshaven chin, which I've let grow out a little more than usual. The way she keeps playing with it, I think she likes it.

"I imagine when you have someone to look up to, someone you respect, it's hard not to be affected by that. The most beautiful part," she says, "is that you're changing these kids' lives without forcing anything down their throats. Before my sister realized she wanted to act, modeling was her dream and I believed it was mine too, but that's because it's the only option I ever explored. And when it got taken away, I was lost."

I frown. "Don't look at it like someone took your dreams from you. You're the only one in charge of those. If you wanted to model, you could, but I know that's not what you want. Cakes, I'm confident you've chosen the perfect path for you."

I must say the right thing because she slips her smooth fingers under my shirt and lifts the fabric over my head. Her sultry eyes zero in on my chest before her lips press against it. She's kissing the skin directly above my heart, and I swear it starts to beat out of my chest.

"Thank you." Her voice is soft, making my throat constrict with emotion.

I kiss her head. "When do classes start?"

"June."

She tells me about the classes she'll be taking, and I fall in love with her a little more every second she speaks excitedly about her future.

Monica has been through a lot with her father, her mother, her sister. Hell, her entire family abandoned her—but she's far from given up. She's making her own life, and while there have been roadblocks along the way, she's continued moving forward. That's the most important part. I think she's finally starting to put her dreams above her fears now that she understands what her dreams are.

Parallel

Monica

Every night, no matter how exhausted we are from the day's events, we sneak off to the bleachers once the girls are asleep. We lie on our makeshift bed, me tucked snugly in Zach's arms, and tonight is no different. It's Thursday, giving us only two more nights together before the week I promised him is over. He hasn't brought it up since the first night, but I know the conversation is coming. We're both in too deep at this point to bury these moments in the past and call it quits.

We talk about growing up, mostly. He tells me stories of his high school football days. The scouts that wanted to meet with him. The schools he debated between. In the end, he didn't want to leave Texas since his brother and mom were still there, and the University of Texas gave him an opportunity he couldn't turn down: a full ride, and with the current quarterback graduating the following year, chances were good that Zach would get a lot of time in the spotlight.

"If it wasn't for Coach Reynolds, none of this would have happened," he says with pride.

I can tell there's a part of him that thinks about this often. That wonders what would have happened if this man hadn't saved Zach and Desmond from destroying their futures with reckless behavior, if he hadn't shown them how to work together instead of against each other.

"He sounds like a very important part of your life," I say softly.

Zach nods and swallows, and I wonder if he's getting choked up. "He gave me a chance I don't think I deserved."

I reach for his arm and latch on, squeezing. "Of course you deserved it. I'll bet he's proud of giving you that chance too. Just like you gave Desmond a chance. You paid it forward. And look at what you're doing for these kids."

He smiles. "It is cool how it all played out. See, Cakes," he says as he tilts my chin so I'm staring into his eyes. "Not all of us football players are bad. Some of us learn early in life that there are certain things you don't mess with: dreams, family, and love. I learned that when I was sixteen. I had a great mentor."

My heart sinks. "Not all of us are that lucky, Zach."

"Yeah, we're not always lucky," he admits, rubbing circles on my back with his palm. "But sometimes life offers you second chances in ways you don't expect. What if I'm yours? I'm not your father. I know what he did to you broke your heart. If I could change that for you, I would. I'd carry your pain forever if it meant you'd open up to love again." His hold tightens around me and my breath catches in my throat. "Let me love you, Cakes. Tell me you're ready for this. For us." He tightens his hold around my waist as if afraid I'll vanish. "I can't imagine all of this ending in two days."

His words cut deep, latching onto the innermost parts of me. Looking back into his eyes, I take a ragged breath. It feels like everything I've been through has led me to this moment. A moment where I have a chance to choose between the future and the past. That's a choice I'd never given myself before Zach. How could I possibly look to the future when my past still haunts me?

"You can't love me, Zach." Tears fill my eyes. He only clutches me harder.

"Too late."

After I get my breathing under control, I roll onto my back and look up at the rows of bleachers beneath the tarp. Since the day I took Zach to my field, the memories have been freshly present at the forefront of my mind.

"One of my favorite things to do on Saturdays was hang out with my dad at the high school football field near our house. He'd run the track and I'd play on the bleachers. It was raining one day. I was skiing across the top step, slipped and fell through the division in the stairs. I landed all wrong and the fall knocked me out."

"Jesus," Zach mutters. "Your dad must have been scared shitless."

I laugh, because looking back on that day—the look on his face as he was running toward me like he knew something awful was going to happen...

"He was terrified. He couldn't get to me through the bleacher steps. The space was too narrow. So he grabbed a pair of shears from his truck and ran around to the back of the stands." I feel Zach's body go rigid, but I continue. "There was a fence, so he had to cut his way in."

I wait for it, because I know he's making the connection. "Um, Cakes. What field did you say that was?"

I bite my lip. "It was Brighton. The shared high school stadium in Dallas."

When he pulls away, his eyes are a bundle of confusion. My heart is going crazy in my chest.

"I thought you were from Rockwall."

I nod. "We moved from Dallas after my parent's divorce."

"That's the same field I—" He pauses to assess my reaction and sees that I've already made the connection. "You knew?"

I sigh. "When you told me your story that day on the field … I figured it out, yeah."

"And you never said anything to me?"

My jaw opens but words don't come out. He gives me a reprieve, rolling onto his back and moves his hands through his hair as he considers everything he knows. When he turns to face me again, his expression is full of emotion, and I'm not sure how to make sense of it.

"I always wondered who made that entrance. Hoped one day they'd come back so I could thank them. That first night Desmond chased me, I was scared shitless, and I swear I thought I was going to die."

He stares at me, still registering everything. We lived in the same town at some point. We didn't know each other then, but we're connected—because of those damn bleachers that almost killed me, and saved him.

"That was you?" he asks.

I nod, and then let out a soft laugh. "Well, it was my dad."

He swallows. "I knew there was something about you, Cakes." His finger moves to my cheekbone, running over it gently before pressing his lips to mine. "It's serendipitous. They should make a movie about us."

My laughter falls into his mouth because he doesn't know the half of it, and then he's kissing me again. I pull away slightly to speak against his lips. "Sorry to break it to you, but *Serendipity* is already a movie."

He grins. "Then call ours *Under the Bleachers*. And don't even think about turning it into a drama. It's a rom-com. The guy gets the girl in the end. I won't have it any other way."

My smile falters as my heart thrums in my chest. "You don't get to direct your own movie, Zach."

He kisses me again. "I'll do whatever I have to do, Cakes. I'm not letting you go. One day, you'll trust that."

In a heartbeat, the mood changes from light to heavy as my feelings for Zach take hold of every part of me. There's no denying this.

I swallow. "When I woke up in the hospital there was a nurse talking to my dad. I remember how nice she was … and so incredibly beautiful … but I just got this strange feeling when I saw them together. My mom was away on a shoot with my sister. Just a few towns over, but my accident wasn't enough to bring them home." I swallow, because this might tear me apart to speak aloud. "That was the day they met."

"Who, Cakes?" His hand gently caresses my arm, but nothing can soothe this knot in my stomach and weight on my heart that I've carried for so long.

"My dad and his new wife. He married the nurse, Zach. When she opened the door for Maggie and me—I figured it out. If I hadn't fallen from the bleachers that day…" I stutter through the thickness in my throat and the liquid filling my eyes. "It's all my fault."

He holds me tightly, kissing my cheek with trembling lips. "No, baby, no," his husky voice demands gently. "Look at me, Cakes." He wipes the tears as I pull my head up to face him. "Your father made some shitty decisions and that's not your fault."

I don't know why it feels good to hear someone say that, but it does.

"I'm not him," Zach says. "I would never, *ever* hurt you like that. Do you still doubt that after this week?"

I shake my head as another tear rolls down my cheek, knowing exactly what I need to do now. "No, Zach. I do trust you. That's why I've made a decision." I swallow. There's so much at stake now, but Zach can't know anything else until I do this. "I'm going to talk to my father."

Monica

It's Friday, the night before the scrimmage. Monica and I have spent every night this week wrapped up in each other's arms, confessing the secrets of our pasts under the bleachers.

It's fitting. It's like we've been living succinctly parallel lives, just waiting for our paths to finally meet. Monica is what I've been waiting for my whole life. I know it.

I try to push down the ball in my throat as I imagine what her life must have been like without the man she'd adored for so long. How it must have felt to see him happy and living life with a different family. One she was never invited to be a part of. Not only was the man remarried with two children, but he'd obviously started that family while he still had another. Disgusting. No wonder Monica has such little faith in men.

"How are you going to find him?"

"I know where he lives," she admits.

And there it is. The unfinished business she's been holding onto so tight. Everything is starting to make sense.

"He's the reason I moved to Washington. It's been almost three years, and I haven't been able to confront him yet."

"Are you sure you're ready now?"

She nods, her eyes flitting between mine as if trying to tell me something she doesn't want to say. "I don't have a choice. I need to let him go somehow, and confronting him is the only way."

"I think it's the healthiest thing you can do."

"I think so too." She sighs. "My mom is furious at me for coming here. She doesn't want me to see him. And my sister—we still talk, but she doesn't get it." Monica shudders in my arms. I can't imagine living with a secret like this.

"Baby, I'm sorry." My voice is raspy as the burn licks flames into the back of my throat. I'm a fucking wreck over this girl. "You're making the right decision." What else can I say? There's nothing I can do or say to take that pain from her. I can love her. I want to love her, but will she let me?

"Look at me."

She wipes her tears and looks up, her eyes begging for something, although I'm not sure what. It crushes me that I don't know how to make any of this better. I'd do anything.

"He fucked up," I say, my voice stronger now. "And he lost the two greatest things that ever happened to him. I'm holding one of them now, and I can't even imagine how or why he could let you go." I shake my head. "I'm not him."

My voice cracks, and I pull her closer, planting my mouth in her neck.

"You're it for me, Cakes. I love you. Every single piece of you. Broken, whole, I don't care. As much as you've tried to push me away, it only helped me get to know you better, and I love you. Everything about you—your cluttered apartment, your lack of cooking skills…"

I kiss her neck again as she laughs.

"Every laugh," I add softly as I lean back to look in her eyes, then I touch her lips with the tip of my finger, skimming their outline. "Every word that comes out of this sexy mouth." I swallow. "I could kiss these lips forever."

And then I do kiss her, and I can feel her surrender beneath me.

Layer by layer, she allows me to peel her clothes from her shaking body and kiss every inch until I'm sliding between her legs, slow and deep. But she only lets me lead for so long before nudging me onto my back like it's the most natural thing in the world. It is. And I can feel her response as her soft and beautiful body rides me. She might not be ready to say she loves me yet, but I feel she does and that's enough for now.

I shift, lifting my upper body until my back is pressed against to couch to bring us closer so I can kiss my favorite spot on her neck. As always, she smells and tastes like wild strawberries and mint. So fresh and sweet I have to stop myself from devouring her whole.

I cup her breasts, pulling one into my mouth as I wrap an arm around the small of her waist, tugging her down so I'm filling her whole.

She's gasping my name and telling me she's close.

"Not yet, baby," I plead, raking my fingers through her hair and gripping her neck. I watch her eyes close and feel her hips slow their pace. "Good girl."

I'm pulling her lips onto mine, greedily licking into her mouth as if teasing a flame with a stick of dynamite. It doesn't take long for the rush of adrenaline to claim us. Monica trembles with her release, muscles contracting around me until my head is bursting with lights.

I feel everything she's giving me: desperation and passion. And then I'm filling her with my everything, because there's no question that this is us loving each other in the most intimate way possible.

Ready or Not
Monica

It's up to me to finally let go.

What I realize now is that my fear of confronting my father is less about feeling rejected by him all over again, and more about the fact that there will be closure—whether that closure is good or bad. But I'm finally ready to handle either outcome.

I'm no longer a teenager who needs her father to complete her. I've proved that I can adult just fine on my own. What I'm looking for is a way to accept my past, because until I do, I won't be able to accept my future.

I've never told a soul about falling through those bleacher steps. Because I've always felt like that was the moment everything in my life changed. My dad's accident was a week later. I had just gotten out of the hospital wrapped in arm and leg casts. It was like the fall knocked me out and I woke up to a completely different life.

Although I hadn't planned on opening up to Zach this week about my father, it felt like the right thing to do. And it felt good to get it out. Besides, he has every right to understand why there's push and pull on my end. Everything he feels, I feel too, but there's still a line I can't cross. Not until I confront the man who broke my heart nine years ago.

I'm finally ready to trust in someone's love. I'm ready to let Zach love me.

I smile as I throw on my Under the Bleachers production crew shirt, ignoring the impatient pleas from Trinity and Gracie for me to hurry up while Meredith taps her foot by the door. She's given me nothing but glares this week because she knows. Everyone knows. But at this point, I don't care. I'm tired of hiding.

"I just need to use the bathroom," I lie. "I'll meet you at the field." Finally, they leave me be.

It's the last day at camp, and I'm pumped to shoot the all-day scrimmage. Everyone will be here to cheer on the kids, and then afterwards will be the ceremony to celebrate everything the kids and coaches have accomplished this week.

But before I walk out of the room, there's something I need to do. *Let me love you, Cakes,* he'd said. *Tell me you're ready.*

I grab a pencil and scribble two words on a piece of paper before folding it and shoving it in my pocket.

I'm ready.

I rush out the door to find my cabin mates huddled together, whispering about something. Based on their silence when they see me, my guess is that something is me. I smile at them as if I couldn't care less—because I couldn't—and keep walking.

Luckily I haven't been forced to spend much time with the gossip queens this week, what with my busy work schedule and the fact that I've spent every free moment with Zach. As tired as I've been each morning, I haven't cared an iota. I love falling asleep in his arms every night, waking up just before dawn to scramble back to our cabins.

"Where did you run off to last night?" Gracie calls from behind me. Her voice is causal, but I know better to assume her question is innocent.

"Nowhere," I say, my tone even with hers. "I was asleep in my bed the entire time." My back is to them so they can't see my smile.

"We saw you leave with him, Monica," Trinity says, her nasally voice grinding against my ear drums. She sounds proud of herself, as if she's uncovered some vast conspiracy. "How long have you been seeing Zach?"

My face heats. "That's none of your business, Trinity. I'm not trying to be rude, but please stay out of my personal life."

Trinity doesn't like my honesty. Her eyes narrow, and then she flips her hair over her shoulder. "I couldn't care less about you. *Zach*, on the other hand, is our business. We get paid to know these things, so enough with the niceties. Is it serious between you two? Because if it is, it's not something we can ignore."

"Stop!" Meredith cuts in. "All of you."

She narrows her eyes at me. "No one's going to say anything because there's nothing going on. Right, Monica?"

I shrug, averting my eyes.

Meredith laughs dryly. "Of course nothing is going on. Zach wouldn't be caught dead dating a PA with no life goals. That would make for horrible press, wouldn't it?"

A surge of anger rips through me, and I whip my head around to face her. "Excuse me?"

Her mouth twists in a wicked grin. "You heard me."

I narrow my eyes, cueing up the darts and locking in on my target. "Not everything is a tabloid opportunity, Meredith."

"Oh please, calm down." She rolls her eyes. "No one would believe you two were together, anyway." She shoots a look at Trinity and Gracie. "Which is why we aren't going to dig any further."

I wish I could believe her. "You know what? You *will* ignore it because it's none of your damn business," I snap. "You're not here to snoop on Zach and get material for a gossip column. He's paying you to capture the event. Do your job and stay out of our business."

"Zach *is* my business, honey. Watch your tone."

My body courses with adrenaline. I take a step in her direction, lowering my voice as I focus on checking my emotions. "You don't get to call the shots in either of our personal lives."

She sneers. "Everyone knows Zach has a thing for his publicist. I'm afraid that's the story we're going to roll with. His fans are already speculating, and knowing Zach, he'll do anything to please them. And me."

I don't have a chance to retort. She pushes into my shoulder with hers and stalks off toward the field. The girls follow, flipping glances at me over their shoulders and giggling like freaking twelve-year-olds.

As heated as I am about the exchange with Meredith, it's not the time to dwell on it. It's scrimmage day and we're expecting buses to start rolling in this morning with family and friends of the kids. Everyone's already on the field preparing for the day we've all been waiting for.

I'm surprised to spot Gavin and Chloe near the bleachers, talking to an animated Zach. I knew they were coming, but didn't expect them until later.

"Chloe!" I squeal.

I run toward them, throwing my arms around my best friend and hugging her until she's peeling me from her body. I've missed her so much.

She laughs. "Nice to see you too."

Zach moves behind me and Chloe's eyes immediately widen and pan between the two of us. I grin. "So," she grins. "How's everything going?"

I reach behind my back for Zach's hands and wrap them around my waist. "The week has been perfect."

He tightens his hold and nuzzles into my neck. "Perfect, huh?"

"Mhmm," I say, turning to kiss his lips.

It was just supposed to be a chaste kiss to let him know I'm not hiding this and neither should he. But he pulls me in and straightens, lifting my feet from the ground. Relief floods my body, and I'm not exactly sure why. Maybe it's because I'm finally letting myself fall in love. Or maybe it's the liberating feeling of not caring who's witness to our affection.

I hope Meredith is watching now. I'll deal with her wrath later. And if it gets back to Sandra, I'll deal with that too.

When Zach sets me down, I take the folded piece of paper from my pocket, reach around him and wedge the note between the elastic of his briefs and his skin.

"Whoa, handsy lady!" he jokes. "There are kids here."

I roll my eyes and pat his waist over the letter. "Open that later."

He leaves me with a grin and a kiss on the head and then takes off.

My heart feels lighter than it has in years, and I know it's because of Zach. I watch him jog toward the approaching kids and sigh, oblivious to the stares Gavin and Chloe are giving me.

"Does this mean you'll have season tickets again?" Gavin's always got jokes. I laugh and watch as his face turns serious. "Don't you dare give them away."

Chloe pushes Gavin to the side and steps in front of him. "Hey, friend, care to tell me when you started sucking face with Zachary Ryan in public?"

"About five seconds ago." I smile. "I'll tell you everything later. I promise."

She grins. "You look happy."

"That's because I am." I jump and turn toward the bleachers where the crew is setting up for the first set of interviews. "I'm gonna go find Richland."

My jog to the other side of the field and under the bleachers only takes a few seconds, but that's all the time I need to spot him. Staring at the field through the bleacher steps, much like I did six years ago at Brighton's homecoming game, it's déjà vu.

Standing in the end zone across the field is Coach Reynolds. *My father.*

I don't move a muscle as I watch Zach toss him the football, which lands safely in his hands. I'm frozen as I observe the celebration that follows as my heart freefalls into the pit of my stomach, landing with a solid thud.

All this time spent pushing Zach away was out of fear that our worlds would collide before I was ready. And here it is.

My dad moves around the field with Zach, smiling brightly and introducing himself to the excited young players as they arrive—as if he's some sort of damn hero.

It's been a long time since I've seen that smile in person. Even after everything that's happened, I find it just as magnetic as ever. That smile—directed at the man I've fallen completely head over heels for.

They're walking with their arms around each other toward the bleachers now, and I realize Zach's searching for something. Me?

Shit.

When they start walking toward me, I panic and start off in the opposite direction. To where, I have no idea. All I know is that I'm walking away from an inevitable confrontation.

Five minutes ago, I was slipping a note in Zach's waistband, ready to move forward and finally confront my father. Only then would I tell Zach the rest.

When I moved to Washington to confront my father, I never expected three years would pass before I would work up the nerve to talk to him.

Falling in love with Zach was never part of the plan.

One thing is clear now: I'm not ready. For any of it.

Coach

Monica

It's easier than I expected to hide from Zach and my dad the entire day. At one point they step under the bleachers to record an interview, and I excuse myself to go to the bathroom. No one questions it.

As soon as the games are done, the award ceremony begins, and Richland points for me to stand on the side stage. "I'd rather hang back here," I argue.

"What's up with you today?" he asks. "It's not a choice. I need you on the side stage with Buddy. Go."

I groan and follow Buddy and his camera, doing my best to use him as a shield. The peculiar sideways glance he gives me tells me he finds my behavior strange. Doing my best to appear normal, I stand back, jotting down time codes and listening for cues in my headset.

Everything is going smoothly until the players pass by us with Coach Reynolds leading the pack. I duck behind Buddy, and he eyes me strangely. "You are extra weird today."

I just need to get through this day.

Not long after, the event officially kicks off and Zach takes the stage to give his opening speech. For a few minutes, I get so wrapped up in all the excitement I almost forget my dad is here. That is, until Zach calls him up onto the stage.

"This week has been about many things," Zach says into the microphone, looking out over the crowded bleachers.

Richland mentioned they counted over fifteen hundred attendees today, not including media. That's got to make Zach happy.

"It's about stepping out from under the bleachers, standing up, and leading when you're on *and* off that field," Zach says, scanning the audience.

"I think we've all learned a lot this week. I know I have. And I'd like to share something a little personal if that's okay. Is that okay?"

Everyone cheers, including the young players sitting scattered around the field and everyone sitting in the bleachers.

"Most of you know Coach Reynolds, right?"

More cheers.

"For the last four years, he's taken Seattle through two Super Bowls and a division win."

Still more cheers erupt from the stands.

"But Coach Reynolds and I go way back. I knew him before I even moved to Seattle, back when we both lived in Dallas."

Knots form in my stomach as Zach motions for my dad to come up to the stage.

"When I was growing up, I was a scrawny kid. You know the kind: full of dreams, but with none of this." He holds up his arm and flexes, causing a roar of laughter to break through the crowd. I smile, unable to help it.

"Unfortunately, there was a kid at my school who thought it would make him feel better to pick on me because of it. He tormented me. I sat alone during lunch every day. I'd hide under the bleachers to watch the games, because you better believe I wasn't missing a single one." He grins and puts a hand on my dad's back. "I lived in fear. But guess what happened next?" He pans the crowd.

"I got tired of the torment. I ran the track after school to get faster. Worked out a lot to bulk up. I did all of this not so I could play football, but so I could run faster when my bully came after me again." The crowd is still, immersed in his every word.

"Why didn't he give this speech at Heroes and Legends?" a voice whispers in my ear.

I jump, surprised to find Chloe standing behind me. "Why aren't you with Gav?" I whisper.

She shrugs. "He's helping Richland out with something." We both turn back to the stage as Zach continues.

"It worked," Zach says. "I became bigger than my bully, and I was faster too. But here's the thing: I thought fighting this kid with my fists was the answer. I was wrong. The reality is, you can't fight a bully by being one." Zach looks at Coach Reynolds and laughs. "This guy right here taught me that. He sat us kids down and said something I'll never forget.

"He said, 'Imagine what you could do if you were on the same team.'" Zach nods emphatically. "Yeah. Imagine that. And then he showed us what he meant. This guy right here put me and the kid who threw me in trash cans more times than I can count on the same team. He gave us a break. He gave us a family." Zach pats my dad's back, his voice cracking. "And he taught us how to be leaders.

"If it wasn't for Coach Reynolds I might still be lost." Zach smiles as my dad squeezes his shoulder in a warm acknowledgement.

Seeing the affection between these men that I love—one who wants nothing to do with me and the other who wants to share the world with me—creates a physical ache in my chest. Tears are streaming down my face before I can stop them because my reality is staring me painfully in the face. Coach Reynolds—my father—is Zach's hero in every sense of the word. How can I take that away from him by telling him the truth?

Now it's my father's turn to speak. "I couldn't be prouder of ya, Zach," he says. "It's true, you know, what this guy tells you about leadership. He's one of the best leaders I know. He seized an opportunity and made magic out of it. Not everyone can do that. Not everyone recognizes an opportunity when it's handed to them. This week was one of the many opportunities you'll get in this life, so don't take it for granted. You learned from the best this week. I know because I coach 'em."

Everyone laughs.

Then my father turns to Zach and hugs him from the side. "I'm proud to call you family, son."

Family.

Son.

Then a thousand things seem to happen at once, setting off a chain reaction that will change everything. Applause breaks out. Chloe tries to get my attention because she knows something is very wrong, but I'm unable to respond. Zach steps off the stage and spots me. It's too late for me to hide again.

Everything is happening in slow motion, and all I can do is watch.

"Hey, Cakes! There you are." Zach takes me in his arms and hugs me. "That was pretty intense, I know."

It's at that moment, with my cheek flattened against Zach's chest, that our eyes connect for the first time in nine years. Both of us are speechless. At least he recognizes who I am.

Zach is wiping the tears from my face, but I'm too numb to react.

Then he hooks his arm around my shoulders and turns to my father. "Coach, this is the girl I was telling you about. Monica, this is Coach."

I step backwards, nearly smacking right into Chloe.

My dad steps forward, pain breaking through his shocked expression. "Monica..."

I step back again and Zach looks between us, confused. Then something in his face changes as he starts to put the puzzle pieces together.

"Cakes..." He reaches for me unsteadily, waiting for me to confirm it all.

I take a final step back, giving him nothing.

And then I turn and run to my cabin.

Left Behind

Monica

Chloe's on my heels, but hers are the only footsteps I hear, so I keep running. I get to the cabin a few seconds before her and start throwing clothes into my suitcase.

I need to get out of here. Now.

As I wedge in a pair of shorts to make them fit, I suddenly begin sobbing all over again. I'm not even sure why I'm crying. It's not like it was a surprise to see Zach and my father together. It's not like I didn't know what I was getting into with him. It's all my fault because I knew, and I kept it from him for so many different confusing reasons.

The next thing I know, Chloe's arms are around me and she's guiding me to the nearest bed. "Monica, oh my God. what just happened back there?"

I throw myself back into the pillow and hiccup through a few breaths before I think I can speak. "It's awful. *I'm* awful."

"No, you're not," she says gently. "Whatever's going on will be okay. I promise."

"You don't even know!" I wail.

She gives me a moment to regain the tiniest bit of composure, and then I give her the bullet point version of the story. As I speak, I can almost hear the questions roaming through Chloe's head, but she's silent until I'm done.

"But you're from Texas."

I groan. "So is Zach. We're both from Dallas. After my parents' divorce, my dad got a coaching job at the local high school, and my mom took my sister and I to Rockwall to live with my grandma."

I want to scream, so I do. I grab the nearest pillow to muffle most of the sound. Chloe, being her amazing self, doesn't even flinch.

"It's complicated, Chlo," I continue. "Jerry Springer complicated. The same year Zach was getting saved by my father, my sister and I were getting our hearts broken. It was awful. We showed up on his doorstep after not seeing him for two years only to find him living happily ever after with his new family."

"Jesus," she breathes. "What do you want to do? We could go. I'm sure Richland will understand. Gav and I could drive you back. I'll stay with you tonight."

I sit up and nod. "I can't stay here. I'm not ready to face either of them right now."

The knock on the door is loud and commanding. I know it's Zach. But why? The ceremony can't possibly be over yet.

Chloe jumps up and opens the door before I can say anything, and Zach pushes his way inside. He just stands there near the door, staring at me wearing a look of hurt, confusion, and anger.

Anger. He's pissed at me for knowing and not saying a word to him. After all the nights we've spent together, confessing everything. He thought he knew *everything*.

And he has every right to be angry. He's only ever asked for the truth.

"Can you give us a minute, Chloe?"

"Zach, I don't think—"

"Just a minute. I have to get back to the field." He turns to her again, pleading. "Please."

I give Chloe a nod, so she steps out the door and shuts it behind her.

Zach doesn't move, and I don't know what to say.

"You could have told me," he finally says.

I cringe. "I was going to tell you everything after I talked to him. You didn't tell me he was coming here."

"I didn't think I had to!" he yells. "Coach Reynolds is your father?"

A tears slides down my cheek and I nod.

"God damn it, Monica. Coach? He's a good man to a good family. The man you talk about is evil and heartless. I hate that man!" he yells. "How could you keep that from me? I told you I loved you!"

The reality of his words hits me hard. I've always known there was a chance he wouldn't want to be with me after he found out the truth. That's exactly why I kept pushing him away.

"Were you planning to end this all along?"

Shit.

I shake my head emphatically. "Not after this week. I told you I wanted to confront him, and I meant it. I knew it was the only way I could finally move on. But you need to understand something. When you told me how much he meant to you, what he did for you—as much as it hurt me, I knew it would hurt you even more to know what I know. He doesn't deserve the pedestal you've put him on. But I have no right to tell you that, do I? Your experience with him is at the other end of the spectrum from mine. The man you know *is* different. I have no right to take that away from you. I don't want to."

Zach bows his head and clenches his fists. "What about last night?" Then he reaches into his pocket and pulls out the note. "What about this?" He throws the paper at me, letting it flutter angrily to the floor. "You're not ready. You'll never be ready."

I cover my face with my hands, and my shoulders shake as I release another sob. "I *was* ready."

"I thought you told me everything. I thought that's what this week has been. But no, you've kept the most important part of yourself from me."

I wipe the tears from my eyes with back of my hand. "You think *he's* the most important thing about me?"

"You know what I mean, Monica."

"This isn't something I go around bragging about to people, *Zachary*."

"But it's not people. It's me!" he roars.

"I know!" I shoot back. "I'm doing the best I can. I moved here to forgive that man, but it's been almost three years now. *Three years* of me trying to get up enough courage to see him, and then he just shows up here. I wasn't expecting to deal with this today."

"You think I was?"

I've never seen Zach furious. And the fact that his anger is directed at me hurts even more. "I warned you this wasn't going to work. I tried to tell you."

"No, Monica. You tried to lie to me. Never once did you try to tell me anything. It was always me prying information from you, wanting nothing more than to protect you from this pain." His face darkens even more. "But you're right about one thing. You did warn me to stay away. I'm sorry I didn't listen."

I gasp at the same time he turns for the door and throws it open. It bounces against the closet and swings back with a slam.

A moment later, Chloe bursts in to find me shaking. "That didn't go so well?"

"Of course not," I heave. "He's just like my father. Selfish and heartless. And once again, I'm the one getting left behind."

And then I wipe my tears and march to the closet to pack the rest of my things.

Too Much History

Monica

"You're not, you know?"

Chloe's driving us home in Gavin's truck while he stays back to help Richland since I got violently ill on the job. At least that's the story we're going with.

It's been silent for a while now. After telling Chloe everything, she's been giving me time to reflect on the morning's events.

"Huh?"

She looks at me briefly before turning back to the road. "You're not getting left behind. You said that earlier, and I can't stop thinking about it. I hate that you would even think that. Everybody loves you, including those two men back there. There may not be a simple resolution, but I can see in their eyes that they want to fix this."

My head falls back against the seat and I turn to inspect my best friend for damage. "You're way too optimistic, Chlo. What do you think happened back there? My dad showed up, horrified to see me once again, and Zach hates me for ruining his happily ever after. Sure, I could have spilled my guts before to prevent this day from happening, but *this day* was never supposed to happen."

Chloe reaches across the armrest and grabs my hand. "Trust me," she says, "I know why you kept this from Zach. It was your secret, and you barely knew him. There came a point where maybe you should have told him, but Monica, none of this is your fault. It's nobody's fault. It's just a result of years of heartache that finally came to a head."

"Now you're being too nice. If I'd just come out with it, Zach and I could have talked through everything. At least then he would have known the truth before falling in love with me."

Chloe shivers. "This feels all too familiar." I know she's thinking about her explosion of a fight with Gavin after she found out he'd been keeping something huge from her.

"You're right," she concedes. "It's good that you can admit when you're wrong. But at the same time, it's not black and white, so stop beating yourself up over it. Here's what it comes down to: either you and Zach are destined for each other, or you're not."

"You really believe in that shit, don't you?"

"Yes," she responds firmly. "I do. I also believe that things happen when they're supposed to. All of this, what happened today, is a result of what your father started years ago. If anyone should be carrying blame and guilt around, it's him. Not you."

There's a burning in my chest and I pound on it. There's no way I'm spilling more tears over this disaster that's become my life. "You know what really snaps my heels?"

Chloe laughs. "What?"

"The fact that in any other situation, if my father hadn't 'saved' Zach"—air quotes around saved—"then he would have never walked away from me back there. He would have been on my side, consoling me. He'd be furious at the man that left me, just like he was when I told him the stories."

"See?" Chloe looks over at me. "You're blaming yourself again. You can't compare this situation to anything else. Think about it from Zach's perspective—"

Oh my God, I'm going to scream. "I have!" I let out an aggravated noise. "Every single time I wanted to tell him, I thought about his reaction. And surprise, never once did my predictions include us driving up into the clouds in a red Ford convertible."

Chloe laughs. "You should really stop watching that movie so much."

"There's nothing wrong with *Grease*. Anyway, I could say that same thing to you about *Teen Witch*." I raise an eyebrow. Got her.

"Fine. Go on."

I smile half-heartedly. "I think I was making a point."

"You were worried about his reaction."

"Yes!" I smack the leather on the door and throw myself against the seat again. "You should hear the way he talks about my father. He worships him."

Chloe gives me a curious glance, and I know what questions are coming next. "Tell me this: how long were you aware of Zach's friendship with your father? Did you connect the dots along the way, or—?"

"Since I was sixteen." I swallow. "When I got my license, I would drive to Dallas to see my dad's high school team play. Not every home game, but most of them."

"Holy shit."

"I don't know what to do, Chlo."

Chloe's expression softens, and she squeezes my hand. "I know. And I'm going to be here for you the same way you were there for me. Whatever happens, Monica, at least now it's all out in the air."

I snort. "It's in the air, all right. Let the shit storm commence."

Chloe and I have already gone through the bottle of wine and the box of chocolates I had stashed above the refrigerator while talking through three movies, and now we're curled up on the couch. My eyes feel heavy and I think I hear her snoring when I try to let myself relax and just go to sleep. Having Chloe here has been the best distraction. I'm not ready to be alone with my own thoughts.

As I feel myself drifting off to sleep, male voices on the other side of the door put me on alert. I pull myself off the couch and peek through the peephole. I see Zach and Gavin arguing on the other side, but their voices are too muffled to make out.

I can't ignore the lurch in my chest when I see him. After he walked out of my cabin earlier, I didn't expect to see him for a while—if I ever saw him again.

The guys' voices get louder, and Gavin steps into Zach's personal bubble. *Great.*

I fling open the door. "Can you two stop bickering?"

Gavin turns to me to speak, his words dripping with annoyance. "Sorry, Monica. The bus dropped us off at BelleCurve and I was coming by to get my keys when I saw this guy."

"Thanks for the escort," Zach responds, just as irritated. "I'll take it from here."

I narrow my eyes at Zach while stepping aside so Gavin can go find Chloe. Once the door closes, I let it all out.

"Wow," I start. "You're really committing to being an asshole today, aren't you?"

He backs up slightly and tilts his head. "Excuse me?"

Crossing my arms across my chest, I tilt my chin up. "You heard me."

"I came here to see you."

"Why?" I feel my breathing quicken, but I hold my ground.

He searches my eyes and then takes a step toward me, leaning against the doorframe. "To talk," he says sincerely. "To apologize. I don't really know."

My bottom lip trembles, so I take in another deep breath to get ahold of myself. Zach steps closer. Next thing I know, my back's against the door and his forehead lands on mine. We're both breathing angry, heavy breaths, challenging each other with our eyes.

"I should have never said what I said," he whispers gruffly.

I sigh, wishing this brought me some relief. "There must have been truth there if it came out of your mouth. You didn't even hesitate. Go ahead, think the worst of me."

He smacks the doorframe with so much intensity that the walls shake behind me. Then he pushes away, stepping back until he's up against the opposite wall. "You want to know what I was thinking?"

I shake my head, because he can't take back these words that are about to leave his mouth, and I'm too chickenshit to welcome them.

"Too bad. We're finally being honest with each other, so I might as well tell you the truth. I was wondering why God would be so cruel as to play us against each other when all I want is to love you. To protect you." He shakes his head adamantly. "I can't do any of those things now. My happiness is your pain. My hero is your villain. I hate the man you've told me about with a passion. He watched his life crumble around him, and then he turned away from the only thing he had left: his family.

"But that man isn't the same one I know. I can't hate him, Monica. I feel like that's what I'm supposed to do here. I'm supposed to be *your* hero. But he's—"

I can't take it anymore. "Then why did you come here?" My seething words are quiet, but firm. "It's all out in the open now. You know everything about my life: my past, my present. God only knows what my future will be like. You shouldn't have come here."

He covers his hands with his face and drags them down before dropping them, helpless. "What do I do, then? Tell me. He's still my coach, and that's not going to change anytime soon. We can't erase either of our pasts, Monica. We're parallel lines that magically derailed and hit a crossroads. That collision was the best thing that ever happened to me—"

"Until the debris cleared and you had a decision to make, right? Is this your way of telling me you've made your choice?"

His eyes are bloodshot. His hair disheveled. Shirt wrinkled. For the first time since I've known Zach, he looks lost and defeated. "I lose either way, right?"

The pain in my chest is as real as it was that day I saw my father with his new family. This is it, all over again.

"You're doing it, Zach. The one thing you promised me you would never do. You're making the same choice that he made. You're breaking my heart." I try to contain my shoulders from shaking and the panic in my chest, but it's taken over my body.

The tears begin to spill down my cheeks as he watches me with shock and pain. "How the hell did I break something that was never even mine to break?"

"That's cheap," I spit out. "You've been trying to get me to fall in love with you for weeks, and then I do, and you act like it never even happened." I push off the wall. Now it's my turn to sound defeated. "Go home, Zach. The sooner you do, the sooner we can forget any of this ever happened."

Give Me Tonight
Zachary

I don't know who should be mad at whom. I'm shaking when I leave Monica's apartment, and I'm still shaking when I arrive at my Jeep. After talking myself out of going straight back to her place to dish it out some more, I force myself into the car and slam my fists into the wheel.

That wasn't what I wanted to say at all back there. The apology, yes. But then I was going to kiss the hell out of her and tell her that we had to make this work. I was going to tell her that I never expected her to come along and steal my heart, but she did. And I only ever wanted to protect her. Why didn't I say any of that?

The truth is, all my feelings from earlier today came tumbling back the moment I saw her face. But she didn't give me a chance to make a choice. She lied. And now we're left with the fallout.

I hate myself for being the exact person she was trying to shield her heart from. That's not me. She's worth so much more than the way I'm making her feel right now. I should have stayed, forced her to talk to me.

"God damn it!" My fist flies into the seat beside me, the cushion taking the impact of my blow. Even pissed off at the world I'm able to think about my throwing hand.

A set of headlights appear, distracting me from my own head. When I see a couple through the front windshield, I look closer, recognizing Gavin's truck. I take it as a sign.

They both left, which means Monica's alone. Without a second thought, I jump out of the Jeep and run back to her apartment. I use the code she entrusted me with when I was picking her up for our last date—the one that involved chocolate covered strawberries—to let myself into the main building, and then I jog upstairs to the second floor and knock on her door.

Seconds later I hear footsteps and then silence. "Cakes, I can hear you. Let me in."

Silence. I wait.

Finally, I hear the latch click. The door opens. Just one look at her puffy eyes and the tissue in her hand destroys me. I may not have been the one who initiated the pain, but I'm the one twisting the knife. This may be the end of me and Monica, but I'm not going down without a fight.

I step inside and let the door shut behind me. We stand only a foot apart, but I make no move to touch her. Not yet. After a single deep breath, our fearful eyes gripping each other, I finally speak.

"I choose you." My voice cracks with every emotion that's been building all day. "I'll always choose you. But it's not me that needs to make a choice. It's you. Are you letting go or holding on? Your past can't be your future too."

Her head moves back and forth, stubborn as hell. "I need time to sort this out, Zach. It's too much right now. We haven't even had time to think."

"What's to think about? I want you in my life." When she's silent, I sigh again. "You don't have to make any decisions tonight." I move in, using both hands to tilt her head to look up at me. I press my lips to hers. They're lacking some of that firmness that I love, so I deepen the kiss, feeling her come alive beneath my grip. She responds with a shudder. That's when I finally pull away. "Give me a chance to leave you with a reason to choose your future. Choose me back."

Searching her eyes, I'm silently begging for her to say yes. She's owned me from the second her eyes met mine above that dessert cart, but it's time I take some of that control back. At least for tonight.

She nods, and I give her no time to rethink her acceptance. My mouth is back on hers and I'm giving her everything I've got. Not a second later she's kissing me too. We're devouring each other, our hands in a frenzy, ripping off each other's clothes. And as soon as our shields are cast aside, I carry her into her bedroom and lay her down gently, never taking my mouth from hers.

We make love without uttering a single word. We don't need to. Our connection grows more intense with each second that passes. There's nothing rushed about tonight. We take our time, the pleasure as sweet as it is heartbreaking. She's my world, and if I only have tonight to show her that, there will be no holding back.

She lets me take complete control—something I need tonight. Maybe it's my fear of losing her. Maybe it's to show her that despite everything that's happening, I can still love her deeply. And as much as I need to give, she needs to take. Tonight, she's different. Tonight, she's raw. Tonight, she's completely mine.

I'm aware of every breath and sound that passes her lips. Her moans only fuel my adrenaline. I'm attuned to every touch as her fingers skim the length of my back and then dig into my skin when the intensity becomes too much. And I know with each arch of her back that she needs my mouth where she can feel it reach her core. I read her like I read poetry: slowly, admirably, intensely, until I'm reading her all over again, because once is never enough.

I give her everything I think she wants. Everything I know I need. But it will never be enough—not if I can't have her forever.

Respect
Zachary

The training facility is quiet, but I know Coach is in his office. It's where he can be found most days whether we have practice or not. He always says he thinks best when surrounded by the dream. It's why he was there that day to break up the fight between Desmond and me. He was studying the next opponent, visualizing plays and preparing pep talks. Little did he know he would find two lost souls battling it out on the field.

The door to his office is open, but I knock anyway. He stares off into the distance as if he's in some sort of trance, and he doesn't react to my approach.

"Coach."

My voice makes him jump. He sits up, pulling his shoulders back as he addresses me a little too formally. "Zachary, this is unexpected."

Although we're close, Coach Reynolds is the ultimate professional. Favoritism doesn't exist in his world. It's always about the team—when we're at work. Everything changes when I'm stopping by for dinner or attending one of his daughters' events. That's when I take on the role of a family member, and life is just as it should be. Those are the moments that have always meant the most. The moments that replaced the deep tunnel of loneliness that swallowed me after my father's death.

"Sorry, Coach. I'm sure the last thing you want is another surprise." I hesitate for a second and decide not to take a seat. I'm not in a cordial mood, and I'm not planning to stay.

He lets out a breath—not a sigh or a laugh, just a breath. "I'm going to guess this visit is a personal one."

I nod, giving him complete honesty. "It is." Except I don't know how to start. There's so much I want to ask. So much I want to say.

I guess all I can do is start. "Nine years ago you saved me from a troubled life. From a hole so dark I didn't think there was a way out. I'd lost hope. At sixteen, that darkness can set the precedent for the rest of your life, but you didn't allow that to happen to me. You took me in. Gave me a team. Opened your home to me, and then to my brother and my mom. I'm forever grateful for those gifts, Coach. For the first time in a long time, I knew what a family was supposed to feel like.

"I've looked up to you … in football, sure, but as a husband and father too. And I'm sorry, Sir, but a man who can leave his children without so much as a goodbye is neither of those things. Monica told me everything about her dad, and I judged him as someone I'd never met. I promised myself if I did ever meet him, I'd let him have it. So…" I swallow. "That's what I'm doing now."

He stares back at me in silence. I see the heavy rise and fall of his chest, and know he's calculating his response, but I don't give him time. He needs to hear this.

"You can see my predicament now, Coach. What you did to those girls was abandonment. It was cruel." My voice is rising with my anger, and I'm not sure how to stop it. "Thanks to you, she may never open her heart to let anyone else in.

Thanks to you, she's broken ties with her family back in Texas to deal with her pain. Thanks to you, she learned what a broken heart was at the ripe age of fourteen. How does that make you feel, Coach? Do you sleep well at night, knowing what you did to them?"

"That's enough!" he shouts, slamming a fist on his desk.

But it's not enough. In the blink of an eye, this man I've looked up to for so long has suddenly become a stranger. A fraud.

"You want to know what she remembers about you?"

Coach stares back at me, face unchanging. *I'll take that as a yes.*

"She remembers the man who taught her how to throw a ball forty yards without breaking a sweat. She remembers her hero on and off the field. Someone she was so proud of. You know, she never lost hope that he'd find her one day.

"Unfortunately, she also remembers the man who didn't take a second glance in the rearview mirror when he drove off to start a new life. When you left, you ensured that no matter how hard a man loved her after that, she'd never believe it. And do you blame her? How could she ever trust any man after what you did?"

My voice cracks and I take in a breath before continuing. "I don't understand. You give *everything* to your team and to your family. Why not Monica and Maggie?"

Coach looks unsettled as he takes short sips of air through his nose. "It wasn't my choice to leave those girls, but I was damned sure I wouldn't let anything like that happen again."

I let out an angry breath. "No choice? That's what you'd call a cop out, Coach."

I can't control the rage blasting through me now. This isn't the man who taught me about integrity and honesty. This isn't the man who forced me into a cold shower when I threatened to pummel Desmond for the second time after he tripped me on the field. This man has no integrity. This man is no leader. No role model. No coach.

"Does Becky know? That you started another family while you already had one?"

Coach stands and narrows his eyes at me, his face redder than I've ever seen it. "Of course Becky knows. There's more to the story than meets the eye."

"So you didn't sleep with Becky while you were married to Monica's mother?" I'm disgusted that he would even try to lie at this point.

"Look, Son—"

"Don't call me that."

He looks at me with surprise, then shakes his head. "You've already crossed the line by coming here. Take a step back."

"No, *you* crossed that line when you cheated on your wife and made countless people suffer for it. How could Becky even look at you after what you did? How could you live with yourself? Weren't you even curious what would happen to your first family? My God."

"That's enough, Zachary."

I can't stop. "She's the most beautiful woman I've ever met!" I yell, because God damn it, he's going to hear me. "She doesn't even have to try. Did you know that? She's good, Coach. So good. She's the first one to lift someone up when they're down, no matter what she's going through. She's selfless, and funny as hell too. Challenging in her own feisty way, but you better believe she'll always treat you with respect. She's brilliant and creative and the most inspiring person I've *ever* been around. Yet she's so incredibly modest that she would never agree with anything I just said, but it's all true." I breathe deeply. "And you can take credit for none of it."

Coach is silent for a while. He's not looking at me, but I'm watching him. I'm not sure if he's trying to picture Monica as the person I just described, or if he just wants me to get the hell out of his office.

"I understand you have a friendship with my daughter, but you are the last person I should be speaking to about all of this." His voice is quiet. I'm taken aback when I read his expression now. Everything about him in this moment reminds me of Monica. The times her walls came down revealing everything she's usually able to hide so well. Now Coach Reynolds' mask is gone, and all that's left is a broken man with unfinished business.

Let's just say I'm here for unfinished business.

Monica's words ring loudly in my head.

"Well too bad, Sir. Because I'm involved now, whether you like it or not."

"And why is that?"

My calming breath does nothing for my emotions. I stay silent instead.

"Do you love her?"

My eyes widen. "That's not why I'm here."

"It isn't?" He steps around his desk. "Then what are you doing here? I understand you have a personal relationship with my daughter and this is a trying time for all of us, but I still expect respect when you walk through that door."

My entire body is shaking. "That's the problem, Coach. I've respected you for as long as I've known you because I thought you were someone else entirely. But who cares how I feel about you? I'm not the one who moved here to be close to a father who never wanted to know me in return."

His face loses color. "She moved here for me? Why?"

I shake my head and let out an exhausted breath. "That's probably a conversation you should have with your daughter."

He loses his edge as his anger transforms to fear, then to sadness, and finally to worry. "I'm not sure what I would say. Nothing can undo the past. We've lost so many years."

"And you'll only lose more if you don't start somewhere. You should go to her. Talk. Let her decide what happens next. At least give her that much."

I walk to the door. I'm done here. I'll deal with my own pain separately. It's insignificant compared to what Monica's going through.

When I first connected the dots as I watched Monica's face unravel in front of her father, revealing all the hurt from years ago, my thoughts were selfish. Why didn't she tell me? Why did it have to be him? Someone I looked up to as a Coach and even as a father figure. I felt as if my whole life was crashing down around me and everything I knew was a lie. I won't make that mistake again.

"Zach, wait."

I stop at the door without turning, my fingers gripping the frame, and wait.

"Why are you doing this?"

I glance at him over my shoulder. "I love her. Unfortunately, she can't reciprocate those feelings. Not in the way I need her to. In her mind, she needs to let one of us go, and her choice was made long before she and I even met."

I turn back around, unable to look at him anymore. "I hope you do something with that information. The rest is up to you, Coach."

STEP SEVEN

Letting Go

"EVERYBODY'S GOT A PAST. THE PAST DOES NOT
EQUAL THE FUTURE UNLESS YOU LIVE THERE."
— TONY ROBBINS

Public Knowledge
Monica

Calm washes over me by the time Monday morning comes. My secret is out. There's nothing left to hide from Zach, and I saw my dad again. For the first time in nine years, he stared into my eyes and said my name. And while the next step would be to confront him with the questions that have riddled my soul for nearly a decade, it's his move.

I'm not sure what I expect as I walk into work this morning, but I'm caught off guard by the wide-eyed and muffled greetings I receive from my peers as I pass them in the hallway. Even Jess looks irritated at my arrival, which is bizarre considering every exchange before now between us has been more than pleasant.

Knots tighten in my gut when I pass Gracie and Trinity talking in hushed giggly voices near the copy machine.

Chloe comes out from her cubicle and when she sees me, her eyes widen too. She drags me down the hall to the production suite and into my office before anyone else can see me.

"What's going on?" I ask, my heart pounding in my throat.

"Why haven't you responded to any of my messages?"

I shake my head. "I turned my phone off yesterday. I just needed some time to think without anyone bothering me."

Chloe looks pale. "Turn on your computer. It's everywhere, Mon."

"What's everywhere?"

She sighs. "You and Zach. Your dad. All of it. There are even photos of you and Zach sneaking around camp. Monica, it's bad. I'm so sorry."

She looks horrified as I push her aside and open my computer. Immediately, notification after notification pops up on my screen. There are messages, comments, friend requests, tagged photos, YouTube videos. After seeing one of the photos of Zach and me kissing in the woods, I push away from my desk and raise my hands to my face.

"What the hell?" I cry softly. And then the bottom of my stomach drops out. "You said there's a story about my dad?"

Chloe drops into the chair across from me and nods. "They're saying you seduced Zach to get close to your father."

"That's not true!" I explode. I stand up. "You know that's not true."

She nods, frantically. "Of course, I know you would never do that. It'll all get clea—"

A firm knock interrupts Chloe, and then the door to my office opens to reveal Sandra. "Chloe, leave Monica and I alone, please."

Chloe gives me a sympathetic look before walking out of my office and shutting the door. Sandra's face is nothing like it did the day she fired me—and then hired me again. This time, she looks exhausted, hurt, and confused. She sits across from me and shakes her head.

"Damn it, Monica. Is it true?"

My voice is shaky. "I-I haven't even seen everything yet, but Chloe briefed me." I swallow. "I didn't use Zach to get to my father. The rest is true—I think. The sneaking. The relationship—if you can call it that."

"And when did this start?"

I just stare back at her. Does she really need to know all the details? Sandra shakes her head as if she can read my mind. "Trust me, I don't want to know everything. I just need to know how long this has been going on."

I swallow. "After Heroes and Legends, we went out. Once. We kissed. But that was all until he came back in March. Even then I tried to fight it. But—"

She holds up her hand. "That's enough. The story has gone viral whether it's true or not, and BelleCurve's name is all over this thing."

My eyes narrow as everything falls into place. "We both know who's behind this." I point to the photo of Zach and me kissing. "Meredith has been after Zach for months. You can ask him. She had her minions following us at camp."

"You don't know that," Sandra says, but she doesn't sound very certain.

"I do," I say angrily. "She confronted me—they all did—and said they knew about us. I told them to mind their own business. What we had was real, and we were tired of sneaking around."

"Was?"

I nod. "It's complicated now, and I really don't want to get into it."

"But your father is really Coach Reynolds?"

I nod again.

"Well that makes things even more complicated, doesn't it? Look, Monica. I'm going to get to the bottom of this. I need to talk to Zach and see where his head is at about all this. I can't accuse them of pushing this story out without evidence, or at least without giving them a chance to answer some questions.

"I have to talk to them, and I need you to take some vacation days while I do it. Once this all settles down, we can talk."

Panic captures me at the thought of losing everything I've worked for. "But Sandra—"

"Honey, this isn't negotiable. I'll call you as soon as I can."

And just like that, I've been kicked out of my own office.

As soon as I get home, I go online and evaluate the dumpster fire that is my life. There are about a dozen photos that were cleverly taken at a distance. There's one of Zach and me holding hands in the woods and another of us kissing. They're hardly condemning—they're actually kind of sweet— but it's the story that accompanies them that has me in tears.

SEDUCED BY THE COACH'S DAUGHTER

The headline is awful, but the story is worse.

Monica Reynolds-Stevens, long-lost daughter of Seattle Head Coach Liam Reynolds, has emerged at the center of an ugly story of lies, deceit, and revenge. After Coach Reynolds abandoned Monica's family when she was twelve years old, she spent nine years plotting her way back into her father's life. This week she finally got to him thanks to a fabricated relationship with Seattle Quarterback Zachary Ryan.

But how did Monica get so close to the star player's heart so easily? The answer is even more twisted and diabolical than you can imagine.

When Monica moved to Washington from Rockwall, Texas, she sought employment at BelleCurve Creative in Bellevue, Washington, the company that manages Zachary Ryan's publicity. It may have taken her three years, but she successfully wormed her way into Zachary Ryan's gullible heart, causing mass destruction in her wake.

I can't read anymore. It all hurts too much. This is what Sandra meant by BelleCurve being dragged into this. She was asking if I applied for the job to get closer to Zach. I heard about BelleCurve because of their work with the Seattle team, and I happened to like what the company offered. I also thought I might run into my father. My intentions were hardly scandalous. I'm afraid it will be hard to convince anyone else otherwise.

My eyes are swimming with tears. I think I've cried more in the past few days than I have in the past nine years. When my shaky hands reach for my phone, my stomach is in knots. I dial Zach's number, but the phone rings twice before going to voicemail.

He hates me. He believes it all, and he hates me.

Monica: Please call me.

Hours later, after officially deleting all my social media accounts, I'm pacing my apartment, restless and tormented with anxiety.

Desperate to reach Zach, I check his calendar only to find that I've been removed from accessing any of it. He's done with me. To him, I'm nothing more than a girl who used him, a calculated manipulator who wormed her way into his heart to get closer to her father.

And the worst part? I can't call myself the victim because I'm the reason we're all in this mess.

Why?

Monica

Today, I decided to revisit the football field. I haven't been back since Zach and I came to brainstorm, but I think it's an appropriate place to ponder recent events. After all, this is where our confessions began.

It's been an emotional week. Even if my secrets hadn't been put out there for public judgment, Zach was right. We could choose each other, but neither of us gets to decide our reality. My dad's wife and daughters have been a part of Zach's life for nearly a decade, and that doesn't just go away. Fully letting Zach into my heart would mean accepting that my father is a part of Zach's life … and I can't do that. I've known that from the beginning.

When his Jeep pulls into the parking lot near the field, my heart feels like it might explode in my chest. I may have no clue what to say to him right now, but I know that I miss him.

He doesn't park, though. He doesn't even get out. Instead, his passenger door opens and out steps a man I thought I would never see again in person.

My dad hasn't made any attempts to speak to me since the scrimmage. Well, technically, he hasn't made any attempts in over ten years, but now isn't the time for technicalities. He's walking toward me. It's been a week, and I'm finally started to accept the fact that my father and I may never have the happily ever after I've been searching for all these years.

Part of me is angry watching my father approach and Zach drive away. Like I'm being abandoned by one man while forced to deal with another. How dare he put me in this situation? How dare he leave without a word, without knowing if this is okay with me? How did he even know I was here?

My father walks toward me with the same long, confident strides I remember so clearly. His expression, laden with discomfort and curiosity, looks a lot like how I feel. I step out from my spot under the bleachers to greet him, feeling shaky and a little out of breath.

"Monica." The familiar sound of his voice hits me hard, sending me full-speed into the past, reminding me of the good and the bad in one fell swoop. The tidal wave of pain only gains more momentum as it topples over me.

What do I call him? *Dad?* That just feels weird.

He stops a few feet from me and lets out a breath as if he can't believe he's standing in front of me. Neither can I.

"Monica." This time his voice carries a decade's worth of emotions. It's enough to knock me to my knees, but I somehow manage to hold my ground. "It's really you. You're a woman now. I can't seem to wrap my head around it."

"That's what happens, Dad." My voice is angry but even. "People get older. I couldn't stay fourteen forever. But maybe you remember twelve-year-old me better."

He seems to accept my anger because he nods and lets out another breath. "This isn't easy. I didn't expend it to be." He shakes his head, buying time before starting again. "Walk with me?"

I nod and follow him to the track. It isn't until we've started our lap that he speaks again. "There's a lot I'd like to explain, or you can ask me questions." He swallows. "There are no rules here. I have nothing to hide from you."

My eyes instantly fill with tears, and I have to stop walking. This isn't a leisurely walk while catching up with an old friend. This is my dad and I finally speaking after nearly a decade of silence.

I turn to face him, forcing myself to search his eyes. As painful as it is for me, it looks to be harder for him. He starts to open his mouth to speak, but I won't let this opportunity go. "Why now?" I demand. "Is it because of Zach? Did he make you come? Because if that's why you're here, I don't want this."

My dad shakes his head quickly. "No, no. He did have a few words for me last week, and he's angry with me for good reason. But I asked to see you."

Silence falls like a heavy sheet over us and he glances around as if taking in our surroundings for the very first time. "You come here a lot?" he asks, a hesitant smile forming on his lips. "It reminds me of the Brighton stadium."

I just nod, temporarily unable to speak.

"It's been a long time, hasn't it?" His voice, though deep, is soft and velvety, just like I remember.

I'm about to nod again, but I don't think I can hold back anymore. He's here, and who knows when he'll disappear again, so I might as well ask the only question I've ever had. The one that breaks my heart again every single time I ask it.

"Why did you leave us?"

His head falls forward slightly and the corners of his mouth turn down. "Nothing I can say will make this right."

"You're right. We were a family." I wrap my arms around myself, unable to stop my own tears from forming. "I know you and mom had some problems, but to just take off like that…" I take a deep breath. "Weren't we enough? How could you leave? How could you stay away? And then to see us on your front porch of your new home with your new family, and not try harder to stop us from leaving." I shake my head, still finding the entire situation hard to believe. "You just stood there and watched as our hearts broke right in front of your eyes, and you did nothing." The tears start to fall. "You were supposed to love us."

"I loved you girls more than anything. I still do. There isn't a day that's gone by when I haven't thought of you. I know that must be difficult to believe, but it's true."

I shake my head, refusing to believe his lies. You can't spend every day for a decade thinking about someone and never reach out to them when *you're* the one who left in the first place. I don't even try to stop the shaking of my body or the tears running down my face.

"No!" I argue. "You disappeared. It was like we never existed to you. You could have picked up the phone. You didn't have to abandon us and start a new family. You already had one."

"I'm so sorry." His grimace as he tries to hold back his emotions fills my chest with a heaviness I'm not sure how to deal with. "Baby girl." His eyes redden as he takes a sharp breath. "You were too young at the time to hear this, but you're an adult now. I'll tell you everything if that's what you want."

I need to hear this, but I also need to sit. Nodding, I leave the track in quick strides, aiming for the bleachers. He follows, but I'm not sure if I want him to right away. Ironic—we haven't shared the same space in so long, and now all I want is to get away.

He sits, leaving only a foot between us. For some reason this fuels my anger more. I turn, locking eyes with his, hoping he can feel my pain as I speak it. "Do you know what it's like waking up every single day of your childhood, wondering if your daddy is thinkin' about you, wondering where he could be, if he's okay, if he loves you, if he hates you? Or maybe, just maybe, is today the day he's coming back? Never in my wildest dreams did I think you went off and found yourself a new family until Maggie dragged me to Dallas that night."

He buries his face in his hands and his shoulders shake. I let him cry since I have no soothing words to comfort him. At least he feels pain. It means he still has a heart and feels remorse.

"Your mom and I weren't the best to one another," he chokes out. "What I felt for your mother was out of this world for so many years. But I don't know, maybe it was the game that got into my head. All that travel, that time away from home. It took a toll on us both. Your mother and I got married so young. I know that's no excuse to cheat, but I was weak." He looks over at me, assessing my reaction, but I give him nothing. "I'm telling you this because I want you to know where my mind was at, but just tell me to stop and I will. I don't want to make you uncomfortable."

That's laughable. I pull my knees up to my chest and hug them, bracing myself for whatever's coming next. "You married the nurse," I say, my tone blistering with an accusation. No need to beat around the bush. "After I fell through the bleachers that day, she was the one with me at the hospital when I woke up."

Color fades from his face, his expression dumbfounded. "I can't believe—" he shakes his head and swallows. "I'm so sorry."

It's not like I need him to confirm it. I was there. "Did you sleep with her then? Is that when it all started? Is it my fault you left? If I had never fallen—" My arms cross tightly around me and my forehead falls onto my knees.

"Shit," he mutters, just a whisper, but I hear it. "You blame yourself? God, Monica, no." He reaches for my hand but I pull it away sharply. Sighing, he shakes his head, but it's a slow, painful movement that clamps down on my heart.

He looks at me again, face completely fallen with his own guilt. Now that he's close I can see the rough lines in his face that age has planted there. I can see the heaviness in his lids where gravity has been unkind.

"Are you sure you want to hear this? It's"—he swallows—"not my proudest moment.

"I don't think it can get any worse."

He sighs and turns his head away, ashamed. "I got injured a week after your accident and I was getting treated at the hospital. I bumped into Becky in the cafeteria and we became friends. I was attracted, sure ... but I never intended for it to go any further."

"But it did." My words feel wobbly in my mouth. "You started a family with her, dad. An entire *family*. While Maggie and I were at home, waiting for you to come back. Did you even miss us?" My voice cracks.

"Yes, baby girl. Every damn day. I *still* do."

Jesus. I can't do this. I can't sit here and listen to him try to justify his actions. "I'm supposed to believe that?"

He lets out an exasperated breath. "It's the truth. After my injury, everything changed. It was my darkest time—losing my career, stuck on bedrest, in physical therapy. Your mother and I were always fighting, and Becky and I—we fell into a friendship that turned the bad into good. I never planned to fall in love. After I cheated..." he pinches his eyes and shakes his head as if the words hurt. Somehow I believe they do. I can't imagine it's easy confessing his sins to the adult daughter he sacrificed for his affair.

"I felt guilty," he says thickly, as if he's pushing peanut butter off his tongue. "I knew I'd gone and done a horrible thing. So I tried harder with your mother. But I was the only one putting in the effort." His jaw tightens. "And then Becky called to tell me she was pregnant. Your mom lost it, with good reason. Forbid me to see Becky. Agreed to pay her child support as long as no one ever found out. But I couldn't do it, baby. I couldn't not see my child."

The irony of this statement hits me hard.

"Becky called when she was in labor, and I went to see her and the baby. Your mother told me not to come home. But I did anyway. I got an apartment in town and came home every weekend. I never wanted to leave you girls. Never."

My throat tightens, my heart wanting to believe him. But he *did* leave us.

"The situation brought out the worst in your mother. She became vindictive and cruel. Writing awful emails to Becky as if they were from me. Threatening to ruin every job prospect I had if I went near her and the baby. Eventually, she threatened to tell you girls I had started a new family. And I wanted to tell you. As hard as that conversation would have been, I wanted it to happen soon … but not like that. Not in a way that would serve as your mother's revenge."

"And during all that time your mom was keeping me away, I was falling deeply in love with someone else. Before I knew it, Clara was six months old and your mom was filing for a divorce and full custody."

I scoff and shake my head. "And you didn't even fight it."

He turns to me, his eyes growing wide. "Oh no," he says with an intense shake of his head. "I fought it for over a year. In the end, she called me an unfit father, an adulterer, and abusive. She told the courts I abandoned you kids even though she was the one who kicked me out. I was stripped of my parental rights. I had no legal right to see you girls at all. And then to top it all off, she took my last name from you. *That* just about killed me."

My throat tightens at the kicking and screaming I did over that name change. It was like the final stone thrown before the death of Monica Reynolds.

My dad pulls something from his pocket and hands it to me. A gold key with m&m engraved on it. It doesn't look familiar, which means he got it after he left. My throat tightens.

"Take it," he prods gently. "It's a spare for my storage unit down the street. There's a cabinet where I put every single returned letter that I wrote to you girls. Your mother blocked my email, so snail mail was the only way. I wrote you every single day to tell you how much I loved and missed you, promising I would fight for you for as long as I had to. And

I'd always write a separate one to your mother, sending her money and begging her to let me come see you girls."

I stare at the key, trying to make sense of his words. "You wrote to us?"

He nods. "I'm guessing that's how you girls found my address. Probably from one of the letters addressed to your mom. Every letter I sent to you girls was returned."

I clasp the key in my hand, but shake my head. "Dad, this is too much. You still left us."

His shoulders fall heavily. "I never thought I'd lose you girls. I knew things were bad between your mother and me, but never in my worst dreams did I think it would come to this. Once I was stripped of my rights, I got a letter from a lawyer saying any correspondence would be seen as harassment. And that was it. When you two came to my door that day, I couldn't believe it. I thought maybe you two knew but wanted to see me anyway. By the time I registered what was really going on, you took off."

"Maggie was furious," I tell him. "I wanted to stay. I wanted to understand. But Daddy, seeing your family like that—"

It's my turn to break down. I'm exhausted, and now that I've heard his story, I'm reliving it all over again. I can't imagine ever forgetting that feeling in my chest when I realized he'd moved on without us—with my nurse, of all people.

I also remember how hopeful he looked when his eyes connected with ours.

"I'll never forgive myself for the hurt I caused you girls. I'm so sorry, baby girl." He reaches out and places a hand on my back, making me break down all over again. Despite the pain, I feel the strength of his touch. It's comforting. "You're always on my mind. It doesn't make up for anything, I know, but you've been with me." He rubs his chest with his fist. "When I saw you at the scrimmage, I wasn't sure if it was real."

"I moved here hoping to run into you."

"Zachary mentioned that." He must see my surprised face. "I'm glad he did. I don't know if I would have had to courage to do this if I didn't think you'd consider talking to me."

I wonder what else they've talked about. Does he know about the relationship Zach and I were building before that awful story flooded the internet?

I look up and meet his eyes. "I've spent close to three years figuring out what I would say when this day came," I admit. "I never did figure it out."

He lets out a small laugh. "I'd say you did just fine."

Seeing my dad smile, I'm able to recall some of our better memories. "I still remember what you taught me." I nod toward the field. "I've got a pretty good arm."

He laughs. "That's what Zachary tells me."

"You two talk about me a lot."

He laughs again, and already some of the tension has lifted between us. "He laid into me pretty good. You have that boy's heart."

As much as I care about Zach, he's not what I want to talk about right now.

"And before you say anything, I'm not here because of Zach. I may have needed the push, but not because I didn't want to see you. I failed you as a father, Monica, and I only ever prayed that you were okay. Happy. Loved. I didn't want to come along and ruin all that."

I wipe another tear from my eye and sigh. "I'm going to be completely honest with you, Dad. I'm not sure if I'll ever forget. It will probably hurt every time I remember the nights I cried over you. The recitals you never came to. The graduations you missed.

"I'll probably be angry every time I think of that day we came to see you only to find out you'd replaced us. And even though I know there's more to the story now, that's probably how I'll always think of it. You replaced us. You moved on, and I'm just now forcing myself to deal with this. That's a lot of years to hold onto this kind of pain, and it's not something you just forget. But I'd like to forgive you. I may have already."

He scoots toward me and wraps an arm around my shoulders. "It's okay if you haven't, M."

The moment he calls me by my nickname, I'm drowning in tears and my heart is full to bursting. I never thought I would hear that name again from his mouth.

"I know this is a lot today, and if you need time to think about it, that's okay. But I'd like to see you again. Over coffee, lunch, a game of catch. Just you and me, M. Any time you want. Can we do that?"

I nod without hesitation. It's like a dream finally coming true, except I'm not a little girl now. Somehow though, it doesn't matter. I *feel* like that little girl when I look at my father, and my chest fills with relief.

"Yeah, I'd like that."

Offense vs. Defense

Zachary

I've played against the toughest defenses in the league, taken some pretty hard hits, and had my ego bruised with every fumble and interception. I've heard the smack talk, the locker room talk, the media gossip. I've seen it all. Heard it all. It's never meant anything to me, because I know it's all part of the game. Monica was right when she called me an entertainer. That's what I get paid for. But in the end, I never expected to be *her* entertainment.

Desmond is the one who sent me the link to the first story. He was sniffing around the Wifey Club again when he saw it all: the photos of Monica and me at camp, photos that under any other circumstance would have looked like two people falling in love. Never once had I considered the possibility that Monica was playing me the entire time to get close to her dad. And as hideous as the accusation is, there are too many coincidences to ignore.

I read the articles, look at all the photos. Am I looking at my beautiful Monica falling just as fast and hard as I was, finally letting her guard down? Or am I looking at a lie?

After the blowup in her cabin, the confrontation at her apartment, and the night that followed, I was certain that no matter what, we would still feel the same about each other. I was ready to give her some time to figure everything out with her father, and then we could have our chance. After months of building something incredible, something I've been waiting my whole life for, I was willing to wait.

I don't know anymore.

I'm certain Meredith handed this story to the press, and I can't say I'm surprised. What I care about is the fact that for the first time since knowing Monica, the puzzle is finally in place, but the picture is all wrong. It's nothing like I imagined.

It's Saturday afternoon and Coach sits in my passenger seat as we pull into the parking lot. I knew she would be here. Both Monica and I learned to use the bleachers to protect ourselves—only I eventually came out of hiding. She's still there, and no one can change that but her.

The pull she has on me is still strong. Part of me wants to stay at the field and have a chance to talk to her, but I'm still pissed. She's made multiple attempts to reach me every day this week, but I can't even bring myself to read her text messages or call her back. I will when I'm ready. But right now, I need time to think for myself.

When it comes to Monica Reynolds-Stevens, I'm not sure who's playing offense or defense anymore.

A New Day

Monica

I finally hear from Sandra that next Monday. Still no word from Zach, though, and I've begun to come to grips with the fact that he may never talk to me again. Now that the secret is out there, he can make up his own mind about me. Unfortunately, his understanding of the situation is filtered through gossip threads and social media, and he probably believes it all. That hurts.

I enter the private conference room to see that Meredith is already there with Sandra, looking annoyed as always. Zach is there too, and my heart gallops at the sight of him. He's sitting a couple seats away from Sandra, staring down at his phone with his jaw clenched, obviously avoiding eye contact.

Sandra waves me in, gesturing to the empty chair beside Meredith. I sit, but not before throwing Meredith a glare and moving my chair a few feet away to make a point. I could have just sat one seat over, but that wouldn't have had the same dramatic flair.

Sandra clears her throat and I swear there's a hint of a smile on her lips. "Let's get straight to the point, shall we? Meredith, you've been with BelleCurve for what, four years now?"

Meredith straightens her back and lifts her chin, her eyes filled with confidence. If it wasn't for the way her fingers are gripping her skirt, I would say she wasn't nervous one bit. "Yes, that's correct."

"And you've been handling Zach's account for three?"

She nods, her eyes darting to Zach and then back to Sandra. "Correct again."

Sandra leans back in her chair. "That's quite a generous amount of time we've given you, considering you clearly have no respect for your client or coworkers."

Meredith's jaw goes slack.

"Tell me, Meredith." Sandra leans in again so her elbows land casually on the conference table. A concentrated smirk is poised on her face. "Who were your sources for this story? As you know, we keep records of those things so we can protect ourselves from liability issues. So, who were your sources?"

Meredith shakes her head. "There were eye witnesses at camp."

Zach's head snaps up, and he looks as if he's about to lunge across the table and strangle her himself. That, I would pay to see. Sandra must see this too, because she gives him a look and shakes her head.

"Well, sure," Sandra says. "The photos speak for themselves. It looks like a young couple in love, doesn't it?"

I'm still watching Zach, searching for any sign that he doesn't hate me, but I don't get one.

"Hardly a scandal," Sandra continues. "What about the story?"

I peek at Meredith out of the corner of my eye.

"We did our research. After we caught her sneaking out of bed every night, we started to dig. It's what we do. And we do it well. It wasn't hard to find out more about our little princess over here. Daughter to an ex-NFL player who left his family to start another. Of course there would be resentment there. And when we learned that Coach Reynolds is her father… Well, the rest was obvious."

"So you made assumptions," Sandra responds, still calm.

Meredith seems confused for a second, and then she shakes her head. "No. Think about it, Sandra. This little twit—"

"Don't call her that," Zach seethes through clenched teeth.

Meredith's face turns beet red, but she continues. "*Monica* happens to show up in town three years ago and seeks out a job at BelleCurve, where coincidentally Zachary Ryan has hired out for his publicity, and then they start hooking up the moment he takes notice of her. Meanwhile, she's been scoping him out, learning about him, weaseling her way into his heart. All so that she can get to her dad, for God knows what reason. He obviously doesn't want her in his life."

"That's enough!" Sandra stands, again leaning over the conference table and peering back at Meredith with disgust.

Zach turns to look at me, and it's not a face I ever dreamed I would see directed at me. It's accusing. *He believes I planned this.* I will not cry in front of Meredith, but I sure as hell want to right now.

"I'm sick of your shit, Ms. Greene," Sandra continues. "Your lack of respect for your coworkers and place of employment is appalling. No one permitted you to run that story. Did it occur to you that your client and the company that signs your checks might just have an issue with your made-up bullshit? Because I certainly have a problem with it."

Meredith shakes her head. "It's my job to run stories that will bring my clients maximum publicity, and that's exactly what I did."

"With zero integrity and not enough facts for your story to hold up. You've broken every possible rule you can break in the powerful position that you've been given. It's unacceptable. You're fired, Meredith. BelleCurve has a zero-tolerance policy for trash news. Trinity and Gracie are done too. I'll deliver the news to them myself. You have five minutes until security escorts you out of the building."

Did I just get a front row to Meredith's demise? I would have paid money for this show.

Meredith stands, eyes blinking between Sandra and Zach, before she finally moves toward the door. Her hand is shaking on the knob when Sandra calls her back. "One second, Meredith. How rude of me." She looks at me. "Monica, is there anything you'd like to say to your former coworker?"

Sandra's a tough act to follow, but hell yeah, I'm taking this opportunity. I stand to face Meredith, getting as close as I can without contracting any of her vile aura. "Go fuck yourself, Meredith."

"You can't talk to me like that." Her words breathe fire but her body shivers like it's starved of heat. I almost feel sorry for her.

Looking to Sandra, I wonder if I crossed the line, but she just shrugs. "I didn't hear anything."

There's a deep chuckle from Zach. Even in his pissed off state he can appreciate this moment. That's progress.

He excuses himself after the show, and as much as I want to chase after him, I know I need to stay to talk to Sandra. Now is not the time to fix my love life.

It's just Sandra and me in the conference room now, and she surprises me with an embrace. I'm shaking, and soon I'm crying. It's relief I'm feeling now, because Sandra believes me. I didn't realize I'd been holding onto that fear until now. Releasing it feels good, but it doesn't take away the fact that there are more people involved in this story.

"Are you going to fire me too?"

Sandra laughs and rubs my back. "No, sweetie. I treat my staff like the adults they are until they act otherwise. And while I don't appreciate all the unwanted attention, I know it's not your fault."

She pulls away, holding me at arm's length while I wipe my eyes. "What about Zach?"

Sandra sighs. "Like I said, you're an adult. If you want to go falling in love with my clients, that's your mess to clean up if it falls apart. As long as you don't drag this company along for the ride." She smiles.

"So I'm not fired?"

Sandra laughs. "Not unless you want to be."

"No." I shake my head.

"Good. Why don't you take this week off, too? Figure things out for yourself and start fresh on Monday morning. I talked to Rich, and he'll be fine without you for a few more days."

Letting out a ragged sigh, I nod in agreement. "Okay. Thank you, Sandra."

Sandra leaves the conference room and I sit in the nearest chair with a thud. The pieces of my life are finally all accounted for, but they're a scattered mess. I don't even know where to start. My job seems to be safe, which is one corner piece locked in tight. School starts in a few weeks, so there's another one. But then there's my family. And not just my dad. My mom and I have never been the closest, but going six months in between a phone conversation isn't something that sits well in my heart. And I miss my sister like crazy.

And then there's Zach … who happens to walk back into the conference room the moment his name springs to my mind. Is Zach coming back in to talk to me, or Sandra? He just looks at me for a second, his eyes darker than I've ever seen them. Then he turns to leave the conference room again.

I launch myself from my chair and catch him, slipping between him and the door. Our eyes meet. He can choose. Talk to me, or push me aside.

He stays.

He's fuming, but he's still here. "I can't talk to you right now, Monica." The formality crushes me, but I'm not surprised.

"Zach," I plead. "We need to talk about this."

"*Now* she wants to talk." He laughs and shakes his head, then clenches his teeth before leaning in without touching me. "For the first time since we met, I don't want to hear it." His hands move to my waist to start to move me, so I just start talking.

"After my sister and I visited my dad, I looked him up. I had his address, so the rest was easy to find. There was so much I wanted to know. Nothing made sense, and my heart was as broken as it could ever get. I thought maybe if I knew everything, I would understand and just get over it. But you know what? I didn't. I just felt worse."

Zach lets go of my waist and moves away from the door to give me space to finish my story. "What did you find?" he asks.

"He got a job coaching football at the high school in our old neighborhood. I drove to Dallas on the night of the homecoming game. You must have been a senior at the time. I just—wanted to see him again. But I knew I couldn't sit in the bleachers. I couldn't do it and risk being seen. My biggest fear was that he'd see me up there and not realize it was me, or worse, he'd see me and go right back to his life as if he hadn't. I couldn't handle feeling rejected again."

"So you sat under the bleachers."

I nod. "I had this dream that I would be brave enough to confront him after the game. That we would have this moment where we'd reunite and cry and everything would be perfect again. That never happened.

"I saw you play. You were amazing." I shake my head. This is not helping my case. "You were in the parking lot with my dad and his new family after the game, looking so much a part of it. I knew then that you were important to him. When you went off to college and then got drafted to Seattle, you were hard to ignore in the headlines. But when I moved to Washington it was entirely for my dad, not to get close to you. That's the part you might have trouble believing, but it's true. BelleCurve is the number one PR company for Seattle, and working for a creative company intrigued me. You hadn't even signed on with them when I got hired." My eyes plead with him, but he turns away. "I tried to stay away from you, Zach, but I just couldn't anymore."

"Well, I guess you got what you wanted in the end. You got your dad and you get to stay away from me. It just took a little bit longer than expected."

My mouth widens and my eyes water. He still doesn't believe me.

"Why do I even bother? I've told you everything." My voice rises as I start to shake. "Is this what you want? To be angry with me so that you can continue on with the family that replaced mine? I'm sorry I ruined that for you, Zach. I really am. But I never asked you to choose."

"Didn't you?" The crease between his eyes deepen and he leans over me. "The night of Clara's recital. The night of the scrimmage. Both times you accused me of choosing someone else over you. But the moment you told me those stories about your dad without telling me *who* he was, you knew I was choosing *you*. How do you think I would feel when it was all out in the open? You tricked me, Monica. And I'm allowed to be pissed about it."

I swipe my tears away and step back. "What did I trick you into Zach? Chasing me? Working so closely with me? Buying me gifts? That was all you. Don't you think if I wanted to trick you, I would have slept with you that first night? And when you offered me tickets to your games, don't you think I would have taken them? What about when you came back to BelleCurve and I tried to stay away from you?" I push into him now because it hurts, and I want him to hurt too. How else can I make him see?

"There's a reason I never told you about him, but it wasn't because I was trying to worm my way into your heart. Sure, I was curious about the boy who had grown so close with my father, but I stayed away from you because of it. Don't you think it fucking killed me every time you spoke about him and how close you were to his daughters, knowing that he left Maggie and me for them? Yeah. It killed me, Zach, but I also was happy for you, believe it or not. What you went through with your father was tragic. My dad was your savior. I never wanted to take that away from you."

We stare at each other, both of us swimming in a swirl of anger and resentment. Both our hearts have been through the ringer lately, and this exchange isn't making things any easier, but I've said what I needed to say.

I step to the side, giving him room to walk away. With a final hardening of his jaw, his eyes flicker to mine and hold for just a second before he tears his gaze away and walks out the door.

"Monica, wait!" Jess calls from the front desk. I've just placed my hands on the glass doors to leave when she runs up behind me. "There's someone waiting for you in your office. Said it was a surprise." She shrugs.

Still reeling from current events, I haven't a clue who could be in my office. When I turn the corner and see her sitting there, feet on my desk, arms crossed as she studies our family photo, my heart soars.

"Maggie?"

She looks up, her perfect features twisting into the beautiful smile I've missed more than I've admitted to myself. "Hey, sis."

Ravaged

Monica

Three weeks later, and my work for Under the Bleachers is nearly complete. The sponsors, the kids, and the families all loved it, and the production team even received special kudos from the execs for an extraordinary event.

Richland and I are sitting in the largest editing bay screening the latest cuts of the leadership PSAs that will be distributed to participating schools when Zach walks in. I had no idea he was invited, but I guess he's here to give final approval. He's wearing dark jeans and a fitted blue V-neck. He looks good—and calmer than the last time we were in the same room.

Richland greets him with a small wave from the other side of the room. "Hey bud, thanks for coming in. Have a seat anywhere."

My entire body stiffens when Zach chooses to sit on the end of the couch furthest from me, resting his arms across the back. He smells different. I noticed his aroma the moment he walked by me, and I can't stop thinking about it. The scent is dark but sweet. Rich, but soothing.

I swallow and meet his eyes, which haven't left me since he strolled in. But the hurt behind his expression completely obliterates any chance my heart has at surviving this moment. I look away.

Richland's hands are on the keyboard, searching through files and selecting the correct video before putting it on the projection screen. "Ready?" he asks.

Zach shifts in his seat to face the screens. "Let's see it."

I should go.

Then the video starts, and Zach laughs at something on the screen, his shoulders shaking a little.

I should stay.

It's almost six o'clock by the time we wrap up. As soon as I can get away, I scurry to my office to shut down and grab my things, hoping to get out of here quickly.

"Can I walk you home?"

Zach's voice jumpstarts my heart. It's a little painful, but it's just what I needed to break out of the misery. Since the day I heard about our story releasing all over the internet, he's not the only one that's been angry. I'm mad at him too. For not trusting me. For abandoning me when things got rough.

"Of course. I have an early morning—"

"I'm just asking to walk you home, Cakes."

I swallow, meeting his eyes, and then nodding.

The warm breeze and night traffic bring comfort to my senses the second we leave BelleCurve. It helps ease the tension as we walk in silence. I only look up once when a door opens at the corner Teriyaki joint and I get a whiff of beef sizzling on the grill. But I can't even think about food right now, not when my stomach is already churning over Zach's nearness.

We both stop before I reach the door to my apartment building, only inches apart, but it's like he's somewhere else. "So you've been seeing your dad." His tone is soft and encouraging, but there's a layer of something else I don't detect right away.

I nod. "Twice now."

"So you got what you wanted." I hear sadness through the cracks of his tone, and heat forms in the backs of my eyes.

"I can hardly say I got what I wanted, Zach." I blink back tears. "Rebuilding my relationship with my father is huge, but none of it matters if you believe I used you to get here."

He cringes. "I don't, Cakes. I was angry. I wasn't thinking clearly." His eyes mist with his pain. Jesus. If Zach cries, I'll lose it.

"You're right," he says, his voice lighter. "I've thought the worst these last few weeks. Coach gave me a family when my world was turned upside down. And not just me—my mom and brother too. He's given me so much and never asked for a thing in return." His voice softens to a whisper. "But I hate what he did to you."

I nod, because I know that Zach has only ever wanted to carry my pain. To take care of me. "And you wanted to believe what was written because then you wouldn't have to choose. You needed someone to be the bad guy." I take a deep breath and say out loud what I've finally come to understand. "There is no bad guy here, Zach. You love him for the same reasons I still love him. You're mad at him for the same reasons I'm mad at him.

"Even after everything, I know he's just a guy who made some shitty decisions. But those shitty decisions led to him meeting you." I smile. "You're allowed to be grateful for that. I know I am."

Zach pulls me in, resting his forehead on mine. "How can you forgive him after what he did?"

I clutch his shirt. "Because he's sorry. Because he's trying. I understand now what he did was probably the shittiest thing in the world, but he's been living with it too, and he wasn't the only one who messed up." I swallow against the lump in my throat.

"My mom may not have initiated the destruction, but she's as much to blame for the fallout as he is. She should have seen our pain and known that being without our father was a fate far worse than us knowing the gory details. Always so damn selfish. For *once*, she should have put us first."

Zach's head falls into my neck, and he holds me tighter as I shake.

I take a heavy breath. "And it would be a much different situation if my dad hadn't shown up on that field to talk to me. If he hadn't called to see me again. He's trying. So I'm going to try too."

We stand like this for a while, me clinging to him, his arms wrapped around me like the warmest blanket. Eventually he takes a deep breath and we straighten our backs, our hands falling between us.

"I'm going out of town tomorrow," he says. "For a week. It's a team thing. We do it every year before the draft."

Blood races through me as he searches my expression. This is the part where we decide we aren't right for each other, isn't it?

He sighs and shoves his hands into the front pockets of his jeans. "Anyway, I'll be back next week, but my schedule picks up when I get back. We've got fittings and promos, training camp… I don't know why I'm telling you all of this. I guess I just want you to know that I'm still around if you need me. For anything, Cakes."

I touch his forearm gently. "You don't need to worry about me. BelleCurve is keeping me busy, and school starts up soon. I've got a lot to work out, and I don't want to be a distraction."

He shakes his head and lets out a quiet laugh. "You not being in my life is the distraction. It's the worst kind of distraction. But I get it. I'll give you space. I just—I hope when I get back to town we can talk more.

"I am here for you. You know that, right?" He tilts my chin up to look me square in the eyes. "I meant it when I said I chose you." He brushes a thumb along the ridge of my cheek. "You need to know that I meant it. If you need more time, take it. But if you want someone to be there with you, to help you through this … if you need a friend. Hell, if you need someone to beat your father's ass, I'll do all of those things."

I smile at his words. Despite our situation, it's a little funny. "That means a lot, Zach. It hasn't been easy … but after speaking with him, I think I've found some peace. I guess I just want to live in it for a while."

Zach smiles. "Okay." He looks tentatively over my shoulder at the main door. "I can walk you up."

Returning his smile, I shake my head. "I don't think that's the best idea. Maggie's in town and she's still flipping out about everything."

He tilts his head. "Really? She's here? Why?"

I laugh. "I'm still trying to figure that out myself. She's the worst kind of mooch. She heard about Dad after it was all over the news and she showed up with her bags, telling me mom's dating some douchebag attorney and she has some auditions lined up here."

His husky laugh fills my ears. "Maybe you can hook her up at BelleCurve."

"Oh no. No way. She's a mooch *and* a diva. Not a good combination."

The air stirs and I get another whiff of his cologne. I smile up at him. "What scent is that?"

The grin that lifts the corners of his mouth answers my question. "It's you, Cakes. Ravaged."

I groan and laugh at the same time.

Zach reaches for my hand and pulls my palm flat against his heart, covering it with his own. "I've missed you, Cakes. Call me. Please." His hand rubs against mine, and I feel his plea. "I'm not expecting us to pick up where we left off. I just—I can't lose you in my life. You've become the most important part of it."

A tear slips down my cheek and I smile. "Of course."

He leans in, letting my head fall to his chest. I breathe him in again, the most delicious richness wafting over me like melting chocolate. As bad as I know it is, I want that scent wrapped around my body, making me forget everything but him.

"No matter what happens, I believe there's a reason we found each other. Maybe reconnecting with your father was it."

I look up again, my eyes filling with liquid. "You've given me more than I could have ever asked for. Things I didn't even know I wanted."

He nods, his arms tightening around me. "It's not over, Cakes."

I shudder, not knowing what to say. I'm hoping he's right, and we just need time to heal.

Although we aren't saying goodbye, it somehow feels like it. His hands shake as he brings our mouths together for a kiss. No matter what happens, I'll never forget these lips. His touch will touch me forever. And our moments ... those will last an eternity.

STEP EIGHT
Love 'em or Leave 'em

"IF YOU WANT SOMETHING YOU HAVE NEVER HAD, YOU MUST BE
WILLING TO DO SOMETHING YOU HAVE NEVER DONE."
— THOMAS JEFFERSON

Cooking Lessons

Monica

For nearly a decade I've gained strength through my suffering, turning sludge to stone to overcome each obstacle. What was once a muddled mess I was left to sort through alone has become my new path. I've learned that there is no grave in which our obstacles decay. They become part of us, dormant until they're awakened.

But what happens when the weight of the struggle becomes too heavy to bear? I'm strong; now what? Where's my prize?

I'm done suppressing the pain. I'm no longer made of stone, but of a massive knot begging for release. For the first time since this all began, I'm choosing to stand still. Eventually this knot will unravel on its own … because I'm letting go.

Maggie and I pull up to the familiar brick building on Pine, and I smile. I don't know what's come over me lately, but these random adventures with my sister have been everything. So far, she's let me drag her to Forks to see what the *Twilight* town looks like … because Robert Pattinson. We've explored a slew of vintage shops for unique clothes instead of relying on the same fancy brand names my sister has always been addicted to. And now, we're trying Zach's cooking school. Because it's something neither of us has ever done.

It might be messed up how I got to this point, but I'm living, unafraid and moving forward. I'm happy.

I think of something Chloe said to me not too long ago: I've been clinging onto my own cocoon of safety for too long, avoiding experiences for fear they would only disappoint me. Now that my world's been blown completely open, I'm craving more risks.

Today, I'm doing something I never thought I'd do— something I'm not sure I even want to do. I'm doing it because I *can*. And I'm dragging Maggie with me.

"This is stupid," she hisses as we approach the door to Edible Desire.

"Shh. You're mooching off me, remember? That makes you my bitch. Suck it up, buttercup."

I bought a month of cooking lessons for us. And I'm expecting nothing less than complete and utter failure.

The moment we enter the building, I start to regret coming. There are reminders of Zach everywhere. But at the same time, I need this. I need to feel close to him. It's been too long. Two months too long.

Although Zach and I promised to keep in touch, we've only been on two lunch dates and we chat via text a few times a week. It's not easy. I miss him like crazy. But this time apart is necessary. For me. For him. After everything that went down, I feel as if I've taken off down a new road—one I need to learn to navigate on my own.

However, I'd be lying if I said that part of the reason I'm at this cooking class wasn't because of Zach, though. Because as much as I want to prove to myself that I'm capable of trying new, uncomfortable things, I want him to know that he's made his mark in my life. Eventually, I hope to show him that.

As I survey the room I haven't seen in close to one year, a cute, enthusiastic girl in a bright blue apron greets us. "Hi! Are you here for the morning class?"

I nod and tug on my sister to get her to smile. "We are."

"Great! If you can come with me, I'll show you to your station and have you sign some waivers, and then we'll get started as soon as the chef is ready."

We're stationed beside each other, bickering about the appropriateness of fake tanning in the summer, when a tall figure with light brown hair and blue eyes approaches. Jesus, my heart skips a beat. He reminds me so much of Zach. But this guy has dirty blonde hair on his face and head, and a slightly darker shade of ocean in his eyes. Not to mention a smirk that exudes a dangerous amount of confidence.

What's worse, he's staring straight at my sister as if he's found his next meal. I've seen that look before when Zach is picturing me naked. Uh oh.

"Ladies." His smile grows wider. He extends a hand to Maggie first. "Chef Desmond Blake. Welcome to my kitchen."

My eyes grow wide. Desmond. Holy shit.

"I'm Maggie," my sister says. "And this is my sister, Monica."

The sound of my name seems to yank Desmond's eyes from my sister for the first time, and he smiles like we're old friends. "No shit. You're Cakes."

I cringe. Desmond makes my name sound so slutty.

"I am. Hi, Desmond."

He gives me a once over now, but I can see that, unlike how his eyes roamed my sister, my clothes remain on, thank goodness. He's assessing me, possibly gathering information to relay to Zach. I'm not sure, but after a few more seconds, he's excusing himself to prepare his station for today's lesson.

"Shit," I mutter softly when he walks away.

"What was that about?" Maggie looks angry, and I know she thinks her future husband just hit on me.

"That's Zach's best friend."

"You haven't met him before now? He's hot, M. That's a guy you let ruin your lipstick, right there. He should be on television—or in my dreams. Either way, he'd be the star."

Despite my horror over meeting Desmond like this, I laugh. "You are a freak."

Maggie sticks her tongue out, but I'm too consumed with my thoughts of Zach to react. Instead, I walk to the main kitchen where Desmond stands at the island.

He swivels to face me, a grin already plastered on his face. "It's about time I meet you. I was starting to think those pictures were a sham."

I blush.

"Don't worry, he's said all good things, I promise."

I let out a breathy laugh. "Somehow I doubt that, but thank you." I look around, unsure of what I want to say to him. "Um. I'm not ready for Zach to know that I'm here. We're not really dating right now, and—"

He nods, his expression changing from a cocky to something a bit sweeter. I don't know for sure, but I think I can trust him. "I won't say anything, Monica. Your secret is safe with me."

It seems like he might say more, but the bell to the front door rings, and his eyes are pulled in that direction. "You'll have fun here. I promise." He winks and then excuses himself to greet the new students.

I believe him. I can feel it already. The excitement of something new. The rush of adrenaline facing the unknown. To some, it's just a cooking class. To me, it's the beginning of many changes to come.

m&m

Chloe

My smile is huge as I run home from school to change my clothes. After receiving a message from my dad asking to meet at our favorite coffee shop, I'm flying high.

"I can't believe you're going to see him again. What is that now, five times?"

Maggie is lying on her stomach on my couch with a magazine in front of her, legs up in the air, wearing nothing but a pair of boy shorts and a sports bra. Not a single ounce of fat on her. Not that I can be too jealous after seeing what she does to stay thin. It's disgusting. Salad with no dressing should be a felony. Not even salt and pepper to give the damn leaves some flavor. She's like a frickin' rabbit. But she also doesn't exercise, something I actually enjoy.

"Maggie," I warn.

She sighs. We went over this the last time I left to meet up with him too. I never keep it from her, and I always give her a chance to come, but she's not ready. She may never be ready, and I'm fine with that. I'm doing this for me, not for anyone else.

"Don't lecture me about mooching again," she warns, because that's always where the conversation leads. She tells me she doesn't understand how I can give our father a chance after what he did, and I tell her she can't come here, mooch off me, and then tell me how to feel.

"Then don't lecture me about Dad."

She sits up so that she can fully face me, her expression carrying the same worry it always does. "It's just weird, M. After what he did—"

I shake my head. "It's not like that, Mags. We're just meeting for coffee. It's not a big deal. It's kind of nice being in the same room with him again. I can't explain it. But he's trying. You can't be mad at him forever, especially if you can so easily forgive Mom for her part in it all."

Maggie frowns, and for the life of me, I can't understand why the steel wall of resistance. She should be mad at mom.

"She was hurt and trying to protect us like mothers do, M. Stop blaming Mom. She isn't the one who left us for another family."

"No she wasn't, but I wouldn't call 'cutting off ties with me because I want to see my father again' protecting me."

"She doesn't understand why you need this," Maggie pleads. "After everything she did to make sure he wouldn't hurt us again, you just threw it in her face by moving here."

This is the part of the conversation where I always get upset. "She shouldn't have kept him from us, no matter what."

Anger heats her skin. "He *cheated* on her and started a new—"

"Maybe she didn't appreciate him. Did you ever think about that? The point is, he didn't willfully leave us."

"He's brainwashed you, sis. He was a grown man. He chose to leave."

"She kicked him out! And then had his rights taken away." I place my hands on my hips. "She made us change our names, Mags. I can't keep doing this with you. If you don't want to see him, I won't make you. But if you're going to live here, then don't you dare tell me what to do or how to feel."

She pouts and then rolls her eyes. No one would ever know she was the older sister by her behavior. Once a brat, always a brat. "Fine. Have a nice afternoon with Daddy Dearest."

With a grunt and a slam of the door behind me, I'm out. This would have been so much easier if she had just stayed in California. I'm tempted to say her timing is awful, but I know why she's really here. She came after hearing about my run-in with Dad, and she wanted to protect me.

I love my sister, but we don't need to live together. She's been here for three months, and her job search has turned up null so far. She just hangs around my apartment, watches television, and goes to one failed audition after the other. She's taken over every room in my house, and somehow she's managed to slip into my bed every night. Girl is clingy too, always trying to spoon me.

And how the hell does she manage to fit into all my clothes? Sure, everything a little too short and baggier on her, but she makes it work as if it was made for her.

The last thing I need on top of all that is her opinion on how I handle this relationship with my father. The truth is, I'm happy. Nothing can ever undo the past, but the forgiving part is easier than I ever imaged—especially after reading all the letters he wrote Maggie and me. I don't think Maggie has even opened one, but I'm confident she'll give in eventually. I know her too well.

I find Dad in the back of the café, his head hidden under his Seattle hat. As I approach, he glances up and smiles. "Hey,

M." Then he looks down and immediately starts laughing when he sees my shirt. "One of your new creations?"

I look down too, almost forgetting I had a presentation in my concept development class today. A giggle bursts from my throat when I think of the positive reaction I got from my peers. My burnt out tank is simple enough, but it's the logo I designed that stands out. We were supposed to create a brand identity that spoke to our personalities. Mine was written in script: *Some people eat their feelings. I just eat cake.*

As I notice the hot cup sitting in front of my empty seat, my eyes widen. "What is this?"

He chuckles. "Hot chocolate. Isn't that what you always get?"

I smile and put the steaming cup to my mouth. "You can never go wrong with hot chocolate. Thank you."

His smile reveals the age lines around his eyes, but other than that, he still looks the same as I remember him. Short, stocky, and baby faced, no matter how much he ages.

"I know it's only been a few months," he says, "but you should know these meetings mean the world to me, M. You've always had the biggest, most forgiving heart. I'm just sorry I wasn't the one to find you first."

"Dad, it's okay. I don't want to dwell on all of that. I just want to move forward."

He swallows and nods. "Becky thought—and I—well, we'd love to have you over some time. I've already started talking to the girls about you and Maggie. They don't know all the details, but they know they have sisters." He swallows again. "And they want to meet you. Both of you." His eyes search mine. "I don't suppose Maggie would—"

I shake my head, wanting to roll my eyes at the conversation I just had with my sister. "She's not ready. But I would like to meet them."

His entire face lights up. "Okay, then we'll make plans."

I smile back and nod.

"Now that we got that out of the way," he says, and we both laugh "I wanted to give you this." He pulls out an envelope from his back pocket and slides it against the table until it reaches me. "For you and your sister, if she'll accept. There's an extra pair too in case you want to bring some friends. I hear it's been a long time since you've been to a game. You should come."

My jaw drops when I open the envelope to reveal a packet of Seattle home game tickets. "Dad," I say through my tightening throat. "Why?"

"I don't know what's going on with you and Zach, and it's none of my business. But I know that boy almost as well as I know my own kids, and he hasn't been the same lately. I saw you two together. I heard the way he talked about you, M. I'm not telling you what to do, but I do hope you'll use these tickets to figure out what needs to be done for you both to be happy."

"Thank you." Gratitude in exchange for thoughtfulness. That's one thing I've learned over the past few months. Zach would be so proud.

My dad gives me a soft smile. "It's my gift to you because you've given me something I never expected to get. You've given me you."

Tears cloud my eyes, and I set the envelope down to hug him.

We stay embraced for the longest time while I let the rush of happiness flow through me.

I know exactly what I'm going to do with these tickets.

He kisses the side of my head. "I just want you to be happy, baby girl. I just want you to be happy."

Win, Lose, or Draw

Monica

At Seattle Stadium on game day, the excitement is palpable. When the house shakes, you can feel it coursing through your body like everything surrounding you is interconnected. Your heart is the drums; your veins, the strings; and your soul, the center of everything. Because that's what it feels like to be here, among this crowd, watching this team. It's everything.

Our seats are incredible, but who needs seats when you can stand practically on the field in the southwest corner of the stadium, watching your team score a touchdown only thirty yards away? Maggie will be pissed she missed this. We've already been approached by three players offering to snap photos with the eager fans beside us. Even Chloe, Miss I-Don't-Understand-Football, is getting her fangirl on and going selfie crazy.

"Have you seen him?" she asks, eyes wide and scouring the field.

I shake my head and wring my hands together nervously. "Not yet." Even if I do see him, it doesn't mean he'll see me.

"Hey, M! You made it." My father approaches the short rail with a grin and I respond with a bigger one, my chest filling with pride. It's hard not to get choked up being here. This is my first NFL game since my dad played with Dallas so many years ago. It's surreal.

"Dad, this is my best friend Chloe."

They shake hands, and Chloe's smile is endearing as ever. "It's so nice to finally meet you, Sir. The seats are incredible."

"Is it just you two?"

I shake my head, frowning, because I know he was hoping I'd bring Maggie. I turn to find Gavin and Justin, who are walking down the steps toward us. Chloe introduces them while I slyly scan the field in hopes of spotting Zach. There's still enough time before the game to see the team run some warm-ups.

As if on cue, Zach walks out to the field, stopping every so often to toss a smile and wave at the crowd. When I take in his uniform, my heart fills my ears with its erratic pounding. His already large build looks massive due to the padding under his purple and gold jersey. No one has ever been sexier.

My dad jogs off just as a familiar figure comes toward us with a wicked grin on his face. "No shit. The daddy's girl is here."

I roll my eyes. "Hi Balko." I quickly introduce him to my friends before focusing in on Zach. I expect him to say something that will set fire to my blood, but his expression is different from the one I remember at camp. It's kinder.

"Well, you sure shocked the hell out of all of us, didn't you?"

I blush. "Yeah, well, I didn't mean for all that to happen."

He waves it away. "It was entertaining; that's for sure. You and Nut-Zach still together after all that?"

I hesitate before shaking my head. "No. We're doing our own thing now." His face changes again, back to cocky Balko, but I stop him in his tracks. "Don't even think about it, Balko. Zach would still kill you."

He laughs. "You think I care?"

When he jogs away, I'm still smiling. Chloe hugs me from the side, as if she can sense my emotions. I'm not trying to hide them. Not anymore.

He's chocolate and I'm cake. Okay apart, but so much sweeter together.

Monica

"Nut-Zach, you've got a crazy fan waiting for you in the southeast corner. She'll stop at nothing to get a photo."

I eye Balko and ball my fists. "Oh, yeah? She turn you down?"

He smirks. "I think you'll like this one. Go on; don't disappoint her. She might claim you're her baby daddy and then you'll have another media scandal on your hands."

I walk away. I don't need this shit today. I woke up with a stiff neck after falling asleep scrolling through Monica's new Instagram account. I know she had one before, but she must have gotten rid of it after the PR disaster. This feed is filled with new photos. Photos of her new clothing designs, her new friends. There's even one of her at home in an apron. To be honest, that one kind of pissed me off.

Although we've kept in contact, the boundary lines are thicker than ever. She's happy building her new life, and I'm happy that she's happy. But I'm resentful of the fact that she can't seem to fit me in beyond the occasional cute selfie when I ask for it.

I'm also tired, and I need to figure out how to turn my attitude around to win us this game.

I've had a lot of time to think about everything that evolved after camp. My biggest regret is ever doubting Monica. She wasn't using me. There's not a scandalous bone in her body. It was always me pushing for more until she finally admitted she wanted more too.

A strong hand lands on my shoulder, dismantling my thoughts. "Where's your head, Zachary?" Coach asks, his tone terse but gentle. When I don't answer, he reaches up to place his arm around my neck and drags me away with him, my body still stiff with anger. "Walk with me for a second."

I let him drag me across the field, not questioning a thing. We're about to kick off pre-season, but everything feels wrong. Like I'm missing my heart.

Finally, I sigh and turn to him. "I'll be fine, Coach. Just dealing with some things, but I'll get it out of my head before the game. Promise."

His nod is slow and measured. "Would it help or hurt if I told you my daughter came to the game today?"

Shit. There's a storm in my chest at just the thought of seeing her again. "Depends why she's here, Sir."

"Southeast corner. You have ten minutes to find out, and then I want your head in the game, ready to throw some rockets."

Coach winks and walks away, leaving me on the sidelines with lightning and thunder sounding off inside me. I'm not sure if I'm walking into the storm or away from one.

Either way, I take off, jogging to the southeast VIP seating. I spot her immediately. Heavy breaths don't slow my adrenaline, and neither does seeing the way she laughs with Chloe as they snap a photo together.

My Cakes. That smile.

God, I've missed her.

As she sees me approach, her smile fades but her eyes brighten. "Hey you," she says like she's been expecting me. *Is she here for me?* "Guess there are benefits to being the coach's daughter after all."

I smile. A giant smile that grows from the inside and blooms just for her. My fingers land on the rail beside her hand, but I make no move to touch her. My name is being called from all directions, but my focus is on the girl in the number four Seattle jersey. Is it awful to love my own jersey so much?

"Guess so. Glad you could make it to a game."

When a soft finger lands on mine, I intake air sharply in surprise. My eyes flicker down to where she's touching me, and then back up to her face. It takes everything in me not to yank her down from the rail and kiss those soft lips. It's all I want, but I still don't know if she wants the same thing.

"I have something for you," she says nervously as she pulls a light blue envelope from her back pocket. She starts to hand it to me then pulls it to her chest. "I can hold onto it if you want to grab it after the game."

Well, this is promising. "Okay, then. I'll come by as soon as I can."

"Okay."

I turn to go, on an instant high from just a few seconds with her.

"Wait, Zach. One more thing," she calls.

I jog back, pressing myself against the rail. "What is it, Cakes?"

Her smile is beautiful as she responds to the nickname. She leans in, taking my breath away when she touches her cheek to mine and speaks into my ear. "I came to see you win, so … good luck." I feel her lips curl up into a smile as they press firmly into my cheek. "No pressure."

When I pull away, the air is sizzling with a chemistry that never went away. Of course it didn't. It's just been patiently brewing this whole time, waiting for that last ingredient to activate.

My Fight, My Future

Monica

I've never been one of those girls who dreamed of her own fairytale, of a guy sweeping her off her feet. I still don't believe in fairytales, but for the first time in a long time I believe in love. And I believe that Zach has owned my heart from that very first night we spent together, when he wanted to peel away something other than my clothes. No one has ever cared to look that close.

This afternoon when the game ended, he came straight for me and didn't stop until his lips were on mine. When he stepped onto the rail and pulled me in for the kiss that would be the envy of millions of women everywhere, I knew that was it.

This is what it feels like to get swept away.

My footwork is quick as I prepare the last of the four-course meal. Green apple salad, house-smoked salmon, and grilled mahi-mahi. And of course ... dessert.

Desmond gave me a list of Zach's favorite dishes and let me have full use of the kitchen for the night. As freaked out as I am to be using a kitchen sans supervision, I only needed to call Desmond for help three times. So I'm kinda killin' it.

After Zach took my breath away with that very public kiss, I handed him the envelope, slapped him on the butt, and sent him on his way to talk to reporters. Not five minutes later, I had a text message accepting the invite to dinner.

When I see Zach's shadow reach the door right before seven, happiness and nervous flutters wreak havoc in my stomach. The food is warming, the table is set, the salad is tossed, our wine is on the island, and dessert is ready.

I'm ready.

He lets himself in and closes the door behind him before looking around the kitchen. The look of shock on his face is more than I was ready for. Now I'm a little embarrassed.

"Cakes?" he asks, before his eyes lock on mine. "What are you up to? How did you get in here?"

I laugh and run my hands down my red apron with lace edges, a piece I made especially for this night. Zachary likes me in red; he told me that once. When a man tells a girl she looks good in something, that might be all she ever wears again.

"Desmond," I say, vaguely. "Surprise." I lift my arms a little to gesture around me.

His eyes are on the lit-up oven and then the decorated table. "It smells amazing in here."

"Thanks. I've been taking lessons."

He steps toward me and tilts his head to the side, his lips curling slowly. "Cooking lessons? Here?"

I nod and place my hands on my hips. "Yes."

"Should I be jealous that you've been spending time with Desmond?"

I throw my head back and laugh, then shake my head. "Nope. I think he's into my sister."

"So if I open that oven I won't find a pre-cooked meal?"

I snort-laugh. "No, Zachary Ryan. I did not invite you here to eat a meal prepared by someone else. A long time ago you got me a present, and I wasn't able to appreciate it. That stuck with me. I wanted to finally show you how much I appreciate it."

He's in front of me now, and his hands move to my cheeks, brushing them lightly with his thumbs. "Those words, Cakes—that's the best present you could have given me."

I bite my lip and shake my head. "There's more."

Tugging on his hand, I lead him to the dining table and point to the bench. "I'll bring the wine. Sit."

Rushing off, I gather our drinks and sit on the bench across from him. "I'm impressed. How long have you been taking classes?"

I grin. "One month, but I signed up for another one. I know. I'm kind of addicted."

His eyes widen in surprise. "Wow. You must be good. I can't believe Desmond never told me."

"I asked him to promise not to say anything. I wanted it to be a surprise."

There's an obvious break in conversation while Zach thinks over what I just told him. "One month, huh?"

"Yup," I say, nonchalantly.

He pauses before clearing his throat. "What else have you been up to? You know, besides trying to become more perfect than you already were."

I roll my eyes, but there's a fluttering in my chest that lifts me. "I've been hanging out with my dad. Once a week now. Sometimes twice." I shrug before smiling. Even though I left my life in Texas to move here with hope in my heart, I

413

never expected to feel so ... fulfilled. "He wants me to meet Becky and the girls."

My eyes flicker up to meet Zach's, to gauge his reaction. There's a twitch of his lips that tells me he wants to smile. "Is that what you want?"

I nod with my swallow. "Yeah. I think so. I mean, it will be weird at first, but I want to. It's just ... complicated with Maggie here now." I shrug, because this isn't what I want to talk about right now. Going on about Maggie's issues could fill a book.

"Would you come with me?" I ask. "To meet them?"

He sucks in a deep breath. "Of course, Cakes."

My cheeks heat but I can't stop smiling. "Are you ready for the first course?"

I know he wants to ask more questions, but he also trusts whatever is happening right now. His eyes speak to me when his words don't. It's the same with me. I love that about us. "Let's see it."

With a sly smile, I walk around the table to straddle the bench beside him. He moves so he's facing me, and I take his hands in mine. "Three months has been too long without you. I'm sorry it's taken me this long to do this." I peer up at his kind eyes that are searching mine, and I smile. "It didn't take me that long to realize how perfect you were for me. I knew that long ago."

I place his hand on my heart and close my eyes. "Once upon a time you told me that you were after this." Taking a stuttered breath, I lift my lids to peer back at him. "It's yours. If you still want it."

Zach doesn't give me a chance to consider any other possibility. He pulls me in, kissing me firmly, then softly before finally pulling away. "I do, Cakes. And you're right; three months is way too long, but my feelings for you have only grown. You may not be ready to say it, but if we're going to do this, we're going all in. No more holding back." He grabs my hands, squeezes and looks at me with the most heartwarming expression. "I love you with everything I've got."

He smiles, then waits, eyes pleading for me to respond. "What do you say, Cakes? Are you ready?"

I nod, squeezing my eyes tight. I can't mess this up. Pressing my lips to his, we're lost for another moment until I remember I have a question to answer. Laughing, I pull away, nodding to the silver catering platter on the table.

"First course. Will you do the honors?"

Zach sighs, disappointed, but he lifts the handle anyway and lets out a throaty laugh. "Um. Dessert is our first course?"

I shrug and take the lid from him, setting it aside. He still hasn't looked at it. "Figured if I'm slaving away in the kitchen, we're going to do this my way. Dessert first." I wink, then nod my head at the cake. "Did you read it?"

He looks down. It's the most beautiful sight as he inhales then exhales, and his shoulders relax. If there was any tension left, it all melts away.

The cake is shaped like a football with white frosting decorating the top layer like it's lacing the icing together, but it's the words in the middle that say it all.

I love you more than chocolate cake.

Nothing could be more simple, more true.

Zach's hand massages my thigh, but he doesn't take his eyes off those words until I speak.

"I love you, Zach."

His eyes float to me.

"I've wanted to love you for a long time now, but I'm more than ready now. I've been scared for a long time, too." I feel my chin start to quiver. "But a smart man once told me that I should stop letting fear rule my life."

"You done hiding under the bleachers, Cakes?" His tone is teasing and loving—a perfect reminder of why it's so easy to love him back. He understands me so well with no effort at all. He's always seen me, even when I couldn't see myself.

I smile and lean in to touch my lips to his. "Yes, smartass. Every home game, I'll be in the stands, right where you can see me."

His grin melts my insides. "That's great news."

His mouth moves with mine. It's a kiss that melds us together with the promise of a kind of love that can't be defined as kismet. We weren't lucky to find each other; we were *meant* to find each other.

Zach said it before: we were two parallel lines that magically derailed and hit a crossroads. Except, I still don't believe we have magic to thank for this. No alternate path along the way or chain of events could have kept us from each other.

What's meant to be … simply *is*.

Let's Connect!

Dear Reader, I hope you enjoyed Monica and Zach's story! If you have a few minutes to spare, please consider leaving a review on Amazon and Goodreads. Reviews mean the world to an author. You can also connect with me on social media and sign up for my mail list to be sure and never miss a new release, event, or sale!

K.K.'s Website & Blog: KK-Allen.com
Facebook: Facebook.com/AuthorKKAllen
Goodreads: Goodreads.com/KKAllen
Twitter: Twitter/KKAllenAuthor

SIGN UP HERE FOR INSIDER INFORMATION:
(New Releases, Exclusive Giveaways, ARCs, Sneak Peeks, More!)
smarturl.it/KK_MailList

JOIN K.K.'S INSIDERS GROUP, FOREVER YOUNG!
Enjoy special sneak peeks, participate in exclusive giveaways, enter to win ARCs, and chat it up with K.K. and special guests ;)
Facebook.com/Groups/ForeverYoungWithKK

Thank You

It's that time again when I get to thank some very important people who made *Under the Bleachers* possible. Writing and publishing is not a one-man job. It truly takes an army, and I'm so blessed to have a team that cares about my characters as much as I do.

First, I want to take a second to say that *Under the Bleachers* was the hardest novel I've written so far. After the emotional story that was *Up in the Treehouse*, it was a challenge to get to know these characters right away. I relied heavily on the people I'm about to thank for good reason, and they deserve all the accolades.

To my family, all of you. To my friends, old and new. There are pieces of you in all my stories. If you ever read something that triggers a memory we share, then it probably inspired me enough to write about it.

Shauna Ward. Again. You are more than an editor and I thank you for the continuous rounds of reviews and answering questions, and helping me transform every story into something worth reading. Also, and most importantly, for making me a better writer by always challenging me to do better.

Richard Duerden. I'm honestly not sure I would be here without your encouragement when I was a debut author struggling with a fantasy series. You were a wonderful teacher then and continue to be. Thank you for allowing me to trust you with my first and worst drafts.

My dream team beta readers!! Adore isn't even the right word to tell you how I feel about you. You challenge me, you're honest, and you take time out of your busy lives to give me critical feedback. Beta reading is not an easy job. Joy, thank you for having the creative foresight to see Zachary and Monica together while reading *Up in the Treehouse*! They have been my favorite couple to write so far. Sue, once again you came in and helped me build elements to this world I didn't even know were missing. You are truly fantastic! Anna, coming in like that to beta in the last hour. You are a doll and I can't thank you enough.

Helene (aka Mom), what would I do without your proofreading skills? Once again, I'd have a lot of missing words. I can't wait for you to read what I've got coming next. You're a huge inspiration for it!

Kristen Puckhaber!!! I couldn't put you in any one category. You simply stand on your own. You are my real-life fashion stylist, an inspiration to so many, and you'll always be my sis. Thank you for not only jumping into this project with both feet, but going above and beyond anything I imagined. I asked for some fashion suggestions and you came back to me with story feedback and a freaking style board! I love you more than any words in any book could ever express.

Ashleigh Wilson. When you signed on to be my assistant I'm not sure you agreed to all that came along with it (ha!). You, my friend, are a blessing. Every day, you surprise me, and I truly love having you on my team! So, as promised, Zachary Ryan is yours. ;) But does that mean I get Tebow?

Lowell Hofer of @LHPoetry on Instagram, thank you a million times over for allowing me to insert your beautiful words into this novel. It truly fit Zachary and Monica's love like nothing I could have written myself. Never stop writing!

To my cover artist, Sarah Hansen of Okay Creations, thank you again for creating the perfect face for my story. I truly love working with you!

To the Sassy Savvy Fabulous team, specifically my publicist, Linda! I am so grateful for your support during this book launch! Thank you for putting up with my never-ending questions, and for kindly batting away my need for control. We did it!

To every book blogger and reader who accepted an advanced copy of *Under the Bleachers*. I am so appreciative of your time and support. A special thanks to Derna from Always Books, the moderators at New Adult Book Club, Lucy and the Words We Love By team, Lindsey from Linz Reads, Kylie and the Kylie's Fiction Addiction bloggers, JoDeen from JoJo the Bookaholic, Cassandra from Bookish Crypt, Jennifer and Roxie at Schmexy Girl Book Blog, The Rock Stars of Romance team ... and so many others! You're all amazing at what you do and you're appreciated more than you know.

To my reader group, Forever Young! What the heck did I ever do without you? I love hanging out with you every single day and sharing our love for books, food, and boys (hehe). Love you all!

And of course—this book would not be complete without a quick shout out to the Seattle Seahawks and the 12s who have made my love for football everlasting. There is nothing like standing in the bleachers at CenturyLink Field. Nothing.

My readers. Wow. THANK YOU from the bottom of my heart for taking the time to read Monica and Zachary's story. I'm not done with this crew. Stay tuned.

To everyone. Keep reading. Keep reviewing. Keep spreading the love. Until the next time.

Much Love,

K.K. Allen

Other Books

UP IN THE TREEHOUSE (CHLOE AND GAVIN'S STORY)

Want to find out more about Chloe and Gavin from Under the Bleachers?

Up in the Treehouse is an emotional and beautiful romance— grown from childhood friendship, sustained with passion ... and threatened by forbidden love. *Up in the Treehouse* is best categorized as 'the perfect imperfect love story' and deals with many important themes, like bullying, family, death, acceptance, and memories.

When Chloe Rivers awakens to the looming eyes of the Rhodes twins, she escapes their treehouse mortified. But after a bully attacks Chloe at school, Gavin and Devon Rhodes befriend her, cementing an instant bond. The three become inseparable, but as years go on, their friendship becomes entangled in secrets and betrayals that will plague them for years to come.

Four years after high school graduation, still haunted by the past, the friends are forced to come to terms with all that has transpired ...

Sometimes, love is messy. People make mistakes. In the end, can deep-rooted connections survive the destruction of innocence?

THE SUMMER SOLSTICE SERIES

The Summer Solstice Series is a Contemporary Fantasy / Romance series inspired by magic, nature, and love. Rich with Greek mythology, romance, and friendship, the community of Apollo Beach is threatened by something dark … someone deadly.

SOARING (A SHORT STORY)

On an Alaskan cruise in the dead of winter, Emma and Luke find each other under the aurora borealis, a phenomenon that bonds them in the most unlikely of ways. While Luke teaches Emma what it means to soar, she gives him a reason to stay grounded, but as their journey nears its end memories of a forgotten past surfaces, challenging their future—if a future for them still exists.

About the Author

K.K. Allen is an Interdisciplinary Arts and Sciences graduate from the University of Washington who writes Contemporary Romance and Fantasy stories that "Capture the Edge of Romance." K.K. currently resides in Central Florida, works full time as a Digital Producer for a leading online educational institution, and is the mother to a ridiculously handsome little dude who owns her heart.

K.K.'s publishing journey began in June 2014 with the YA Contemporary Fantasy trilogy, *The Summer Solstice*. In 2016, K.K. published her first Contemporary Romance, *Up in the Treehouse*, which has been highly rated and nominated for two 2016 Reviewers' Choice awards (Best New Adult and Best Review Source) from *RT*BookReviews.com. Her latest novel, *Under the Bleachers* is available now! More works in progress will be announced soon. Stay tuned for more by connecting with K.K. in all the social media spaces.

www.KK-Allen.com

CPSIA information can be obtained
at www.ICGtesting.com
Printed in the USA
BVOW08s0715120317
478397BV00001B/326/P